P9-DXE-648

## Praise for bestselling author Lucy Monroe

"*The Sicilian's Marriage Arrangement* is one of those stories that I couldn't wait to finish, but already started to miss when I turned the last page."
—*Romance Junkies*

"If you are a fan of Diana Palmer's, like I am, you definitely need to give Lucy Monroe a try."
—*Thebestreviews.com*

## Praise for *USA TODAY* bestselling author Jennie Lucas

"With this touching story of how past tragedies can mar the present, Lucas has written another winner with a surprise ending that is sure to satisfy."
—*RT Book Reviews* on *Tamed: The Barbarian King*

"Talented Jennie Lucas is the queen of gorgeous alpha male characters and the passionate women that tame them."
—*Cataromance.com*

Award-winning and bestselling author **LUCY MONROE** sold her first book in September of 2002 to the Harlequin Presents® line. That book represented a dream that had been burning in her heart for years... the dream to share her stories with readers who love romance as much as she does. Since then she has sold more than thirty books and has hit national bestseller lists in the U.S. and England.

She really does love to hear from readers and responds to every email. You can reach her at lucymonroe@lucymonroe.com.

## JENNIE LUCAS

had a tragic beginning for any would be writer: a very happy childhood. Her parents owned a bookstore, and she grew up surrounded by books, dreaming about faraway lands. A year after graduating from Kent State University with a degree in English, she started writing books. Jennie was a finalist in the Romance Writers of America's Golden Heart contest in 2003 and won the award in 2005. A fellow 2003 finalist, Australian author Trish Morey, read Jennie's writing and told her that she should write for Harlequin® Presents. It seemed like too big a dream, but Jennie took a deep breath and went for it. A year later, Jennie got the magical call from London that turned her into a published author. Since then, life has been hectic—juggling a writing career, a sexy husband and two young children—but Jennie loves her crazy, chaotic life.

For more about Jennie and her books, please visit her website at www.jennielucas.com.

# Lucy Monroe

# The Sheikh's Bartered Bride

USA TODAY Bestselling Author

# Jennie Lucas

# The Greek Billionaire's Baby Revenge

**Harlequin**®

TORONTO NEW YORK LONDON
AMSTERDAM PARIS SYDNEY HAMBURG
STOCKHOLM ATHENS TOKYO MILAN MADRID
PRAGUE WARSAW BUDAPEST AUCKLAND

Recycling programs
for this product may
not exist in your area.

ISBN-13: 978-0-373-68822-7

THE SHEIKH'S BARTERED BRIDE &
THE GREEK BILLIONAIRE'S BABY REVENGE

Copyright © 2011 by Harlequin Books S.A.

The publisher acknowledges the copyright holders of the individual works
as follows:

THE SHEIKH'S BARTERED BRIDE
Copyright © 2004 by Lucy Monroe

THE GREEK BILLIONAIRE'S BABY REVENGE
Copyright © 2007 by Jennie Lucas

# CONTENTS

To Isabelle...
You are more precious to me
than words can ever express and I thank God daily
for giving you to me as a very special gift.
With love, Lucy

# THE SHEIKH'S BARTERED BRIDE

Lucy Monroe

# CHAPTER ONE

"Miss Benning."

She wasn't Miss Benning. She was Catherine Marie, captive of The Hawk, a sheikh who still lived by the code of the desert, where only the strongest survived.

He was coming now. She could hear his deep, masculine voice as he spoke in a tongue she did not understand to someone outside her tent. She struggled against the cords that bound her hands, but it was useless. The silk scarves were soft, but strong and she could not get her hands free.

If she did, what would she do? Run?

Where?

She was in the middle of the desert. The sun beat against the tent, heating up the cavernous interior. She wouldn't last a day in the vast wasteland on her own.

Then he was there, standing in the entrance to the room in which she was held. His features were cast in shadow. All she could see was his big body encased in the white pants and tunic typical of his people. A black robe, his *abaya*, fell from his massive shoulders to midcalf and his head was covered with the red and white *smagh* that denoted his position as sheikh. The headband holding it in place was made of twisted black leather.

He was less than fifteen feet away, but still his face

was hidden from her by the shadows. Only the strong line of his jaw denoting his arrogance was discernible.

*"Miss Benning!"*

Catherine Marie Benning's head snapped up from where it had been resting against her fist and her eyes slowly focused on her surroundings. Tent walls hung with faded silks, to be replaced by cool gray cement, relieved only by the posters advertising the upcoming book drive and literacy event. They were the walls of the break room in the Whitehaven Public Library, much closer to a cold and wet Seattle, Washington, than the blistering hot deserts of the Sahara.

Fluorescent light cast a harsh glow over the pointed features of the woman standing in front of her.

"Yes, Mrs. Camden?"

Straightening her double-knit polyester blazer, almost identical in color to the library's walls, Mrs. Camden, Catherine's superior, sniffed. "Your head was off in the clouds again, Miss Benning."

The disapproval in the older woman's voice grated against Catherine's usually limitless patience. Perhaps if the man in her fantasies would ever show his face, she wouldn't be feeling so frustrated, but he did not. This time had been no different. The Hawk was as elusive to her imagination as he was in it.

"I'm still on break," she gently reminded the older woman.

"Yes, well, we all do what we must."

Recognizing the beginnings of a familiar lecture, Catherine stifled a sigh at the knowledge her lunch break was to be cut short. Again.

Hakim bin Omar al Kadar walked into the library and scanned the reference area for sight of Catherine Marie Benning. Her picture was indelibly printed on his mind. His future wife. While arranged marriages were not uncommon in the royal family of Jawhar, his was unique.

Catherine Marie Benning was unaware that she was to become his wife. Her father wanted it that way.

One of the stipulations of the deal between Hakim's uncle and Harold Benning was that Hakim convince Catherine to become his wife without telling her about the arrangement between her father and the King of Jawhar. Hakim had not asked why. Having been educated in the West, Hakim knew that American women did not view arranged marriages with the same equanimity the women of his family did.

He would have to court Catherine, but that would be no hardship. Even in an arranged marriage, a royal prince of Jawhar was expected to court his intended bride. This marriage would be no different. He would give her a month.

Ten weeks ago, his uncle had been apprised by Harold Benning of the probable deposits of a rare mineral in the mountains of Jawhar. The American had suggested a partnership between Benning Excavations and the royal family of Jawhar.

The two men had still been negotiating terms when Hakim had been attacked while out riding in the desert in the early hours of the morning. Investigations had revealed that the assassination attempt had been made by the same group of dissidents responsible for his parents' deaths twenty years before.

Hakim was unclear how marriage for Catherine had become part of the deal. He knew only that his uncle considered it convenient. Should the need for long-term living visas arise for the royal family, Hakim would be in a position to sponsor them as the spouse of an American. There would be no need to go through regular diplomatic channels, thus preserving the privacy and pride of his family.

The royal family of Jawhar had not sought political asylum from another country in the three centuries of its reign and they never would. Already overseeing the family's interests in America, Hakim had been the logical choice for the alliance.

Harold Benning also saw the marriage as beneficial. His concern over the continued single state of his twenty-four-year-old daughter had been obvious. According to him, she never even dated.

The result of the older men's negotiations had been a Royal Decree: Hakim was to marry Catherine Benning.

He spotted his quarry helping a small boy on the other side of the room. She stretched to pull a book from the shelf and the button-up black sweater she wore above a long, straight skirt caught his attention. Molding her breasts, it revealed a surprisingly lush feminine form and he felt himself stir.

This was unexpected. Her picture had revealed a pretty woman, but nothing like the exotic beauties he had bedded in the past. That he should react so readily to such an innocent sight made him stop in his journey toward her.

What had so aroused him? Her skin was pale, but

not alabaster. Her hair was blond, but a dark blond and twisted up on the back of her head as it was, it looked drab. Her eyes were a shock, a gentian-blue that had startled him with their intensity in the picture and were even more unusual in person.

Aside from the eyes, nothing about her stood out and yet his body's response could not be denied. He wanted her. While he had experienced this sort of instant physical attraction before, it had been with a lot more provocation. A certain way of walking, dressing or an alluring look. Catherine Benning exhibited none of these.

It was a puzzling, but not unpleasant surprise. A genuine physical attraction on his part would make the job of her seduction that much easier. He had been prepared to do his duty regardless of personal attraction. Country came first. Family came second. His own needs and desires last of all.

He walked forward, stopping a little to her left. As the boy walked away, her dark sapphire gaze did a quick survey of the room, skimming over him, and then settled back on a man who had come to stand in front of the desk.

But even as she pointed to something on her computer monitor, her gaze flicked back to Hakim. And stayed. He met her eyes, noting peripherally the man she had been helping walk away. The next person in line went unnoticed as her attention remained on him.

She appeared poleaxed and he smiled.

Her entire body went taut and her cheeks pinkened, but she did not look away.

His smile went up a notch. Fulfilling his duty would

be a simple matter of turning that attraction into a desire to wed.

"Miss Benning! Pay attention. You have patrons to serve."

The martinet haranguing Catherine was no doubt the dragon of a boss Harold Benning had mentioned when briefing Hakim on his daughter.

Catherine's head snapped around and her blush intensified, but she did not stammer as she answered the older woman. "I'm sorry. My mind wandered." She turned to the next person in line, repeated her apology and asked how she could help them, effectively dismissing her superior.

The older woman harrumphed and marched away like a petty general deprived of his battle spoils.

He waited until the last of the line had walked away before greeting Catherine. "Good afternoon."

She smiled, her eyes even more startling up close. The blush was back. "Hi. What can I do for you?"

"I am interested in antique telescopes and the history of stargazing. Perhaps you can direct me to a good reference."

Her eyes lit with interest. "Is this a new hobby for you?"

"Fairly new." As recent as the discussion Hakim had had with her father. Although Hakim's own father had shared Catherine's passionate interest in ancient stargazing, since his death, his books had remained unused in the observatory in the Kadar Palace.

"It's one of my personal interests. If you've got a few

minutes I'll show you the right section and point out a few books that I think are particularly good."

"I would like that very much."

CATHERINE SUCKED IN AIR, trying to calm her racing heart as she led the handsome and rather imposing man to the proper nonfiction area of her library. The aura of barely leashed power surrounding him was enough to send her pulse rocketing, but the fact that he physically embodied every characteristic of her ideal fantasy tipped her senses into dangerous territory.

At least a couple of inches over six feet, his muscle-honed body towered above her own five foot seven in a way that made her feel small beside him. Even knowing she was not. The silky black hair on his head was only a shade darker than the color of his eyes and if he didn't speak with such impeccable English, she would think he was the sheikh of her fantasies.

A wave of totally unfamiliar desire swept over her, leaving her even more breathless and confused.

He hadn't touched her and somehow she had always believed this level of sexual awareness could only accompany touch. She'd been wrong.

They stopped in front of a row of books. She pulled one off the shelf and handed it to him. "This is my favorite. I have my own first-edition copy at home."

He took the book and his fingers briefly brushed hers. She jumped back, shocked by the contact. Her body throbbed in a way she hadn't experienced before, but she desperately tried to look unaffected by his nearness.

"I am sorry." His black gaze probed her own, leaving her even more unsettled.

She shook her head, but could feel that infernal blush crawling along her skin again. "It's nothing." Less than nothing. Or at least it should have been.

He flipped open the book and looked at it. She knew she should go, but she couldn't make her legs move in the direction of the reference desk.

The book shut with a snap and his dark gaze settled on her again. "Do you recommend anything else?"

"Yes." She spent another ten minutes pointing out different books and suggesting a couple of periodicals he might be interested in ordering.

"Thank you very much, Miss…"

"Benning, but please call me Catherine."

"I am Hakim."

"That's an Arabic name."

His mouth twitched. "Yes."

"But your English is perfect." What an inane thing to say. Lots of Arabic people lived in the Seattle area, many of them second or third generation Americans.

"So it should be," he drawled in a voice programmed to melt her insides. "The royal tutor would be most displeased if one of his pupils should speak with anything less than complete mastery."

"Royal?" The word came out sounding choked.

"Forgive me. I am Hakim bin Omar al Kadar, prince in the royal family of Jawhar."

She was breathing, but her lungs felt starved of oxygen. A prince? She'd been talking to a prince for more than ten minutes. Lusting after him! Heavens. Her half-formed idea of inviting him to attend the next meeting of the Antique Telescope Society died a swift death. Unfortunately the attraction he held for her did not.

She swallowed. "Can I help you with anything else?"

"I have taken up enough of your time."

"There's a society for people interested in antique telescopes in Seattle," she found herself blurting out, unable to let it go at that. She wouldn't invite him to meet her there, but she could tell him about the meeting.

"Yes?"

"They meet tonight." She named the time and place.

"Will I see you there?" he asked.

"Probably not." She would be there, but she sat in the back of the room and he was not the sort of man content to enjoy anything from the sidelines.

She wasn't wholly content, either, but she didn't know how to break a lifetime of conditioning.

"You will not attend?" He actually looked disappointed.

"I always go."

"Then I shall see you."

She shrugged. "It's a big group."

"I will look for you, Catherine."

She barely stopped herself from blurting out the question, "Why?" Instead she smiled. "Then maybe we *will* run into each other."

"I do not leave such matters to fate."

No doubt. He was much too decisive. "Until tonight then."

She turned to go and was only marginally disappointed he did not call her back. After all, he'd said he would look for her.

He checked the books out she had recommended and left the library a few minutes later.

Catherine watched him go, certain of one thing. The sheikh of her fantasies would no longer be faceless.

He would have the features of Hakim.

## CHAPTER TWO

CATHERINE WALKED INTO the meeting room in one of Seattle's posh downtown hotels. Though she was early, over half of the seats were already taken. She scanned the crowd for Hakim while butterflies with hobnail boots danced an Irish jig on the inside of her stomach.

Would he be here?

Would he really be looking for her?

It was hard to believe. Even harder to accept the sensations she felt at the mere thought of his presence.

A scar-riddled face and subsequent laser treatments had meant she'd missed out on dating in both high school and college. Her shyness had been so ingrained by then that the *late blooming* her parents had expected never materialized. She thought she'd come to terms with the fact she would most likely die a maiden aunt in the best tradition of little old ladies with white hair and homes filled with other people's memories. She was too shy to pursue men and too ordinary to be pursued. Yet something about Hakim compelled her to step outside her comfort zone.

And that scared her.

No way would a guy like that return her interest.

"Catherine. You have arrived."

She knew the owner of the deeply masculine voice, even as she turned. "Good evening, Hakim."

"Will you sit with me?"

She nodded, unable to immediately voice her acceptance.

He led her to a chair in the middle of the room, much closer to the front than she usually sat. Taking her arm, he helped her into the seat with a courtesy that was both captivating and alarming. Alarming because it meant he touched her and the feel of his warm fingers on her arm was enough to send her senses reeling.

Several pairs of eyes turned to watch them take their seats, the curiosity of the onlookers palpable. She smiled slightly at an elderly woman whose stare was filled with avid interest. Catherine remembered talking to her at the last meeting. She was nice, but a bit nosy.

Catherine moved her own gaze to the front of the room where tonight's speaker stood talking to the president of the society.

The speaker was the leading authority on George Lee and Sons telescopes. He was supposed to bring along one from his collection for the society members to look at up close. She couldn't wait to see it and thought the red silk covered shape in the front of the room must be it.

She was proved right forty minutes later when the silk cover was removed and the general assembly was invited to come forward and take a look.

"You wish to see it?" Hakim asked her.

She shrugged.

"What does this shrug mean?"

She turned her head, allowing herself the luxury of a full-on look. The impact was that of a bomb exploding in her brain and she almost gasped, but held back the revealing sound.

She smiled wryly, knowing herself. "The shrug means I'll probably forego the pleasure."

"I will accompany you."

Like a security blanket? "It's not that," she denied, even though it was exactly that. "I'd just rather not wait in line. Do you see how many people are already waiting to look at it?"

Hakim looked toward the line of society members and then back at her. "Are you quite certain you do not wish to see it?"

Even a George Lee and Sons telescope could not compete with Hakim for her interest, she admitted to herself. "Very sure."

"Then, perhaps you would consent to dinner with me this evening and we could discuss my new hobby. You appear highly knowledgeable in the subject."

"Dinner?" she parroted.

"Are you concerned about sharing a meal with a stranger?"

The quite justifiable concern had never entered her mind, but then she'd never been in a sheikh's company before, nor had she ever experienced the debilitating cocktail of feelings being near him elicited in her body.

"No," she said, shocking herself and making his eyes widen fractionally.

"Then you will allow me to buy you dinner this evening?"

"I don't know…"

"Please." The word sounded much more like a

command than any sort of pleading, yet it affected her just the same.

"I suppose I could follow you to the restaurant in my car." She should show at least a rudimentary level of self-protection.

"Very well. Is seafood to your liking?"

Her mouth watered at the thought. "I adore it."

"There is a beautiful restaurant not a block from here. We could walk."

"I think it's just starting to rain," she said.

His lips tilted in a sardonic smile. "If so, I will lend you my raincoat."

She laughed at the instant picture she had of herself in a raincoat several sizes too big. "That won't be necessary. I just thought you probably wouldn't like to walk if it was wet out."

"I would not have suggested it otherwise."

"Of course."

It was a short walk and though the gray clouds were heavy with moisture, it did not rain.

They spent dinner discussing her favorite hobby. She was surprised at his knowledge and said so.

"I read the books you gave me this afternoon."

"Already?"

It was his turn to shrug. "Most of them."

"Wow. I guess you didn't have to go back to work."

"We all must have our priorities," he said with a smile.

"I wouldn't have pegged you as someone who put his hobbies above his work."

"There are times when the unexpected takes precedence in our lives."

She wondered at the mysterious statement, but did not know him well enough to ask about it.

They both declined dessert and he walked her back to her car. He took her keys from her and unlocked it. Opening the door, he indicated she should get inside.

She stopped before bending down to get into the driver's seat. "Thank you for dinner."

"It was my pleasure, Catherine."

TWO DAYS LATER, Hakim invited her to attend a Saturday showing of a journey among the stars at the theater. It required spending the whole day together as well as a three-hour drive to Portland. The prospect of all that time with just her and Hakim in the enclosed space of a car had her nerves completely on edge. She jumped when the security buzzer rang to announce his arrival.

She pressed the button on the small black communications box. "I'll be right down."

"I'll be waiting." His short reply came; his voice even sounded exotic and sexy over the apartment building's tinny intercom system. She was still finding it difficult to believe that such a gorgeous man had a serious interest in her. Grabbing her hold-all and purse, she left the apartment.

When she got downstairs, she found him waiting in the lobby.

"Good morning, Catherine. Are you ready to go?"

She nodded, while her eyes devoured the sight of him. Wearing a snug-fitting black sweater and tan trousers that managed to emphasize his well-developed muscles, he made her mouth go dry with desire.

She licked her lips and swallowed. "I've got everything I need."

"Then, let's go." He took her arm and led her outside where a long, black limousine waited.

"I thought you were driving."

"I wanted to be able to focus my attention on you. There is a privacy window. We will be as secluded as we desire."

The way he said it made totally inappropriate images swirl through her head and her nipples tightened almost painfully. It was such an unexpected sensation, she gasped.

"Are you well?"

"F-fine," she stuttered before practically diving into the backseat of the limousine.

As a tactic to hide her discomposure from him, it was no doubt a dismal failure. Most of his escorts probably waited for him to help them into the car. Of course, these same escorts most likely had a love life outside of their fantasies and could handle the close proximity of such a sexy man with equanimity.

Not so her.

She was in over her head and the man had never even kissed her. When he took the seat opposite her, her breasts swelled at his nearness.

And his smile was positively lethal to her self-control.

"Would you like some refreshments?" He flipped open a small door in the side console of the car to reveal a fully stocked fridge.

"Some juice would be nice." She was really proud of herself when her voice came out fairly normal.

He poured her a glass of cranberry juice and handed it to her. "So, are antique telescopes your only hobby?"

"Oh, no. I'm an avid reader. I guess that makes sense, me working in a library."

"I think I expected that, yes."

She returned the droll smile. "Right, but I also love hiking nature trails."

His brows rose at that and she couldn't help a rueful shrug of acknowledgment to his surprise.

"Maybe I should have said ambling through the woods."

"Ah." He sipped at his mineral water. "And do you daydream as you walk, I wonder."

She could not hide her own surprise that he had guessed something so private about her quite accurately. "Yes. Being outside and away from people is sort of magical."

"I too like the outdoors, but prefer the desert to the woods."

"Please tell me about it."

And he did, but he deftly directed the conversation back to her on several occasions and they spent the long drive talking about subjects she rarely discussed with anyone but her sister. Hakim seemed to understand her shyness and was not bothered by it, which made it easier for her to be open with him.

He also never dismissed her views as her father was so adept at doing. Hakim listened and as he listened, Catherine found herself falling under the spell of his personality.

He took her to lunch at a restaurant that overlooked the Willamette River. The food was superb, the view of the river amazing and his company overwhelming to her heart and her senses. She was very much afraid that she was falling deeply and irrevocably in love with a man that was far out of her league.

WHEN THEY'D SETTLED into their seats at the theater, Hakim slipped his arm over Catherine's shoulders, smiling to himself when she stiffened, but did not pull away. She was not used to a man's touch, but her body gave all the signals of being ready for a sexual awakening. The latent and untapped passion he sensed in her would play to his advantage, making it easy for him to seduce her into marriage and fulfill his duty.

His specialized training had made it possible to save himself from the recent assassination attempt, but his parents had not been so lucky. He had been unable to save them and the knowledge still haunted him.

The fact that he had been ten years old at the time did nothing to assuage his need to protect his family now, whatever the cost.

He could still remember the sound of his mother's scream as she watched her husband shot before her eyes, a scream cut short by another gunshot. His little sister had whimpered beside him and he'd taken her hand, leading her out of the palace via the secret passage known only to members of the royal family and their most trusted servants.

Days of grueling heat in the desert sun had followed as Hakim had used the knowledge taught him by his Bedouin grandfather to seek shelter in the wild for him and his small sister. He had eventually found his grandfather's tribe. He and his sister had survived, but Hakim would never forget the cost.

A small sound from Catherine brought him back to the present. He realized he had been caressing her neck with his thumb. Her eyes were fixed on the huge screen, but her body was wholly attuned to him and hummed with sexual excitement.

A month of seducing her toward marriage might very well be overkill.

CATHERINE REVELED IN THE FEEL of Hakim's arms around her and pretended it meant more than it did. It was only natural that he ask her to dance with him. After all, he was her escort for the evening and everyone else was dancing.

The black-tie charity ball was to raise money for St. Jude's Children's Hospital. She'd invited Hakim to be her escort, half expecting him to say no, but he hadn't. He'd agreed to bring her and even to have dinner with her family beforehand.

Her mother and sister were completely charmed by his exotic charisma and enigmatic presence. Even in a business suit and tie, the man exuded sheikhness.

"Your sister is very kind."

She let her body move infinitesimally closer to his and fought the urge to lay her head on his shoulder and just breathe in his essence. "Yes. She and I are very close."

"This is good."

"I think so." She smiled up at him.

His expression remained serious. "Family is very important."

"Yes, it is."

She wasn't sure where this was headed.

"Having children, passing one's heritage from one generation to the next is also important."

"I agree. I can't imagine a married couple not wanting children."

Finally he smiled. "Perhaps there are those that have their reasons, but you would never be one of them."

She thought longingly of marriage and family, specifically with this man and it was all she could do to keep her smile pasted in place. "No, I'd never be one of them."

She was unlikely ever to be married at all, but why bring up that depressing thought?

His thumb started a caressing rotation in the small of her back and her thoughts scattered, even the depressing ones.

Closing her eyes, she gave into the urge to let her cheek rest against his chest. He'd probably never ask her to dance again, but she just couldn't help herself.

Instead of acting offended by her forwardness, Hakim settled her more fully against him and danced with her until the music changed to a faster beat.

He didn't ask her to dance again that evening, but he didn't neglect her, either. Using his easy sophistication to deflect the interest of other women who approached them with the intention of flirting with him, he kept his interest fixed firmly on her and her heart gave up the battle.

She was in love.

Hopelessly.

Helplessly.
Completely.

CATHERINE OPENED THE CARD attached to the flowers.
It read, "For a woman whose inner beauty blooms with
more loveliness than a rose."

Tears filled her eyes and it was all she could do not
to cry. She and Hakim had spent the night before at a
benefit concert. Catherine had gotten up and spoken on
behalf of the children and their hopes and dreams. She'd
been shaking with nerves, but she'd felt compelled to
make a plea on the foundation's behalf.

Afterward, Hakim had told her that her obvious
love of children and compassion for them had shown
through even her nervousness. She'd been warmed by
the compliment, but the long-stemmed red roses totally
overwhelmed her.

She put the vase on the corner of her desk where
both she and the rest of the librarians could see them
easily.

Picking up a pile of papers that needed filing, she
contemplated the crimson blooms. He made her feel so
special, even if they were just friends. Sometimes it felt
like more than friendship and her hopes would soar, but
what else could it be when he never so much as kissed
her?

They spent a lot of time together and her attraction
for him grew with each occasion, but he appeared unaffected on a physical level by her.

She wasn't surprised.

She was hardly the type to inspire unbridled lust in
a man like Hakim, but her desire for him continued

unabated. Growing with each successive meeting, both it and the desire to be in his company became gnawing needs within her.

Her thoughts stilled along with the rest of her as Hakim walked into the library. She should be used to his arrival by now, it happened often enough and every time since the first, he'd made it clear he had come specifically to see her.

He walked toward her with an unconscious arrogance that she found rather endearing. He was just so sure of himself, but then he was rich, gorgeous and had been raised a prince. Why wouldn't he be?

She remembered the papers in her hand just as he reached her desk and leaned over to put them away quickly.

HAKIM STOPPED IN FRONT of Catherine's desk, just as she bent to put something away in the lowest drawer.

"Catherine…"

Her body straightened and her intense blue gaze met with his, her mouth twisted in a rueful grimace. "Sorry, I just remembered I had to file these—" she waved a sheaf of papers in her hand "—when I saw you."

"And it could not wait until you had greeted me?" he asked with some amusement.

"I might have forgotten easily."

Did she realize what she was giving away with that admission? He already knew he had a definite impact on her ability to concentrate, but a more sophisticated woman would not have admitted it.

"Then I shall have to content myself conversing with the top of your head while you finish."

"Sometimes, you sound so formal. Is that because the Arabic language is a more formal language, or is it because English is your second language and therefore you don't slip into slang as easily?"

Not for the first time, her rapid change in topic left him slightly disorientated. "French is my second language," he said in answer to her question, "I did not learn English until I had mastered it."

She tilted her head to one side. "Oh. I've always thought French would be a lovely language to learn. I studied German and Spanish in school, but I have to admit I don't have a facility for it."

"I did not come to discuss my fluency in other languages."

"Of course you didn't." She smiled. "Why did you come?"

"To see my friend."

Something flickered in her eyes at the word *friend*, but was gone too quickly for him to interpret.

"Oh," she said again. "How many are you?"

"How many what, little kitten?"

Her face heated to rose red as he knew it would at the small endearment. Such words were common in his culture between a man and the woman he intended to marry. They were nothing more than an admission of his intent, but they flustered Catherine a great deal.

"How many languages are you fluent in?" Her voice was breathless and he had the not so shocking urge to steal her breath completely with a kiss.

He could not do it of course. Not here and not yet, but soon. He smiled in anticipation, causing her eyes to widen.

"I'm fluent in French, English, Arabic and all the dialects of my people, little kitten." He repeated the phrase on purpose just to watch the effect it had on her, which was perhaps unfair of him.

It was startling. She sucked in air, grimaced and then whispered, "Hardly little."

While she was maybe an inch above average in height for a woman, she often made comments as if she saw herself as some kind of Amazon. He stepped toward her until he stood only a few inches from her and reached out to brush the smooth curve of her neck with one fingertip. "To me, very little."

She trembled and he smiled.

Very soon she would be his.

Her head tilted back and she eyed his six-foot two-inch frame with unmistakable longing. "I suppose so."

He wanted to kiss her. It took every bit of the self-discipline developed in his training with the elite guard to step back and drop his hand.

"I came to see if you would like to join me for dinner tonight."

Her mouth opened and closed with no sound issuing forth. They had known each other for three weeks now and eaten numerous meals together, as well as attending several formal functions. Yet she acted shocked every time he asked her out.

"Come, this is not such a surprise. We had lunch together only yesterday."

She smiled whimsically. "That's why I'm surprised. I thought you'd want to spend time with…"

Her voice trailed off, but her eyes told him what she

had been about to say. *Other women.* She had so little concept of her own value. While he should be relieved his duty would be so easy to see through, it made him angry she dismissed herself so easily.

"I want to spend time with no other woman."

He had no difficulty reading her expression now. Her eyes were filled with both joy and hope. Yes. She was ready. He had courted her long enough.

"I would love to have dinner with you."

"Then I shall see you this evening." He turned to go.

"Hakim."

He stopped.

"You could have called. It would have saved you an hour of driving here and back to Seattle."

"Then I would have foregone the pleasure of seeing you."

She looked ready to melt at that assurance and he smiled before walking away. His duty would be fulfilled very soon.

## CHAPTER THREE

HAKIM TOOK CATHERINE to his favorite restaurant on the waterfront for dinner. The ambiance was quiet and elegant. Perfect for proposing to his future wife.

He'd thought about taking her to the restaurant at the top of the Space Needle. He'd been told it was considered the height of romance, but sharing a noisy elevator with tourists on the way up held no appeal. At least not for tonight.

She smiled at him as he held her chair for her at the table. She'd worn a black dress with long sleeves, a peasant neckline and gathered waist. The full skirt swirled around her legs as she sat down. He let his fingers trail along the exposed skin of her shoulders above the wide neckline and she shivered. Satisfaction that his mission would soon be accomplished settled over him as he dropped his hand, moved around the table and took his own seat.

Even in the dim light of the restaurant, he could tell she was blushing again.

"Surely such a small touch is not cause for embarrassment?"

She smoothed her already perfectly coiffed hair. She'd worn it up again. Though he liked the view it gave him of her slender neck, one day soon, he would remove the clip and see what the dark honey strands looked like tumbling against her shoulders.

"I'm not embarrassed. Not exactly." Her sigh lifted her breasts against the soft fabric of her bodice, revealing the source of her blush.

His little virgin was excited. Two unmistakable ridges under the black material gave her away. They also apprised Hakim of the fact she was not wearing a bra. The knowledge had a by now predictable effect on him.

"What are you exactly?" he asked, wondering if she would admit anywhere close to the truth.

"Stupid."

He shook his head. Little did she know, but her desire for him would soon be fulfilled. "Jewel of my heart, you must not say such things."

She dropped her focus to her lap, where she straightened her burgundy napkin against the black fabric of her skirt. "You shouldn't call me things like that. I know you're just saying it because it's the way you talk, but…"

He reached across the table to tip her chin up with his finger. "It is not merely the way I speak. Do I use such terms with other women in your hearing?"

Her bottom lip disappeared between her teeth and her eyes reflected confusion. "No." It was a bare whisper.

He wanted to kiss those trembling lips. Her vulnerability called to primitive instincts inside him.

"They are words meant for you alone."

It was as if she stopped breathing and she went utterly still, the look in her eyes a revelation of emotions so volatile he was shocked by them. Then her eyelashes lowered and she sucked in air too quickly, choking.

He offered her a glass of water as she sought to get the small coughing fit under control.

"Thank you." She drank the water and he watched as her throat convulsed gracefully with each swallow.

"You have a beautiful neck."

The water glass tumbled and only the quick action of a nearby waiter saved her dress from a drenching. Considering her reaction to his last statement, Hakim decided it would be best to wait until after dinner to propose.

BY THE TIME HAKIM pulled his black car to a halt in the parking garage of her apartment building, Catherine's nerves were stretched tighter than an overtuned violin string. They wound one notch tighter when he insisted on seeing her inside.

She watched his dark hands as they unlocked her door and turned the knob to open it. Such masculine hands and yet so fluid in their movement, she desperately wanted them on her.

He pushed the door open and ushered her inside, one of the hands she found so fascinating secured around her waist. Her lungs stopped working while her heart went into overdrive. He closed the door and locked it, indicating he wasn't leaving any time soon and her already racing heart went turbocharged.

He led her toward the living room and she was surprised when her legs were able to move. She felt like her bones had all melted to jelly.

When they reached her bright yellow couch, he gently pushed her down onto the overstuffed cushions and then sat beside her. So close beside her that her shoulder was pressed against the hard wall of his chest. "I wish to speak with you."

"Oh," she squeaked.

He laid the hand that was not attached to her waist on her thigh, succeeding in surrounding her completely with his body and putting her on the verge of hyperventilating.

What would he do if she turned to him and did what she'd been longing to do for so long, touch the black silkiness of his hair and kiss the sensual line of his mouth? She clasped her hands firmly together in her lap to stop them from taking liberties that might end in her humiliated rejection.

For several seconds, neither of them spoke, the rush of air going in and out of her lungs at such a rapid rate the only sound in the room. He started to draw small circles on her thigh with his forefinger, sending awareness arcing up her leg and to the center of her being. She stifled a gasp of pleasure. She couldn't move. Nor could she look at him. Her attention was firmly fixed on that darkly tanned hand as it moved lazily against the black knit of her skirt.

Still he said nothing.

The quiet became unbearable. "Hakim?"

His silence beat against her and she sensed he wanted something from her, but she did not know what. Finally, when she could not tolerate one more second of the torturous anticipation, she raised her head and tilted it backward to look at his face.

It was what he'd been waiting for. Eye contact.

Dark ebony bored into her. "You have enjoyed these past weeks in my company, have you not?"

"Yes."

"Am I a fool to believe you would like our association to continue?"

"No." She had to clear her throat before she could get more words out. Necessary words. "You could never be a fool."

"Then I would also not be out of bounds to hope you might want to deepen our relationship?"

*He wanted to be her boyfriend?* Her mind couldn't quite grasp the concept, but she nodded her head in agreement anyway.

"Yes, I would be out of bounds, or yes you want to deepen our relationship?"

"I want…" She forced her halted lungs to pull in a breath of air. "I want to deepen our relationship."

Would he kiss her now? The mere thought sent her pulse on a ride like a runaway stagecoach.

"Marry me."

She was daydreaming. She had to be.

But there was something wrong with the fantasy. "But you've never even kissed me."

"I have not had the right."

"What do you mean? Were you… Were you attached to someone else?"

"No, not that, but I was not as you put it *attached to you*, either. It would not have been right for me to kiss you before formal declarations were made."

Did he mean declarations of love? No. He'd said formal declarations. "Do you mean you have to be engaged in your country to kiss?"

His hand moved from her thigh to her cheek and

he cupped it, his expression almost tender. "To kiss a virgin, yes."

Was her lack of experience so obvious? She supposed it was. "But this is not Jawhar."

"Nevertheless, I will treat you with the respect due you."

That was nice. "If I say I'll marry you, will you kiss me then?" This was by far the strangest daydream she had ever indulged in, only she knew on some level it was all too real.

A distinctly predatory light entered his obsidian eyes. "Yes."

"Yes," she repeated, not ready for the fantasy to end.

"You will marry me?"

"Yes." He couldn't really mean it and she would say just about anything to experience his mouth on hers. "Now you can kiss me."

He lowered his head, until his lips were centimeters from hers. "I can?"

"Yes." When he didn't close the gap, she said, "Please."

The kiss was as soft and fleeting as a butterfly flitting from one flower to another, but he did not move his head away and their breath continued to mingle.

The scent of his cologne mixed with a fragrance that could only be him. Male. It called to the primordial woman in her. She wanted to claim this man.

"Are you teasing me?" she asked, wondering why he had not kissed her again, more thoroughly.

"I am teasing myself."

His admission was flint to the gunpowder of her self-control. To say such a thing implied he wanted her and that was as exciting as having his body so close she could feel his heartbeat. She closed the gap of those few centimeters, her mouth locking to his with enthusiasm, if not skill.

He didn't seem to mind. His grip on her tightened and he took control of the kiss almost immediately. His mouth moved against hers, his tongue running along the seam of her lips. She opened her mouth on a small rush of air and he took possession of the interior. She'd thought of kissing like this before of course, but it had seemed messy.

It felt wonderful.

He tasted like the tiramisu he'd had for dessert at the restaurant. He also tasted like Hakim and it was a flavor she could not get enough of.

She moaned and sucked on his tongue.

He growled, his grip on her going painfully tight now and she found herself in his lap, her breasts pressed against his chest.

She wanted to touch him. She had to touch him. Her hands landed against his shoulders and stayed there for a full five seconds while the kiss went on and on. But just feeling the heat of him under her fingers was not enough. She wanted to explore.

First she let her fingers trail through his hair. It felt soft, almost like silk and she explored the shape of his head through it. He was so male, even his head felt a particularly masculine way to her searching fingers.

A sense of desperation, laced with fear that this would end soon and she would miss having touched the rest of his body, she brought her hands down on either side of his face, slowly sliding them toward his neck, then shoulders. With each centimeter of movement, she memorized the feel of his warm skin against the pads of her fingertips.

Sliding her hands down the polished cotton of his shirt, under his jacket, she outlined each muscle, each ridge and valley on the masculine torso so close to her own.

He shuddered and she rejoiced that she could affect him.

His hands were kneading her backside and she could feel a growing ridge of hardness under her hip.

In the back of her mind, she registered that meant he was getting excited which sent her emotions careening out of control and the impossible feelings she harbored for this magnificent man poured out through her lips and fingertips.

As if the release of her emotions had freed something in him, his ardor increased and the kiss went nuclear.

His tongue dueled with hers, demanding a submission she was only too willing to give. While he conquered her mouth, she tore at the buttons on his shirt, getting enough undone to slip her hand inside and feel the smooth, hot flesh of his naked chest. It was at that point that she accepted this was not a waking dream. No fantasy could possibly be this good.

And somehow because it was real, it was more. More intense. More feeling. More excitement. Almost too much.

She broke her mouth from his and sucked in air, trying to breath as her world spun around her in a kaleidoscope of feelings she had never experienced, but nonetheless recognized.

She wanted him.

Desperately.

"Do engaged people get to make love?" Her own boldness shocked her, but she waited tensely for his answer.

The kneading action on her bottom stopped and his forehead fell against hers. "No."

"Is it because I'm a virgin?" she asked, feeling tears of frustration already burning at the back of her eyes.

Hakim was going to wake up to whatever insanity had prompted his proposal and withdraw. And she would *still* be a virgin. Life was so unfair.

"It is true. This is part of it."

"But I don't want to be a virgin," she wailed and then felt mortified color drench her face, neck and even the breasts achingly aware of the proximity of his body.

He didn't laugh. He didn't even smile. He kissed her, hard and quick against her mouth. "We must wait."

"I can't."

He groaned like a drowning man going under for the last time. The hardness under her thigh twitched and his mouth locked with hers again, this time not waiting for her to open her lips, but forcing them apart for the entrance of his tongue.

His hand came up and cupped her breast, his thumb brushing over her achingly erect nipple. She arched into his touch while squirming her backside against his hard maleness. She loved him so much. Loved what he was doing to her. Loved the anticipation of more. For the first time in her life Catherine was glad she had never been with another man.

She wanted Hakim to be her first.

He kissed his way down her neck, stopping to suckle her rapid pulse beat. Arrows of pleasure shot through her limbs and she cried out at the wonder of it all.

Then his mouth was on her collarbone, his tongue caressing her in a way she had not expected. She went completely still when he pulled the stretch neckline of her dress down to expose her braless breasts.

He stopped moving, too, pulling back until he had an unfettered view of her exposed flesh. There was a lot on display. Her figure in no way resembled the boyish shapes so popular in today's media.

She felt another blush crawl up her skin as her senses prickled with heat and heady excitement.

Dark fingers caressed her pinkened flesh, making her moan and shake in response.

"So beautiful. So perfect." His words registered with the same sensual impact as his touch had done.

"I'm—" She'd meant to say something about how she was not exactly cover model slender, but he forestalled her with a finger against her lips.

"Exquisite. You are exquisite."

Then his head lowered, his lips touched her sensitized flesh and she lost her sense of place and time. He tasted her. All of her, covering each square centimeter of her naked curves with tantalizing attention. By the time he took one of her nipples into his mouth, she was shaking and inexplicable tears were running hotly down her temples and into her hair.

It was too much. The pleasure was too great.

"Hakim, darling, please!"

She didn't know what she was begging for, but he seemed to as his hand trailed down her body until it reached the hem of her skirt. His fingers brushed against her stocking clad leg and moved upward, slowly, ever so slowly.

Combined with his tasting of her breast, this tormenting slowness was driving her mad. But then his hot fingers were on the skin above the top of her stocking, curving toward her feminine center. His fingertip brushed against the silk of her panties where it covered her most tender flesh and sensation exploded inside her like a nuclear reactor.

Her body bowed. She screamed. She thought Hakim cursed, but she couldn't be sure. Nothing but the agonizing pleasure of her body was registering completely.

His hand slipped inside the waistband of her panties, down to flesh that had never, ever felt a man's touch and she cried out in an overload of sensation as he touched that bit of feminine flesh that other women talked about, but she had never even experimented with finding.

She went rigid and then shook in convulsions that were so strong, her muscles ached from supporting them.

He continued his ministrations until her entire body went limp from the strain.

He pulled her close to his chest, wrapping her in his embrace with strong, sure arms. The tears that had been a trickle became a torrent and she sobbed against his chest with as much abandon as she had given to her pleasure.

He comforted her, whispering soothing sounding

words in a language she did not recognize. It didn't matter that she couldn't understand the words, their tone was what she needed.

"That was too much," she said between hiccuping sobs.

"It was more beautiful than the desert at sunrise," was his response.

"I love you," she confessed, her heart left unprotected by the amazing experience she had just gone through.

She was hopelessly in love with a man who could have any woman he wanted and that scared her. Refusing to admit it did not change it and there was a certain amount of relief in letting the truth out.

His hands caressed her back and she shivered with another convulsion. If it had been an earthquake, she would have called it an aftershock. It had been close enough.

He picked her up, carrying her as if she weighed no more than one of the throw pillows off the sofa. When they came into her bedroom, he flipped on the small light by her bed, casting a warm glow in the room.

Stopping beside the bed, he bent to lay her down, but she clung to his neck. "Please, don't leave."

She couldn't bear being alone after *that*.

He tensed.

"Please," she begged again.

"Do not plead. If you want me to stay, I will stay."

She let go of his neck and let him lay her down on the bed. He straightened to stand beside her. "Prepare yourself for bed and I will return to hold you."

"Aren't we going to make love?" she asked, not at all

sure she could stand another dose of pleasure like what she had just gone through, but willing to try.

"Not until we are married."

She still didn't believe for a minute they were actually going to end up married. "But…" She could see the hard ridge still pressing against his slacks.

He shook his head decisively. "We will wait."

She couldn't expect him to hold her all night in that condition.

"I could…" She blushed without completing the offer, knowing he was a smart enough guy to figure it out.

"I'll take a shower."

"You're going to take a cold shower?" The thought of a sexy man like Hakim having to take a cold shower over her was somehow very appealing.

He smiled as if he could read her thoughts. "As you say. Prepare yourself for bed. I will return in but a moment."

She nodded and silently watched him walk into the en suite. It was only when she looked down that she realized her chest was still exposed. Her nipples were still hard and wet from his mouth. Oh, my. The sight paralyzed her for a full minute before she was able to get up and find a nightgown to wear to bed.

HAKIM STOOD UNDER the warm jets of water, his body buffeted by the pain of unrequited passion, his mind filled with pleasure at how successfully his campaign had gone.

Catherine had agreed to be his wife.

His uncle would be pleased. Her father would be pleased. Hakim was pleased.

Marriage to Catherine would be no hardship.

Under the shy exterior, she was so passionate, so beautifully sensual. It had been harder than he ever would have thought possible to pull back from making love to her completely.

She'd liked that. His sweet little wallflower had liked thinking he was in here taking a cold shower because of his desire for her. The shower wasn't cold, but only because he'd never found that an effective deterrent to desire. He had found that warm water could sometimes soothe the physical ache of wanting what he could not yet have.

It wasn't working right now though. His sex was so hard, he was in pain.

He could not banish the image from his head of how she had looked with her dress pulled down, her breasts swollen and quivering with her desire. And the way she had exploded…her entire body bowing with such strong contractions, he had found it most difficult to keep his jewel on the couch. He groaned as his male member throbbed at the memories.

Maybe a cold shower would help.

Turning the knob all the way to the right, he was soon blasted with an icy spray. He gritted his teeth, practicing a self-discipline technique he had learned while training with elite guard in his uncle's palace.

Catherine would have to marry him very soon.

She would not demur at a simple civil ceremony, he was certain. She was too happy to be marrying him.

She loved him.

Though it was not necessary, it pleased him, it pleased his pride that his future wife loved him.

Her shock at his proposal underscored the reality that she had reached the age of twenty-four without once having had a serious relationship, or even a steady date. Or so her father had asserted and Hakim had no reason to disbelieve him.

Her virginity had been an important issue to Hakim's uncle. According to the old man, no royal prince of Jawhar could marry a woman of uncertain morals. Hakim felt a certain primitive satisfaction in Catherine's untouched state, but he hardly placed the importance on it that his uncle did.

After all, he'd been prepared to marry once before and the woman had not been a virgin. Undoubtedly his uncle would not have approved.

And right now, when he wanted very much to bury himself in the silken wetness of Catherine's body, her innocence was more barrier to pleasure than benefit.

REENTERING THE BEDROOM, he found Catherine sitting up in the bed wearing a virginal, almost Victorian gown in white and her dark honey hair hanging over one shoulder in a thick braid. He smiled at her innocence.

As he got closer to the bed however, his smile slipped. He doubted very much that she realized it, but the gown was borderline sheer and the dark aureoles of her nipples were visible as well as the outline of her gorgeous breasts. He wished he'd left his slacks on as the benefits of the cold shower disappeared and the silk of his boxers shifted with his growing erection.

Catherine didn't seem to notice. Her blue eyes were

unfocused as she stared at something beyond his right shoulder. Her lips were slightly parted and he could see the sweet, pink, enticing interior of her mouth.

As he climbed into the bed beside her, she jumped as if startled.

"Hakim!"

"You were not expecting me?"

Soft color flooded her cheeks and she scooted down into the bed so that the quilted spread covered her to her neck. "I was thinking about something."

"And was I this something?"

Expecting a shy affirmative, he was surprised and chagrined to see her shake her head in a jerky motion.

"What were you thinking of?"

She started. "Just, just a story that's all."

"A story?"

"Sometimes I like to tell stories in my head."

"Our lovemaking was not enough to keep your mind occupied?" The fact his innocent fiancée had been able to dismiss their lovemaking from her thoughts when he had not, irritated him.

"I didn't want to think about it."

Offended, he demanded, "Why not?"

And only realized as she pulled back that he was leaning over her in a most intimidating fashion. He did not move back however. He wanted an explanation.

"You said we couldn't make love until we're married."

"Yes. This is true."

"Well, then what would be the point of letting myself get all worked up if you aren't going to let anything happen?"

It was a good question. One he wished he could answer, but he had not been so successful in tamping down his own desires. He was rock-hard and the only thing saving his pride were the blankets covering them both. Even so, had he not had his body tilted toward her, his erection would have tented the covers and given him away.

It shamed and frustrated him that his usual ice-cool restraint was letting him down. With all his training, she had more control over her desires than he did his. He did not like weakness, even that of a purely sexual nature.

"So you told a story in your head?" What sort of story would have been sufficient to take her mind off of the pleasure of their lovemaking?

"Yes."

"And it was not about me." He felt his irritation turn to irrational anger at the thought.

"That would defeat the purpose, wouldn't it?" Her tone said her words should be obvious to even the simplest of minds.

He glared at her. "I thought you wanted me to stay with you tonight."

Suddenly the pragmatic tilt to her mouth disappeared and searing vulnerability beamed at him from the startling blue of her eyes. "Yes. Are you going to leave because I was daydreaming?"

She had much to learn about him. "I made a commitment to stay. I will stay."

She chewed on her bottom lip, still red and full from his kisses. "Do you always keep your promises?"

"Always." He repeated the word in his mind, reminding himself he had given her his word to wait until their marriage to receive the gift of her purity.

# CHAPTER FOUR

"IN OUR MARRIAGE, you will always know that when I promise a thing, it will be done."

Catherine stared at him. Their marriage? This joke had gone far enough. "Stop teasing. We're not really going to be married."

Hakim's black eyes snapped at her and the darkly dangerous side to his nature she had first suspected became all too real. "When you promise me something I expect the same from you. We will be married."

"But why?" It had to be obvious to him that he didn't have to marry her in order to make love to her. She was way too vulnerable to her desire for him and after what had happened on the couch, he had to know it.

He tapped the end of her nose with his forefinger. "Are you so uncertain of your own appeal you must ask this question?"

"But you're a sheikh for goodness' sake. Don't you have to marry a princess or something?"

"We are not quite so medieval in the royal family of Jawhar. Catherine, it is my desire to marry you."

A twenty-four-year-old children's librarian who had never even been kissed by a man before that night? "I don't think so."

The gentle touch of his palm against her cheek mesmerized her. "I want you, Catherine. I thought that was obvious."

Was it true? Felicity had told Catherine many times that she was no longer the girl too tall for her age or whose face was pockmarked with severe acne. But Catherine had never stopped feeling like that girl.

He tilted her head toward him. "Accept that it pleases me very much to make you my wife."

But why did it please him? The only logical answer that she could think of was so beyond the realm of reality, she felt shock thrill through her even contemplating it. Yet, she could think of only one reason for a man like Hakim to marry a woman like her. She had no diplomatic pull, could not increase his cachet with his people and while her father was wealthy, Hakim was wealthier.

Love.

He had to love her. It was the only thing that made any sense of their situation. He'd never said the words, but maybe that was a cultural thing. Or an alpha guy, totally in charge and too cool to admit to really tender emotions kind of thing. Whatever.

When she remained silent, stunned by the thoughts racing through her mind, he sighed and rolled onto his back. "The time has come for me to marry. It is my uncle's wish I marry now."

"And you picked me."

"You are my chosen bride, yes."

She thought of the years since her laser treatments during which her father had thrown men at her head, men interested only in what they would gain materially from the marriage. Men who had not stirred her emotions or her senses as Hakim did. Not only did he stir her emotions, he returned them.

A glorious smile broke over her face. "I want children." Family who would love her and accept her love unconditionally.

"As do I."

Then a sudden thought assailed her, one she could not dismiss. Not when he'd withheld the words of love so there was this little niggle of doubt way down, deep inside. "You have to be faithful. No mistresses. No other wives."

He didn't smile, didn't make a joke of it as some men would have. In fact, his expression turned even more serious, his mouth set grimly. "Polygamy is not practiced in Jawhar and to take a mistress would be to compromise my own honor as a prince among my people."

"Then I will marry you." Even as she said the words, she had a hard time believing them.

"Then I am content."

The words were a little disappointing. *I am content* did not sound nearly as romantic as *I love you*, but what did she expect with a sophisticated guy like Hakim? A brass band?

"It is time we slept." He kissed her briefly and it was all she could do not to follow his lips as they pulled away from hers.

"All right."

Although, he did not pull her into his body, he did lay one arm across her stomach and it felt so nice, she wasn't even tempted to slip into fantasizing herself to sleep. For once, reality outshone anything her imagination could conjure.

A FEATHERLIGHT TOUCH on his cheek woke Hakim. He waited to open his eyes to see what she would do.

Her small hand settled on his chest, her fingertips touching his collarbone. And then nothing. No movement of any kind, but he could feel her gaze as if it were an electric current directed at him. Opening his eyes, he found her looking not at his face, but at her hand against his chest.

"Good morning."

Her gaze rose to his and the wonder in the blue depths of her eyes did strange things to him. "Good morning, Hakim."

She was closer than she had been last night, her warm, womanly body pressed against his length and his morning erection tightened to urgent need in the space of a heartbeat. She could not help but notice, the small gasp and perfect "O" of her lips confirming she had indeed felt his body's response to her nearness.

He needed to move away. Immediately.

This was much too dangerous.

"Do you…"

He waited for her to finish her question, but she didn't. Instead, her hand, which had been immobile for several minutes, now started a slow slide down his chest.

He should stop her. He knew he should stop her, but that hesitant little hand turned him on as no woman performing the *raqs sharqi* after years training in belly dancing had ever done. He waited with heart-stopping impatience for her hand to reach its destination. She stopped when her fingertips reached the top of his boxer shorts. He would not ask her to continue, but waiting to see if she did so was driving him wild.

One tentative fingertip outlined the hard ridge. His sex twitched. Her exclamation drowned out his moan. She yanked her hand back and rolled away from him. Her breath was coming out in little pants.

She stared up at the ceiling, her fingers gripping the blankets with white-knuckle intensity. "I've read romance novels, you know? Some of them have pretty steamy love scenes."

"And?"

"Experiencing it is different than reading about it." She sounded so perplexed, he smiled.

"Yes."

"I mean, I didn't expect to be so nervous."

"You are a virgin, little kitten."

Her head turned and gentian blue eyes pinned him. "Why do you call me that?"

"Your name."

"My name?"

"Catherine. Cat. Only you do not act like a cat. You are more like a kitten. Inquisitive. Sometimes shy. Innocent."

"Oh. Are all virgins so jumpy about touching male flesh?"

He did not know. He had never bedded one. "You did not touch my flesh."

Catherine whipped over to face him fully.

Her braid landed heavily against her unfettered breast and he found his attention riveted by the hardened nipples pressing against the almost transparent fabric of her nightgown. So he did not catch her words at first. His brain had to play them back for him to make sense of them.

She had said, "I did touch you."

He reached out and brushed the back of his fingers against the nipple that tantalized him so. "This is touching you through your gown." Then he untied the ribbon holding the neckline of her gown together, slowly pulling the ends until the bow unraveled.

She stopped breathing.

He parted the edges of the gown and gently cupped her naked breast, palming the excited peak.

"Oh, my gosh!"

He could not quite smile. He was in too much pain from his need, but he felt the smile inside. She was so responsive to him. So perfect. "This is touching your flesh."

Her, "Oh," came out choked.

He knew he was teasing them both because he did not believe he could give her completion without taking her. His control was too close to the edge. Yet, he tormented himself playing with her nipples and caressing the swollen skin around them.

"Can I… Can I…" She repeated the phrase with each rotation of his hand, but did not complete her thought.

"Can you what?"

"Touch your flesh." The word *flesh* came out a long, soft moan.

He wanted it. He wanted it very much, but if she did, they would consummate their marriage before the wedding. This would be wrong. He had made a promise.

He must keep it. His mind knew the truth, but his libido argued that this was America, not Jawhar. She did not care about the standards to be adhered to by a sheikh of his people, would not care if he broke his word on this.

"It would not be wise."

*"Hakim."* Her tortured cry was loud in the silent room.

He reluctantly pulled his hand from her soft curve, moving to lie on his back. He felt as if he had been hiking in the desert under the noonday sun.

"You go to my head." He should not admit such a thing. It gave her power over him. Her innocence and eager response to him was too much of a temptation.

Her soft laugh had him turning his head to look at her. Her smile was that of an imp. "I was under the impression I *went to* other parts of your body."

"That too."

She looked so happy with herself, he was tempted to kiss the lips curved so sweetly. Then a wrinkle formed between her eyebrows and she frowned as if in thought. "Are you sure it's me?"

"I see no one else in the room."

She bit her bottom lip. "I mean, I read that men wake up feeling that way. Maybe it was just your normal morning reaction, you know?"

He couldn't help it. He burst out laughing.

The uncertainty in her gaze contained his mirth. He reached out to brush her cheek because he could not prevent himself. "You know book knowledge, but as you said earlier, the reality is quite different. I want you, Catherine, I am throbbing with need, I assure you."

That had her smiling again. "Good."

HAKIM HAD BEEN GRATIFYINGLY complimentary over the Belgian waffles and scrambled eggs seasoned with her own special combination of spices that Catherine had made for breakfast. It was the first time she'd made breakfast for a man. The entire morning had been filled with firsts for her. The first time waking up beside a man. The first time she had to share a toothbrush. She'd been surprised when the fastidious Hakim had so calmly asked to use hers.

It had seemed like such an intimate thing to do.

*Like what they'd done on the sofa and then in her bed hadn't been*, she chided herself.

She finished putting the dishes in the apartment's small dishwasher while Hakim wiped down the counters and table.

"You're awfully domesticated for a sheikh."

"I lived alone for most of my university years."

"You said most, does that mean you had a roommate for a while?" Her mind boggled at the thought of rooming with a sheikh. Of course she would be doing that soon. As his wife.

His expression closed. "Yes. I had a roommate for a while." He tossed the dishcloth in the sink.

She rinsed it, wrung it out and hung it over the sink divider. "It didn't work out, huh?"

She could remember horror stories from friends at college who had shared their dorm rooms with impossible people.

"No. It did not work out."

Something in his voice alerted her that he wasn't talking about getting rid of a roommate because he was a slob.

"Was it a woman?" she asked before thinking better of it.

Hakim's face tightened. "Yes."

She had to know more. "Were you a couple?"

"Yes," he said again, but offered nothing more.

She swallowed an inexplicable lump in her throat. "Was it serious?"

"We considered marriage."

"But you broke up."

"She did not fancy life in a backwater like Jawhar." The way he said the words, Catherine got the impression he was quoting the faceless woman he had once considered marrying verbatim.

"But you live in Seattle."

"At the time, my plans were to return to my homeland."

"She refused to go with you?" Catherine was incredulous. How could any woman who loved him turn down a lifetime with Hakim, no matter where they lived?

"Yes. When do you plan to tell your parents of our engagement?"

Knowing he had loved another woman enough to want marriage hurt, even though she knew it shouldn't and she was more than willing to go along with his abrupt change in conversation.

Nevertheless, his question caught her unawares. Tell her parents? What would happen if he backed out? She still couldn't quite believe Hakim wanted her, wanted to marry her.

*Stop it right there*, she firmly told herself.

She wasn't going to live in fear of rejection for the rest of her life. She had to stop reacting like the emotionally scarred preadolescent or physically scarred teenager she had been and start acting like the future wife of a sheikh.

"I can tell my mother this morning."

A strange expression crossed his face. "What of your father?"

That would concern Hakim. Parental approval was a big thing in his culture…in hers too, really. They just went about different ways of getting it. He asked beforehand while she'd learned it was easier to get her parents blessing on a project than their permission before starting it.

She looked at the clock which read seven-thirty. "He's already at work, but Mom will be home for another couple of hours."

"Then let us call her."

They did and Lydia Benning was ecstatic at the news her youngest daughter was finally getting married. Catherine grimaced at the phone. *Twenty-four was not that old*.

"You'll have to bring him for dinner tonight. I'll call right now and invite Felicity and Vance," she said, naming Catherine's sister and brother-in-law. "I can't wait to welcome the man who wants to marry my little girl. He's a sheikh—that's just so romantic."

After gushing for another full five minutes, she cut the connection.

Catherine smiled at Hakim. "I hope you don't mind, but I've agreed to dinner at my parents' house tonight."

"So I gathered. I will pick you up here."

"We could just meet there. They don't live all that far from your penthouse building."

"I'll be here at six-thirty to escort you."

"So, SHE'S AGREED has she?" Harold Benning made no effort to disguise the satisfaction he felt at the news Hakim had recently imparted. His brown eyes fairly sparked with it.

"Yes."

Harold's hands rubbed together. Of average height, he had the look of one of his miners. Even his suit, made by an exclusive London tailor, did little to hide the raw musculature of Hakim's soon-to-be father-in-law. He looked like what he was, an extremely wealthy self-made man.

He never apologized for that fact, either. At no time during negotiations with the King of Jawhar had Harold Benning showed the least discomfiture at the prospect of his daughter married to the Sheikh of Kadar.

Hakim wondered briefly how such a self-assured man could have raised Catherine, who was so insecure.

"You haven't told her about our little arrangement, have you?"

"No."

"Good." Harold's graying red head bobbed twice in acknowledgment. "She wouldn't understand. Her mother and I have been concerned about her lack of a social life for quite a while. Sure, it was understandable when she was younger, but since the laser treatments, she's been as reclusive as ever. And she balks at every attempt Lydia and I make to introduce her to men."

Laser treatment? He would have to ask Catherine about that. "She sets great store by her independence." Something that would naturally change with their marriage.

"Yes, that she does. She can be stubborn."

Hakim could not picture the shy Catherine being willful, but did not bother to disagree with her father. "Is your wife aware of the arrangement between my uncle and your company?"

Tugging at his collar, Harold grimaced. "Not exactly. I told her I was looking to fix a husband up for Catherine, but she wouldn't understand the business side of it any better than my daughter. Women are romantics at heart, the lot of them."

"You would know your family best." His sister knew to the coin how much dowry money had exchanged hands upon her marriage to a prince in their mother's father's Bedouin tribe.

Yet, she had been brilliantly happy on her wedding day. He wanted his bride to be equally pleased and if keeping certain details from her was conducive to such happiness, that was what he would do.

## CHAPTER FIVE

HAKIM APPROVED of the understated décor and Queen Anne furnishings in the Benning's Seattle mansion. Catherine's mother, Lydia, had excellent taste and it showed from the gloss black grand piano in the living room to the subdued upholstery on the dining room chairs.

They were in the dining room now, just finishing dessert. The evening had been illuminating. Catherine's mother and sister could have been twins with their petite builds, pale blond hair and gray eyes. And while Catherine and her sister were obviously close, there was a distance between mother and daughter he found disturbing.

Despite this, Lydia Benning appeared genuinely pleased her daughter was happy. *And Catherine was happy.* It radiated off her in waves, her enticing lips constantly curving in one sexy smile after another.

He watched as she took a bite of her crème brûlée, his temperature spiking when she closed her eyes and licked the spoon.

There was a small bit of burnt sugar on the corner of her lips and he reached out to gently wipe it away with his fingertip. She went still at his touch and suddenly what had been simple became complicated as her eyes reflected the desire he felt.

Laughter around them broke the sensual link.

"The wedding had better take place soon, if that look means anything." Vance's voice was full of amusement.

Hakim agreed with the sentiment completely. "I believe the waiting period in the state of Washington is one week."

"Actually it's three days." Catherine's voice was husky. "But what difference does that make? It will take at least six weeks to put together a church wedding."

Hakim turned to face his fiancée. Their eyes met again, hers had gone the color of the night sky in the desert. "Do you really want a formal wedding?"

She was much too shy to desire to be the center of attention at such a gathering.

"Why not?"

Her question shocked him. "Have you forgotten the meeting of the Antique Telescope Society we attended together?"

She looked puzzled. "What does that have to do with our wedding?"

"You refused to examine the telescope because it required going up in front of the others to do so." She had denied that was the case, but it had been obvious her shyness had held her back. "You shook like you'd been standing in the cold when you gave that small speech at the charity reception. You would be a nervous wreck put on display in front of several hundred wedding guests."

The glow of happiness surrounding her dimmed a little. "You want to marry in a civil ceremony?"

Perhaps the thought of being wed by a judge did not

sit well with her. "We can arrange a midweek ceremony with a clergyman if you prefer."

Her eyes flickered, but she did not smile in gratitude as he expected. In fact, her smile disappeared altogether.

"You don't mind being married in a church?" Vance asked.

Hakim looked away from Catherine reluctantly, disturbed by her sudden lack of animation.

"My grandfather's tribe is one of the many Bedouin tribes converted to Christianity centuries ago."

"But I thought all the Bedouins had converted to Islam," Felicity remarked.

"Not all." Hakim didn't really want to get into a discussion of religious history among the Bedouin people. He wanted Catherine to smile again. "You are all right with a small ceremony?" he asked her.

Catherine thought a certain amount of arrogance must be bred into men like Hakim. Even his question came out like a command.

What could she say? That she had dreamt of her wedding since she was a little girl? That those dreams had not included a poky wedding held in the middle of the day in the middle of the week with only family as guests?

He was right. Considering the way she reacted to being the center of attention, there was no reason for him to have suspected she wanted anything more than a few words spoken in a judge's chamber.

But her dreams were not limited by her fears and knowing that Hakim wanted to marry her had given her confidence. He was a special guy. Sexy. Gorgeous. He was a sheikh, for Heaven's sake. And he loved her. That knowledge had given her a desire to fulfill the secret dreams of her heart.

Before she could answer, he reached out and touched her. His look was intimate and full of promise. "I want to make you my wife."

The unspoken message was clear. He wanted to make love to her and he'd already said that would have to wait until after the ceremony.

She wanted him, too, even more than the fairytale wedding trappings. She forced a smile. "All right."

"Catherine!" Felicity's voice registered shock and a certain amount of disappointment.

Felicity would have fought for the flowers. In fact, she had. Not that Vance had even hinted at anything less than a full production when they'd gotten married, but then he had loved her sister. He had not even balked at Felicity's insistence on having her sister for a bridesmaid. At the time, Catherine's face had looked like she had a perpetual case of severe chicken pox.

In the end, it had been Catherine who begged her sister to allow her to be the candle lighter instead. She hadn't wanted to stand in front of a church full of people during the ceremony or be in any of the wedding photos. Her mother had been more than willing to give instructions to that effect to the photographer.

Shaking off the painful memories, Catherine smiled reassuringly at her older sister. "You can help me put it together."

Felicity's mouth opened and shut, her porcelain fine features drawn in lines of rejection. "Sweetie, you wanted a horse drawn carriage, oodles of flowers, music—"

Catherine cut in before her sister exposed her childish fantasies completely. "That was when I was nine years old." A year before she'd become *Amazon Girl*, growing five inches in one summer and towering above her classmates the following September. Boys and girls alike. For one reason or another, the next ten years had been hell on Catherine's self-confidence.

"But—"

"Do you want to go shopping with me tomorrow? I need a wedding dress."

That caught her sister's attention. "Of course, but don't you have to work at the library?"

"I'll take a personal day." She'd never taken one. She was due the concession.

"What about a honeymoon?" Vance asked.

Catherine shook her head decisively. "Not possible."

"Why not?" Hakim asked. He had planned to take her to Jawhar immediately to meet his family.

"I can't leave the library in the lurch like that. We don't have enough time to schedule someone to cover all of my shifts."

"That's ridiculous. I'll hire a temp if that's what you need," Harold inserted, his first contribution to the wedding plans.

Catherine shook her head. "Reference Desk librarians don't generally hire out through temporary agencies, Dad."

"You could always quit your job." Lydia smiled tentatively at her daughter. "Hakim will need your attention once you are married. You'll want to establish a firmer social footing."

Hakim agreed with Lydia. Not necessarily about the social scene, but he wanted to come first in his wife's priorities. The narrowing of Catherine's eyes and straight line of her mouth said she did not think much of her mother's suggestion.

"I'm not quitting my job," she said tightly, "I like it."

"And if I told you that was what I wanted?" Hakim asked, testing how much in common his fiancée had with his former live-in lover in regard to the importance they placed on their careers.

"Is that what you want?" she asked, turning the tables back on him and giving nothing away with her expression.

"I would like to know you are available to travel with me when the need arises."

"With sufficient notice, I can travel with you now."

And one week was not sufficient notice. "Then we will have to plan a trip to Jawhar after you've given proper notification for your vacation time at the library. I want you to meet my family."

"Won't they be coming for the wedding?" Felicity accepted a fresh glass of wine from her husband. "Surely your parents would not want to miss it."

"There is only my sister. She and her husband will be delighted to meet my new wife when we travel to the desert of Kadar."

"Don't you have any other family?" Felicity asked.

"Some. There is my mother's father. He is the sheikh of a Bedouin tribe." He paused. "There is also my father's brother, the King of Jawhar, as well, and his family."

"Your uncle is a king?" Felicity demanded, her eyes round.

"Yes." He caught Catherine's hand to his mouth and kissed the small circle of her palm. "Grandfather will be pleased. He has been encouraging me to marry since I graduated from university."

Of course the old man had thought marriage would bring Hakim home to the desert and it would not.

"Why can't your family come?" Felicity asked, clearly unwilling to drop the subject.

Grimness settled over him. "There is a faction of dissidents in Jawhar that oppose my uncle's leadership. He fears to leave the country now would be to put it at risk from this group of rebels."

"But I thought your family had been the ruling sheikhs for generations." Catherine's expression was clouded with confusion. "It seems odd there would be serious opposition after all these years. Your uncle is loved among the people of Jawhar."

She had been studying his country. The knowledge pleased him. "This is true. Nevertheless, dissension arises from time to time. Twenty years ago, there was an attempted coup. It failed, but many were left dead." Like his parents he thought bitterly.

"What does that have to do with today?" she asked.

"The remnant which survived that attempt have been gathering forces outside Jawhar for the past five years. My uncle is concerned they will once again attempt a removal of our family from power. He cannot risk leaving the country, nor can my cousins."

"What about your sister?"

"She is married to the man that will one day succeed my grandfather as sheikh of his tribe and will meet you when we travel to the desert for our Bedouin marriage ceremony."

Catherine's eyes widened. "We're going to be married a second time in Jawhar?"

"Yes." It would be necessary to fulfill his obligation of respect toward his grandfather.

Catherine was quiet in the car on the way to her apartment. She and Hakim were to go for the wedding license the first thing the next morning. She was still finding it difficult to assimilate that bit of information.

And her mind continued to play with images of long ago dreams. Lights flickered over the dark interior of the car as Hakim passed a semitruck on the freeway, but it barely registered as Catherine's thoughts slipped into a fantasy of the perfect wedding.

She was standing at the altar in a gown of the most exquisite lace and Hakim looked at her the way a man in love gazed at the woman he was about to marry. That was definitely a dream. They were surrounded by candles and flowers. Bunches and bunches of flowers, all white, all in perfect bloom.

A soft sound escaped her lips.

"What are you thinking, Catherine?"

She was so lost in her daydream, she answered without thought. "Flowers. Lots and lots of flowers."

Then she realized what she'd said and felt the warmth

steal into her cheeks. At least he would not notice in the dim interior of the car.

Hakim sighed. "Tell me about the horse drawn carriage and oodles of flowers your sister mentioned."

"It was just something we used to talk about when we were little."

"And something you were thinking about just now." He sounded resigned. "Tell me, Catherine. I want to hear."

Why not? He'd asked. It wasn't as if she was demanding they go through with her long ago plans. "Felicity and I used to talk about what our dream weddings would be like. I think a lot of little girls imagine themselves in a beautiful gown, riding in a carriage with Prince Charming at their side. It was all just silly fantasy, nothing that applies to this marriage."

"Am I not your Prince Charming?"

She couldn't help smiling at the question as she was sure she was meant to. "Well. You are a prince in Jawhar and you are charming, so I suppose it would be appropriate to call you my Prince Charming."

"So, it is only the fantasy wedding you find impossible."

"It's not something you can throw together in a week." She couldn't help the slight wistfulness in her tone.

"It is something that takes a minimum of six weeks?"

He had remembered her comment from dinner.

"I don't know." She'd never planned one and Felicity's wedding had been organized over several months.

"With sufficient financial and manpower resources

at your disposal, do you think you could put together this dream wedding in less than six weeks?"

"How much less?" What was he getting at?

"Could you do it in under a month?"

"Are you saying you're willing to wait?"

"It pleases me to make your dreams come true." He sounded so arrogant, but could she blame him?

He *was* making her dreams come true.

"Three weeks?" she asked, as if she were bartering a deal.

"You will take sufficient time off after the wedding to visit Jawhar?"

With three weeks' notice, she could arrange it...just. "Yes."

His smile flashed. "Then it is a deal."

THE ENGAGEMENT DINNER was more like a party. Her mother had invited a hundred of her nearest and dearest, arranging for the meal to take place in an upscale Seattle restaurant with a live orchestra and dance floor.

Catherine circled the floor in her father's arms and listened while he listed off Hakim's attributes.

"Boy's got a good head for business on his shoulders."

She wondered how her sheikh would feel being referred to as a boy. Suppressing a smile, she nodded her agreement.

"He's considerate. Look at how he changed his mind about the wedding."

Finally her amusement found vent in a small laugh. "Dad, you don't have to sell Hakim to me. He's not one of your matchmaking attempts." *Thankfully.* "I chose him and he chose me. I want to marry him."

Satisfaction coursed through her at the knowledge that her father had had nothing to do with her and Hakim meeting. She wasn't a pity date, or being eyed as a possible way into her father's good graces. Hakim wanted nothing from her father, needed nothing from Benning Mining and Excavations. His desire for her might be physical, but at least it was for her. He wanted her, Catherine Marie Benning, and nothing else.

HAKIM WAITED FOR HIS BRIDE at the front of the church. Organ music swelled and he turned to face the massive oak doors at the back of the church. They swung wide and Catherine's sister came into view. Hakim felt shock lance through him. The filmy fabric of her dress was the color of a robin's egg, but that was not what held Hakim motionless. It was the *al-firdous* style of the dress. It had been embroidered and beaded in traditional Middle Eastern patterns with thread and beads the same color as the dress. Felicity wore the matching sheer scarf looped over her pale blond hair much the same way his own sister would have done.

Hakim felt his pulse increase as he waited to see his bride. He barely noticed the flower girl as she came forward, dropping rose petals along the white runner, or the small boy wearing a traditional tuxedo bearing the rings.

Each of the attendants had taken their place when the music halted for the count of several seconds. When it began again, the organ played the strains of the "Wedding March." And then she was there, framed by the open portal of the two massive doors. Hakim's mouth went dry. She had brought together east and west with mind-numbing effect.

The traditional white wedding gown fit snuggly against her body, accentuating the feminine curves to her hips and then flared out in a skirt that rustled as she made the slow march toward him. But the hem, the edges of the medieval sleeves and the off the shoulder neckline had all been embroidered with gold geometric patterns. The semitransparent veil had matching embroidery around its edges, a veil worn in the tradition of his homeland covering all but the exquisite gentian blue of her eyes. Which as she came closer he could see had been outlined with kohl, giving his shy little flower a look of mystery.

Her lips were curved in a smile behind the soft white chiffon covering her face. She reached his side and her father put her hand into Hakim's. He curled his fingers around hers. Her skin was cold and the hand holding her white bouquet was shaking. He squeezed, offering the assurance of his presence. She had wanted this large wedding, but that did not mean a lifetime of shyness had dissolved in a fortnight.

They spoke their vows, he in a firm steady voice, she almost in a whisper. Then he was sliding a white gold band to accompany the large ruby in a Bedouin setting he had given her after she agreed to marry him. The ring had belonged to his mother.

The pastor gave Hakim permission to kiss his bride and everything around them faded to nothing as he reached out to unhook her veil and expose her face. He did it slowly, wanting to savor the moment of unveiling. Then he lowered his head until their lips barely brushed.

He liked this particular Western wedding custom. Her mouth parted slightly and he pulled her to him for a kiss that staked his claim on the beautiful woman before him for all the wedding guests to see.

When Hakim lifted his head, he knew his sense of satisfaction and accomplishment radiated off of him.

He had fulfilled his duty and had for a wife a woman who would satisfy his passions.

He was content.

"WHAT ARE YOU THINKING about, Catherine?"

Catherine turned from the window whose only view was a night-darkened sky and smiled at Hakim. "Nothing."

She'd been thinking about the night ahead, but could not have said so to save her life.

He'd been in the cockpit with the pilot for takeoff which had given her some much needed moments to herself. Ever since he had informed her there was a bedroom on the plane, with the implication they would make use of it, she had been vacillating between fear and anticipation.

She wasn't sure which one she was feeling now. "Tell me, will you insist on overseeing the landing as well?" she asked to avoid the probing look in his dark as night eyes.

He shrugged broad shoulders. "Probably."

"Your uncle's pilots must love flying you."

He flashed her a smile. "They have made no complaints in the past, but then I had been content to remain in the cabin for takeoffs and landings."

"So, what's so special about this flight?"

"You need to ask? My wife is on the plane. I must always see to her safety."

Emotion caught in her throat and she had to take a deep breath before speaking. Sometimes she forgot he didn't love her and basked in the feelings his naturally protective nature caused. "Your wife is a lucky woman to be so well looked after."

His hand cupped her cheek and anticipation overwhelmed fear in the space of a heartbeat.

"I am hoping she thinks this is so."

"She does." Involuntarily her head turned and her lips kissed the center of his palm. The scent of his skin and the warmth of it against her lips tantalized her senses. "I do."

He leaned across her and unbuckled her seat belt. Taking her hand, he pulled gently until she stood. "Come little kitten, we have a bed that awaits our pleasure."

Was it just her, or did his speech become more Eastern when his passion was engaged?

She nodded, her throat too tight to speak. It was time.

It occurred to her that she should have gone to the bedroom earlier, so she could greet him in the sensuous white satin nightgown Felicity had given her to wear tonight, but that was not to be. Catherine wasn't sure how she felt about that. Part of her was a bundle of nerves at the thought of parading herself in front of him in something so revealing. Another part of her did not wish to miss out on any of the traditional aspects to her wedding night.

Which was a silly response probably, so she said nothing.

He led her into the small bedroom at the back of the plane and she stopped, stock still, unable to believe her eyes. The bed was the first thing to arrest her interest. It was covered with quilted silks and tasseled pillows. There were flowers everywhere, all white and red. A silver ice bucket with a bottle of champagne stood beside the bed and red silk scarves covered the wall-mounted lights, giving a warm but subdued glow to the room.

"It is to your liking?"

Her eyes misted over. "Oh, yes. It's just beautiful." She turned to face him.

Heat radiated from his eyes. "I am glad to have pleased you. For today you have given me great delight."

"You liked the dress." She smiled. She'd known he would.

His hands settled on the shoulders of her bright blue suit jacket. "I loved the dress, but right now I would like very much to see you without even this most charming outfit you chose for traveling in."

She looked down at the suit and then back at Hakim. "You want me to take it off?" Somehow she had pictured him doing that for her.

"You have something else you would like to change into?" He sounded like he wouldn't mind seeing that nightgown Felicity bought her after all.

She looked around the small room uncertainly. Did he expect her to disrobe in front of him?

"There is a bathroom through there." He indicated a

door in the wall of the bedroom. "However, you would be more comfortable changing in here, I think. I will make use of it to undress."

He'd seen her practically naked, but her nerves didn't recognize that salient fact and she smiled her gratitude at him.

## CHAPTER SIX

HAKIM CAME OUT of the tiny bathroom, having given his bride time to prepare for him.

Catherine sat in the middle of the bed surrounded by several Turkish pillows. Her glorious hair was unbound for the first time of their acquaintance and its dark honey strands cascaded over her shoulders.

She had her arms locked around her drawn up knees and the expression on her face was rueful. "I didn't know if I should be standing or lying down. So, I compromised and sat."

"Are you embarrassed for me to see your body?"

She shook her head causing her hair to ripple and he felt an instant reaction coursing through his body.

"Yet you are curled up like a small kitten."

"Small?" She laughed. "Perhaps you haven't noticed, but I'm a good deal taller than most women."

"Surely not. You are perhaps a shade above average in height, but to me, you are quite small." He wished he understood this tendency she had to refer to herself as if she were a giant.

"Yes, well, you are pretty tall aren't you?" The fact seemed to please her.

He shrugged. "Truthfully, among my people I am considered so." He had not thought to spend any portion of his wedding night discussing their relative heights, but if it relaxed her, he was willing to be tolerant.

"Kids used to tease me when I was little. They called me Amazon Girl, beanpole and other horrible names."

He sat down on the bed and laid one hand over her clasped ones. "Talk to me."

"I don't want to ruin tonight with bad memories."

He wanted to banish the remembered torment in her eyes. "Share these memories and I will help you dispel them."

"You're so confident."

So she had said before, or rather that he was arrogant. He shrugged. "I am a man."

She shook her head.

"I assure you this is true."

She laughed softly. "I'm not doubting you."

Unable to resist, he reached out and let a swath of her hair slip through his fingers. "Tell me." He waited in silence while she made up her mind to do so.

"When I was a little girl, I grew five inches in one summer. I didn't stop growing until I was taller than all the other children at school. I was thirteen then and some of the boys were beginning to catch up, but I remained taller than most of them for at least another year."

"It happens to many girls, it's not so bad."

"*It was.* I suppose it's hard for you to understand, but I went to coed school. The boys teased me about being a giant and the girls pitied me. I was shy and didn't make friends easily anyway, my sudden height just made everything worse."

"But as you say, the boys grew taller and the girls—many of them—would have caught up."

She shut her eyes. "I don't want to talk about this anymore."

There was something else. Something she did not want to share, but he had a need to know everything about this woman he had married. A memory teased his conscious. "Your father said something about laser treatments. What were they for?"

She looked confused and not at all happy. "When did he mention them?"

Remembering the conversation, Hakim considered how best to answer without revealing his secret and could see no way of doing so and speak only the truth. There was a proverb among his people, *lying in its proper place is equal to worship.* It applied now. "We were discussing the upcoming wedding."

His lie was one of omission only.

"Oh." A look of profound sadness crossed her features. "When I was thirteen, I started to get acne."

"This is not unusual for an adolescent."

"No, but mine was horrible. The doctors tried antibiotics, acne skin treatments…the works. Nothing helped. My face was discolored with the purple scars from acne and fresh breakouts for five long years. The fresh breakouts finally cleared up when I was eighteen and I started the laser treatments on the scarring when I was nineteen."

He rubbed his thumbs along the perfect smoothness of her cheeks. "You are beautiful."

She grimaced. "Hardly that, but I'm no longer a social

embarrassment to my parents and an object of pity to my peers."

Tension snaked through him at her words. "Surely your parents were not concerned about your looks to that extent."

She shrugged, but it was anything but a casual gesture. "They couldn't make it better, so they ignored the problem."

He sensed there was more to it than that and remained silent, hoping she would share it with him.

She looked into his eyes for several seconds, hers glazed with memories he could not see. But he could feel the pain of their impact in her.

Then she spoke. "There was only one way for them to close their eyes to the problem and that was to avoid me as much as possible. We didn't take family photos for those five years. They frequently entertained away from home rather than risk having their disfigured daughter the cynosure of all eyes."

Her eyes shone with tears she blinked away. "Felicity was the only one who didn't let it matter. She often invited me to stay with her and tried to help me out of the shell I'd crawled into to avoid possible rejection."

The picture Catherine painted was a chilling one.

"What happened after the laser treatments?"

"They went on a campaign to get me married. I think they believed that once I got a husband it would prove their genes weren't damaged after all."

"You resisted." Harold had said Catherine had refused to consider any of the men he'd brought to her attention.

"I didn't want pity dates or to be married as a means

to an end in procuring a rich and influential father-in-law."

Hakim's body tensed. "I do not want your father's wealth."

Her smile was dazzling. "I know."

He could never tell her of the plans associated with their marriage. She would not understand. But he could show her what a desirable woman she was now, erasing the painful perceptions shaped by her past.

He stood up beside the bed and looked down at her. She tilted her head back and returned his gaze.

"You said you were not embarrassed for me to see you."

"I'm not."

He put his hand out to her. "Then come."

She hesitated only a fraction of a second before placing her small hand trustingly in his and allowing him to pull her up from the bed.

Sleek, shimmering white satin settled around the generous curves of her body, accentuating each dip and hollow in a way that sent his thoughts scattering to the four winds.

Forcing himself into movement, he turned and poured a glass of champagne. He took a sip of the bubbling wine and then grasped her shoulder, pulling her body into his so that the gentle roundness of her bottom pressed against his thighs. He placed the glass against her lips at the exact spot from which he had sipped.

"Share with me."

She allowed him to pour the champagne onto her tongue and then she swallowed. His hand drifted from her shoulder to cup her left breast. The nipple beaded against his palm, straining against the silky fabric and she let out a small moan.

He fed her another sip of champagne while squeezing the soft flesh in his hand. He continued the sensual torment until her head tipped back on his shoulder and her breath was coming out fast and strong. He transferred the glass to his other hand and began the same kneading motion on her right breast. He put the champagne to her lips, smiling as she drank mindlessly while her body writhed to his touch.

By the time the glass was empty, her moans were loud and her tender peaks were hard like pebbles. He dropped the glass to the carpet and cupped her creamy fullness with both hands, drawing his fingertips together until both her nipples rested between a thumb and forefinger. He pinched, gently.

She screamed, arching her body into his touch.

He rotated the excited flesh, ignoring her pleas to desist, to do it harder, and finally to make love to her. He wanted to draw this out, to give her more pleasure than she could imagine. His own body ached for a release he refused to give it.

"Please, Hakim. Please… Please… Oh, you have to stop. No. Do it harder." Her head thrashed from side to side against his shoulder. "I can't stand it!"

"But you can. Your body is capable of great pleasure." He whispered the words into her ear, knowing the warmth of his breath would add to her passionate enjoyment.

"Then please me," she implored.

Without warning, he dropped one hand down to her thigh and discovered something he had not noticed before. Her gown was slit all the way up her hip. Primitive satisfaction flowed through him as he delved beneath the satin to tangle in the dewy curls at the juncture of her thighs.

"Oh!" She tipped her pelvis toward his hand and his forefinger slipped onto the slick bud of her femininity.

He circled it once. Twice. And she came apart, her scream echoing in the room as her body shuddered in ecstasy against his own. He continued to touch her until she convulsed again and then shook with each light stroke of his finger.

"Oh, Hakim, it's too much." Her tormented whisper came just before her entire body went limp in his arms.

She would have fallen but for the intimate hold he had on her. He just held her, his sex hard and hurting, but the satisfaction in giving her pleasure so deep, he had no real desire to let go.

Her head turned and her lips pressed against his neck. "I love you." Her whisper against his flesh was finally too much for his control.

"I WANT TO MAKE YOU MY WIFE." Hakim's growl against her temple barely registered in Catherine's pleasure sated state.

But being spun around and kissed to within an inch of her life did.

Unbelievably his passion sparked renewed life in the erogenous centers of her body, causing extremely sensitive nipples to tighten almost painfully and swollen flesh to throb. She opened her lips, wanting his tongue. He did not disappoint her. He conquered her mouth with a sensual invasion that took the strength from her limbs and she sagged against him.

He swept her high against his chest and soon she found herself being lowered to the silk covered bed. Breaking the kiss, he loomed above her, his expression sending jolts of pure adrenaline through her body.

"You belong to me."

Tears of intense emotion burned her eyelids. "Yes."

This time when his lips touched hers, the passion was laced with a sense of purpose. He peeled off the silk robe he'd worn out of the bathroom and laid his completely naked body along hers. Hot satin skin inundated her senses everywhere their bodies collided. She started to tremble as if she'd been playing in the snow too long, uncontrollable shivers of sensation racking her body.

Her reaction did not seem to concern him. Warm masculine lips never parted from her own while talented fingers skimmed the sleek smoothness of her nightgown. She felt as if the air she was taking in was devoid of oxygen.

Breaking the kiss, she tossed her head against the pillows. *"Hakim."* She could not form another word, just his name.

He reared up above her, gloriously naked, gloriously male. "It is time."

The words were ominous. Her eyes widened as he leant forward and began the process of pulling her nightgown up her body. She was glad for the subdued lighting as the sudden memory of her physical imperfections rose up to taunt her.

He sensed her miniscule withdrawal immediately. "What is it?"

He'd see soon enough anyway. Perhaps if she told him, the scars would not come as such an unpleasant shock.

"I have marks." She couldn't bring herself to say the ugly word *scars*. "From the summer I grew so fast."

She could tell nothing from his expression as he finished removing her white satin covering. He then did something that took her completely by surprise. He rose, moving until one foot rested on the floor and one knee on the bed. Then he reached out and pulled one of the scarves from a wall sconce increasing the light in the room by almost tenfold.

Flinching, she felt the desire drain from her like water draining from an unplugged cistern to be replaced by dismay.

"Hakim, please…"

But then her gaze settled on his fully naked, fully aroused body and she forgot to worry about his reaction to her scars in the new and more gripping concern over making love for the first time. Was he as big as he looked or was that her inexperience showing? She wasn't about to ask him.

That would be mortifying.

New brides did not ask questions like that of their husbands but she had to.

"Are you oversized, or am I just worried?" The words blurted out of her mouth, halting the tan hand reaching toward her.

His head snapped up and she could tell she'd surprised him. That was fine with her. She'd downright shocked herself. Could she have gotten more gauche?

He gestured with both hands toward his erect flesh, a

rueful expression on his face. "I am what I am. I do not measure myself against other men." He sounded deeply offended by the very thought.

Well, good on him, but that didn't answer her question, did it? And anxiety ridden or not, she was beginning to have deep misgivings about proportionate sizes. For the first time since she was ten years old, she felt very small and fragile. It was not an entirely pleasant feeling.

Her gaze skittered to his face. He didn't look like one iota of his desire had deserted him. In fact, he was looking at her like a ravenous wolf ready for its first meal after a long, hungry stretch. The shaking she had experienced earlier came back, but this time it was liberally laced with anxiety.

Despite his apparent hunger, when he touched her it was with a featherlight fingertip.

He brushed along the thin ridge of raised flesh at the juncture between her arm and body, then reached across her and traced the matching one on her other side. "They are barely an inch long and very narrow. From your concern, I thought they would be much bigger."

"They're ugly."

"No, they are not."

There was no arguing with such an implacable tone and she didn't really want to. Was it possible the blemishes truly didn't bother him?

"I have some on the sides of my knees as well." She never wore short dresses because of them.

His attention was no longer on the old flaw. It had strayed along with his hands to the generous curves of her breasts. She felt them swell and tighten in response and a small moan escaped her. He bent down, lowering his head until she had no doubt of his intention.

Her breath froze in her chest as she waited for the incredible pleasure of his mouth on her. Only when it came, it landed first on one of the scars. His tongue traced where his fingertip had before and her moan this time was much louder. His mouth swiftly braced over her body until he closed it over one now turgid peak and her body involuntarily bowed off the bed, pushing her excited flesh more firmly into his mouth. Her eyes closed on the exquisite pleasure. She cried out when his hands grasped her rib cage, keeping her pressed against his mouth while he kissed, nibbled and sucked in an ever increasing circular pattern over first one breast and then the other. He was very thorough, giving every centimeter of sensitized flesh erotic attention.

He lifted his head and she gasped in protest at the loss of his pleasurable ministrations.

"You said your knees have these small marks as well?"

"What?" She got no further as his fingers began a comprehensive inspection of the area around her knees, pressing her legs apart so he could touch the stretch marks on her inner knees as well.

"I must admit, when I am here, such tiny scratches cannot hold my attention. I find other things of far more interest."

Catherine knew exactly what he meant as his fingertips started a slow glide up her inner thigh and she had to admit her stretch marks had stopped mattering to her with the first stroke of his tongue several minutes ago. Just remembering what it had felt like when he had touched her between her legs before had her aching, burning and squirming against the silk coverlet.

"Hakim?"

"Hmm?" His fingertips were on the hypersensitive flesh just before the juncture to her thighs.

"Could you put the scarf back on the lamp?"

She felt vulnerable, open and naked to his gaze and the harsh light only increased that feeling.

"Is that what you really want?" As he asked the question his fingers trespassed her most intimate flesh, finding tissues wet and swollen in preparation for their joining.

"Oh…my…gosh…" she panted as one masculine digit slid inside her untried body.

He pressed forward until she flinched with pain. He did not draw all the way out, only far enough that the discomfort left. "You are very responsive."

He delighted her too, but she couldn't get the words past the constriction in her throat.

"I want you so very much, but you must be made ready." There was no mistaking the sincerity of his statement. His voice sounded tortured.

*"I'm ready now,"* she fairly screamed as he began moving that one finger in and out, stretching her, exciting her.

"No, but you will be. It is my responsibility as your husband and your lover to make it so."

She would have answered, but his thumb had found her sweet spot and her vocal chords were only capable of moans.

"There is an ancient tradition among my grandfather's people for the women to prepare the bride for her husband by dispensing with the maidenhead. Thus there is no pain on the wedding night." His deep voice mesmerized her. "However, I must admit to a primitive satisfaction in knowing you have left this privilege to me."

"You're not going to do it so long as it's only your hand on me." It had been a struggle to get the words out.

His laughter was low and rich. "Ah, little kitten, you are so innocent. I could indeed, but I prefer to wait for my complete possession of you."

"Are we—"

The feel of a second finger joining the first inside her cut off the question of whether he intended to wait all night to make that possession.

She felt full and only slightly uncomfortable as he made the same motions with two fingers he had made with one. Tension built inside her, a now recognizable strain toward fulfillment. Just as she felt the precipice near, he withdrew his hand.

Her eyes, which had been closed in ecstatic pleasure, flew open and she looked at him, but all she saw was the top of his head as he did something she was totally unprepared for. As his mouth settled over intimate flesh she instinctively tried to arch away, but strong fingers held her hips in place.

"Hakim. *Oh, Hakim.* Please… Oh, my gosh! It's too much. Don't stop, please don't stop!"

It was unlike anything she'd known, even in his arms. The intimacy of his action mortified her on one level, but the physical sensations more than conquered her mental misgivings.

Pleasure built. Tension increased. Her body strained against his mouth, her hips against his hands. Her mouth opened on a silent scream. She thrashed. Her hands gripped the quilt. Her heels dug into the bed.

All the while, the sensual torment continued.

Then it all coalesced into a crescendo of delight so intense, she screamed wildly with the joy of it.

It was then, at that moment of intense delight that he moved up her body and slid inside her, breaking through her small barrier with a pain she hardly acknowledged. Her body was too busy dealing with the aftermath of what he had just given her.

She looked into his black eyes, her own swimming with tears and said the words she knew he was thinking. "I'm yours now."

"Yes."

She smiled at that one arrogant word. "You're mine too."

"Can you doubt it?"

And he started to move and incredibly it all began again. This time when her body convulsed, his feral shout joined her feminine whimpers as the overwhelming pleasure ignited a crying jag of monumental proportions.

He was no more affected by this than he had been by her shaking earlier. He hugged her close and whispered to her in a mixture of Arabic and English, every word and caress seemed to be assurance and praise for her femininity and passion.

Her tears finally subsided and he carried her to the bathroom where he showered with her, washing her body with meticulous care and then groaning in delight when she insisted on returning the favor.

She discovered that a soapy hand and curiosity could end in a very male satisfaction.

She was still smiling at her own daring and success when they exited the shower and he began drying her with a towel.

"I can do that."

"But it gives me greater pleasure to do it than to watch."

"Are you going to let me dry you?" she asked, grinning cheekily at him.

He laughed out loud. "You are flushed with your triumph in the shower, are you not?"

She felt herself blushing, but nodded. "It's nice knowing you aren't the only one giving the pleasure around here."

He stood up and placed his hands on her shoulders, his expression terribly serious. "The joy your response gives me is greater than any I have ever known."

Her breath caught in her throat. She could definitely get used to the flowery and extravagant way of talking passion seemed to elicit in him. "Thank you."

They went back into the bedroom and he brought forth that same uninhibited response in her three more times before they fell into exhausted slumber, wrapped tightly in one another's arms.

# CHAPTER SEVEN

MYRIAD IMPRESSIONS stamped Catherine's awareness through the tinted windows of the stretch limousine on their way from the airport to the Royal Palace of Jawhar. The gray of the window glass muted the harsh light glinting off the desert sand and roads that seemed to stretch into nothingness. Yet Hakim had assured her that they were quite close to the Royal Palace as well as the capital city of Jawhar.

Both would be found on the other side of the tall sand dunes that appeared to swallow the road on which they traveled.

She was grateful for the air-conditioned car as her skin already prickled with the heat of nerves. She would be sweating if the car matched the heated temperatures outside.

Catherine adjusted the long chiffon scarf draped over her hair for the tenth time in as many minutes and the fragrance of jasmine tickled her senses. This time she crossed the filmy fabric at her neck, letting the excess dangle down her back. She was glad women in Jawhar did not wear veils. Hakim had told her she didn't even have to wear the head covering, but she had wanted to out of respect to his uncle. The King.

The car topped the sand dunes and suddenly her

vision was filled with the massive domed structure of the Royal Palace.

Hakim had grown up here since the age of ten. He'd shared that bit of information over breakfast, but had not told her why and she hadn't asked, being too awed by the prospect of meeting the rest of the royal family. What if they didn't like her? How could an American woman be their first choice for Sheikh Hakim bin Omar al Kadar? For here, he was a sheikh, not just an extremely wealthy businessman.

And he looked the part. Her gaze strayed momentarily from the rapidly approaching palace to the man she had married less than twenty-four hours ago.

Hakim in full Arab mode was somewhat intimidating. Dressed much as the sheikh in her fantasies, he wore white, loose-fitting pants, a long white tunic over them, and a black *abaya* that looked like a cross between a robe and a cloak over that. His head covering was the only deviation. It was white like his pants and shirt with a gold *egal* holding it in place, the ends of the golden rope twisted and tucked into the band that circled his head.

She'd seen a red and white checkered head covering in his suitcase and couldn't help wondering if he wore it when he was amidst his grandfather's Bedouin tribe.

Her eyes flicked between him and the home of his youth. Even the gray tinting on the windows could not disguise the bright colors of the domes, walls and revealing archways of the huge complex.

Her heart started to hammer.

She was going to meet a king in less than five minutes.

She smoothed a miniscule wrinkle out of the over-dress of the caftan ensemble she was wearing. She'd adored it on sight. The underdress was the simplest component. It was floor length and cream in color with wine roses embroidered around the hem and sleeves. The matching overdress had a V-neck outlined in the roses and was sleeveless. Both sides were slit up to her waist for ease of walking, and to expose more of the underdress's fancy work.

It, along with several other gorgeous things to wear while on their honeymoon in his homeland, had been Hakim's gift to her that morning.

She tugged her sleeves so they fell past her wrists.

"If you don't stop fidgeting, your dress will be in tatters by the time we reach my uncle's palace."

She gave Hakim a wry grimace. "I've never met a king before."

"Now you are married to a sheikh. It is expected."

"Have you noticed that since arriving in your country, you've gotten more arrogant?" And that was saying a lot. She thought he'd been pretty imposingly confident before.

He smiled. "Is that so?"

"Even your voice has changed. You've always had a certain air of authority, but since getting off the plane you just exude power."

"I am considered one of the rulers of my country. I am the only remaining sheikh of Kadar."

"I'm surprised your uncle encourages you to live in the States then."

"There are some duties only family can perform."

Those were the last words between them before the

limousine slid to a halt outside the Royal Palace of Jawhar.

Hakim helped her from the car, but then removed his hand from her arm and maintained a distance of at least ten inches between them as they made their way inside the palace.

The incredible splendor, vibrant colors and grandiose size surrounding her, registered even as she kept her eyes fixed firmly on the huge wooden double doors they were headed toward. Just before they reached them, a servant wearing a headdress and flowing garments stepped forward to open the one on the right so that she and Hakim could walk through.

If the entranceway had been impressive, the formal reception room was overwhelming. Mosaic patterns interspersed with ornate carpets dyed a predominant red covered the floor that stretched at least fifty feet in each direction. Her eyes only skimmed the furniture and no doubt original statuary surrounding the room, before they settled on the man sitting in a chair that could only be described as a throne on a raised wooden dais.

"Bring your bride forward, Hakim."

Hakim took her hand then and led her forward until they stood only a foot from his uncle, the King.

The next two hours were a complete haze as she was first presented to King Asad bin Malik al Jawhar and then introduced to Hakim's other relatives on his father's side and expected to converse with them. Where her wedding had been both exciting and terrifying, this was worse. She did not know these people, did not speak their language and every single one of them had their attention fixed firmly on her.

She'd been shy all her life and her first instinct was to hide behind a wall of reserve or a nearby pillar, but she refused to let Hakim down. So, she forced herself to smile and talk to the intimidating strangers.

King Asad came up and hugged Hakim at one point. "Your duty is more pleasing than you at first expected, hmm?"

"Yes, Uncle. I am content."

Since both men were looking at her, Catherine assumed the comment was directed to her in some way and felt herself blushing at its implications.

"She is charming." The King's tendency to speak of her as if she wasn't there made her want to smile. He was much more traditionally Arab than Hakim, who had been educated in France and then America. "Her fair skin reveals her blushes and innocence I think."

"Can you doubt it?"

She felt like melting through the floor. They couldn't be discussing what she thought they were discussing, but after the big deal Hakim had made over her virginity she suspected they were. He'd said it was important to his family, she remembered.

"No, I do not doubt it. Assurances were made."

Assurances were made? What the heck did that mean? She wasn't about to ask in front of his uncle, but she was going to find out if Hakim had told the older man that she'd admitted to being a virgin. Just the thought of them talking about her like that made her skin heat with a truly mortified blush.

*"Hakim."* Her voice came out strangled and not at all *charming.*

Hakim's expression had turned wary, as well it should be. "Yes?"

"If you and your uncle are talking about what I think you are talking about, things could get ugly very quickly."

As threats went, it appeared to be very effective because Hakim excused them on the pretext that she was tired from the long journey.

"Stop by Abdul-Malik's office on your way to your apartments. He has the final geologist's report for you to review before Mr. Benning can begin his excavations."

Catherine stopped walking at the second mention of her father. "My dad's mining company is coming to Jawhar?"

"Yes."

"Why didn't you tell me?"

"It is not important to us, unless you wish to visit him when he is here."

"Yes, women should not concern themselves with business."

She chose to ignore the king's chauvinistic remark. There were still men among her father's generation who agreed with him, not to mention her own mother's willful ignorance of her father's business dealings.

However, she was determined to discuss the issue with Hakim when they made it to their private apartments.

Hakim's seemingly limitless ardor prevented any conversation but that which occurred between lovers from taking place as he made love to her throughout the lazy warm hours of the afternoon.

SEVERAL HOURS LATER, she was dressed for their official wedding celebration dinner and waiting for Hakim to finish a business call when she noticed the geologist's report again. She wasn't surprised her father had moved quickly to take advantage of his new connection to Hakim's resource rich, if small country.

She picked up the report, wondering what type of mining her father planned to do here. She didn't recognize the named ore, which was nothing new. Geology had not been one of her strong suits in school. Her interest had always been books and teaching children to appreciate and use them to their advantage.

As she scanned the first page, the date of the initial inquiry caught her eye. At first she wondered if it had been a typo, but other dates coincided with that being the initial query. The problem was that it was for a date significantly *prior* to her meeting Hakim for the first time at the Whitehaven Library. Her brain scrambled to understand what her eyes were telling her.

Hakim had known her father before they met.

She shook her head. No. This report was for Jawhar. His uncle had surely had business dealings with her father, but that did not mean Hakim had been apprised of them until later.

It seemed like such a huge coincidence though. Why hadn't her father or Hakim mentioned it? He obviously knew now. When had he found out?

The questions were still whirling through her mind when she looked up to find Hakim's gaze locked firmly on her. His face was completely expressionless and for some reason that really worried her.

She laid the report down, feeling an inexplicable need

to make sure it lay in the exact spot from which she had originally picked it up. "It's dated for some time before we met."

"That report is confidential." The words were hard, clipped, unlike any tone she'd heard from him before.

"Even from your wife?"

"I do not expect you to concern yourself with my business dealings."

"You sound just like your uncle."

Hakim's head cocked arrogantly in acceptance of that fact.

"I don't believe women are too stupid to understand business dealings and you'd better accept that I'm not going to pretend ignorance to feed your male ego."

That made his eyes narrow, but she ignored the reaction.

"Why didn't you tell me you had met my dad?" She made the accusation as a wild stab in the dark, hoping he would deny it. She wanted to believe the original business had been conducted between his uncle and her father.

"Harold thought it would be best."

A mixture of raw emotions swirled through her, but chief among them was confusion. Why would her father suggest keeping their business dealings a secret from her? "Did he think I might reject you once I knew you two were business associates?"

"I believe that was his concern, yes. You had shown that marked tendency for the past several years."

"But *you* had to know my feelings for you were genuine, that I wouldn't turn away from our relationship just because you and my father knew each other." She felt like she was navigating her way through heavy fog without the aid of headlamps.

"It was not a risk I was willing to take."

Because he was falling in love with her and hadn't wanted to risk losing her? For a guy with Hakim's arrogance, such an explanation just did not ring true, no matter how much her whimpering heart wanted it to.

She tried to make sense of everything while her husband watched her, his expression wary. Hakim had known her father before meeting her at the library.

"My father set us up."

Something flickered in his eyes and she had the strangest sense he was going to lie to her.

"If you won't tell me the truth, then don't say anything at all."

He jolted, his black eyes widening fractionally before the emotional mask once again fell into place. "Not all truth is desirable."

"I don't care. I won't be lied to by my husband."

"Your father arranged for us to meet, yes." The words came out grimly and gave no satisfaction at all.

He was right, some truth was unpalatable.

As unpalatable as having her virginity discussed between her husband and his uncle. Almost as if she were watching a movie screen, the scene in the reception room played over in her mind.

His uncle, looking pompous with a bearded face and white robes of state. *Her fair skin reveals her blushes and innocence I think.*

Hakim's expression sardonic. *Can you doubt it?*

Herself standing there, blushing painfully.

The King taking a deep breath and letting it out with

an expression of supreme complacency. *No, I do not doubt it. Assurances were made.*

And suddenly she understood what assurances had been made and by who. "You asked my father if I was a virgin before you asked me to marry you!"

In a very peripheral way, she realized she was yelling. She never yelled. She was the quiet one, the one who stayed in the shadows and was content to do so, but she didn't feel like being quiet. She felt like screaming the place down.

"He volunteered the information."

"Is that supposed to make me feel better?" Why in the world would her dad have felt the need to tell Hakim she'd never had a serious boyfriend? "It's not like you couldn't have made an educated guess on your own."

Her lack of experience around men had to have been obvious.

"I did not know you then."

*"Are you telling me that you discussed my virginity with my father before we ever met?"* Dread was curling its ugly tentacles around her heart even as she hoped against hope that he would deny the charge.

Hakim's eyes closed as if he was seeking an answer and then he opened them and jet black glittered at her with hard purpose. "This is not something you truly wish to know. It will only upset you to discuss this further and it will serve no good purpose. We are married. That is all that matters now."

No way. "My being able to trust my husband matters."

He drew himself up, his expression going grim. "You have no reason to mistrust me."

"If you've lied to me, I do."

"There is a proverb among my people. *Lying in its proper place is equal to worship.*"

She felt the words like a slap. Was he admitting to lying to her? "Well, there is a proverb among my people. A lying tongue hides a lying heart."

"Your father and my uncle discussed your innocence prior to our meeting the first time." He bit the words out. "Does that please you to know?" The sarcasm hurt.

"You know it doesn't." She wasn't yelling anymore. In fact, she could barely get more than a whisper past the tears now aching for release. "I was just a pity date."

And not even a pity date arranged between her father and Hakim, but one arranged between two old men. Had she not been a virgin, she had the awful feeling even a pity date would not have occurred. It was medieval and felt like the worst kind of betrayal.

"Why didn't you tell me?"

He reached out, following her when she backed up and took both her shoulders in a gentle but firm grip. His thumbs rubbed against her collarbones. "You are my wife. Does the reason we met mean so much?"

*Of course it mattered*, her mind screamed. "He fixed us up. He even told you I was a virgin! *You don't think that matters?*" she asked, trying not to choke on the words.

"Are you saying you would have been content to give your innocence to another?"

How dare he sound offended?

"Stop trying to sidetrack the issue! You lied to me. My father lied to me. I feel manipulated and it hurts, Hakim. It hurts more than you can imagine."

"It was a lie of omission only." His hands moved to cup her face. "Was this so terrible? If I had told you the truth, you would have rejected me like you rejected all the others. We would not be married now. Is that what you want?"

He wasn't putting it back on her like that. She yanked her face from his grasp. "I love you. I wouldn't have rejected you because of the truth."

"Like you are not rejecting me now?"

*"I'm not rejecting you,"* she screamed, out of control and in emotional pain, "I'm rejecting being lied to, being betrayed by the man I love."

How could he not understand that? "How would you like knowing I had colluded with your family behind your back? How would you like knowing you'd been made a total fool of?"

"How did we make a fool of you? Do you consider it folly to have married me?"

They stood facing each other, two combatants on a battlefield of emotional carnage.

Her shoulders slumped, all energy draining from her as she acknowledged the truth that came from knowing he had been dishonest with her. "Yes, if it meant tying myself to a man I cannot trust."

"You are making more of this than it is," he retorted coolly.

"Am I?" Two words whispered so low, she didn't know if he heard them, but he moved.

"Yes."

She shook her head. Denial? Confusion? She didn't know, but it served to loosen the hot wetness gritting behind her eyes. He pulled her into his body again as she started to cry, great gulping sobs that sounded as awful as they felt. She struggled, but he was too strong and she gave in, letting the grief take over. He didn't try to quiet her, but just held her, seeming to realize she had to have this emotional outburst.

Eventually the tears subsided and he handed her a handkerchief to mop herself up. She stepped away from him to do so.

He watched her broodingly. "How we came together is no longer important. You must believe this. We are husband and wife. Your father's interference has no bearing on our future. We make of our marriage what we choose to make of it."

The crying had calmed her enough to really take in what he was saying and his words made her stop and think.

She'd been rebelling against her dad's interference in her life since reaching adulthood, but could she really regret meeting Hakim just because Harold Benning had a hand in it? Or even his uncle for that matter? Two old men had played matchmaker and discussed private affairs of hers they had no business discussing, but in the end she had married the man she loved. No one had coerced her.

Unlike the other men her father had fixed her up with, Hakim didn't need anything from Harold Benning.

No matter what had brought them together, he had married her for her own sake and he loved her. But a man who loved her would not have lied to her, would he?

"It hurts that you hid this from me, that you didn't trust my love enough to believe I wouldn't let it matter.

A-And…a lie by omission is still a lie." She was trying not to cry again and her words came out stuttered.

"It was not my intention to hurt you."

"But you did."

"This I can see. I made a mistake." She could sense this was not easy for him to admit.

"You didn't trust my love."

"I did not see it that way."

If he hadn't seen it that way, then, *"Why did you lie to me?"*

"It was your father's wish."

It was chauvinism at its worse for her dad to think he had the right to ask Hakim to keep the secret and for Hakim to believe he had an obligation to do so. Maybe how they met wasn't so important, but where she stood in his list of priorities was. So was knowing he would never lie to her again.

"My wishes should come first with you. I'm your wife and you made promises to love and cherish me. My father has no place in our relationship."

"That is what I have been saying."

"Then promise me that from now on I come first in your considerations." She meant between her and her father. She knew she could not come first over everything for a man in Hakim's position.

"This I will do."

"Do you *promise*?" He always kept his promises.

He brushed the wetness from under her eyes with his thumbs. "I promise."

"You're big on keeping your promises. I remember you telling me that."

"This is true."

"Then promise me one more thing."

He looked wary. "What?"

"That you will never lie to me again."

He hesitated and she glared at him. "I don't care if you think the truth will upset me. I can't trust you if I believe you'll lie to me, even if it is to protect my feelings."

"Then I promise this also."

She nodded, feeling a sense of relief that he had agreed so easily. If she couldn't trust him, she could not stay with him, no matter how much she loved him. "I need to fix my makeup."

He drew her forward and dropped a soft kiss on her lips. It felt like an apology and she took it as such.

He released her. "Be quick. The dinner will have started without the guests of honor."

# CHAPTER EIGHT

LATER, SITTING BETWEEN her husband and the wife of one of his cousins, she thought the dinner would go on forever. It wasn't that the company was not entertaining. They were. Hakim's cousin's wife was sweet and everyone had been very kind to Catherine, but her husband was driving her crazy.

He seemed to have gotten it in his head that she needed reassurance regarding their marriage. Physical reassurance.

Since it was considered unseemly among his people for a husband and wife to touch in public, all of his touches were surreptitious. And dangerous. Under the cover of the table, he caressed her thigh through the black lace overlay of her dress.

He had told her to dress in Western style for the dinner. She'd been glad she'd followed his advice when she arrived to find the other women similarly attired, although the men wore traditional Arab costume.

However, when she felt Hakim's foot brush the inside of her calf under her long skirt, she wished she was wearing more than a pair of sheer stockings. Her body was humming with the excitement only he could generate and no way to appease it. They could not leave the dinner until his uncle excused them.

She turned her head to tell him to stop it and found herself mesmerized by a pair of obsidian eyes.

"Hakim."

"Yes, *aziz*?" His foot moved and sensation arced right up her leg to the very core of her.

She gasped.

He smiled.

She was still smarting a little from their earlier argument, but he had promised never to lie to her again. "If you don't stop it my foot is going to make contact with your leg as well, but it will still have a shoe on and its sharp toe will be the point of impact."

He laughed and popped a grape into her mouth. "Your impact on my body is sharp indeed."

She couldn't help smiling at him.

He removed his foot and winked.

She sighed with exasperation and turned to her other dinner companion, Lila.

The other woman turned to her and smiled warmly. "You and Sheikh Hakim are well matched."

"Thank you."

"It is good to see him find pleasure in a duty that must have been hard to accept."

"Yes." The more time she spent around Hakim in Jawhar, the more she realized how much he had sacrificed of his personal happiness to oversee the family's business interests abroad.

"In my opinion, it was not necessary. It seems reactionary to believe the dissidents could force the family into fleeing the country. And, after all, marriage to an American would be difficult for the more traditional members of our family, but Hakim is content." Lila leaned forward and whispered, "My husband would never approve my having a career."

Considering the fact the woman's husband was the Crown Prince of Jawhar, even Catherine could understand his reasoning. Being a queen would be a full-time job.

Catherine didn't know what her marriage had to do with politics. "Does King Asad really believe a coup could succeed?"

"I do not think so. I believe he assigned Sheikh Hakim his duty to be prepared in case it is so, but not out of real necessity. The dissidents have less support than they did twenty years ago and that uprising failed."

"It's too bad the king will not trust anyone but family to oversee the business interests. Hakim would be happier living here in Jawhar." Catherine was certain of it.

"Perhaps my honored father-in-law could be persuaded to assign a trusted advisor to oversee the business affairs for the family, but he would only trust family to fulfill the duty assigned to Hakim."

Catherine didn't understand. Was the language barrier the problem, or was Lila implying that Hakim had additional duties in the States?

"After all, only a family member could be trusted to sponsor the others for living visas in the United States. I think your government may even require it to be a relation. You would know better than I."

Catherine's confusion at finding the date on the geologist's report was nothing compared to what she felt now. "I don't understand," she admitted.

Lila smiled. "I found it rather complicated when my

husband told me about it as well. It pleases me that he shares so much with me. In some ways he is very traditional, but he does not dismiss my intellect."

Catherine would have felt more empathy if she wasn't so puzzled. "Can you explain it to me?"

"Why don't you ask Hakim? I, too, prefer not to admit to my husband when I don't understand something he has explained. I suppose it is an issue of pride." She sighed, then smiled. "It's quite simple, really. Once Hakim married you, he was then eligible through you to sponsor long-term living visas for members of his family provided he could guarantee their income. Which, of course, is no problem."

"Long-term living visas?" Catherine choked out.

Lila nodded and went on. "Then of course there is the mining partnership. King Asad wants to realize the benefit of the geologist's findings. He is convinced your father's company is key to making that happen."

"Mining partnership?" Catherine asked, her voice faint to her own ears.

Lila missed the question and leaned forward confidingly. "My husband thought King Asad would surely bring forth a more distant relation for the marriage alliance until he realized that, as usual, his father had other benefits in mind."

"Long-term living visas." The words came out of her subconscious as Catherine dealt on a conscious level with the other things Lila had told her.

Lila nodded. "King Asad is a sharp negotiator."

Catherine's mind was still stuck on the concept that a marriage had been part of the mining deal. *Her mar-*

*riage?* "You mean Hakim's duty was to marry me?" Catherine whispered in dawning horror.

Lila's brow furrowed. "Well, yes. You could put it like that."

Catherine wondered if there was any other way of putting it. "The further benefits of my marriage to your husband's cousin were the long-term living visas in case political dissidents made them necessary?" she asked, clarifying it in her mind as she spoke.

This time Lila did not answer, seeming to finally latch onto the fact that what she'd been saying was news to Catherine. And not welcome news.

For her part, Catherine was finding it almost impossible to wrap her mind around the idea that her marriage had been arranged as part of a business deal with Benning Excavations. That the man she believed had loved her had lied to her and tricked her. No love there.

Lila looked worried. Really worried.

Catherine felt sick to her stomach and had to swallow down bile as her throat convulsed. Everyone at the dinner probably knew that she was the albatross around Hakim's neck. Necessary for him to fulfill his duty, but *not* a wife he truly wanted and desired. Certainly not a loved wife.

Humiliation lanced through like a jagged edged sword.

"Does the whole family know?" she asked, needing confirmation of the worst.

Lila shook her head vehemently. "No one outside of King Asad, Abdul-Malik, my husband, Hakim and you know of the plan."

Learning that the mortifying truth was known by

only a select few did not lessen the pain threatening
to engulf her in a tide of black anguish. She'd been
betrayed on every level. Her father had lied to her. Her
husband had lied to her. She'd been used as a means to
an end by a king she'd never even met before today.

She'd been used to fulfill his duty by the man seated
next to her. The swine. The no good, double-dealing…
She couldn't think of a word bad enough to describe
him.

She hated him.

She hated herself more. She'd been such a fool.
Twenty-four-years old and still too stupid to realize
when she was being manipulated and used. Hakim did
not love her. He didn't even care about her. You didn't
use people you cared about. What did that say about her
dad?

She felt another wave of sickness wash over her.

Did her mother know?

Did Felicity? No. Felicity would have told her.

"Are you all right? You've turned very pale." Lila's
concerned voice barely penetrated the fog of pain surrounding Catherine.

Lila leaned around Catherine. "Sheikh Hakim. I
think your wife is ill."

Hakim turned, his duplicitous face cast in a false
show of concern. "Is something wrong?"

"You don't have a heart." Venom born from an unbearable pain laced each word. "I hate you."

He reeled back as if she had struck him. Lila's
shocked gasp barely registered. Catherine just wanted
out of there. She was breaking up, her heart shattering

into jagged pieces inside her chest. She went to stand, but Hakim caught her and held her to her chair.

"What is going on?"

"Let me go."

"No. Explain what has you so upset."

"You lied to me."

"We discussed this. You understood." Even now, he wasn't going to admit the full truth.

"I'm the duty. You *had* to marry me." Her voice rose with each successive word until she was practically shouting. "It was part of some mining deal with my father!"

Hakim's gaze slid to Lila. "What did you tell her?"

Catherine answered for the other woman. "She told me the truth, something my husband and father did not see fit to do."

She could hear King Asad inquiring about what the problem was. Her husband's answer and his anger both registered in the peripheral of her consciousness. As did Lila's profuse apologies. It was all there, but none of it was real. She couldn't take it in.

She'd felt the pain of rejection many times in her life, but nothing had ever been like this. To know she was nothing more than a commodity to be bartered by her dad and a means to an end to the man she had loved. To know where she had believed herself loved, she had been merely tolerated. It was too much. Too much betrayal. Too much pain to take in.

She tried to stand again, forgetting Hakim's iron grip on her arm. She looked at his hand curled around the black lace sleeve. It hurt to see it, to know he was touching her. She didn't want his hand on her, but her voice would not work to tell him so. So, she looked away, letting her gaze roam over the rest of the room.

Shockingly no one seemed to notice the holocaust of emotion at the head table.

Then she realized that everyone else had kept their voices down, their expressions bland. Even Lila, whose eyes registered remorse wore a plastic smile on her lips. Hakim was no longer talking to King Asad.

He was talking to her, but the words weren't registering over the rushing in her ears.

"I want to go to our room," she said, right over the words coming out of her husband's mouth. "Please tell your uncle I am not feeling well and must go."

She wondered if he would argue with her.

He didn't.

She watched dispassionately as he turned to his uncle, spoke a few words in the other man's ear and then turned back to her.

"He will give his official blessing to our marriage and then we will be free to go."

She did not respond.

She simply sat, wishing Hakim would let go of her arm, while the King stood and spoke his official blessing. When he was done, he instructed the newlyweds to retire to their apartments, saying they had better things to do than listen to old men tell jokes well into the night. The room exploded in laughter, but Catherine's sense of humor had vanished.

Hakim pulled her to her feet.

She swayed. Stupid. She refused to let her body be so affected by her emotional devastation. That is what she told her mind, but the woozy feeling persisted.

Suddenly Hakim swept her into his arms, making a comment about following Western tradition and carrying his bride over the threshold. That was supposed to happen in their new home, but she didn't correct him. She doubted anyone cared.

They were all too busy cheering her bastard of a husband's seemingly romantic action.

SHE SAID NOTHING all the way down the long hallway, up the ornate staircase, down another hallway and through the door into their apartments. Silence continued to reign as he released her to sit on the gold velvet covered sofa, but when he went to sit beside her, she spoke.

"I don't want you near me."

He ripped his headgear off and tossed it on the desk. It landed smack on the offending mining report.

"What has changed, Catherine? I have not changed. Our marriage has not changed. We discussed this before the dinner. How we met is not important to our future. It is already in the past."

She glared at him, wishing looks really could singe.

He sighed heavily. "There is no need for you to be so upset."

"No way did you just say that."

His jaw went taut, his expression frustrated.

"I find out that I've been manipulated by people I should have been able to trust above anyone else in my life, my husband and my father, and you don't think I should be upset?"

He'd grown up in Jawhar, not another planet...even if he was a sheikh. He couldn't be so dense.

"I did not manipulate you."

"How can you say that?"

"Did I coerce you into marriage?"

"You tricked me."

"How did I trick you?"

"Are you kidding?" She threw her hands in the air and even that hurt, like her muscles were as bruised as her emotions. "You made me believe you were marrying me because you *wanted* to marry me. Whereas in reality it was all some plan your uncle had cooked up with my father." Her jaw ached from biting back the tears. "I thought you loved me."

"I never said I loved you."

Her heart felt like it shattered in her chest. "No. You didn't, but you knew I believed it was me you wanted."

"I did want to marry you, Catherine."

"Because it fulfilled your duty to your uncle and because my father made it part of his filthy mining deal with an opportunistic king."

Hakim tunneled his fingers through his hair and clasped the back of his neck. "It also fulfilled my desire, little kitten."

"Don't call me that! It doesn't mean anything to you. All those endearments you use. They're just words to you. I thought they were more, but they aren't."

He crossed to her in two strides and fell on his knees before her. "Stop this. You are tearing yourself apart, imagining the worst and it is not true. It pleased me to make you my wife. It pleased you to marry me. Can you not remember that and forget the rest?"

Ebony eyes compelled her to agree.

She wanted to, if only to stop the drumbeat of pain remorselessly pulsing through her. She tried to stifle a whimper, but the broken sound escaped her.

He groaned and pulled her to him. "Why I asked you to marry me is unimportant," he said, speaking into her hair. "The only thing that matters now is that we are married. We can be very happy together."

He was wrong. So wrong. "It is important."

"No." His hand brushed her back. "Many marriages are arranged among my people and they are very happy. It is what we give to our marriage that will determine what it becomes for us. Trust me, jewel of my heart."

She'd been listening right up to that moment, wondering if he was right. Wishing it could be so, but it couldn't.

"I can't trust you." And she wasn't the jewel of his heart. He didn't love her, therefore she had no place in his heart. Rage born of betrayal welled up in her. She pushed on his chest. *"Get away from me!"*

Again he had that look like she'd smacked him. "I am your husband. You will not speak to me like that."

His arrogance wasn't in the least attractive at that moment.

"You're only my husband until I get home and file for divorce." What that wouldn't do to all his uncle's and her father's machinations.

She supposed that none of them had taken into account the possibility that the worm would turn. They probably thought that she'd stay married to a man who had lied to her and manipulated her. After all, what else did she have to look forward to?

She might not be the kind of woman who haunted

men's dreams, but that didn't mean she was willing to live the nightmare of loving someone whose whole purpose in pursuing her had been to use her.

He jumped to his feet and towered over her. "You do not mean that. I will not allow it."

"I don't know how things work in Jawhar," she said with dripping sarcasm, her heart hemorrhaging with grief, "but back home I can file for divorce without the approval of my sheikh husband." Or her deceiving father for that matter.

"You are tired. You are not thinking rationally." He rolled his shoulders as if trying to lessen the tension surrounding them.

She could have told him it wouldn't work. Nothing would work. The tension was born of anguish and it was anguish that had no respite.

"You're wrong. I'm thinking more rationally than I have for the past six weeks."

He shook his head, as if he could negate her words. "You need rest. We will not discuss this further right now."

She crossed her arms over her chest. Was he for real? Okay, maybe that was the way things worked in Jawhar, though she took leave to doubt it. But he'd gone to school in both France and America, both countries hotbeds of feminism. And although she had never considered herself a raving feminist, that didn't mean she was going to let her husband treat her like a child.

"*That's it?* You say we aren't going to talk about it and I'm supposed to shut up and go to bed?"

He rubbed his hand over his face. "That is not what I meant, Catherine. If it pleases you, I am tired, as well. I would be most grateful if we could wait to discuss this further until we have both had a chance to sleep."

As hard as she tried, she could not detect a single note of sarcasm or condescension in his voice. He looked tired, too. Considering how little sleep they'd had the night before and the way they had spent the afternoon, she could even understand why.

But a cynical doubt needled her already agitated brain. Was he just trying to take their battle to a location he had shown his mastery in so well already?

If he was, he had a rude shock coming.

"You're right. I am tired." And heartsick. "I would like to go to bed."

He looked relieved.

"But there is no way on this earth I'm sleeping with you." She said each word as it were its own sentence, spacing them succinctly so there could be no confusion about her intentions.

"You are my wife."

She didn't feel like a wife right now. She felt like a dupe. "I'm your means to an end," she derided.

His body tightened and he pulled himself to his full height, his chilling expression of outrage making him look bigger than his already tall six feet two inches.

"You are my wife," he gritted out between clenched teeth, more angry than she had ever seen him. "Several hundred guests bear witness that this is so. I have legal documents that state you are no longer Miss Catherine Benning, but Catherine bin Hakim al Kadar. Do not ever again say you are not my wife or attempt to deny my name."

His vehemence shocked her. He looked ready to spit ·

nails. Good. She shouldn't be the only one hurting here. Though, she doubted sincerely he was hurting. Angry more like. Apparently it offended his male ego in a very big way for her to deny the reality of their marriage.

"Legal documents don't make a marriage. They're just paper. They don't prove anything." Even in her anger, she doubted her own words. Being married meant something, but not the same thing to her and Hakim evidently.

"The consummation of our marriage is a fact."

She went hot then cold as his words sank in. "Are you saying you only made love to me so that I would consider myself married to you?" she asked wildly, realizing that she was fast approaching the irrational state he'd accused her of earlier. If she wasn't already there.

The question seemed to stun him because his head jerked back and then he stared at her with incredulity in every line of his face. "You dare ask me such a question?"

"Why not? You married me for reasons I knew nothing about. As far as I'm concerned, all your motives are suspect."

She watched in a furious kind of fascination as he visibly took control of his anger until his face was a blank mask.

He spun away from her, his hands fisted at his sides the only indication that his emotions were not completely controlled. "Very well. I will sleep on the divan in here."

Even in the agony of her devastation, practical considerations asserted themselves. He was way too tall for the smallish divan.

"You can have the bed. I'll sleep out here." She sincerely doubted she'd get much rest anyway.

"Either we share the bed or you sleep in it alone." He still hadn't turned back to face her, but from the sound of his voice, she didn't doubt he meant what he said.

"Fine." If he wanted to suffer, let him suffer. She'd offered a better solution. It was his own fault he was too stubborn to take it, but why he had refused to take it niggled at her conscience. "I'll sleep alone."

A slight inclination of his head was the only indication he had heard her words.

She got up and went into the bedroom. She stopped at the doorway and compulsively looked back at Hakim. There was something incredibly lonely about his stance by the window. He looked as isolated as she felt.

But he'd chosen this path, her mind cried. She hadn't. It had been chosen for her by men who thought she was unworthy of truth and honest consideration. Unworthy of love.

# CHAPTER NINE

CATHERINE WOKE TO THE smell of coffee.

Her eyelids fluttered, but did not open.

"Good morning. I have brought you breakfast."

The sound of Hakim's voice was a welcome intruder into her slumber until the pain she had escaped for a few short hours in unconsciousness rushed back in a wave so strong she actually moaned.

Masculine fingers tunneled through her hair to cup her scalp. "Are you all right, little kitten?"

The shock of the stupidity of the question brought her eyes wide open and her gaze to the source of her torment.

He was sitting beside her on the bed, wearing a *thob*, but clearly having just woken himself. His hair was mussed, his jaw darkened with morning stubble, his eyes faintly shadowed from what must have been a near sleepless night for him as well. She'd known the divan was too short for him.

How could a man look so very masculine and appealing in something that could be mistaken for full-length robe or dress? Yet, he did. The typical Arabic lounging garment accentuated Hakim's maleness rather than detracting from it. And she didn't want him looking attractive.

She'd come to some very difficult decisions in the

long hours of the night. Being reminded of just what she was giving up did not help her resolve or lessen the ache in her heart.

Determined to ignore his blatant maleness, she struggled into a sitting position. She tucked the blankets around her, covering the sheer fabric of her nightgown. She didn't want Hakim thinking she was extending any invitations.

His brows rose at the gesture, but he said nothing and laid the rattan breakfast tray across her lap.

There were two croissants on the plate and two demi-tasse cups of dark, fragrant coffee as well as a small bowl of figs.

She picked up one of the cups of coffee. "Thank you."

"It is my pleasure."

Seeing no reason to put off telling him of her decision, she dove straight in. "I want to go back to Seattle."

He waited to answer until he had finished chewing a bite of his croissant. "We will, inevitably return as planned. My business is there, your job as well."

She placed her cup carefully back on its small white saucer. "I meant today."

The ridge of his jaw became more pronounced. "That is not possible."

"Your jet is broken?"

Rather than respond to the sarcasm in her question, he answered it as if it had not been rhetorical. "No."

"Then I don't see the problem."

"Do you not?" The silky menace in his tone reminded her that this was a man who had been trained since birth to exercise a great deal of authority.

Still, "No," she insisted stubbornly.

"Have you forgotten the wedding ceremony among my grandfather's people?" He asked the question conversationally, as if they were discussing their social schedule rather than the end of one of the shortest marriages on record.

She wasn't about to play the hypocrite. "It would be ridiculous to go through yet another wedding ceremony when I intend to go home and file for divorce, don't you think?"

That elicited a reaction, albeit a subtle one. His entire body tensed as if prepared for battle. "There will be no divorce." So decreed Sheikh Hakim bin Omar al Kadar.

"I don't see how you can stop me." She wasn't one of his subjects.

The expression on his face said she didn't have a very efficient imagination and as much as it shamed her, she shivered. "I mean it, Hakim. I won't stay married to a man who sees me as nothing more than a convenient means to an end."

"You are not a convenience. You are my wife."

"So, you keep saying. Funny, I don't feel like a wife."

Something feral moved in his eyes. "I can take care of that small problem."

She knew just what he meant and she shook her head vehemently. "I'm not going there again."

"Where?" he asked in a honeyed drawl that made her wish she was fully dressed and sitting across a table from him, not a small breakfast tray.

Nevertheless, she refused to let him see how intimidated she felt. "Bed," she said bluntly.

"But we are very compatible in bed." His fingers brushed down the curve of her breast.

She sucked in air, but it didn't help the goose bumps instantly forming on her flesh or the tightening of two erogenous bumps she hoped did not show through the blankets. Her heart felt dead inside her, why didn't her body follow suit?

"That's sex and I'm sure you've been *compatible* with other women before."

"Never like with you."

She wished she could believe him. It would have been some small assuagement for her lacerated pride. But after yesterday, she didn't trust anything he said. "Tell it to the marines."

He laughed at that, though it was a harsh sound. "I have no interest in making love to anyone but you."

"It's not making love when you don't love me."

His superior smile made her want to scream. "Then what is it?"

"Sex, or if you'd rather…" She said a blunt Anglo-Saxon term she had never used before in her life. Then she picked up her croissant and forced herself to take a bite to show she wasn't affected by the conversation.

"Crudeness is unbecoming in you."

She finished chewing her food before speaking. "I'm not interested in what you find becoming. Not anymore."

With a gesture of frustration, he stood up. "Enough."

She glared at him. "You can't order me around like a child."

"Why not? You are behaving like one."

"In what way am I acting childishly?" she demanded.

"You are happy married to me. You love me, yet you threaten to dissolve our marriage on the flimsiest pretext."

"I do not consider betrayal a flimsy excuse!"

"I did not betray you!"

She'd never heard him shout before. She didn't like it.

He took a visible hold on his temper. "When we married, you were so filled with joy, you glowed."

She opened her mouth, but he held his hand up.

"Do not deny it."

"I wasn't going to."

"Good. Finally, we move forward."

"I'm not happy *now*."

"That is apparent, but not something that cannot be changed."

"It will never change," she said with all the despair eating away at her emotions. She'd been happy because she believed the man she loved also loved her. He didn't. End of joy.

He shook his head, the movement decisive. "This I do not believe."

"It may come as a shock to you, but being used by both my father and my husband does not make me happy and since that reality cannot be altered, I don't know how you expect my feelings to change."

Time was supposed to heal all wounds, or so the old saying went, but right at that moment the future stretched forth in one bleak ribbon of pain.

"It is not a matter of being used. I know you resent your father's interference in your life. You have said so, but it is a father's prerogative to find a suitable husband for his daughter. And all the pleasure we found in one another's company awaits only your acceptance of the truth."

"Sex without love is degrading and a father concerned for his daughter's well-being does not sell her in exchange for a mining partnership."

"He did not sell you."

Tears that should be impossible considering how many she had shed in her lonely bed the night before welled and spilled down her cheeks. "Yes, he did. I'm nothing more than a duty wife, bought and paid for."

It hurt so much, she felt as if her heart was being squeezed by a vice.

She turned her face away, not wanting him to witness her grief.

The tray was lifted off her lap. A moment later, she was being pulled into his strength. "Don't cry. Please."

She didn't want him to comfort her. He was the enemy, but there was no one else and the pain was just too heavy to bear alone. His hands rubbed her back, his mouth whispered soothing words while she wept silent tears, soaking the front of his *thob*.

"You are more than a duty wife."

"You don't love me." Her voice broke on each word as the tears competed with her mind for control of her tongue. "You married me because your uncle told you to."

His arms tightened around her, but he did not deny it.

She pressed her face into his chest, wanting to blot out reality. But reality would not be ignored. She was only putting off the inevitable, she realized, allowing Hakim to hold her because she knew it was the last time.

Taking a deep breath, she hiccuped on a sob, but eventually managed to gain control of herself again. She pushed herself from his arms. "I need to get up."

He frowned. "This conversation is not finished."

"I need to get ready to travel."

He searched her face, but she refused to meet his gaze.

Finally, he sighed. "You are right. We need to prepare for our journey to Kadar. We go by helicopter. As much as it pains me to see your hair bound, you should braid it."

Hadn't he heard a word she had said? "I'm not going with you to the desert. I'm going home," she spelled it out as if to a slow-witted child.

"You are wrong." His expression was carved in granite. "You will come with me to *our* home in the desert."

"I won't."

"You will." Standing beside the bed, he looked every inch the Arab prince, his belief in his own authority absolute.

"You can't make me."

"Can I not?"

Frissons of unease shivered along her spine, but she defied him with her eyes. "I'm not going through a second sham of a marriage."

"There is nothing fake about our marriage."

"That's your opinion and you are entitled to it, but it won't change mine."

"I have had enough of this. We will participate in the Bedouin ceremony tomorrow as planned. I will not allow my grandfather to be shamed before his people. Nor will I allow you to dismiss our marriage."

With that, her even-tempered, civilized husband stormed out of the room.

TWO HOURS LATER, Catherine was dressed in a sleeveless fawn sweater and doeskin pants for traveling. It had a matching calf-length cardigan that made it perfect for the transition in weather from Jawhar to Seattle. And she was going to Seattle, regardless of what her arrogant, deceitful wretch of a husband had decreed.

She checked to make sure her passport was still in her handbag and nodded in satisfaction at the sight of the small blue book. She had cash, her credit cards, everything she needed for departure from Jawhar.

She'd called the airport minutes after Hakim had stormed from their apartments that morning. Then she'd called for a car, reasoning that he was too arrogant to have put a moratorium on her going anywhere. She'd been right. There'd been no problem ordering a car to take her to the airport.

Hakim had assumed she'd wait for him.

That they would continue discussing their marriage.

But there was nothing left to discuss.

She hurt in ways she hadn't known it was possible

to hurt and she was not sticking around for more of the same.

She'd come out onto the balcony to wait for a servant to announce her car was ready.

The sights and sounds of Jawhar's capital were open to her as their apartments were on the outer wall of the Royal Palace. While the city was much smaller than Seattle, the cacophonous mixture of voices, beeping horns and tinkling bells that rose to her was more impacting on her senses than Seattle's downtown district. The sun beat against her skin, warming her body while leaving her heart a cold lump in her chest.

A sound in the sitting room alerted her to a servant's arrival.

The trip to the airport was uneventful.

As a member of the royal family, getting a seat on the next flight to a major airline hub was a cinch and within short order she found herself in a first class seat waiting for the plane to take off.

The door closed and then the pilot announced their departure. They taxied to the runway and then stopped, no doubt waiting in line for their takeoff slot.

It seemed a long time coming and other passengers began talking among themselves, asking the flight attendant about the delay. Unfortunately, the conversations were in Arabic and she had not yet learned enough to interpret them fully.

But as the minutes ticked on a premonition of dread began to assail her.

When the outer door opened, she watched with almost fatalistic detachment as her husband's form came into view.

His eyes caught hers immediately and the rage she saw in the black depths made her mouth go dry.

He didn't bother to come to her row, but barked out a command to the flight attendant who quickly removed Catherine's bag from the overhead compartment.

Catherine didn't move, but glared her defiance at him.

He could take her bag. She didn't care. She wasn't getting off this plane. "I'm going home."

Hakim did not respond. He spoke again to the flight attendant, this time his voice not so harsh, but the implacability of his tone was apparent even to Catherine, who could not understand what was said.

The flight attendant approached Catherine. "His highness has decreed we cannot take off until you leave the plane, madam."

She didn't need the immediate and quickly escalating grumbling to tell her defeat was staring her in the face. She could not hold everyone back. There was no doubt but that Hakim had the power to ground their plane indefinitely and the hard-faced stranger standing by the open doorway would do it.

She unbuckled her seat and stood up. Hakim turned and left. She followed him off the aircraft, stepping gingerly down the portable stairway that had been transported to the runway for her husband, the sheikh's benefit.

When she reached the bottom, one of the black clad security men led her to a waiting limo.

She climbed into the backseat. She refused to look at her husband. She was both furious and frightened. The

THE HELICOPTER WAS HOVERING above an oasis surrounded by tents when Hakim leaned next to Catherine and spoke into her ear so she could hear him. "Put your sweater on."

The desert's evening air was chilly, particularly so far above the ground, so she acquiesced without argument. Besides, even furious with him, her body responded to his nearness in a disastrous way. She didn't want to encourage more of it by arguing and keeping him close to her. She could smell his unique scent, the one her body identified with her lover, her mate and longing that should be as decimated as her heart, but wasn't, went through her.

Using the excuse of pulling her sweater into place, she maneuvered farther away from him.

Once the long cardigan was on, he eyed her critically and then leaned forward again until his mouth practically touched her ear. "Can you close the front?"

She shivered as his breath intimately caressed the inside of her ear. He had no right to do this to her. He knew how easily she responded to him. Was he tormenting her on purpose? She shrugged him away with her shoulder.

"It's meant to be worn open." She had raised her voice to a near shout in order to be heard without having to move into his close proximity again. If her traitorous lips got anywhere near his ear, there was no telling what they would do.

The helicopter started to descend.

He said something she couldn't hear. She shook her head to let him know she hadn't gotten it.

He waited to speak again until they were landed

and he'd pulled her from the helicopter to stand on the pebbled sand a hundred feet from the oasis and encampment. "It would be better if you could close it. My grandfather is very traditional."

*His grandfather?* Her attention skittered to the tents within her line of vision. Some were as small as a potting shed and others as large as a cottage with several rooms. They were all cast in a pink glow from the setting sun. One of those dwellings belonged to his grandfather.

"I thought we were going to your palace."

She was in no mood to make nice with more of his family.

"I changed my mind."

"Then change it again. I don't want to meet any more of your relatives."

"That is unfortunate because you are about to."

Who was this man?

He was not the man who had agreed to wait so she could have the wedding of her dreams, nor was he the man who had been so patient with her shyness, who had tempered his passion with gentleness the first time they made love…and every time since.

This man was a stranger.

"I don't know you at all," she whispered.

His body jerked and his eyes narrowed. "I am the man you married."

"But you are not the man I believed you to be. The man I met in Seattle would not have kidnapped me against my will and dropped me in the middle of the desert."

"And yet I am that man. I have been forced to measures I would not have otherwise taken by your irrational behavior."

"That's not true." How dare he say she was not rational?

"Enough of this? You see no perspective but your own. We will talk when you have calmed down."

Judging by the tight rein he had on himself, Hakim had some cooling down to do.

"At least tell me why we're here instead of your palace." They had not planned to come to the Bedouin encampment for another two days.

Her sense of being married to a stranger increased as the shadows cast by the setting sun gave him a hawklike appearance.

He raised his hand and with a flick of his wrist, the helicopter lifted into the air again. His expression was bleak. "There are no phones here."

Her gaze moved from his face to follow the disappearing helicopter. "And no source of transportation?"

But she knew the answer to the question before she asked it. He wasn't taking any chances on her running away.

"Not unless you know how to ride a camel."

She looked away from the sky and back at her husband, expecting dark humor or triumph to be glinting in his eyes after that comment. Neither mood was in evidence in the predator sharp lines of his face.

She licked lips that felt dry. "You know I can't."

"Yes."

"So, in addition to kidnapping me, you intend to make me your prisoner?"

"If that is necessary, yes."

She frowned. "I'd say it is already a fact."

"Only if you choose to see it that way."

"What other way is there to see it?" she asked belligerently.

"You are my wife. You are here to meet my family. It is something we planned days ago. There is nothing sinister in that," said the man who had just sent the only form of escape available to her flying off into the rapidly darkening sky.

"Eventually you will have to take me back to Seattle."

"Yes."

She would have said more, but a shout from behind them silenced her. Hakim raised his hand and called out in Arabic.

"Come, let us go meet my grandfather."

She turned away from him and using the scarf that matched her outfit, she fashioned it like a belt around her waist, pulling one edge of the sweater over the other increasing the modesty of the outfit significantly. "All right."

He surprised her by taking her hand and began leading her toward the largest tent and the delegation that had gathered to meet them. Torches cast light on those assembled. Standing in the center was a man almost as tall as Hakim. The wrinkled leather of his skin and red checked covering on his head worn by sheikhs indicated he could be no other than Hakim's grandfather.

He stepped forward to greet them. "You are welcome among my people." He had spoken in English, clearly for her benefit and she was impressed by the courtesy coming from a man so obviously used to authority.

Hakim stopped a few feet from the other man, released Catherine and then stepped forward to embrace his grandfather. "Father of my mother, I am grateful for your welcome."

He came back to her side, taking her hand in a firm hold once again. "Grandfather, this is my wife, Catherine."

The old man's eyes narrowed. "Your bride, you mean."

Catherine looked to Hakim for an explanation, but he wasn't looking at her. His attention was fixed on his grandfather. A quick dialogue in Arabic commenced. Hakim sounded angry. His grandfather sounded adamant.

It ended with Hakim releasing her hand.

A beautiful woman stepped from behind the man to the old sheikh's right. She wore the traditional dress of a Bedouin woman, the garment black, but embroidered with red, her head and neck covered completely by a black georgette scarf.

She smiled at Catherine. "I am Latifah, wife of Ahmed bin Yusef, sister to Hakim. You are to come with me."

Again Catherine looked at Hakim for understanding.

This time, he was looking at her, his expression grim. "My grandfather does not recognize our marriage because he did not witness it. It has been decreed that you will sleep in my sister's tent tonight. You are no doubt pleased by this turn of events." He inclined his head in acknowledgment of that reality.

"You must go with my sister." His hand reached out

as if to touch her, but then dropped back to his side. "Grandfather has decreed that since I am not yet your husband in the eyes of him and his people, to touch you would dishonor you among them."

The words disconcerted her, but it seemed she had an unwitting ally in the old sheikh.

Still smiling, Latifah touched Catherine's arm. "Come. We have much to do, much to talk about."

## CHAPTER TEN

BY LATE AFTERNOON the following day, Catherine thought *much to do* an understatement of monumental proportions.

Evidently a Bedouin wedding was every bit of a production as the one they had already gone through. She wondered when she would see Hakim. She had been cloistered in his sister's tent since her arrival and when Catherine had asked, Latifah had smilingly shrugged. Whenever their grandfather allowed him to visit appeared to be the answer.

She wondered if he arrogantly assumed she was going through with the ceremony, or if he was worried she would follow through on her refusal.

She didn't know her own mind right then. Too much had happened, her emotional wounds too fresh for her to do anything more than try to make it through the day without bursting into tears. Luckily Latifah made it easier, assuming agreement from silence and happiness where there was none.

Throughout the day and while they made preparations for a wedding Catherine was not reconciled to, Latifah talked. She was extremely kind and extremely friendly. She'd told Catherine about growing up in Kadar until she was eight. She had also told Catherine why Hakim had gone to live with King Asad and Latifah had gone to live with her grandfather. Catherine shivered at the memory of what Latifah had told her.

The attempted coup twenty years ago had left their parents dead. She and Hakim had almost died, too, but the ten-year-old boy had managed to spirit his sister out of the palace under attack and had tracked his grandfather's tribe in the desert. When they had found the Bedouins, both children had been suffering from dehydration and hunger, but they had been alive.

Catherine thought about a small boy who had lost his parents and taken the responsibility of his younger sister's safety. Her heart ached for him. Because from what Latifah said, Hakim had not only lost his parents, but latter arrangements had effectively severed him from his remaining closest relative.

Latifah had been raised Bedouin and Hakim had been raised to be the Sheikh of Kadar, trusted adopted son to King Asad.

His feelings of obligation toward his king stemmed from more than a simple sense of honor, they stemmed from his emotions as well. How could it be otherwise when the King had become the only consistent entity in Hakim's life?

"And these troublemakers, they are the same ones who threaten the royal family now?" she asked Latifah.

Latifah's dark brown eyes snapped with anger. "Yes. Though smaller in number. The sons took over where the fathers left off. It is criminal. They have no popular support and still they attempt these horrendous things. They would have succeeded in their assassination attempt on Hakim had he not been so well trained in combat."

Unwelcome fear jolted through Catherine. "They tried to kill Hakim?"

"Yes. Did he not tell you? Men. They hide these things and believe they are protecting our feelings. Women can give birth. Do not tell me we are too weak to know the truth."

Catherine agreed, but right now she wanted to know more about the assassination attempt, not discuss the misconceptions between the sexes. "When did this happen?"

"On Hakim's last trip home to Kadar. It upset my grandfather very much and for once he did not complain when Hakim returned to America."

He'd married her, not only out of duty, she now realized, but out of a very real need to protect his family from the horror of the past. For him, these living visas represented an opportunity to protect his family. Something he could do personally, not just pay for with his great wealth.

She understood that.

She also understood that the concept of barter being exchanged at a marriage was not the same for him as it was for her. That had been brought home as Latifah helped Catherine sew several gold coins onto her headdress for the wedding. It was a dowry provided by the old sheikh in order to show her value to his people.

Among these people, such an exchange was not only acceptable, it was expected.

Her father and King Asad's deal that centered on her marriage to Hakim was in no way out of the ordinary.

In one sense, she could truly comprehend his view of their marriage, but understanding did not lessen the pain. She had believed he loved her and he didn't. She felt betrayed by him, by her father and by her own mis-reading of the situation. She'd talked herself into believ-ing he loved her, but he'd never used the words. It had all been in her own mind and that made a mockery of the wealth of feeling she had for him.

"What about love?" she asked Latifah as the other woman finished affixing the final coin to the fabric.

Latifah's brows drew together. "What do you mean?"

"Does love have no place in marriage among your people?"

The other woman's eyes widened in shock. "Of course. How can you doubt it? I love my husband very much."

"Does he love you?" Catherine could not help asking.

Latifah's smile was secretive and all woman. "Oh, yes."

"But…"

"Love is very important among our people." Latifah lifted the headdress and admired it.

"Yet your marriages are based on economic gain." Catherine was trying to understand.

Latifah shrugged. "It is expected for love and affec-tion to grow after marriage."

"Does it always?" Did Hakim expect to come to love her? Was he open to the possibility?

Latifah carefully laid the headdress aside and sur-veyed Catherine. "It is the duty of both husband and wife to give their affection to one another. You must not worry about this. It will come in time."

Catherine met Latifah's exotic eyes with her own. Could a woman so beautiful comprehend her own insecurities? She did not see how. Latifah's husband had probably found it very easy to fall in love with his wife. They shared the same background, the same hopes and expectations and she was stunning to look at.

Hakim, on the other hand, was married to a woman who had been raised very differently from himself. The fact that she was also ordinary and shy only added to the mix of Catherine's insecurities.

THAT EVENING, she was allowed to see Hakim under the sharp eyed chaperonage of his grandfather. They had no opportunity to talk about anything of a private nature, which frustrated her. She understood many things about Hakim that had eluded her, but she needed to talk to him before she would commit to going through with the Bedouin marriage.

The fact she was even considering it spoke volumes about the effect his absence from her life for two nights and a day had on her. She missed him and if she missed him this much after such a short absence what would the rest of her life without him be like?

Although the marriage had clearly been a business arrangement, he had made the effort to develop a personal relationship between them. He had shared his time with her, proving to her that they enjoyed one another's company. His friendship was as hard to let go of as his lovemaking.

And that was saying something.

Her body was now permanently addicted to his, the craving he engendered in her a constant pulsing ache in her innermost being. It shamed her she could be so affected by physical need, but when she considered how gloriously he fulfilled those needs, she wanted to weep.

What did she have to look forward to if he let her go? She knew she'd never love another man as she loved Hakim. No matter what he felt for her, the feelings she had for him were too deep, too permanent to ever be repeated with someone else.

When she went to bed that night, it was with a great deal of frustration. The wedding was to take place in two days' time and if those days followed the pattern of this one, she would not get a chance to talk to Hakim.

She lay in the bed of silk quilts and cushions, listening to the sounds of the desert and camp nightlife outside. A group of men walked by and their masculine laughter filtered through the thick wall of the tent. The camels were silent, but not all the animals had gone to sleep.

The air had cooled significantly and she snuggled into the blankets, glad for their layers between her and the cold.

She was on the verge of sleep when a hand closed over her mouth. Adrenaline shot through her system, sending her into fight or flight mode and she jackknifed into a sitting position, only to be trapped in a steel-like grip.

"It is I, Hakim."

As his voice whispered directly into her ear penetrated her terror, she relaxed, her body going almost boneless from relief.

He removed his hand from her mouth.

"What are you doing here?"

"Shh." Again he spoke straight into her ear, his warm breath fanning the always current flicker of desire in her to a small flame. "Do not speak loudly or we will be discovered."

"Okay," she whispered, "but what are you doing here?"

"We must talk."

He helped her to stand and the cold air quickly penetrated her thin nightgown, but he was wrapping her in a cloak that smelled of him before she could voice her discomfort.

He led her outside the tent, via a passageway she had noticed earlier. It surprised her to discover there was more than one entrance to the outside in the large, but temporary dwelling. Once they were outside, she realized she had forgotten shoes as her tender feet came into contact with sharper objects than sand.

Once again, Hakim seemed to know before she spoke and he swung her up into his arms, carrying her beyond the light cast by the torches of the Bedouin camp.

He stopped and sank gracefully to the ground, keeping her close as he did so. She found herself in her husband's lap and felt the unmistakable evidence of arousal against her hip.

She tried to move away.

He tightened his grip on her. "Relax."

"You're…" She couldn't finish the sentence.

"I know." He sounded disgruntled and angry, but at least she knew his desire for her was real.

She also liked knowing he'd felt the need to talk

before the ceremony. It meant he wasn't completely sure of her. His arrogance actually had limits.

She waited for him to talk, but he seemed preoccupied. One hand wrapped in the strands of her hair and his face was averted, as if he was contemplating the stars.

Finally he spoke. "We are to be married by Bedouin ceremony in two days' time."

"So I've been told."

He faced her. "According to Latifah's husband, you have been engaged in preparations all day."

"Yes." If he wanted to know if she planned to go through with it, he could ask.

"Have you considered you might be carrying my child?"

The question was so far from the one she expected that at first, she did not take it in. When she did, she stopped breathing for several seconds.

Could she be pregnant? With a sinking sensation in the region of her heart, she had to admit it was likely. Their marriage had coincided with the most fertile time in her cycle. It had not been planned that way, but the result could very well be another al Kadar. Her baby. Hakim's baby. *Their* baby.

Her plummeting heart made an unexpected dive for the surface. The thought of carrying Hakim's child was not an unpleasant one, but she could hardly divorce the father of her child before it was even born.

"No."

"No you have not considered it, or no, you are not pregnant?"

"I hadn't considered it."

"That is funny, for I have thought of little else since the first time I planted my seed in your womb."

She went hot all over at his words, becoming even more keenly aware of the hardness under her hip. "You don't know they got planted."

"Considering how frequently we made love, I would say it is very likely."

She couldn't deny it, so she said nothing.

"Is the thought of having my child an unpleasant one?"

She had asked him for truth. She refused to prevaricate herself. "No."

She could feel tension drain from him and only then did she realize how uptight he had really been.

"Will you love my child?"

"How can you ask that?"

"It is not so unreasonable to believe the hatred you hold for the father could be transferred to the child."

"I would never hate my own child." Or any child for that matter. The comment that she hated him, she refused to answer.

"For the sake of our child, will you go through the ceremony in two days' time?"

"We don't know there really is a child." But the thought was a sweet one.

"We do not know there is not."

"It would really shame you if I refused, wouldn't it?" That had become very apparent the more time she spent observing the Bedouin life.

"Yes. It would also cast shame on the child of our union."

He'd latched onto her weakness right away and was obviously intent on making use of it.

"I cannot say vows I don't mean."

"There is no vow of love in the Bedouin ceremony."

He really believed she'd stopped loving him. She wished it was that simple to turn off emotion. It wasn't, but she was not about to share that knowledge with him.

"You married me as part of a business deal."

"I cannot deny this, but that does not negate the reality of the marriage."

She wasn't so sure about that, but she decided to pursue another grievance. "You kidnapped me."

"It was necessary."

"For you to get your way you mean."

"For your safety."

"That doesn't make any sense." How could she be in danger going home to Seattle?

"Threats were made against your life the day after our marriage."

"What? How?"

"A letter to the palace. King Asad showed it to me the day we left."

While she had been making her plans to leave him. No wonder he had had the plane held at the airport.

"It is my duty to protect you. I could not let you go."

"Duty," she said with disgust. She was coming to hate that word.

"Yes, duty. Responsibility. I learned these words very

young. I am a sheikh. I cannot dismiss my promises as easily as you do your wedding vows."

That infuriated her and she jumped off his lap to land on her bottom in the cooling desert sand. She scrambled to her feet. "I'm not dismissing them."

He stood, too, casting a dark and ominous shadow in the moonlight. "Are you not? You threaten divorce hours after promising me a lifetime."

Okay, maybe from his perspective she was dismissing those vows, but they didn't count. "I was tricked into them."

"You were wooed."

"How can you say that?"

"It is the truth."

His truth.

She sighed. "I should get back before your sister realizes I've left the tent."

"We are not done talking."

"You mean I haven't agreed to your plans."

"I want your promise you will go through with the ceremony."

"I want some time to think."

"You have two days to think."

"What will you do if I say *no*?"

Instead of answering, he kissed her. Anger pulsated in that kiss, a fury she had not even realized he was holding in, but there was passion too. Desire. And seduction. When he pulled back, she was limp in his arms and barely standing. "You will go through the ceremony so that you are my wife in my grandfather's eyes. Then I will make love to you and you will forget this talk of divorce."

His complacent belief that he could seduce her utterly to his will made her angry. So she lashed out. "Why not? We've already been through one sham wedding. Why not another?"

She fully expected him to explode, but he didn't. Tension filled his body, but he merely said, "Indeed."

He scooped her up into his arms and then carried her back to the tent, not putting her down again until he reached her bed. He leaned over and spoke with his lips so close, their breath mingled. "Good night, *aziz.*"

Then he kissed her. She expected another passionate assault on her senses. More anger. More seduction. She got a gentle caress that left her lips tingling.

Then he was gone.

CATHERINE WRINKLED her nose, both from the sight and the smell of the camel kneeling on all four legs before her.

Latifah had informed Catherine that her husband had ridden this animal to victory in the past three camel races. The knowledge was small comfort as she climbed into the boxlike chair on the camel's back. She'd never even ridden a horse and here she was, getting ready to ride a camel.

She adjusted herself on her seat, gasping as the box swayed with her movements. It was tall enough for her to sit fully erect, but she had to curl her legs under her because there was no place else to put them.

She was supposed to ride in this rather daunting conveyance to her wedding. Evidently this was the Bedouin equivalent to the romantic horse and carriage she'd dreamed of and been forced to discard as impractical in the rainy winter weather of Seattle.

The old sheikh led the camel himself, saying that since her father was not there to do it, he would be pleased at the honor.

She felt as if a thousand eyes were on her as the camel made its sedate pace toward where the ceremony was to be held.

Catherine kept her head down, but peeked through her lashes at the desert people who had gathered to watch her and Hakim marry according to their tradition. Small silver bells on the ornate necklace she wore made a tinkling sound as her body moved with the jarring gait of the camel.

When they reached the site for the marriage, the old sheikh helped Catherine down from the camel and led her to take her place beside Hakim. She didn't look at him during the ceremony, but kept her gaze focused downward as Latifah had instructed.

The ceremony itself didn't take very long, but the Mensaf, a dinner prepared to celebrate their union, did. The men and women ate separately and came together only afterward for the entertainment. They sat in the open air with fires going around them. The wood was so dry, hardly any smoke was emitted from the fires, but the scent of burning chicory filled the air. Men played instruments and women sang, their voices beautiful in their Eastern harmony.

Hakim interpreted the words for her, his voice husky in her ear, his fingers curled around her wrist.

She could not ignore the way his touch affected her and the growing desires in her body, not after four nights away from their marriage bed. By the time Latifah led Catherine to Hakim's quarters in his grandfather's tent, it was quite late and she was jittery with pent-up feelings.

Lit with hanging lanterns, the room was surprisingly large. Richly colored silks covered the interior walls of the tent and the floor was made of the beautifully woven rugs the Bedouin women had become famous for. Hakim's bed was in the center of the room.

It was too elaborate to be called a pallet even though the large cushion for sleeping reposed on the floor with no frame under it. A multitude of pillows indicated the head of the bed. They were framed by billowing white silk that draped from a round frame hanging from the tent's ceiling.

It was like a tent within a tent.

Other than the impressive bed, there were few other items in the spacious room. Big Turkish pillows, obviously for sitting, were arranged around a small table.

She opted to sit on one of the pillows rather than the bed to wait for Hakim. Unfamiliar with the customs of his grandfather's people, she had no idea how long her husband would be. She could hear the revelry continuing in the camp and then she heard the unmistakable tenor of her husband's rich voice just outside the wall of the tent.

As her attention fixed on the doorway through which he would come, it struck her how like her fantasy her current predicament was.

She'd been kidnapped by a sheikh and waited for him to have his way with her, but unlike the daydreams,

Hakim was flesh and blood. She could touch him and he would touch her.

She shivered in anticipation at the thought.

HAKIM PAUSED OUTSIDE the entrance to his chamber.

Catherine waited inside. She'd charmed Latifah with her sweetness, impressed his grandfather with her humility and scandalized the women who had helped Latifah prepare Catherine for the wedding by refusing to have her hair hennaed.

However, she had been very quiet throughout the evening's festivities. At least she had not refused to go through with the wedding. He had not been sure until he saw his grandfather leading the camel that she would actually go through with it, but then she considered it a sham. *Another* sham.

He would show her tonight there was nothing fake about their marriage.

He brushed aside the covering over the opening into the room and went inside.

The sight of her sitting on a pillow on the far side of the room stopped him. She had removed her headdress and it rested in her lap. Her hair hung loose, its dark honey strands glistening with sweet smelling oil. He inhaled the fragrance, taking in her distinctly feminine scent as he did so.

"My grandfather is pleased with you."

Her eyes flickered, their blue depths turbulent with emotion. "Does he know why you married me?"

"He does not know of my uncle's arrangement with your father, no."

She lifted the gold laden scarf. "Latifah told me this

is considered quite a dowry for a bride, even the bride of a sheikh."

Hakim wished he knew what she was thinking. "Grandfather values you."

She looked down, her hair falling to shield her face from his gaze. Her small, feminine fingers traced the patterns on the coins for several seconds of silence.

Her hand stilled and her head came up. "Do you?"

"Do I value you?"

"Yes."

"Can you doubt it?" She was his wife. Someday, God willing, she would finally understand what that meant to a man raised as he had been raised.

"If I didn't doubt it, I wouldn't be asking."

The reminder of her mistrust angered him, but he forced himself to speak in a mild tone, without recriminations. "On the day we arrived in Jawhar, I made you a promise."

She frowned, her lovely skin puckering between her brows. "You promised never to lie to me again."

"And I have not."

She nodded, apparently accepting that at last.

"I made a promise before that, little kitten."

Her face showed her confusion. It was a mark of how impacted she had been by later revelations that she had forgotten something that had been very important to her at the time.

"I promised to always put your needs and desires first from this time forward. Tell me how I could value you more?"

"Are you saying that if it came between something your family wanted and what I wanted, you would

choose my wants over theirs?" Her voice was laden
with skepticism.

"Yes. That is what I am saying."

"So, if I said I didn't want you to sponsor their living
visas?"

"Could you say that and mean it if their lives were in
danger?" he asked instead of answering her question.

Her head dropped, her face hidden from him again.
"No."

Her continued refusal to see the good in their
marriage and in him, frustrated him. "You are very
pessimistic."

She jolted, her head coming up. "What?"

"You see only the negative."

## CHAPTER ELEVEN

CATHERINE FELT HAKIM'S words like an arrow piercing her. "I don't see only the negative." But even as she said the words, she wondered at their truth.

His expression told her he didn't have to wonder. He knew she was lying. "You would dismiss our marriage as nothing because of an agreement that has no bearing on our lives together. You seek new evidence at every turn to justify your mistrust of me and your cheapening of our marriage."

"I did not cheapen our marriage!" How dare he say that? She had loved him. It was his and her father's deceit that had cheapened the marriage and she said so.

"I did not dismiss you as nothing and demand divorce the day after we were wed. I did not refuse you the comfort of my body or the affection of my heart. You are angry because *love*," he said the word scathingly, "did not motivate my proposal of marriage. Yet you professed your *love* for me and then rejected me and threatened to dishonor me before my people. What is this love?"

Each charge affected her conscience like a prosecuting attorney's court indictment. He had never said he loved her and yet he had treated her with consideration. She had said she loved him, but then threatened divorce within thirty-six hours of their marriage.

"I…" She didn't know what to say.

His words were true and yet it had not been a weakness in her love that had made her do those things, but the strength of her pain. Of her sense of rejection, but he had never actually rejected her.

"You are no doubt sitting there right now planning to tell me not to touch you. No matter that you are my wife. You do not care if I ache with wanting for you. No doubt you will rejoice in the knowledge I am suffering."

"No, I—"

He rode right over her words. "You can easily spurn the intimacy between us."

*"It's not easy,"* she cried.

He snorted, clearly unimpressed with her response. "I have promised you honesty, do I not deserve the same?"

"I'm not lying."

"Are you saying you plan to share my bed?"

"Yes." She had already decided that for the sake of her pride, she would not fight him on this. She would rather walk back into intimacy with Hakim under her own steam than deny him and be seduced into his bed anyway. She loved and wanted him too much to deny him.

That fast, his eyes heated with a desire that burned her. He started walking toward her, but she put out her hand.

"Wait."

He stopped.

Before another storm of anger could rise between them, she quickly held up the headdress still clutched in her other hand. "I need to give you this."

His brows drew together in puzzlement, his eyes glittered with wariness. "Why?"

She took a deep breath and then let it out slowly, gathering her thoughts and courage at the same time. "In essence, you bought me with a mining permit."

She had taken a bit to work this all out in her head, but though her father had suggested the marriage, she felt as if she had been bartered in a business deal. She needed to redress that before she could share her body with Hakim again.

When he would have protested, she waved him silent.

"When you accept this gold," she said, indicating the heavily weighted headdress, "I am buying you. It makes us even."

She prayed he would understand and not make fun of her or remind her that his own grandfather had provided the dowry.

He did neither. He looked at the gold and then back at her face. "This is important to you? That we are even?"

"Yes."

"And when I accept your dowry, it is so?"

She nodded.

His eyes darkened with comprehension and he put his hand out to receive the gold. "May you find as much contentment with the exchange as I have done."

He meant as he had done before she found out the truth, but she didn't correct him. She wanted this night to be free of the weight of her father's bartered deal or even Hakim's cultural expectations of such a marriage. She wanted to make love on a level playing field.

She released the headdress into his hands.

Then she untied the gold belt around her hips, letting it fall to the woven rug beneath her feet.

Hakim went completely still, his black eyes fixed on her with almost frightening intensity.

She took advantage of his stillness to remove her dress and the garment under it, letting both glide down her body to pool around her feet. She wasn't wearing a bra and the way his gaze locked onto her naked torso told her he appreciated that fact.

Her nipples, which had already peaked in anticipation of her husband's touch, puckered into firmer rigidity under the heat of his look, stinging with the need to have his mouth on them. Her unfettered breasts swelled, making her skin feel tight and sensitive while other intimate tissues became inflamed, pulses of anticipatory pleasure vibrating trough them.

She walked toward him, the tiny silver bells on her necklace and anklets jingling with each step, her breasts swaying in a way that should have made her blush. For the first time, it didn't. It only increased her sense of feminine power because his eyes locked onto that swaying movement and he began to breathe faster.

When she reached her husband, she pushed his *abaya* off his shoulders. "Let me undress you."

He allowed her to remove his head covering and *egal*.

She let her fingers run through his thick, but short curling hair, reveling in the silky feel against her skin. Reveling also in her right to touch him in this way, to see him as no other woman in Jawhar had the right to see him.

He helped her remove his white tunic, the muscles of his chest rippling as he stretched to take it off.

The flat brown disks of his male nipples drew her attention and her desire. She brushed her fingers over them, feeling her own pleasure as they responded immediately to her touch.

"Yes. Touch me. Show me you desire me as I desire you."

His words sent excitement arcing through her and a determination to do as he said, to show her desire. She leaned forward and licked each nipple, then swirled her tongue around them, tasting the saltiness of his skin, smelling the masculine scent of his body.

His hands clamped on either side of her head. "The sultry air of the desert has turned you into a temptress."

She smiled and took the small, hard nipple into her mouth, sucking on it until he crushed her body to his with an agonized groan. She wiggled against him until her fingers could reach the drawstring on his loose fitting white pants. She tugged at it and it came undone so that the only thing holding them up was the way her body was pressed so tightly against his.

Tilting her head back, her eyes met his. "Take them off."

"You think because you have bought me, you can order me like a slave?" The warm humor in his eyes told her he was joking and not offended.

She gave him her best haughty look. "Of course."

His brows rose, but then they lowered and his look became predatory. "Then you are my slave also."

She found herself swallowing nervously. The game was taking a turn she hadn't expected. "Yes."

He said nothing, but he let her go to step back and push his pants down his thighs. Sleek satin hardness sprang up to greet her.

Remembering the pleasure she felt when he was inside her was exciting her.

"Take off your last covering." The way he said it sent shivers of desire and trepidation down her limbs.

All of a sudden it felt as if the small bit of lace was indeed her last covering, or protection, against him.

But she didn't need protection against him. Not now. She wanted what was about to happen. Very much.

She pushed the scrap of fabric down her thighs, exposing damp blonde curls.

"Come to me."

She took the step forward that separated them, stopping so close to him that the tip of his manhood brushed the soft skin of her stomach.

He reached down, grabbed her hand and led it to the rigid shaft between them. "Touch me."

She allowed her trembling fingers to curl around him. The hardness encased in warm satin fascinated her and she stroked him to the base. He made an incoherent sound of need and his head tipped back, his hands clenched at his sides.

She reversed her stroking and allowed her thumb to flick over the end of him.

His entire body racked in a giant shudder. *"More."* Both demand and plea, she found it impossible to deny him.

She did not want to deny him.

Touching him with gentle then firm strokes, she gave him more…and more…and more.

His entire body had drawn taut when he grabbed her wrist to still her hand. "Enough."

He took several deep breaths, his body shuddering. "Now it is your turn."

For him to touch her?

"To command," he clarified and she smiled.

They were still playing their game.

She didn't think she had the temerity to tell him to touch her. "Carry me to bed." It was where she wanted to be.

He didn't hesitate. He lifted her in strong arms and carried her to the bed in the center of the room. He knelt on the coverlet with her still in his arms and then released her legs so they knelt facing each other, his arms locked around her waist. He lowered his head and kissed her.

The kiss seared her lips with heat and touched something deep inside of her.

He was her husband and she wanted him, would always want him.

His lips broke away from hers to trail down her neck.

"I need you, Hakim."

His head came up, ebony eyes blazing into her own. "I have ached for you."

"You have me."

Triumph flared in his features. "Yes. I have you. I will never let you go."

She didn't want to think about the future. She wanted to concentrate on the present. She pulled his head down and kissed him, opening her mouth in invitation against his lips. The warmth of his tongue invaded her and soon the kiss was devouring and carnal.

Their game forgotten, Hakim made love to her with his hands, his mouth and ultimately, his body. When he exploded inside of her, she almost fainted as her own orgasm joined his.

Afterward, they lay entwined, their bodies sweat soaked.

He disengaged himself from her clinging arms and she moaned in protest, too wasted to actually form words with her mouth.

"Shh, little kitten. I want only to make you comfortable."

Soon, she found herself tucked under a silk quilt, surrounded by Hakim and pillows. He had extinguished the lights and released the cord on the bed hangings so it fell in a circular tent around them, an extra layer of privacy.

She snuggled into his side.

"Little kitten suits you well. You cuddle like a small cat, content to warm yourself with my flesh."

"You make me feel small."

"It is only in your mind that you are some Amazon creature."

She kissed the warm brown skin of his chest. "I know, but I like how you make me feel just the same." Because he didn't just make her feel small. He made her feel cherished.

"I am pleased this is so."

Playing idly with the black curling hair on his chest, she asked, "How long are we staying here?"

"We can go to our home in Kadar as soon as you like."

"Will it offend your grandfather if we do not stay longer?" Their short stay in King Asim's palace had been planned as part of their journey, but they had originally discussed staying among his grandfather's people for a few days.

"He would prefer we stayed long enough for me to race his favorite camel."

"When are the races?"

"In two days' time. Two other encampments will participate."

"I don't mind staying if you don't." She liked his sister and found the Bedouin way of life fascinating.

He hugged her to him in blatant approval. "It would please me to stay."

"Will you teach me to ride a camel?"

"Are you sure you want to learn? You looked very nervous today as you rode in the bride's coach."

"The box swayed. I thought it might fall off."

"I would never allow you to be at such risk."

For the first time, it struck her that this stranger he'd become was no stranger at all. He was Hakim. A complex man with many facets to himself. At once hard and unbending and then tender and protective, but always at the core the man she had fallen in love with, her sheikh.

CATHERINE ENJOYED the next two days very much.

Latifah was a wonderful companion and she laughingly taught Catherine the rudimentary moves of Eastern dance while Hakim spent time with his grandfather.

The second lesson was a little more difficult than the
first as it came after Catherine's first lesson riding a
camel. She was sore from the exercise, but the dance
limbered up her muscles and Hakim's sensual massage
that night completed her recuperation.

Dancing and camel riding weren't the only things she
was learning while staying in the encampment. Hakim
took great pains to teach her the extent of pleasure her
body was capable of experiencing each night. When
they were making love, she found it easy to forget the
real reasons for their marriage.

As she watched her husband and Ahmed vie for first
place in the camel race, ulterior motives for her marriage were the furthest thing from her mind. She was
too terrified to think of anything else.

"I didn't know camels could move that fast."

Latifah laughed. "They are magnificent, are they
not?"

"But what if the camel stumbles? What if Hakim is
thrown?"

More laughter met her questions. "Hakim?" Latifah
asked with clear disbelief.

"He's a man like any other, made of flesh and blood,
bones that can break." Okay, maybe he wasn't like any
other man, but he was still breakable.

Latifah became serious. "You care very much for my
brother, do you not?"

"Yes," Catherine admitted, without tearing her gaze
from the racing camels. "I love him. It's why I married
him."

"I am glad. He deserves this love, I think."

Catherine sucked in a terrified breath as Hakim made a move with his camel that looked incredibly risky.

"He is an excellent rider," Latifah tried to reassure her. "He often wins the race, much to my husband's chagrin. It is good for Ahmed not to win every time."

It was Catherine's turn to laugh at Latifah's complacent statement.

Latifah laughed with her. "I am not disloyal, but my husband has been known to be insufferable after winning a race."

"Arrogance runs in the family, does it?" She'd learned that Ahmed and Hakim were cousins.

The other woman's eyes twinkled. "Yes."

"So, you're wishing the insufferable winner syndrome on me instead?"

"I believe my brother already considers himself the winner. He is well pleased with you for his wife."

TWO HOURS LATER, Catherine and the winner of the camel races boarded another black helicopter. Again, there was little opportunity for communication as the helicopter flew through the sky, but unlike before, Hakim took Catherine's hand firmly in his, keeping it captive for the entire flight.

Her first view of Hakim's palace was an aerial one. Nowhere near as huge as the Palace of Jawhar, it was nevertheless an impressive structure. Domed roofs and tinted sandstone gave the hilltop structure a distinctively Middle Eastern look.

The helicopter landed in a flat valley several hundred

feet from the palace. Men wearing the distinct black of King Asad's private guard were there to meet them along with an SUV to drive them and their luggage to the palace.

HAKIM INSISTED on giving her a tour of the palace right off. She was correct that it wasn't nearly as big as his uncle's palace, but she was still overwhelmed by the time he led her up a winding staircase. It seemed to go on forever before it ended at the entrance to a glass domed room.

It was an observatory, obviously built many years ago. Books on stargazing lined one wall. Some were in English, some French and some Arabic.

However, the books could not hold her attention long, not when in the center of the room sat a table and on that table resided a vintage George Lee and Sons telescope in perfect condition. She walked toward it as if drawn by a force greater than herself, her hand outstretched to touch.

Her fingertips brushed along the barrel. "It's beautiful."

"I believed you would like it."

She spun around to face him. "I thought, you know, that you faked your interest in ancient stargazing so we'd have something in common."

His mouth twisted in a grimace. "The telescope was my father's as was the passion for this hobby, but I soon found myself interested beyond pursuing it merely as a means to get to know you."

Why they met was taking on less and less significance the longer she stayed with him. She was sure that had been his plan when he kidnapped her. "Will you continue to attend meetings for the Antique Telescope Society with me?"

"I would enjoy the opportunity to do so."

She smiled.

"I meant to present the telescope to you as a gift before our wedding in the desert. It would have pleased my father for a true devotee of his favorite hobby to have it, particularly his daughter by marriage."

"I don't know what to say."

He took her hands in his, his eyes compelling her agreement. "Say you will accept it."

She sensed that in accepting it, she was tacitly accepting the permanence of that marriage. Was she ready to do that?

No matter what he felt for her, ultimately, it came down to life with Hakim and life without him. The possibility that she might carry his child weighed heavily against life without him. It was much too soon to tell, but she could not shake the feeling she was pregnant.

But even without a baby, the last few days had shown her the richness of life with him. Did she really want to return to the colorless life she had without him in it?

"You've fought very hard to keep this marriage," she said.

"I will never let you go."

"I have a say in it, Hakim."

He spun around and pounded one fist into the other

palm. "When will you cease to fight me on this? You are my wife," he raged, shocking her into stillness with his unexpected anger. "I will not let you go. You are the mother of my children. Even now, you could carry my baby. Do you consider this when you make your plans to leave me?"

"I haven't *made* any plans." At least not since the first attempt to leave Jawhar on her own.

She laid her hand over her belly, a warm feeling suffusing her, even in the face of her husband's anger. "Do you think I might truly be pregnant?"

He spun around to face her. "If not, it is not for lack of trying on my part."

The admission stunned her. "You'd do anything to keep our marriage."

"Believe it."

He'd promised her fidelity, honesty and that she would come first in his consideration. It was a better recipe for marriage than many she'd seen and according to Latifah, love came later. Even so, there was no guarantee he would ever come to love her.

And if he had loved her, what was the guarantee he would always do so? In Hakim she had a husband who would always keep his promises.

"I don't want to end our marriage. I don't want to leave you."

His smile sent her pulses racing. In that moment of her capitulation, he looked marvelously happy. He could not be so happy if she personally meant nothing to him.

She put her hand out. "Let's get a little more practice in at starting a family."

Rich, deep laughter reverberated around her as Hakim led her to their room and a night of loving unlike any they had yet shared.

## CHAPTER TWELVE

A LITTLE OVER THREE weeks later, they flew back into Sea-Tac, greeted by the typical gray skies and wet weather of a Seattle winter. Catherine mourned the loss of the warm sunshine of Hakim's desert home. Her husband clearly reveled in his Kadar lifestyle. Being honest with herself, she had to admit she had as well.

A great deal of it had been Hakim. He'd been so attentive and wanted to share every aspect of his life as a sheikh with her. She'd visited the settlements in his region, learned the only library available was at the palace and discovered an instant rapport with the people they came into contact with.

She had enjoyed their warmth and unreserved welcome for their sheikh's wife. The only downside had been the many requests the people made for Hakim's return. His political responsibilities were being seen to by a cousin from his father's side of the family, but his people wanted the Sheikh of Kadar to come home permanently.

She didn't understand his refusal to even discuss it. Could King Asad truly be cruel enough to expect Hakim to give up his homeland to oversee business interests? It didn't fit with the man she'd observed on their second visit to the capital.

Hakim drove them home from the airport in his Jaguar.

"We will have to arrange a visit with your parents now that we are back in Washington."

She noticed he never called Seattle home.

She swallowed a sigh. She'd have to face her father sometime. "Does Mom know? About Dad's deal with your uncle I mean."

Hakim's jaw clenched and he shook his head once in negation. "He did not think she would understand."

Just as Catherine had not *understood*, but she was glad her mom had not known. It would hurt that much more to think both her parents had been so willing to barter her life away.

"I'll call Mom and schedule something in a couple of weeks."

"Your father is scheduled to travel to Kadar the week after next to investigate the most likely mining sites."

He certainly wasn't letting any grass grow under his feet. "I guess we'll have to wait to see him until after he gets back."

With a little luck, it would take him several weeks to choose a site. By then she might have her emotions under control enough to see him without going totally ballistic.

"Why not before he goes? Surely this can be arranged."

She sighed. "I'm not sure I want it arranged."

"I thought you had reconciled yourself to our marriage."

Her gaze snapped to him. His jaw was taut, his expression unreadable.

"I am."

"Then why do you not want to see your father?"

"Because he betrayed me."

"As you believed I betrayed you."

She couldn't deny it. "Yes." She hated this. Everything had been fine until he brought up her father.

"And you cannot forgive."

That stopped her. She'd forgiven Hakim because forgiveness had been necessary to the healing of the wound in their marriage. But she'd never told him, assuming he knew because she'd stayed with him.

Apparently he didn't.

"I do forgive you."

"And your father? He wants only what is best for you."

"He made my marriage into a business deal."

"I have only met him a few times, but this seems to be his way. To do what he knows. To believe he knows best."

It was an accurate summation of her father's take-no-prisoners approach to business and life. And no doubt about it, he understood business better than people.

"Catherine?"

What could she say? She could not regret having Hakim in her life. Her heart had been shredded by the men's deceit, but it had not ended with the pain and the past few weeks had given her hope that perhaps one day her marriage would truly be one of love, not a business deal. "I'll call Mom and get something scheduled. I want to see Felicity too."

"You and your sister are very close."

"She's always been there for me."

"This is a good thing. Latifah is very important to me, but after the attempted coup we were no longer raised in the same household. We are not close."

It always surprised her when he opened up with something like this. He kept his deeper emotions under guard so much of the time, except in bed. Then his passion was as volatile as a live volcano.

"What about your cousins?" He'd been raised with them. Had they taken the role of brothers?

"It was determined early on that I would accept the role of diplomat and so I was educated abroad from the age of twelve."

"It must have been lonely growing up being part of a family, but having a destiny that placed you on the outside in many ways."

He shrugged, his powerful shoulders shifting with the movement. "I am no longer alone. With you, I am very much on the inside."

The sexual innuendo made her blush, but at the same time, her eyes filled with unaccountable tears. She'd been extremely emotional the past week and couldn't help wondering if the fact her menses were two weeks late had something to do with it. Had all Hakim's concentrated efforts paid off?

She blinked away the moisture and went for an expression of amusement. "I'll say." She gave him her best version of a lascivious wink and squeezed his thigh.

Deep, masculine laughter erupted around her as he caught her hand in his. "Behave, wife."

"I thought I was behaving, *husband*." She drew the word out in a long, slow, intimate breath of sound.

His fingers laced with hers. "We are fully reconciled, are we not?"

"Yes."

He was silent for a couple of miles. "You are no longer considering divorce?"

She was surprised he felt the need to ask. "No. I told you I was committed to our marriage."

"And you do not think I am lower than the underside of a lizard in the desert?"

That shocked a giggle from her. "No. I don't think that."

"Then why have you not repeated your avowal of love since the day after our wedding?"

Tension seeped into her body, making her muscles contract. "You didn't marry me for love."

"Does this negate your love for me?"

What difference could it possibly make to him?

She pulled her hand from Hakim's and turned to look out the window. Gray sky and wet concrete made an uninspiring view. "What do you want me to say?"

"I want you to tell me you love me."

The blatant request buffeted nerves that she thought had settled. She could make her own demand for the same thing and did not doubt he would comply. It was his duty to come to love her, so he would will himself to do so, but she didn't want a duty vow. She wanted the same hot cauldron of emotions that seethed inside her to churn in him.

When she didn't answer he brushed her cheek. "Is it so hard, little kitten?"

"I'm not sure this is the best place for this discussion."

She could see him return his hand to the steering

wheel out of the corner of her eye. His jaw clenched for the second time in twenty minutes. "Perhaps you are right."

She hated feeling like all the rapport they had shared for the past few weeks was going up in smoke.

How could she explain that telling him she loved him made her feel vulnerable? That somehow keeping the words locked inside protected her heart from his indifference.

Only he *wasn't* indifferent.

He wanted to hear her words of love. Could it be that he was coming to love her? Did he feel just as vulnerable as she did because she hadn't told him she loved him since learning of the real reasons behind their marriage? Perhaps by trying to protect her own feelings, she was not leaving room for him to express his, or at least to allow his to grow into something stronger than dutiful affection.

She turned to look at his tense profile. "I do love you." Her voice was low, almost a whisper, but he heard her.

His grip on the steering wheel tightened until his knuckles showed white. "You are right. This is not the place for such declarations."

Hurt by the apparent rejection of her words, she demanded, "Why?"

"Because I now want to make love to you with painful fervor and it will be at least fifteen minutes before we reach our home."

CATHERINE CALLED HER father's office the next day. They needed to talk. But he had flown to South America on business and wasn't expected back for several days. Catherine made an appointment to see him before he left the country again, this time to the Kadar Province in Jawhar.

THE DAY BEFORE HER appointment with her father, Catherine was in the living room of her and Hakim's penthouse, curled up on the sofa, a book on ancient astronomy in her lap. She traced a picture of a telescope very similar to the one Hakim had given her after their wedding and remembered their days in Kadar.

Hakim had spent the first ten years of his childhood in that palace. She could imagine him as a small boy, learning to ride a camel, teasing his little sister as boys do, climbing into his mother's lap for a cuddle when he was tired.

Catherine gently touched her stomach and pictured the same things with her own child. Only she was having a really hard time picturing them here in Seattle. The palace in Kadar had felt like a home, a grand one, but a home nonetheless. Their penthouse felt like a yuppie launching pad. It wasn't just the difference between Hakim's penthouse apartment and the palace in Kadar, either.

It was more. It was millennia of tradition, family and political responsibilities, an entirely different way of life to the one her child would know here.

A way of life she thought she could embrace. A way of life she knew her husband missed.

"Hello, little kitten. Did you have a good day at the library?"

She'd been so lost in her thoughts, she hadn't heard him come in.

She looked up and smiled. "Hi. It's been a wonderful day. Come and sit by me and I'll tell you all about it."

He shrugged off his suit jacket and loosened his tie before tugging it off. By the time he joined her on the couch, the top two buttons on his dress shirt were undone. Dark hair peeked out of the opening.

She reached out and brushed a fingertip along the open V. "You're a sinfully sexy man, Hakim."

Ebony eyes burned with instant desire. "It pleases me you find it so."

Her own eyes fluttered shut as he lowered his head to kiss her, his customary greeting when they'd been apart for longer than a few minutes. There was something desperate in his lips she didn't understand and she automatically sought to sooth with her response, surrendering completely to his touch.

Ten minutes later, she was lying across his lap, the small pearl buttons on her sweater undone along with the front clasp on her bra. His hand gently cupped her breast, one thumb brushing over an already hardened nipple.

"To come home to such a greeting makes up for a lot." His words whispered against her neck between small, biting kisses.

"And what am I making up for, the lousy traffic in downtown Seattle?" she asked, breathless with rapidly spiraling desire.

He husked a laugh and hugged her tightly to him.

She leaned back a little, wanting to see his eyes. "I've got news."

His brows rose. "Do not hesitate to tell me."

Her lips tilted in a smile. She loved it when he talked all sheikhlike. "As of Monday, I'll be part-time at the library and I've explained that if you need to travel for business I am going with you."

She wasn't sure how black eyes could darken, but his did...with pleasure. "I like this news very much."

"I thought you would." She also hoped he would feel free to make more trips to Jawhar if he knew she could go with him on short notice.

She snuggled more firmly into his lap, reveling in the feel of his hardened flesh under her bottom. "There's more."

He groaned and the hand on her breast contracted. "Perhaps it can wait."

She wiggled again for good measure, but shook her head. "I want to tell you now."

His hands locked on her hips to stop their movement. "Then tell me before I ravish you here on the sofa."

"There's a reason I wanted to go part-time."

His head had fallen back and his eyes were closed, his nostrils dilated with arousal. "What is that?"

"All your effort paid off."

His eyes flew open and he looked at her with reproach. "I did not demand you cut your hours at work."

"I didn't go part-time because you wanted me to," she assured him.

The twist of his lips said her answer had not reassured.

"I altered my work schedule to accommodate an upcoming change in our family." She leaned forward and kissed his lips very softly, then with their mouths only separated by a breath, she said, "I'm going to have your baby."

If she had not known better, she would have thought a spasm of pain crossed his face, but it was gone in a flash to be replaced by unadulterated joy.

"Thank you," he whispered against her lips and then he kissed her.

It was the most tender expression of affection he had ever shown her. Then he broke into speech in Arabic, his hand moving to cover her belly, his mouth kissing her all over her face, neck and chest.

He cupped her breast. "My baby will suckle here," he said with awe.

Tears filled her eyes. "Yes."

He pressed a gentle kiss to one rigid peak and then the other. He moved until he had her laid out on the couch before him; somewhere along the way, their clothes had disappeared. He paid homage to her breasts again, then moved his mouth to press a ring of kisses around her navel. "My child is nourished and protected here in the warmth of your body."

Her fingers tangled in the thick black hair on his head and tears of love, joy, and pleasure swam in her eyes.

His mouth rested over the blond curls at the apex of her thighs. When his tongue darted out to part the folds of her femininity and seek her pleasure spot, she arched up off the couch. "Hakim!"

He pressed her thighs apart and continued to make love to her with his mouth until she was shuddering in exquisite release. He moved up her body, taking possession of her with one sure thrust. "From this pleasure we made life between us."

"Oh, darling…Hakim. My love."

His lips cut off any more endearments, but her heart continued to utter them, beating out a rhythm of her love that he had to have felt.

He established a pace that soon had her arching in renewed tension, but this time when she went soaring among the stars, he was with her.

Afterward he collapsed on top of her and she brushed her hands down his back, petting him, loving him. "I love you."

His head came up and his face wore the most serious expression she had ever seen. "Do not stop loving me, I beg of you."

"Never," she promised fiercely. "I will always love you."

The warmth of his desert home was in his smile. "Then all is worth it, jewel of my heart. For the gift of your love, the gift of our child makes every sacrifice of no consequence."

"What sacrifice?"

But he was kissing her again and any thought of conversation melted under the fire of his physical love.

CATHERINE DRESSED for success for her meeting with Harold Benning. Her straight black skirt, short-sleeved black sweater and hip-length hound's-tooth jacket gave her badly needed confidence. She hadn't had a heart-to-heart talk with her parents since before puberty.

He looked up from his desk, a telephone pressed to his ear, when she walked in. Wariness chased shock across his features.

He said something into the phone and then hung it up. "Catherine."

Now that she was here, Catherine didn't know where to start.

"Would you like a cup of coffee, something to drink?"

She shook her head. "Not really. I want to talk to you."

"About your marriage." It was a statement, not a question.

"How did you know?"

Her dad leaned back in his leather executive chair, his pose relaxed, but his expression watchful. "Hakim called from Jawhar to tell me you knew about the mining deal."

Her hands clenched at her sides. "It isn't exactly your average mining deal, though is it? Instead of paying for the privilege to mine in Jawhar, you bartered your daughter like some medieval tyrant."

Her dad's brown eyes snapped with reproach. "It wasn't like that."

She sat down in one of the chairs in front of his desk and crossed her legs, trying to project an air of casualness she did not feel. "Why don't you tell me what it was like?"

"You know your mother and I have been worried about your lack of a social life for years. When this business with King Asad came up, I saw a way to kill two birds with one stone is all. I didn't do a damn thing to hurt you."

She shot to her feet and leaned across his desk until their faces were inches apart. "You didn't do anything to hurt me? Just how do you think I felt when I discovered the man I loved didn't love me, that he married me as part of a business deal? Let me tell you. It hurt! It hurt a lot."

Her dad sank back into his chair like a puppet whose strings had been cut, but he didn't say anything.

She didn't need him to.

She was in full throttle now. "Let me tell you about hurting. I found out that both my husband and my father had lied to me. I knew I wasn't as important to you as Felicity, but I never thought you saw me as an expendable possession!"

He flinched and passed his hands across his face. "You aren't expendable to me. I didn't sell you into slavery in a third-world country, Catherine. I fixed you up with a business associate."

"Without telling me."

His expression turned belligerent at that. "Hell no, I didn't tell you. You would have run a mile in the opposite direction."

"So you told Hakim how to manage an *accidental* meeting."

He shrugged. "It seemed the best way to get you to give him chance. Listen to me, Catherine. The laser treatment got rid of the scars on your face, but that wasn't enough. Your mom and I thought once the scars were gone, everything would be okay, you'd date like your sister, get married one day. Have a life."

She looked away, not wanting to see the years-old pity burning in his eyes.

"It didn't work that way, though. You don't trust people, especially men. Hell, maybe that's my fault. I ignored you because I couldn't fix your problem. And you felt rejected because of it. I was wrong, but I can't change it now. Maybe you were afraid of being rejected again. I don't know, but until Hakim, you kept your emotions locked up tighter than the Denver Mint."

"I trusted Hakim."

"You fell in love with him. Don't hold the arrangement against him, Catherine. The kind of deal we made is pretty common in his part of the world."

"I figured that out. The fact that I am a means to an end for him doesn't lessen my value in his eyes."

"Well, as to that, I'm sure you've heard there won't be any need for long-term living visas."

"What?"

"Didn't Hakim tell you? His uncle's intelligence sprang a trap on the leaders of the dissidents. They're in jail awaiting trial for treason right now."

Why hadn't Hakim said something? "When did this happen?"

Looking relieved by the change in topic, her dad said, "I got word yesterday."

Yesterday. She remembered the desperation in Hakim's kiss, his mention of sacrifices and there was that initial flash of pain in his eyes when she told him she was pregnant.

She stumbled to her feet. She needed to think. "I've got to go." She walked quickly toward the door of his office.

"Are you okay?" She hadn't heard her dad get up from his chair, but his hand was on her shoulder.

"I'm fine. Why wouldn't I be?"

"I'm sorry, Catherine. If I could change the way things happened, I would."

She believed him.

WALKING INTO THE PENTHOUSE fifteen minutes later, she was still trying to make sense of what her father's revelations meant for her and Hakim. She couldn't forget that small flash of pain. What had it meant?

There was no longer any need for long-term living visas. Did he regret their marriage now that the personal benefit to him was gone?

The blinking light on the answering machine caught her attention as she tossed her purse on the table. She couldn't listen to the recording, not yet.

So many thoughts were crowding her mind, she didn't think she could take another one in. Not even a phone message.

She sat down and started dealing with the kaleidoscope of impressions one by one. The foremost was the very first time she and Hakim had shared passion. They hadn't made love, but he'd wanted to, had been aching with the need to have her.

The next image she examined was his reaction to her demand for a divorce. He hadn't just been angry. He'd been furious on a very personal level. And he'd done everything in his power to change her mind. The fact that he'd been successful considering how betrayed she had felt meant something.

Then she thought of her life together with him over the past weeks. Happy. Content. Pleased with one another's company. Sexually insatiable. In harmony.

*They fit together.*

She didn't know what that small flash of pain meant, but she was absolutely positive it had not resulted from his discovery he was stuck with her. The fact that he hadn't told her about the capture of the rebels yet indicated that, in his mind, that aspect of their marriage was incidental to their relationship.

With that tantalizing thought swirling through her mind, she got up to push the play button on the answering machine.

Hearing the voice of the King of Jawhar was a little unsettling, but hearing his request that she, not Hakim, return his call was enough to make her knees go weak.

# CHAPTER THIRTEEN

AFTER TAKING SEVERAL deep breaths, she picked up the phone to call the King. Her nervousness only increased when Abdul-Malik insisted on sending her call straight through even though the King was in a meeting.

Their greetings were a little stilted, but it didn't take King Asad long to come to the point. "You have heard the dissidents have been arrested?"

"Yes." She didn't bother to tell him her father, rather than Hakim, had told her the news.

"There is no longer a need for long-term visas."

"I gathered that, yes."

"Another could oversee our business interests abroad. Hakim could come home."

Catherine felt her mouth curve into a smile at the wonderful news and then the King's wording struck her and the smile slipped a little. "Why are you telling me rather than Hakim?"

"I have told my nephew." She could hear the royal impatience clearly across the phone line. "It is my will and the will of his people that he return to rule the Kadar province."

"He didn't mention it." Why hadn't he?

"He refuses to return."

*"What?"* She couldn't believe it. Then she realized she'd just shouted into the ear of a king. "I'm sorry, Your

Excellency, but I cannot understand this refusal. My husband wants to return to Jawhar, I know he does."

"I am certain of this too, jewel of his heart."

What in the world? Why had he called her that? "Then…"

A heavy sigh and then, "He is convinced you would be unhappy living in Kadar."

"That's ridiculous. I loved our time there. He knows I did."

"I think, perhaps I should tell you a confidence."

She wanted to hear anything that would make sense of this bizarre situation. "Please do."

"It is not something I would share with the wife of my nephew in the usual circumstances, but his stubbornness leaves me no choice."

"I understand," she said with a fair bit of her own impatience.

"Very well. When he was at university, Hakim had a relationship with a woman he believed he loved. A woman he believed loved him."

Maybe Catherine didn't want to hear about this.

"Hakim asked this woman to marry him, to return to Jawhar and live as his sheikha. This was before it was decided he would oversee our business holdings in America."

"She turned him down. He told me."

"She told my nephew that no matter how much she loved him, no Western woman would willingly give up her career, her lifestyle and her country to move to a backwater like Kadar." The King's voice dripped acid. "This woman told Hakim he had to choose between his position as a Sheikh of Kadar with life in Jawhar and her."

"He chose his position," Catherine said, stating the obvious. After all, the two had not married.

"But with you, he has found the true jewel of his heart. He chose you over his duty to his people."

"What do you mean?"

"He believes your happiness lies in Seattle, therefore he has refused to return to his homeland and his people."

Catherine's body started shaking and she had to sit down. "But I didn't ask that of him. He never said anything."

"He does not wish to distress you. He told me that he thought you might sacrifice your happiness for his, but he would not allow you to do so."

"But I'd be happier in Kadar. I want to raise our babies in his palace. I like the sunshine. The people are wonderful. I could learn to race camels." She was babbling, but so stunned from the news that Hakim had chosen her over his duty that she couldn't control her tongue.

"Babies?" the King inquired with meaning.

"Oh… I…"

"Perhaps you will have good news to share when you and my nephew return to Jawhar?"

"But Hakim said he doesn't want to come."

"No, Catherine, he said you do not wish to come and therefore he will not."

She bit her lip. What was the King thinking now? "Are you angry with me?"

"No. I spoke to Lila and many whom you had contact

with on your visit to Jawhar. I am convinced this problem my nephew believes exists is in his head, not your heart."

"You're right, but what should I do?"

"Tell him your feelings." The King sounded a bit exasperated with her dull thinking.

She smiled. "I want to do more." Hakim deserved a gesture that showed how much she loved him, how much she wanted to live in Jawhar with him. "Maybe you could help me out…"

HAKIM OPENED THE DOOR to the penthouse with a sense of anticipation he had never had prior to his marriage. She would be waiting. His Catherine. His little kitten.

Perhaps she would be curled up on the sofa as she had been yesterday. He smiled at the thought. Such a welcome did indeed make up for a lot. It made up for everything. He could live the rest of his life in this damp climate if it meant basking in the warmth of her love.

There would be children. Sooner than later. His heart pounded at the thought. She already carried his child, perhaps a son, the next Sheikh of Kadar. A son who would be an outsider to his people like he had been in the Palace of Jawhar after his parent's death. But the child would belong in their family. He would fit with Catherine and Hakim. It was enough. It had to be enough.

The sound of soft music from the bedroom drew him, but he found the room empty. Eastern music played from the built-in sound system and the door to the lavish en suite bathroom stood open. He walked in to find his wife lounging in the deep sunken bath, the fragrance of jasmine surrounding her, a subtle lure to his senses.

"It would take a man very secure in his masculinity to share his wife's bath when the water has been scented with the oil of fragrant flowers."

Her beautiful head turned, the cupid bow of her mouth tilted in a beguiling smile. "It's lucky for me I'm married to a very macho guy then isn't it?"

His fingers were already at work on the buttons of his shirt. "It is I who am blessed, my jewel." She glittered like the most precious stone with beauty and fire. "To have such a wife is all any man could ask."

Soft pink colored her cheeks and she averted her eyes. "I never know how to respond when you say stuff like that."

He finished undressing and slipped into the hot water with her. His legs brushed the silken smooth skin of hers. "It is my hope you will accept my words with the flowering of joy in your heart."

She peeked at him through her eyelashes, her expression coquettish, the feel of her foot insinuating itself between his thighs not. "I am very happy with you, Hakim."

And it was true. She radiated with the same glowing joy she had on their wedding day. What had wrought this change? Was it her pregnancy?

Her small, feminine toes caressed his male flesh and he felt an immediate and overwhelming response.

She reached out and brushed the tip of his shaft. "Mmm... Very masculine."

He laughed and launched himself at her.

Later, she snuggled in front of him, her breathing still a little ragged. "I think you drowned me."

"You offered an invitation too appealing to pass up."

"Are you sure it was an invitation? Maybe I was just trying to unwind in a nice, relaxing bath."

He laughed. She often gave him the gift of laughter. "It was a shameless invitation and you know it." He tweaked a still rigid nipple.

She squealed and batted his hand away. "All right. I admit it. Sexy invitation all the way."

"You are that."

"What?" she asked, cuddling more snuggly against him.

"You are incredibly sexy."

"You make me feel like it. You make me feel beautiful." She said it with such surprise.

"Your beauty surpasses that of any other woman."

She sighed and laced her fingers with his across her stomach.

Would she accept his avowal of love now? He had wanted to tell her of his feelings, but although she had admitted she still loved him, she held something back. Her trust. When he told her of his love, he wanted her to believe him, to trust him. If she believed his words of love were insincere, it would hurt her and he could not bear for her to be hurt anymore.

Her kiss surprised him and her lips were gone before he could take advantage of it.

"Your uncle called today."

Tension filled him. "What did he have to say?"

"One of your cousins just got engaged."

This he knew. His uncle had told him that along with the news about the dissidents being captured. "She is not technically my cousin. She is my uncle's niece through his wife."

"He still wants us to come to Jawhar for the betrothal celebration."

His heart ached as it always did when he thought of his home. "Do you wish to go?" They had just gotten back. It was a long journey to take again so soon.

"Oh, yes."

"Then we shall go."

Her smile was all woman and somehow mysterious. He gave up wondering what it meant when her lips once again covered his own. This time he was ready to take the advantage.

A WEEK LATER THEY BOARDED the same jet that had taken them to Jawhar the first time. Hakim was very attentive on the journey, asking Catherine repeatedly how she felt and if she needed anything. Thankfully, she had experienced only the slightest form of morning sickness with her pregnancy and the flight was no problem at all. Which was a relief considering the plans she had for when they reached the airport.

Hakim led her to the helo pad, believing they were taking a short helicopter ride to his cousin's home province. Catherine kept him occupied with a totally inappropriate display of affection he did not seem to mind in the least and it was an hour before Hakim realized they were headed in the wrong direction.

He tapped the guard seated next to the pilot and

yelled something in Arabic. The guard answered and Hakim turned to her, his expression furious.

"What the hell is going on?"

The smug smile she'd meant to greet him with withered in the face of his wrath, but she kept her cool. He couldn't go totally ballistic. After all, being pregnant did have its uses.

"I'm kidnapping you," she shouted above the sound of the helicopter's blades.

His eyes snapped black retribution, but he didn't say another word until they had landed near the Kadar Palace. The same SUV was there to transport them, even the same guards. Catherine smiled at them, trying to ignore the glowering man by her side.

Hakim kept his silence until they had reached the privacy of their bedroom in the palace.

Then he turned to her, menace written in every line of his body. "What is happening?"

"I kidnapped you."

"So you said."

She clasped her hands together in front of her to stop their shaking. This was supposed to be easy. Tell him how she felt about living here, he would be pleased and everything would be fine. Only he was mad, really mad.

"Why are you so angry?"

"You usurp my authority among my people and you have to ask this?"

She hadn't considered that angle. "You have to stop taking yourself so seriously. Your consequence hasn't suddenly taken a nosedive, if that's what you're worried about. As far as everyone else knows, everything has been done according to the will and authority of King Asad. It's no big deal."

Hakim did not look particularly reassured. "And what exactly is this *no big deal*?"

She was getting a little frustrated with his anger. "You had no right to refuse to return to Jawhar without consulting me. I'm your wife, not a mindless bed warmer who has no say in the decisions that affect me. And I'm definitely not that stupid woman you lived with. My thoughts and my feelings are my own. You should have found out what they were before refusing your duty to your family and your country."

She crossed her arms over her chest and glared at him, a little of her own anger coming to the surface as she remembered how he'd made such a major decision without her input.

Hakim rubbed the back of his neck, his expression turning resigned. "My uncle convinced you to sacrifice yourself for me, for the good of my country." It wasn't a question, but she treated it like one anyway.

"No, he did not. He simply told me that you had refused to come home when the capture of the dissidents made it possible."

"We will not be staying." He spun as if to leave the room.

He made her so mad sometimes she wanted to spit. "Hakim!"

He stopped.

"I know you can ride a camel. Heck, you can order a helicopter faster than I can order dinner."

His body tensed. "What is the point of this?"

"I can't hold you here against your will. I can't stop

you from leaving by dropping you in a desert encampment from which you have no easy escape."

He turned to face her, his expression not so much unreadable as full of conflicting emotions. "So?"

"I have only one thing to hold you here." If he loved her, it would be enough.

"What?"

"Myself."

He shook his head and she squelched the tiny doubt that tried to intrude on her certainty that he loved her. He had to love her to have chosen her over his duty. A man with his strong sense of responsibility would only make such a decision under a powerful influence of emotion.

"This is not about you." He swung his arm out indicating the room, the palace, Kadar. "This is about my uncle manipulating you into sacrificing your happiness for my duty. I won't allow it."

"How do you know what would make me happy?" she demanded. "You never asked."

"I made a promise to you, to put you first from the point of our marriage forward. I will keep that promise."

"Are you saying it's a promise holding you here in this room with me?"

He stared at her, his expression that of a man trying very hard to hold on to his temper. "I did not say that."

"Good. Am I enough to hold you?" She wanted the words. She deserved the words.

"There is no binding that could be stronger." He

started toward her, his intent very clear in the obsidian eyes she loved so much.

Her feet started moving of their own volition, taking her to him. They met in the middle of the room. He pulled her into his arms, his hold so tight she could barely breathe.

"I want to raise my children here," she said breathlessly, "I want them to know the tradition of their father's people, to know the warmth of the desert, the love of a family so big I'll probably never learn everybody's name."

He cupped the back of her neck under her hair. She'd left it down and it was wind-blown from the helicopter ride. "But your job…"

She smiled reassuringly. "I'll expand the library in the palace and make it available to the people."

His groan was that of a man who knew his peaceful existence was in danger of extinction. "There are no cities here, no malls, no movie cinemas—"

She interrupted his litany of Kadar's supposed shortcomings. "I told you I'm not that other woman. I don't like shopping. I don't care for city traffic. I was living in a small town by choice when we met. I love this place. I love the people. How could you not see that when we were here?"

He kissed her and she melted into him. Somehow they ended up on the bed amidst a pile of tasseled pillows.

He leaned above her and brushed the hair from her temple. "I want you to be happy, *aziz*."

Her heart constricted with hope and then certainty. "Because you love me."

"Of course I love you. Have I not said this a hundred times?"

She could not recall him saying it once. "No."

"I have."

"When?" she challenged him.

"Do you not know the meaning of *aziz*? I would have thought you would ask my sister or Lila. You had their confidence in every other matter."

She licked her lips, her heart thrilling when his gaze zeroed in on the movement with feral intent. "What does it mean?"

"Beloved. Cherished. How could I not love you? You are all that a woman should be, the jewel of my heart."

Joy suffused her until she was almost sick with it. She grinned. "When did you realize it?"

Hakim hugged her to him. "I was pretty stupid. I did not realize these feelings I have for you were love until the day I gave you the telescope and I thought you were still thinking of leaving me. Before that I knew I did not want to let you go, but in that moment, I realized that if you did go, you would take my heart, my soul, with you."

She started unbuttoning his shirt, wanting to get to the man beneath. "Why didn't you tell me you loved me then?"

"I was afraid you would not believe me, that my avowal would cause you more pain than pleasure."

She stared at him in disbelief. "How could you think telling me you loved me would hurt me? I was dying inside thinking I was nothing more than a means to an end."

"Forgive me, *aziz*, for my many mistakes, but you are and will always be the ultimate means to my end, for I need you to be happy and without you my life would be as arid as the desert and as empty as a dry well."

The words brought tears to her eyes and finally she knew what to do when he said stuff like that.

Later, their naked limbs entwined on the bed, she smiled at him, her heart a melted puddle of feeling from the many words of love he'd spoken during their love-making. "I love you, Hakim."

He kissed her softly. "I love you, Catherine. It will always be so until the stars fall from the heavens and even beyond."

After a lifetime of not fitting in, she had finally found her place. In his arms. Next to his heart.

It would always be.

\* \* \* \* \*

To Pete, the sexiest, smartest and best.
Every day, I love you more.

# THE GREEK BILLIONAIRE'S
# BABY REVENGE

## Jennie Lucas

# CHAPTER ONE

SNOW WAS FALLING so hard and fast that she could barely see through the windshield.

Anna Rostoff parked her old car in the front courtyard of the palace, near the crumbling stone fountain, and pulled on the brake. Her hands shook as she peeled them from the steering wheel. She'd nearly driven off the road twice in the storm, but she had the groceries and, more importantly, the medicine for her baby's fever.

Taking a deep breath, she hefted the bag with one arm and climbed out into the night.

Cold air stung her cheeks as she padded through soft snow and ascended sweeping steps to the gilded double doors of the two-hundred-year-old palace. They were conserving electricity in favor of paying for food and diapers, so the windows were dark. Only a bare thread of moonlight illuminated the dark Russian forest.

We're going to make it, Anna thought. It was April, and spring still seemed like a forlorn dream, but they had candles and a shed full of wood. Once she found work as a translator she'd be able to make a new life with her four-month-old baby and her young sister. After months of hell, things were finally looking up.

She lifted her keys to the door.

Her eyes went wide as a chill descended her spine. The front door was open.

Barely able to breathe, she pushed into the grand foyer. In the shadows above, an ancient, unseen chandelier chimed discordantly as whirling flurries of snow came in from behind, whipped by a cold north wind.

"Natalie?" Anna's voice echoed down the hall.

In response, she heard a muffled scream.

She dropped the groceries. Potatoes tumbled out across the floor as she ran down the hall. Gasping, she shoved open the door into the back apartment.

A figure stood near the ceramic tile fireplace, his broad-shouldered form silhouetted darkly in the candlelight.

*Nikos!*

For one split second Anna's heart soared in spite of everything. Then she saw the empty crib.

"They took the baby, Anna," Natalie cried, her eyes owlish with fear behind her glasses. Two grim bodyguards, ruddy and devilish in the crackling firelight, flanked her sister on either side. She tried to leap from the high-backed chair, but one of Nikos's men restrained her. "They came in while I was dozing and snatched him from his crib. I heard him cry out and tried to stop them—"

Misha. Oh, God, her son. Where was he? Held by some vicious henchman in the dark forest? Already spirited out of Russia to God knew where? Anna trembled all over. Her baby. Her sweet baby. Sick with desperation and fear, she turned to face the monster she'd once loved.

Nikos's expression was stark, almost savage. The man who'd laughed with her in New York and Las Vegas, drinking ouzo and singing in Greek, had disappeared. In his place was a man without mercy. Even in the dim light she could see that. Olive-skinned and black-haired, he was as handsome as ever, but something had changed.

The crooked nose he'd broken in a childhood fight had once been the only imperfection in classic good looks. Now his face had an edge of fury—of cruelty. He'd always been strong, but there were hard planes to his body that hadn't been there before. His shoulders were somehow broader, his arms wider, as if he'd spent the last four months beating his opponents to a pulp in the boxing ring. His cheekbones were razor-sharp, his arms thick with muscle, his blue eyes limitless and cold. Looking into his eyes was like staring into a half-frozen sea.

Once she'd loved him desperately; now she hated him, this man who had betrayed her. This man who, with kisses and sweet words whispered against her skin at night, had convinced her to betray herself.

"Hello, Anna." Nikos's voice was deep, dangerous, tightly controlled.

She rushed at him, grabbing the lapels of his black cashmere coat. "What have you done with my baby?" She tried to shake him, pounded on his chest. *"Where is he?"*

He grabbed her wrists. "He is no longer your concern."

"Give me my child!"

"No." His grip was grim, implacable.

She struggled in his arms. Once his touch had set her body aflame. No longer. Not now that she knew what kind of man he really was.

"Misha!" she shrieked helplessly.

Nikos's grasp tightened as he pulled her closer,

preventing her from thrashing her arms or clawing his face. "*My son* belongs with me."

It was exactly what she'd known he'd say, but Anna still staggered as if he had hit her. This time Nikos let her go. She grabbed the rough edge of the long wooden table to keep herself from sliding to the floor. She had to be strong—strong for her baby. She had to think of a way to save her son.

In spite of her best efforts, a tear left a cold trail down her cheek. Wiping it away furiously, she raised her chin and glared at Nikos with every ounce of hate she possessed. "You can't do this!"

"I can and I will. You lost the right to be his mother when you stole him away like a thief in the night."

Anna brought her hands to her mouth, knowing Nikos could use his money and power and man-eating lawyers to keep her from her son forever. She'd been stupid to run away, and now her worst nightmare had come true. Her baby would grow up without her, living in Las Vegas with a heartless, womanizing billionaire and his new mistress…

"I'm so sorry, Anna," Natalie sobbed behind her. "I tried to stop them. I tried."

"It's all right, Natalie," Anna whispered. But it wasn't all right. It would never be all right again.

A door slammed back against the wall, causing Anna to jump as a third bodyguard entered from the kitchen and placed a tray on the table. Steam rose from the samovar as Nikos went to the table and poured undiluted tea, followed by hot water, into a blue china cup.

She stared at her great-grandmother's china teacup. It looked so fragile and small in his fingers, she thought. It could be crushed in a moment by those tanned, muscular hands.

Nikos could destroy anything he wanted. And he had.

"I've been here two weeks," Anna said bitterly as she watched him take a drink. "What took you so long?"

He lowered the cup, and his unsmiling gaze never once looked from hers.

"I ordered my men to wait until you and the child were separated. Easier that way. Less risk of you doing something foolish."

*Stupid. Stupid.* She never should have left her baby—not even to go to an all-night market in St. Petersburg. After all, Misha wasn't really sick, just teething and cranky, with a tiny fever that barely registered on her thermometer.

"I was stupid to leave," she whispered.

"It took you four months to figure that out?"

Anna barely heard him. No, the really stupid move had been coming here in the first place. After four months on the move, always just one step ahead of Nikos's men, and with money running out, Anna had convinced herself that Nikos wouldn't be staking out her great-grandmother's old palace. Now mortgaged to the hilt, the crumbling palace was their family's last asset. Natalie was trying to repair the murals in hopes that they'd be able to find a buyer and pay off their paralyzing debt. A fruitless hope, in Anna's opinion.

As fruitless as trying to escape Nikos Stavrakis. He was bigger than her by six inches, and eighty pounds of hard muscle. He had three bodyguards, with more waiting in cars hidden behind the palace.

*The police*, she thought, but that hope faded as soon as it came. By the time she managed to summon a policeman Nikos would be long gone. Or he'd pay off anyone who took her side. Nikos Stavrakis's wealth and power made him above the law.

She had only one option left. Begging.

"Please," she whispered. She took a deep breath and forced herself to say in a louder voice, "Nikos, please don't take my child. It would kill me."

He barked a harsh laugh. "That's what I'd call a bonus."

She should have known better than to ask him for anything. "You…you heartless bastard!"

"Heartless?" He threw the cup at the fireplace. It smashed and fell in a thousand chiming pieces. "Heartless!" he roared.

Suddenly afraid, Anna drew back. "Nikos—"

"You let me believe that my son was dead! I thought you both were dead. I returned from New York and you were gone. Do you know how many days I waited for the ransom note, Anna? Do you have any idea how long I waited for your bodies to be discovered? Seven days. You made me wait seven damn days before you bothered to let me know you were both alive!"

Anna's breaths came in tiny rattling gasps. "You betrayed me. You caused my father's death! Did you think I'd never find out?"

His dark eyes widened, then narrowed. "Your father made his own choices, as you have made yours. I'm taking my son back where he belongs."

"No. Please." Tears welled up in her eyes and she grabbed at his coat sleeve. "You can't take him. I'm—I'm still breastfeeding. Think what it would do to Misha to lose his mother, the only parent he's ever known…"

His eyes went dark, and Anna wanted to bite off her tongue. How could she have drawn attention to the fact that she'd not only denied Nikos the chance to experience the first four months of their child's life, but she'd broken her promise about their son's name?

Then he bared his teeth in the wolflike semblance of a smile. "You are mistaken, *zoe mou*. I have no intention of taking him away from you."

She was so overwhelmed that she nearly embraced him. "Thank you—oh, God, thank you. I really thought…"

He took a step closer, towering over her. "Because I'm taking you as well."

HE SHOULD HAVE savored this moment.

Instead, Nikos was furious. For four months he'd fantasized about taking vengeance on Anna. *No, not vengeance*, he corrected himself. *Justice*.

Some justice. His lip curled into a half-snarl. Bringing Anna back to Las Vegas, where he'd see her face across his table every day? That was the last thing he wanted.

He'd intended to take his son and leave, as she deserved. But from the moment he'd first seen his baby son a surge of love had risen in him that he'd never felt before. At that moment he'd known he could never allow his son to be hurt. He'd kill anyone who tried.

For four months he'd hated Anna. But now…

Hurting her would hurt his son. His child needed his mother. The two were bonded.

The payback was off.

He cursed under his breath, narrowing his eyes.

Anna had lost all her pregnancy weight, and then some. Under her coat's frayed edges he could see the swell of her breasts beneath her tight sweater, see the curve of her slender hips in the worn, slim-fitting jeans. There were hungry smudges beneath her cheekbones that hadn't been there before, and tiny worry lines around her blue-green eyes. The tightly controlled secretary was gone. Her long dark hair, which she'd always pulled back in a tight bun, now fell wild around her shoulders. It was…sexy.

Anna slowly exhaled and stared up at him, her eyes pleading for mercy. Even now, she was the most beautiful woman he'd ever seen. Her aristocratic heritage showed in the perfect bone structure of her heart-shaped face, and in every move she made.

Once he'd been grateful for her skills. He'd admired her dignity, her grace. He'd known Anna's value. As his executive secretary, she'd run interference with government officials, employees, vendors and investors, making decisions in his name. She'd reflected well both upon him and the brand of luxury hotels he'd created around the world. Even now he still missed her presence in his office—the cool, precise secretary who'd made his business run so smoothly. She'd made it look easy.

It made him regret that he'd ever slept with her.

It made him furious that he was still so attracted to her.

Misha, indeed. A Russian nickname for Michael? Anna had promised to name their son after Nikos's maternal grandfather, but it didn't surprise him that she'd gone back on her word. She was a liar, just like her father.

"I had Cooper pack your things," he bit out. "We're leaving."

"But the storm—"

"We have snow chains and local drivers. The storm won't slow us down."

Anna glanced from Nikos to the empty crib, and the fight went out of her. Her shoulders sagged.

"You win. I'll go back with you," she said quietly.

Of course he'd won. He always won. Although this victory had come harder than he'd ever imagined, at a price he hadn't wanted. Already sick of the sight of her, he growled, "Let's go."

But as he turned away Anna's throaty voice said, "What about Natalie? I can't leave her here. She has to come with us."

"What?" her sister gasped.

Nikos whirled back with a snarl on his lips, incredulous that Anna was actually trying to dictate the terms of her surrender. Another Rostoff woman in his house? "No."

"No way, Anna!" Her sister echoed, pushing up her glasses. "I'm not going anywhere with him. Not after what he did to our father. Forget it!"

Anna ignored her. "Look around, Nikos. There's no money. I was planning to get a job as a translator to support us. I can't just leave her."

"I'm twenty-two! I can take care of myself!"

Anna whirled around to face her young sister. "You barely speak Russian, and all you know about is art. Mother doesn't have any more money to send you, and neither do I. What do you expect to eat? Paintbrushes?"

The girl's eyes filled with tears. "Maybe if we went to Vitya he would…"

"No!" Anna shouted.

Who was Vitya? Nikos wondered. Another impoverished aristocrat like Anna's father had been? For most of Anna's young life he'd forced his family to live off the charity of wealthy friends. She'd once drily commented that that was how she'd learned to speak fluent French, Russian, Spanish and Italian—begging the Marquis de Savoie and Contessa di Ferazza for book money.

Although of course that had been before Alexander Rostoff had realized it would be simpler to just embezzle the money.

*Aristocrats,* he thought scornfully. Rather than live in the comforts of Nikos's house near Las Vegas, his brownstone in New York, or his villa in Santorini, Anna had kidnapped his baby son and moved from one cheap apartment to another.

His lip curled as he looked around the room. The back of the palace had been turned into a cheerless Soviet-era apartment. It was a little disorienting to be smack in the real thing, especially since Anna seemed to be using nineteenth-century standards to light and heat the room.

"How could you force my son to live like this?" he abruptly demanded. "What kind of mother are you?"

Anna's turquoise eyes widened as she gripped the gilded edge of a high-backed chair. "I kept him warm and safe—"

"Warm?" Incredulously, he looked at the single

inadequate fireplace, the flickering candles on the wooden table, the frost lining the inside of the window. "Safe?"

Anna flinched. "I did the best I could."

Nikos shook his head with a derisive snort as Cooper, his right-hand man and director of security, entered the room. He gave Nikos a nod.

Nikos made a show of glancing at his sleek platinum watch. "Your things are packed in the truck. Are you coming, or should we toss your suitcases in the snow?"

"We just need a minute for Natalie to pack her things—"

"Perhaps I have not made myself clear? There is no way in hell that I'm taking your sister with us. You're lucky I'm bringing you."

Anna folded her arms, thrusting up her chin. He knew that expression all too well. She was ready to be stubborn, to fight, to prolong this argument until he had to drag her out of this place by her fingernails.

"Stay, then." He turned to leave, motioning for Cooper and his bodyguards to follow. "Feel free to visit our son next Christmas."

Precisely as he'd expected, Anna grabbed his arm.

"Wait. I'm coming with you. You know I am. But I can't just abandon Natalie."

He tried to shake off her grip, but she wouldn't let go. He looked into those beautiful blue-green eyes, wet with unshed tears. What was it about women and tears? How were they able to instantly manufacture them to get what they wanted? Well, it wouldn't work on him.

He wouldn't be manipulated in this way. He wouldn't let her...

"You might have to go with him, Anna," Natalie said defiantly. "But I don't. I'm staying."

Nikos glanced at Anna's sister. The girl had fought like a crazed harpy to protect her nephew. Now, she just looked heartbreakingly young.

Something like guilt went through him. Angrily, he pushed it aside. If the Rostoffs were penniless, it wasn't his fault. As his secretary, Anna had been paid a six-figure salary for the last five years—enough to support her whole family in decent comfort.

So where had that money gone? He'd never seen Anna splurge on clothes or jewelry or cars. She bought things that were simple and well made but, unlike his current secretary, she avoided flashy luxury.

Anna's sister didn't look terribly royal either. In her bulky sweatsuit, covered by an artist's smock, she stood by the frost-lined window with a bowed head. She was staring wistfully at the broken pieces of the blue china teacup he'd smashed against the fireplace.

His jaw tightened.

He gestured to Cooper, who instantly came forward. "Yes?"

"See that the girl has all the money and assistance she requires to live here or return to New York, as she wishes." In a lower voice, he added, "And find a replacement for that damn cup. At any price."

Cooper gave a single efficient nod. Nikos turned to Anna. "Satisfied?"

Anna raised her chin. Even now, when he'd given her

far more than she deserved, she was defiant. "But how do I know you'll keep your word?"

That one small question made fury rise tight against his throat. He always kept his word. Always. And yet she dared insinuate that he was the one who was untrustworthy. After her father had stolen his money. After she herself had stolen his child.

He hated her so much at that moment he almost *did* leave her behind. He wanted to do it. But not at the cost of hurting his son. Damn her.

Gritting his teeth, he said, "Call your sister when we reach Las Vegas. You'll see I've kept my word."

"Very well." Anna's face was pale as she knelt beside her sister. "You'll accept his help, won't you, Natalie? Please."

The girl hesitated, and for a moment Nikos thought she would refuse. Then her expression hardened. "All right. Since he's only paying back what he took from Father."

What the hell had Anna told her? Surrounded by bodyguards, he didn't have the time or inclination to find out. He'd tried to spare Anna the truth about her father, but he was done coddling her. It was time she knew the kind of man he really was. He would enjoy telling her.

And more than that, Nikos promised himself as they left the palace. Once they'd returned to his own private fiefdom in Las Vegas he would make her pay for her crimes. In private. In ways she couldn't even imagine.

Oh, yes, he promised himself grimly. She'd pay.

## CHAPTER TWO

RIDING IN THE LIMO from the Las Vegas airport to Nikos's desert estate twenty miles outside the city gave Anna an odd sense of unreality.

In one long night she'd left darkness and winter behind. But it wasn't just the bright morning light that threw her. It wasn't just the harsh blue sky, or the dried sagebrush tumbling across the long private road, or the feel of the hot Nevada sun on her face.

It was the fact that nothing had changed. And yet everything had changed.

"Hello, miss," the housekeeper said as they entered the grand foyer.

"Welcome back, miss," a maid said, smiling shyly at the baby in Anna's arms.

The moment their limo had arrived inside the guarded gate the house steward and a small army of assistants had descended upon Nikos. He walked ahead with them now, signing papers and giving orders as he led them through the luxurious fortress he called a home. Members of his house staff had already spirited away her luggage.

Where had they taken it? Anna wondered. A guest-room? A dungeon?

Nikos's bedroom?

She shivered at the thought. No, surely not his bed-room. But for most of her pregnancy his room had been her home. She'd slept naked in his arms on hot summer nights. She'd caressed his body and kissed him with her heart on her lips. She'd dreamed of wearing his engagement ring and prayed to God that it would last. She'd been so sure that if he left her she would die.

But in the end she'd been the one who left.

Because the moment he'd found out she was pregnant he'd fired her. She'd gone from being his powerful, trusted assistant to a prisoner in this gilded cage. He'd ordered her to take her leisure, practically forcing her into bedrest, although she'd had a normal, healthy pregnancy.

Nikos had taken the job she loved and given it to a young, gorgeous blonde with no secretarial skills. He'd ordered the household staff to block the calls of her mother and sister. Then, during her final trimester, he'd suddenly refused to touch her. He'd abandoned her to go and stay, with his secretary Lindsey on hand, at the newly finished penthouse at L'Hermitage Casino Resort.

That should have been enough to make Anna leave him. That should have been more than enough. But it hadn't been until she'd found those papers showing that Nikos had deliberately destroyed her father's textiles company that she'd finally been fed up. Anna's hands tightened. Running away had been an act of self-defense for her and her child.

But now they were back. As Anna entered a wide gallery lined with old portraits, she could smell the flowers of the high desert. Spring was swift in southern Nevada, sometimes lasting only weeks. Wind and light cascaded through high open windows, oscillating the curtains.

Her footsteps echoed in the wide hall as she followed Nikos and his men.

But a woman was with them, too: the perfect blonde who'd replaced Anna in Nikos's office, and in his bed. Anna watched Lindsey lean forward eagerly, touching his arm. She blinked, surprised at how much it hurt to see them together.

Nikos was impeccably gorgeous, as always. He'd showered and changed on the plane, and now wore dark designer slacks and a crisp white shirt that showed off his tanned olive skin. It wasn't just his height that made him stand out from the rest of his men, but his aura of power, worn as casually as his shirt.

Nikos had always stood out for her. Even now, looking at him, Anna felt her heart ache. It was too easy to remember the years they'd spent working together. In spite of his arrogance, she'd admired him. He'd seemed so straightforward and honest, so different from her former employer, Victor. Plus, Nikos had never tried to make a pass at her. For five years he'd taken time not just to teach her about the business, but also to rely upon her advice. At least until that night thirteen months ago when he'd shown up wild-eyed on her doorstep, and everything had changed between them forever.

But her job had meant everything to her. For the first time in her life she'd felt strong. Capable. Valued. Was it any wonder that, even knowing her boss was a playboy, she'd fallen so totally under his spell?

As if he felt her gaze, Nikos glanced back to where she trailed behind with the baby. His eyes were dark, and a shiver went through her.

"He hates you, you know."

Anna glanced up at Lindsey, who was standing next to her. She had a scowl on her pouting pink lips, though she looked chic in a dark pinstriped suit with a tucked-in waist and miniskirt. Her tanned legs stretched forever into impossibly high heels.

Anna felt dowdy in comparison, wearing the same T-shirt and jeans from last night, with a sweater tied around her waist. Her hair, which hadn't been washed or combed since yesterday, was pulled back in a ponytail. She'd been afraid to leave her baby alone on the plane, even for the few minutes it would have taken to shower.

Next to Lindsey, Anna felt a million years old, worn out from running away, working odd jobs, trying to get by, raising her child. Lindsey was fresh and young, glossy and free. No wonder Nikos preferred her. The thought stung, even though she told herself that it didn't hurt.

"I don't care if he hates me." Anna nervously twisted her great-grandmother's wedding ring around her finger, fiddling with its bent-back tines and empty setting. She couldn't let Lindsey know how vulnerable she felt on the inside, how scared she was that the younger woman would soon take everything Anna cared about. She already had Nikos and her job. Would Misha be next?

Lindsey lifted a perfectly groomed eyebrow in disbelief. "You really think you've gotten away with it, don't you? You actually think Nikos will take you back."

Anna smoothed back a tuft of Misha's dark hair. "I don't want to be taken back. I'm here for my son. Nikos can rot in hell for all I care."

The girl gave Misha a crocodile smile that made Anna's skin crawl. "Yeah, right. As if anyone would believe that." Her perfectly made-up eyes narrowed. "But Nikos doesn't want you. He's got me now, and I keep him very satisfied, trust me. We'll be getting married soon."

Anna couldn't keep herself from glancing at Lindsey's left hand. It was bare. Remembering Nikos's wandering eye when she'd been just his secretary, Anna almost felt sorry for the girl. "Has he proposed?"

"No, but he—"

"Then you're kidding yourself," she said. "He'll never propose to you or anyone else. He's not the marrying kind."

Grinding her white teeth, Lindsey stopped in the hallway, and grabbed Anna's wrist. Her long acrylic nails bit into Anna's skin.

"Listen to me, you little bitch," Lindsey said softly. "Nikos is mine. Don't think for a second you can come back with your little brat and—"

Nikos spoke from behind her. "This is cozy. Catching up on office gossip?"

Lindsey whirled around, spots of hot color on her cheeks. "We...uh, that is..."

Anna hid a smile. But her pleasure at the blonde's discomfiture was short-lived as Nikos turned to her, reaching for the diaper bag on her shoulder.

"I need this."

"What? Why?" Anna stammered. The diaper bag held her whole life. Bought at a secondhand shop, it was overflowing with documents, diapers, wipes and snacks. It was the one item that Anna had taken with her everywhere since Misha's birth.

"For my son." As he took the bag, he brushed her

shoulder carelessly with his hand. An electric shock reverberated across her body. For a single second it stopped her heart.

Then she realized that Nikos was taking Misha away from her.

And handing both bag and baby to her replacement.

"No!" Anna cried out, shaking herself out of her stupor. "Not to *her*!"

Nikos stared straight back at her, as if he were marking her over the barrel of a gun. "Good. Fight me. Give me a reason to throw you out of my house. I'm begging you."

Anna opened her mouth. And closed it.

"I thought so." He turned back to Lindsey. "Take my son to the nursery. I'll follow in a moment."

She tossed Anna a look of venomous triumph. "With pleasure."

As they passed him, Nikos kissed the baby on the forehead. "Welcome home, my son," he said tenderly.

Anna watched as Lindsey disappeared down the hall toward the nursery. She could see her baby's sweet little head bobble dangerously with every swaying step and clackety-clack of the girl's four-inch heels against the marble floor. She wondered if Nikos had destroyed all of Natalie's hand-painted murals and her own carefully chosen antique baby furniture. *He probably ordered Lindsey to redecorate the nursery from a catalog*, she thought, and her heart broke a little more.

As much as she'd hated being on the run, this was worse. Here, every hallway, every corner, held a memory of the past. Even looking at Nikos was a cruel reminder of the man she'd once thought him to be, the man she'd respected, the man she'd loved. That was the cruelest trick of all.

"You don't like Lindsey, do you?" Nikos said, watching her.

"No."

"Why?"

Did he want her to spell it out? To admit that she still had feelings for him in spite of everything he'd done? Not in this lifetime.

"I told you. After you fired me, I got calls at the house from vendors and managers at the worksite, complaining about her cutting off half your calls and screwing up your messages. Her mistakes probably cost the company thousands of dollars. It nearly caused a delay in the liquor license."

Nikos pressed his lips together, looking tense. "But you said those complaints stopped."

"Yes," she retorted. "When you had the house staff block all my calls. Even from my mother and sister!"

"That was for your own good. The calls were causing you stress. It was bad for the baby."

"My mother and sister needed me. My father had just died!"

"Your mother and sister need to stand on their own feet and learn to solve their own problems, rather than always running to you first. You had a new family to care for."

She squared her shoulders. She wasn't going to get into that old argument with him again. "And now you have a new secretary to care for you. How's she doing at solving all your problems? Has she even learned how to type?"

His jaw clenched, but he said only, "You seem very worried about her capabilities."

Oh, yeah, she could just imagine what Lindsey's *capabilities* were. Still shivering from Nikos's brief touch, bereft of her baby, Anna could feel her self-control slipping away. She was tired, so tired. She hadn't slept on the plane. She hadn't slept in months.

The truth was, she hadn't really slept since the day Nikos had rejected her in the last trimester of her pregnancy, leaving her to sleep alone every night since.

She rubbed her eyes.

"All right. I think she's vicious and shallow. She's the last person I'd entrust with Misha. Just because she's in your bed it doesn't make her a good caretaker for our son."

He raised a dark eyebrow. "Doesn't it? And yet that's the whole reason that *you* are the caretaker of my son now…because you were once in my bed."

Their eyes met, held. And that was all it took. Memories suddenly pounded through her blood and caused her body to heat five degrees. A hot flush spread across her skin as a single drop of sweat trickled between her breasts. It was as if he'd leaned across the four feet between them and touched her. As if he'd taken possession of her mouth, stroked her bare skin, and pressed his body hot and tight on hers against the wall.

One look from him and she could barely breathe.

He looked away, and she found herself able to breathe again. "And, as usual, you are jumping to the wrong conclusions," he said. "Lindsey is my secretary, nothing more."

Anna had been his secretary once, too. "Yeah, right."

"And whatever her failings," he said, looking at her with hard eyes, "at least she's loyal. Unlike you."

"I never—"

"Never what? Never tricked a bodyguard into taking you to the doctor's office so you could sneak out the back? Never promised to name my son Andreas, then called him something else out of spite? I did everything I could to keep you safe, Anna. You never had to work or worry ever again. All I asked was your loyalty. To me. To our coming child. Was that too much to ask?"

His dark eyes burned through her like acid. She could feel the power of him, see it in the tension of hard muscles beneath his finely cut white shirt.

A flush burned her cheeks. The day of her delivery, surrounded by strangers in a gray Minneapolis hospital, she'd thought of her own great-grandfather, Mikhail Ivanovich Rostov, who'd been born a prince but had fled Russia as a child, starting a difficult new life in a new land. It had seemed appropriate.

But, whatever her motives, Nikos was right. She'd broken her promise. She pressed her lips together. "I'm...sorry."

She could feel his restraint, the way he held himself in check. "You're sorry?"

"A-about the name."

He was moving toward her now, like a lion stalking a doomed gazelle. "Just the name?"

She backed away, stammering, "But some might say

y-you lost all rights to name him when you—" Her heels hit a wall. Nowhere to run. "When you—"

"When I what?" he demanded, his body an inch from hers.

When he'd ruined her father.

When he'd taken a mistress.

When he'd broken her heart…

"Did you ever love me?" she whispered. "Did you love me at all?"

He grabbed her wrists, causing her to gasp. But it was the intensity in his obsidian gaze that pinned her to the wall.

"You ask me that now?" he ground out. But there was a noise down the hall, and he turned his head.

Three maids stood with their arms full of linens, gawking at the sight of their employer pressing Anna against the wall. It probably looked as if they were having hot sex. Heaven knew, they'd done it before, though they'd never been caught.

He lifted a dark eyebrow, and the maids scattered.

With a growl, he grasped Anna's wrist and pulled her into the privacy of the nearby library. He shut the heavy oak door behind him. The sound echoed against the high walls of leatherbound books, bouncing up to the frescoed ceiling, reverberating her doom.

His dark eyes were alight with a strange fire. "You really want to know if I loved you?"

She shook her head, frightened at what she'd unleashed, wishing with all her heart that she could take back the question. "It doesn't matter."

"But it does. To you."

"Forget I asked." She tried desperately to think of a

change of subject—anything that would distract him, anything to show that she didn't care. But he was relentless.

"No, I never loved you, Anna. Never. How could I? I told you from the start I'm not a one-woman kind of man. Even if you'd been worthy of that commitment—which obviously you're not."

Pain went through her, but she raised her chin and fired back, "I was loyal to you when no other woman would have been. You kept me prisoner. You fired me from the job I loved. When you took Lindsey in my place I should have left you. But it wasn't until I saw what you did to my father…"

"Ah, yes, your sainted father." He gave a harsh laugh. "Those papers you found, Anna, what did they prove? That I withdrew all financial support from your father's company?"

"Yes. Just when he needed you most. He'd been doing so well, finally getting the company back on its feet, but just when he needed extra cash to open a new factory in China, to compete in the global market—"

"I withdrew my support because I found out that your father embezzled my investment—millions of dollars. There was no new factory, Anna. He'd laid off most of his workers in New York, leaving Rostoff Textiles nothing more than a shell. He used my investment to buy cars and houses and to pay off his gambling debts to Victor Sinistyn."

"No." A knife-stab went through her heart. "It can't be true." But even as she spoke the words she remembered her father's frenetic spending in those days. He'd stopped pressuring her to marry Victor, and instead had suddenly been prosperous, buying a Ferrari for himself, diamonds for Mother, and that crumbling old palace in Russia. He wanted to remind the world of their royalty, he'd said, that the Rostoffs were still better than anyone.

"I didn't tell you," Nikos continued, "or press charges, because I was trying to protect you. I cut off his lines of credit and informed the banks that I was no longer responsible. If he'd just asked me for the money I would have given it to him, for your sake. But he stole from me. I couldn't allow that to continue."

She turned to stare blindly at a nearby gold and lacquer globe. Turning the smooth surface of the world, her fingers rested near St. Petersburg. She wished with all her heart that she was still there, in the dark, cold, crumbling palace without a ruble to her name. She wished Nikos had never found her and dragged her back to luxury. Russia was numb peace compared to this hell.

"And so he went bankrupt. Then died from the shame of it." She closed her eyes, fighting back tears.

"He was weak. And a coward to leave his family behind." She felt his hand on her shoulder as he brushed back her hair with his thick fingers. "I'm done protecting you from the truth. You stole from me. Just like him."

Barely controlling her body's involuntary tremble at his touch, she blinked fast, struggling to contain tears that threatened to spill over her lashes. She pressed her nails hard against her palms. *If he sees me cry, I'll kill myself.*

"I hate you," she whispered.

His grip on her shoulder tightened. "Good. We're even."

"Let me go."

Pressing her back against the wall of leatherbound books, he ran his hand along the bare flesh of her arm. "You chose to come back with me. Did you think it would cost you nothing?"

Heaven help her, but even now, hating him, she wanted to run her hands along his back, to touch the strength of his muscles and the warmth of his skin. She wanted to lace her fingers through the curls of his short dark hair and pull him down to her, to taste the sweet hardness of his mouth.

Oh, God, what had come over her? Trembling from the effort, she forced her body to stay still and betray nothing. "You're not some medieval warlord. You can't toss me in a dungeon and torture me into surrender."

He gently traced the back of his hand down her cheek. "We have no dungeons here. But I could keep you in my bedroom. Every night. And you wouldn't escape." He whispered in her ear. "You wouldn't want to."

She sucked in her breath as a hard shiver rocked her body. She couldn't stop it even though she knew, pressed against her as he was, he'd be able to feel the movement.

He rewarded her with a smug, masculine smile. "Would you like that, Anna?" he murmured against the soft flesh of her ear, his breath hot on the tender skin of her neck. "Would you like to sleep against me again? Or would I have to tie you to the bed and force you to remember how good it once was between us?"

She felt his closeness and power over her and she hated it, even as part of her longed for him with all the strength of her body's memory.

"I don't want you," she gasped, but even as she spoke the words she felt her traitorous body slide against him, melding every soft curve against his well-muscled form.

"We'll see."

He leaned forward, lowering his head. Involuntarily she closed her eyes, licking her lips as her body moved against him.

She felt the warmth of his breath. She could smell his skin, a scent of soap and hot desert sun and something more—something she couldn't describe but that made her yearn for him with all the ferocity of her heart, as she'd once hungered for Christmas as a child.

But Nikos was in no hurry. The seconds it took before his lips finally touched hers were exquisite torture. And when he finally kissed her the world seemed to whirl around them, making her dizzy, making her knees weak.

She'd expected him to savage her lips, to try and break her in his embrace. But his kiss was gentle. Pure. Just like the very first time he'd kissed her, long ago, that night he'd shown up at her door half-mad with confusion and grief…

He deepened the kiss, brushing his hand through her hair as his tongue caressed her own. She clung to him, returning his caress with a rising passion.

He lingered possessively in her arms, kissing her neck and murmuring endearments in Greek. A sigh of pleasure came from deep within her as she ran her hands through his dark, wavy hair.

Then, without warning, he released her.

She blinked up at him, dazed. Caressing the inside

of her wrist with a languorous finger, he looked down at her with cold, dark eyes.

"You hate me enough to kidnap my son," he observed coolly. "But then you kiss me like that."

He dropped her wrist and stepped away from her. As if she disgusted him. Rejecting her. Again.

Her whole body went white-hot with humiliation as she realized that his gentle kiss had been more savage than any forceful assault. Nikos was too strong for brute force. All he had to do was give her the chance to betray herself. One loving, lying kiss from him, and all her feeble defenses had burned to the ground.

She took a deep breath, trying to regain her balance. "You surprised me, that's all. It was just a kiss. It meant nothing."

"It meant nothing to me. But to you…" He looked down at her with a sardonic light in his dark eyes. "I own you, Anna. You're mine in every way. It's time you understood that."

She tightened her hands into fists, fighting for calmness, for some vestige of dignity. "You don't own me. You can't *own* someone."

He stepped back from her. His face was a dark silhouette against the sunlight flooding the high library windows. She could see the cruel twist to his sensual lips as he stared her down.

"You're mine. And I will make you suffer for betraying me."

He meant it, too. She could see that. And she knew how he'd make her suffer. Not by hurting her body— no. But by breaking her will. By breaking her heart. By making her desire him, by giving her pleasure in bed such as she'd never imagined until it ultimately destroyed her soul.

He would poison her with love.

A sob rose to her lips that she couldn't control.

"Enjoy your time with our son," he said. He stepped back through the tall library doors, closing them behind him as he departed with a low, grim parting shot. "Because for the rest of your days and nights you are mine."

*REVENGE.*

As Nikos strode down the hall toward the east wing of the house he smiled grimly, remembering the way Anna had melted into his arms. The bewildered look in her eyes after he pulled away. She was putty in his hands. Like the old song promised, that single kiss had told him everything he needed to know.

She still wanted him.

She still cared for him.

That was her weakness.

Now that he knew, making her suffer would be easier than he'd ever imagined. He'd already begun, by telling her the truth about her worthless excuse for a father. She didn't want his protection? Fine. He was done protecting her.

He would see her twist and pant helplessly, like a butterfly pinned to a display. He would see the pain in her eyes every day while he mercilessly pounded her heart into dust. Maybe then, someday, she would understand what she'd done to him by stealing his child.

His son was all that mattered now. He was the one who needed Nikos's protection…and love.

"I waited for you in the nursery," he heard Lindsey

say from down the hall. "When you didn't come, I gave him to the nanny."

He turned to see Lindsey leaning against the wall in a sultry pose. "I was delayed," he replied in a clipped voice.

"That's okay." She skimmed a hand over a tanned thigh barely covered by her short skirt, curving her red lips into a smile. "Finding you alone is even better."

God, no. Another of Lindsey's clumsy attempts at seduction? He was in no mood.

"I gave you the rest of the morning off," he said shortly. "The negotiations for the Singapore bid can wait."

"That's not why I came looking for you."

No, of course it wasn't. Unlike Anna, who'd taken her job so personally, Lindsey would never stick around on a holiday. Her work was barely up to par on regular days.

He hated that he still had Lindsey as his secretary. She wasn't a fraction of the employee Anna had been. He should have fired her long ago. But firing her would have been like admitting that he'd made a mistake.

"What do you want, Lindsey?" he asked wearily.

She toyed with the slit of her short skirt with her long French-manicured nails, making sure he could see the top edge of her thigh-high stockings. "The question is, what do *you* want, Nikos?"

It was the most blatant invitation she'd ever tried.

Once, he might have taken her up on her offer, buried his pain in the sweet oblivion of pleasure. No longer. His experience with Anna had taught him that sex could give a worse hangover than tequila and Scotch.

"Just go to the casino office and wait for my call," he said, walking past her.

Nikos found his son in the nursery, held in the plump arms of his new nanny. The white-haired Scotswoman had recently finished raising an earl's son from babyhood to university, and Nikos had hired her at an exorbitant rate. His son must have the best of everything. "Good morning, Mrs. Burbridge."

"Good morning, sir." She smiled at him, holding up the baby. "Here to hold your son?"

"Of course." But, looking at the baby, he suddenly felt as if he were facing a firing squad. What did he know about babies? He'd never held one before. Nikos had been an only child, or close enough, and he'd never exactly been the sort of man to ooh and ah over the children of friends.

Feeling nervous, Nikos gathered his child from the nanny's protective embrace and held him awkwardly underneath the arms.

"No, er…Mr. Stavrakis, tuck him closer to you. Under his bum."

Nikos tried, but he couldn't seem to get it right. The baby apparently agreed. He looked up at Nikos, and his lower lip started to tremble. He screwed up his face and started to wail.

"I…I seem to be doing this wrong," Nikos said, breaking into a cold sweat.

"Don't take it personally, sir," Mrs. Burbridge said in her friendly Scottish burr. "The bairn is just tired and hungry. He'll soon be right again with a bit to eat. Is his mum about? Or should I make a bottle?"

But Nikos could hardly hear her words over his son's panicked cries. He felt helpless. Useless. *A bad father.*

"He… I… I'll come back when he's not so tired." He thrust the baby back into Mrs. Burbridge's arms and fled.

Or at least he started to. Until he saw Anna standing in the doorway of the nursery, staring around the room with an expression of wonder.

"You didn't change the room," she breathed in amazement. With apparent ease, she took the baby from Mrs. Burbridge and cuddled him close. His cries subsided to small whimpers as Anna looked from the painting of animals and trees on the wall to the soft blue cushions of the window seat. "I was sure you'd have Lindsey redecorate."

Lindsey? Redecorate his house? She could barely manage to type his letters.

"Why would I do that?" Nikos said uncomfortably. "Damn waste of time."

But the truth was he'd loved this nursery. Once. Mostly he'd loved the way Anna's face had lit up when she designed it.

This was the first time he'd been in here since that awful day Cooper had called him to say that Anna was missing. Nikos had been sure she'd been kidnapped. Or worse.

It had been one of the police detectives who'd first dared to ask, "Is it possible the woman's just left you, sir?" Nikos had nearly punched the man for even suggesting it. Because, in spite of his arguments with Anna over her job and her family, Nikos had known he could trust her. He'd never trusted anyone more in his life.

And she'd made him look like a fool.

"Ah, so you're Mum, then? I'm Mrs. Burbridge, the new nanny. A pleasure to meet you, Mrs. Stavrakis."

"I'm not Mrs. Stav— A nanny?" Anna glanced at Nikos in surprise. "Is that really necessary? I can take care of Misha, as I always have."

Nikos stared at the baby. That name still grated on him. He could probably still change it to Andreas. *No*, he thought. Even he thought of his son as Michael now— Misha. Too late to change his name. Too late for a lot of things.

His own son didn't know him. He clenched his hands.

"I'm terribly sorry, Mrs. Burbridge, but we don't need you—"

"Mrs. Burbridge stays," he interrupted, glaring at Anna. "Since I don't know how long you'll be here."

"What do you mean, how long I'll be here?" she demanded. "I'm here until Misha is grown and gone. Unless," she added, "you want to give me joint custody?"

The idea was enough to make him shudder with the injustice of it, but he showed his teeth in a smile. "Your presence here is based upon my will and my son's needs. The day he doesn't need you anymore you'll be escorted to the gate. When he's weaned, perhaps? A few months from now?"

He had the satisfaction of seeing Anna's face go white.

She wasn't the only one. Mrs. Burbridge was edging uncomfortably toward the door. "I…er…now that you're both here with your son, I can see you have much to discuss. I'll go and take my tea, if you'll pardon me…"

Nikos barely noticed the woman leave.

"You can't throw me out," Anna said. "I'm his mother. I have rights."

"You're lucky you're not in jail. You have no idea how much I'd love to hand you to my lawyers. Letting them stomp you like grapes in a vat would give me a great deal of joy."

She looked scared, even as she raised her chin defiantly. "So why don't you do it, then?"

"Because my son needs you. For now." He came closer to her. "But that won't last forever. In the meantime, just give me an excuse, the slightest provocation, and you're out the door."

"You can't force me away from my son!"

"I can't?" He gave her a hard look, then shook his head with a disbelieving snort. "You and your whole aristocratic family really think the world revolves around you and your wants, don't you? To hell with everybody else."

"That's not true!"

"You're too much of a bad influence to raise my child. You're a thief, and the daughter of a thief. Your family mooched off others their whole pathetic lives. Your father was a selfish, immature bastard who never cared about anyone but himself, no matter what it cost the people who loved him—"

He stopped himself, realizing it was no longer Anna's father he was talking about.

She gave him a knowing glance, causing his teeth to set on edge. She knew too damn much. Ever since the night they'd conceived Michael, when he'd been stupid enough to spill his guts, she'd known the chinks in his armor. He hated her for that.

It had been the confusion and pain of finding out about his father that had sent Nikos to her house last year, expecting his perfect secretary to fix the ache as she fixed everything else in his life. But he hadn't expected to end up in Anna's bed. No matter how gorgeous she was, he never would have slept with her if he'd been in his right mind. Anna had been too important to his work—too important in his life—for him to screw it up that way. But, seeking comfort, he'd fallen into her bed and they'd conceived Michael. He'd never had a moment's peace since.

His son started to whimper again.

Anna snuggled the baby close. "You're hungry, aren't you?" With some hesitation, she looked up, biting her lip. "Nikos, I need to feed the baby. Do you mind?"

Itching for a fight, Nikos sat down on the blue overstuffed sofa, pretending to make himself comfortable. "No, I don't mind at all." He indicated the nearby rocking chair.

She stared at him in amazement. "You think I'll do it in front of you?"

"Why not?"

"You're out of your mind."

"What? Are you scared?" He raised his eyebrows. "You have no reason to be. I've seen everything you have to offer."

Although that was true, it wasn't true at all. With her loose ponytail, that left dark tendrils cascading against her white skin, she looked very different from the tightly controlled, buttoned-up woman he remembered. And even in the baggy T-shirt she was wearing he could see that her breasts were larger. They'd been perfect before. He remembered them well, remembered cupping them in his hands, licking slowly across the full nipples, until she'd moaned and writhed beneath him, making love to them after he'd brought her to climax—twice—with his mouth. What were her breasts like now beneath that shirt?

He suddenly realized he was rock-hard.

He was supposed to torture *her*, not the other way around. He willed the desire away. He didn't want her. He didn't want her.

"Fine. Stay. I don't care," she said, although he could tell by the defiant expression on her beautiful pale face that she cared very much. Grabbing the diaper bag with her free hand, she set it down with a plop on the floor by the cushioned rocking chair. Rummaging through the bag, she pulled out several items before she found a blanket. A small vial fell out and rolled across the floor. He picked it up. The label was in Russian.

"What's this?"

"Baby painkiller," she said. "He's teething."

"At his age?"

"It's a little early, but not uncommon." Her fingers seemed clumsy as she used the blue blanket, decorated with safari animals, to cover both baby and breast before she pulled up her T-shirt. The baby's wails immediately faded to a blissful silence, punctuated with contented gulps.

It shouldn't have been erotic, but it was. Every movement she made, every breath she took, seemed electric in Nikos's overcharged state.

He pressed his lips together, remembering how her whole body had trembled when he'd kissed her in the library. The way she'd melted into his arms when he'd brushed his lips against hers.

And before. After they'd found out she was pregnant he'd barely left her side for six months. Every inch of his skin, every cell of his body tingled with the memory. Remembering lovemaking so hot that it had nearly set his bed on fire. Not just his bed. When they hadn't been fighting about the way he'd forced her to relax and take care of herself, they'd made love everywhere—in the kitchen, the conference room, the home theater. Against the wall in the courtyard one rainy day. And in the back of his helicopter the time he'd wanted to fly her over the Grand Canyon. They'd never made it off the ground.

She glanced up at him now, her turquoise eyes so cool and distant. *I'm too good for you,* her eyes seemed to say. She had a royal bloodline of a thousand years. The great-granddaughter of a Russian princess, she was a fantasy of ice and fire. He'd never experienced any woman like her.

Watching her now, nursing his son, he came to a sudden decision.

She deserved to suffer.

But there was no reason to make himself suffer as well.

Tonight. He would have her in his bed tonight.

## CHAPTER THREE

A SLOW BURN SPREAD across Anna's cheeks as Nikos watched her nurse their child. She pulled the blanket a little higher, making sure her breast was covered, but she could still feel his eyes on her. It made her feel naked.

Funny to think she'd once dreamed of this moment, of nursing their baby in the gorgeous, spare-no-expense baby suite she'd decorated, with Nikos sitting beside her. A happy family. She'd dreamed that Nikos would love her, be faithful to her, and someday propose to her.

Now the dream tasted like ashes in her mouth.

Perhaps he hadn't purposefully set out to ruin her father, but he'd kept his involvement in his business a secret. If Anna had known, she could have found a way to save her father from himself, to prevent the depression after his bankruptcy that had caused him to drink himself to death. Nikos should have told her. Instead, he'd tried to shield her from everything, as if she were a helpless doll. It was as if the moment she'd become pregnant he'd suddenly lost all trust in her and in the world around them.

Thank God she'd given up on waiting for him to love her. Too bad it had taken her so long to wise up. After five years as his secretary, watching his revolving door policy with women, she'd been stupid to ever think he would ever change.

But for her to run away had been trading one stupidity for another. She'd dragged her newborn baby from Las Vegas to Spain to Paris, always on the run, living in cheap, tiny apartments with paper-thin walls and mattresses that sagged in the middle. Even in her great-grandmother's old palace there'd been no heat or electricity.

That was no life for a baby. In trying to do better for her child, she'd done worse. Nikos had been right to criticize her. Misha deserved a life of comfort and security.

And he deserved to spend time with the father who loved him.

But how could Anna remain here with him and survive? Nikos had made his intentions clear. He would shred her apart without remorse. Glancing at him now, she shivered at the darkness in his eyes. No, she couldn't stay here. That path led to endless days of seduction…a lifetime of heartbreak.

She silently cursed herself. Last year, when Nikos had unexpectedly shown up on her doorstep, she'd opened her arms…her bed…her soul. She should have slammed the door in his face, thrown all her bags into her car and headed east on Interstate 15. If she had, she might have still been in New York. Working. Single. Free.

But then Misha would never have been born.

That focused her. The past didn't matter. Her mistakes were old news. Her son was all that mattered now. And she wasn't going to let him grow up in this cold house with that cold brute.

But how could someone as small and powerless as Anna fight a billionaire ensconced in his own private fortress? He had money, power, and the added immunity of having no heart. What weapons did she have against him? Her family had no money. Her heart was an easy target.

What power did an impoverished single mother have in the world?

Then she had an idea.

An awful, terrible, dangerous idea.

Nikos touched her knee. She jumped in her seat, causing the baby to give a whimper of protest.

"We need to talk. Alone. We'll have Mrs. Burbridge watch Michael tonight." He gave her a lazy smile that belied the predatory look in his eyes. His strong, wide fingers lightly traced the edge of her knee through her jeans. "We'll have dinner. Discuss our future."

Anna could imagine the type of reacquaintance he had in mind. She felt relatively sure that it wouldn't involve a night of bowling or picquet. She trembled with anticipation and fear. He meant nothing less than full-scale seduction—which she wouldn't be able to resist. Even knowing that he caressed her with a cold heart and punishment on his lips.

She cleared her throat. "I would love to have dinner with you tonight, but, um, I'm afraid I have other plans."

He quirked an eyebrow. "Plans?"

"Yes, plans. Big plans." She swayed furiously back and forth in the plush rocking chair.

"Fascinating. With whom?"

She glanced down at the baby. "With a man."

He followed her gaze with amusement. "Anyone I know?"

She scowled, knowing it was hopeless to continue when they both knew that she was a terrible liar. "All right, I'm going to spend the evening with my son."

"Michael won't mind if his parents spend time alone together tonight. Mrs. Burbridge is trustworthy, Anna. She comes highly recommended and I had her thoroughly vetted, believe me. Michael will be happy with her."

"You called him Michael," she said suddenly.

"So? It's his name."

"You accept that?"

She saw a flash of anger in his face which was quickly veiled. "It is done and over with."

"You know I'm sorry about—"

"Forget about it. I have. Let's talk about tonight. Shall we have Cavaleri serve us dinner under the stars? By the pool?"

Yeah, the pool. Which was conveniently adjacent to the poolhouse, the Moroccan stone fountain, and the manmade waterfall—all places where they'd made love during their brief months of happiness.

*Not happiness,* she reminded herself fiercely. *Illusion.*

"No thanks," she said. "I heard it might rain tonight."

"Would you prefer we have dinner at L'Hermitage?"

Her breath caught at his suggestion. L'Hermitage Casino Resort. All the years she'd spent organizing the details of its creation, and she hadn't even seen the inside since it opened. She ached to see it. In so many ways L'Hermitage was a part of her. She and Nikos had worked on it together. She'd never formally studied architecture, or interior design, but he'd still taken her suggestions to heart. She missed that.

"We'll have dinner at Matryoshka," Nikos continued.

*Yes*, her heart yearned. But she forced herself to take the safe course. She turned away.

"You can do whatever you want," she said crisply. "But after Misha's asleep I will stay in my room alone. I plan to get a sandwich and take a long, hot bath."

He gave her another lazy half-smile, toying with her. "That sounds pleasant. I'll join you."

"You'll find a locked door."

"This is my house, Anna. Do you really think you can keep me out?"

She took a deep breath. He was right, of course. He had the key to every lock. And even if he didn't, he could break down the door with one slam of his powerful arms. He'd find a way into her room, and that would be that.

Of course he wouldn't need violence. One kiss and she'd fall at his feet like a harem girl, without a mind or will of her own.

*Victor.* The name of the Very Bad Idea pounded in her brain. He was her only hope to escape. Her only hope to survive.

*It's too dangerous,* she tried to argue with herself. But her former employer had ties both in Las Vegas and in Russia, and the wealth to employ lawyers who could face the best Nikos had to offer. The two men already hated each other—ever since the day Nikos had stolen Anna away to be his executive secretary. If Victor was still in love with her, he'd be willing to help… For a price. Whose price was worse?

Talk about a rock and a hard place. Would there be any way for her to pit the two men against each other and emerge unscathed, without giving body and soul to either one?

She glanced at Nikos from beneath her lashes. His power seemed like a tangible thing. It scared her. No, she couldn't risk getting Victor involved. It was too dangerous. Someone would end up getting hurt.

With as much grace as she could muster, she gently lifted Misha out from beneath the blanket, pulling down her shirt.

"He's asleep," she said softly. She carefully laid him down on the soft mattress of the crib. Nikos came to stand beside her, and for a moment they watched their child sleep. The baby's arms were tossed carelessly above his head, and his long dark eyelashes fluttered against his plump, rosy cheeks as his breath rose and fell. She whispered, "Isn't he beautiful?"

"Yes."

She bit her lip at his abrupt tone, feeling guilty again about what she'd done. No matter how she hated him, how could she have separated a child from his father?

She took a deep breath. "I…I owe you an apology, Nikos. I should never have taken Misha away from you."

"No." His voice was low.

She licked her lips. Might as well get it all over with. "And I'm sorry for blaming you for my father's death," she said in a rush. "You invested in his company and he took advantage of you. He's the one who chose to drink himself to death. I just wish you'd told me, so I could have tried to do something to save him before it was too late." She paused, then sighed. "I guess we've both made a mess of things in our own way, haven't we?"

He drew back, his eyes cold. "My only mistake was trying to take care of you."

She was trying to be penitent, but his words caused resentment to surge through her anew. She backed away from the crib, keeping her voice soft so as not to wake their sleeping child. "Oh, I see," she said furiously. "So was it for my *welfare* that you cheated on me during my pregnancy?"

He followed her across the room, clenching his jaw in exasperation. He shook his head. "What are you talking about? I never cheated on you. Although at this point I wish I had. Are you trying to make up lies to use against me in court? That's a new low, even for you."

She could hardly believe he'd try to deny it. "What about Lindsey?"

"What about her?"

"You might as well admit she was your mistress. She told me everything." Anna stared blindly at the five-foot-high stuffed giraffe sitting on the powder-blue sofa in the corner. "Lindsey often came here during the last months of my pregnancy, supposedly to ask questions about her job. But I think the real reason was to torment me with details of your affair."

For a moment there was silence in the shaded cool of the nursery.

"Lindsey told you that we were lovers?" His voice was matter-of-fact, emotionless.

"She told me everything." Her throat started to hurt as the pain went through her heart again, ripping the wound anew. "How often you made love. How she believed you'd ask her to marry you."

"It's a lie."

"Of course *that* part was a lie. She was obviously delusional. You'll never propose to anyone." She gave a bitter laugh. "I almost feel sorry for her. You use women when it suits you. But you'll abandon her like you abandoned me."

He became dangerously still. "You think I—abandoned you?"

"I wasn't so sexy anymore, was I? The last three months of my pregnancy you wouldn't touch me, you pushed me away, and finally you just left altogether. You replaced me with a younger, slimmer model."

He looked down at her with narrowed eyes as his nostrils flared. "And that's really what you think of me? After all our years working together you think I would reject and abandon the woman carrying my child."

She pushed away all the wonderful memories of them working, laughing, dancing together. Of nights under the stars. Days spent together in bed.

Wordlessly, she nodded.

"Damn you, it's well known that having sex during the final trimester can induce early labor—"

"I had a healthy pregnancy!" Anna cried. "But you kept me prisoner for nine months. I let you do it because I thought you were just worried about our child. But you kept me away from my family and my work, keeping me helpless and alone. Then you left to live with your gorgeous young mistress. Make up some cockamamie story about early labor if you want, but the truth is you just didn't want me anymore!"

"Anna, you know that's not—"

"I gave you everything, and you broke my heart." She turned away, barely holding back tears as she looked down at her sleeping son. "Go, Nikos. Just leave. That's what you do best, isn't it?"

He grabbed her shoulders, whirling her around. "I can't believe this. *That's* why you kidnapped my son and caused me four months of hell? Because of some damned lies Lindsey told you?"

His hands tightened painfully, and she was suddenly aware of his body close to hers. His breath brushed her cheek, sending waves of heat up and down her body. Her gaze fell to his mouth.

She licked her own lips unconsciously. "Lindsey is your lover. Why won't you just admit it? You didn't hesitate to tell me the brutal truth this morning about my father. I thought you said you were done protecting me!"

He pulled her close, wrapping his muscled arms tightly around her as he whispered in her ear, "Damn you, Anna."

He abruptly released her, striding for the door.

"I'll be back for dinner," he tossed at her without a backward glance. "I expect you to be waiting for me when I return."

She stared after him, still shivering. She had no doubt as to what he expected of her. To be waiting for him in lingerie, holding two flutes of champagne, hot and ready for his seduction. He thought she was weak. He thought that, even though she hated him, she would be powerless to resist.

No, she thought. No way.

Resting one hand protectively on her son's crib, Anna narrowed her eyes.

Whether he was more dangerous or not, Anna had to get Victor's help so she could get out of this house. She had no choice. Because when Nikos had told her that Lindsey's words were lies, she'd found herself wanting to believe him. Aching to believe him.

Being this close to Nikos was killing her.

She'd go to Victor's club tonight. She'd beg for his help. In exchange, she would promise to work for him again—something she'd sworn she'd never do. She'd do anything short of becoming his lover. And once she had Victor's help Nikos would see who was powerless and weak.

She clenched her hands into fists, remembering the arrogant way he'd demanded that she wait for him tonight. She'd be waiting, all right.

Waiting to give him the shock of his life.

NIKOS POURED HIMSELF a small bourbon from the crystal decanter in his office on the fourth floor of L'Hermitage.

He swished the glass and leaned back against the desk, staring out through the wide windows overlooking the Las Vegas Strip. The brilliant blue sky and desert sun were beating down on the palm trees and garish architecture. The blacktop of Las Vegas Boulevard reflected waves of heat on the camera-wielding tourists, the gamblers and the drunken, ecstatic newlyweds.

He took a sip of bourbon. The normally smooth flavor was tasteless. Staring at the amber-colored liquid, he set down the glass and rested his head against his hands.

At last he understood.

He'd thought Anna had left because he'd tried to protect her during her pregnancy. He'd fired her because he'd sworn he'd be damned if his child's mother would ever have to work—not after he'd watched his own mother work herself to death. He'd blocked Anna's phone calls because he'd too often found her pacing while she solved problems at the casino building site, or tried to solve the endless foolish problems of her mother and sister. In both cases she'd been taking on problems that other people should have handled for themselves. Her first priority should have been her child, to the exclusion of all else. Why had she not seen that? Why had she been unable to let the weight of responsibility rest on him? Why had she fought his efforts to keep his fragile new family safe and protected?

Perhaps he should have told her about her father's initial request for an investment, but Alexander Rostoff had asked Nikos to keep it quiet. Later, when Nikos had discovered the embezzlement, Anna was already pregnant, and upsetting her had been the last thing he'd wanted to do. Anna already took too much on where her family was concerned.

But he couldn't believe that his real mistake, what had truly driven Anna away, had been leaving her bed.

She'd been so beautiful in her final trimester, lush with curves and ripe with his child, that Nikos had known there was no way he could keep his hands off her. He'd read in a pregnancy book that late-term sex could be a factor in early labor, so he'd forced himself to leave her, moving to his newly finished penthouse at L'Hermitage. To an empty bed and a lonely apartment. For her sake. For their child's sake.

And she'd taken that as rejection?

In leaving Anna's bed he'd given up the greatest pleasure he'd ever known. He'd even told her why he was leaving, but apparently she hadn't believed him. Instead of being grateful, she'd been angry at his sacrifice.

He clenched his jaw. Hell, how could she have felt otherwise after what Lindsey had told her?

Furious, he rose from his desk and paced his office, crossing to the opposite wall of one-sided windows that overlooked the main casino floor. Leaning against the glass, he stared down at the wide expanse of elegant nineteenth-century Russian architecture, the soaring ceilings with high crystal chandeliers and gilded columns, packed in with slot machines, card tables and well-heeled gamblers.

He spotted Lindsey weaving through the crowds, rushing toward the employee elevator. She was carrying a bag from a high-end lingerie store in the Moskva Shopping Complex within the casino. Even after he'd ordered her to wait for him here at the office she'd taken time to go shopping. Unbelievable.

He missed Anna.

Anna, the perfect secretary. Anna, who'd read his mind. Anna, who'd solved problems before he'd even known they existed.

He'd first met her in New York, when Victor Sinistyn had pitched that ridiculous idea for an Elvis-themed hotel-casino called Girls Girls Girls. The meeting had been an utter waste of his time. With twenty boutique hotels around the world, Stavrakis Resorts were known for their elegance, not for their go-go dancers.

Nikos had noticed Sinistyn's executive assistant, with her cool efficiency and aristocratic demeanor. He'd needed someone who could handle the complex details of running a billion-dollar business while still maintaining the image of his company. He'd needed someone with understanding and discretion, who wouldn't let herself be bullied—not even by him.

Anna Rostoff had been everything he'd wanted and more. Hiring her away from Victor Sinistyn had caused him no end of grief, for the man had been a furious thorn in his side ever since. But Sinistyn's enmity had been a small price to pay. For five years he and Anna had worked together, traveling around the world in his private jet, often working around the clock. She'd never complained. She'd never failed him. She'd never made a mistake. And he'd compensated her accordingly. When he'd found out she was sending most of her salary to support her mother and younger sister in New York, he'd given her a raise that had sent her salary skyrocketing deep into six figures.

He'd known by then that she was indispensable to his empire. Indispensable to *him*.

"I'm here." Lindsey's voice was panting as she leaned against the doorway. She'd stashed the lingerie bag somewhere *en route*, and now brought a hand to her heaving chest. "I was...um..."

"Stuck in traffic?" he said laconically.

"Right. Stuck in traffic." She looked relieved. "You

know Las Vegas Boulevard is a nightmare this time of day."

"Don't worry." Standing over his desk, he leaned forward and gave her a lazy smile. "You're just in time."

"In time?" Her eyes lit up, and her hips swayed as she came toward him. Harsh afternoon sunlight hit her tanned face as she stretched a manicured hand to caress his cheek. "Past time, I'd say."

He removed Lindsey's hand.

"Stop it, Lindsey. It's not going to happen."

The desire for release was strong in him. The desire to forget, to bury himself in flesh and curves and the hot scent of woman. To pull her long hair back, exposing her throat for plunder, to possess her mouth and see the answering spark of desire in her eyes...

He wanted a woman. God, yes. Just not this one.

He wanted the woman who was at home right now, hating him.

Undeterred, Lindsey stroked his thigh. "Why do you think I took this stupid job? I know we'd be perfect together. I'll make you wild. I'll make you so hot and worked up that you'll forget that tramp—"

He cut her off, his tone ruthlessly cold. "You told Anna that we were lovers. When she was pregnant and vulnerable you lied to her. I want to hear it from your mouth."

"All right." Lindsey dropped the seductive pose, and her young, pretty face took on the hard, calculating look of a hustler. "But, the way I see it, I was doing you a favor."

He turned to his desk and pressed a button. Two guards appeared at his door.

"Please escort Miss Miller out of the casino," he said coldly. "Her employment here is done."

The color drained from her face, leaving her pale beneath her tan. "What?"

"A severance check will be waiting for you at the casino office downstairs. You'll find I've been more generous than you deserve."

"You can't be serious!"

"For every minute you argue with me I'll instruct Margaret to subtract a thousand dollars from your check."

She sucked in her breath. "Fine!" She turned on her designer heel and stalked out, grabbing her shopping bag just outside the door. She stopped and glared at him.

"It's not my fault she left, you know. She was having your kid and you still wouldn't marry her. Pathetic." She shook the lingerie bag at him. "And now you'll never see me in *this*!"

He should have gotten rid of her a long time ago, he mused, his ears still ringing with the noise of the slammed door. It took him a moment to realize he was hearing the phone. Shaking his head, he picked up the receiver.

"Yeah?"

"You're not going to like this, boss," Cooper said.

"What's wrong?" Nikos's heart gave a weird thump. "Michael?"

"The baby's fine. With his nanny. But Anna took off. I didn't stop her, since she didn't take the boy. I had her followed, like you said. She took the Maserati."

Nikos nearly choked on his bourbon. Anna had snuck out? Leaving their son behind? When it was almost dusk? Driving his favorite car?

That was her idea of going under the radar?

"Where did she go?"

"That's the part you're not going to like." Coop paused. "She walked into Victor Sinistyn's club ten minutes ago."

"And you waited ten minutes to tell me?" he said tersely.

"Wait, boss. You don't want to go there alone—I'm getting some of the guys—"

"I can do this alone!"

Nikos slammed down the phone and headed for the door. He went straight to his private garage and jumped on his Ducati motorcycle. Swerving through the traffic on Las Vegas Boulevard, he headed downtown.

Fremont Street was gritty, for all of its brilliant lights. This was where the hardcore gamblers came to play, far from the lavish themed hotels and the families with cameras and strollers. This was the original Las Vegas, and its hard-edged glamor showed its tarnish like an aging showgirl.

Victor Sinistyn had turned his failed casino concept into a dance club. Outside of Girls Girls Girls there was a long line of lithe, scantily-clad twenty-somethings, waiting to drink and dance.

Nikos leapt off his motorcycle, tossing his keys to a valet. The bouncer recognized Nikos as he strode arrogantly forward, bypassing the line.

"No bodyguards tonight, Mr. Stavrakis?"

"Where's your boss?" Not waiting for an answer, Nikos pushed past him.

Inside the club, colored lights were pulsing through the darkness to the beat of the music. The place was a cavern, a rebuilt warehouse with an enormous high ceiling, and it shook with the rhythm of the dancing crowd. The air was steamy, hot, redolent of sex and skin.

And then he saw her, wearing a tiny halter top and low-slung jeans that made her look virtually naked.

Dancing with Victor Sinistyn.

The man smiled down at Anna as they danced, running his hands possessively down her bare skin. She gave him a strained smile as she stepped back from him, swaying her body, moving down to her knees before she rose again. She leaned back, arms over her head, and her full breasts strained the fabric, nearly popped out of her flesh-colored top. But apparently Sinistyn wasn't satisfied with just looking.

Grabbing her shoulders, he pulled her bare belly against him and ground his body against hers, nuzzling her neck. Anna didn't struggle, but Nikos had a glimpse of her pale face. She looked as if she were gasping for air. Why was Anna allowing him to manhandle her?

He saw the Russian's hands move toward her breasts. With a savage growl, Nikos started to push roughly through the crowd. All he could think was that if Sinistyn kept touching her he'd kill the man in his own club.

# CHAPTER FOUR

"THERE, WE'VE HAD OUR DANCE." Anna panted, drawing away. "Please can we talk now?"

"The music's not over yet," Victor said, pulling her back close.

That was what she was afraid of—that this music would never end. Her skin crawled where he'd touched her. "But I need to ask you something important, Victor. A life-and-death favor."

"Then you should be trying to please me now," Victor replied, flashing his teeth in a grin as he moved his body against hers. He was handsome, Anna thought, amid the heat and the lights and the pounding rhythm of the dance music. She could see why her sister had had a crush on him since girlhood. Too bad he had such an ugly soul.

Aware that she was playing with fire, Anna wanted to run from him, far away from this dance floor.

But where would she go?

Besides, though he might have hurt business rivals in the past, he would never hurt her, she tried to reassure herself. She'd known Victor since she was eighteen years old, when he'd gone into business with her father and had personally asked Anna to become his secretary. True, she'd spent five years fending him off, but now she had no other choice but to ask for his help. If she didn't want to be completely at Nikos's mercy she needed a favor from the only man who could fight him and win.

"Victor—"

"Call me Vitya, like you used to."

That was Natalie's nickname for him, not hers. "Victor, please, if we could only—"

A hand suddenly gripped her wrist, pulling her away.

"Get away from her, Sinistyn," Nikos said.

"Stavrakis." Narrowing his eyes, Victor wrapped his arm around Anna's waist, pulling her back so hard he almost yanked her off her feet. "You've got some nerve to come into my club and start throwing orders. Get out before I throw you out."

"You? You'll throw me out? Or do you mean one of your goons will do it for you?" Nikos drawled lazily, in a tone that belied the threat in his posture. "We both know you wouldn't have the guts to do it yourself."

Victor smiled at him, showing sharp teeth. He looked over the dance floor. Anna noticed his bodyguards hovering close by. Apparently, this gave Victor courage. "I don't see Cooper with you tonight. It was a mistake to leave your guard dogs at home, you Greek—"

Anna physically came between them, pushing them apart. She felt sick. She'd thought Nikos would wait for his bodyguards, giving her at least thirty minutes to privately conclude her business with Victor. Having him come so quickly, and alone, had shot her plan apart.

"Please, let me go," she said to Victor. "I need to talk to Nikos anyway. I—I'll talk to you more later."

For a moment Victor looked as if he were going to

pummel the smirk off Nikos's face anyway. Then he shrugged and said shortly, "As you wish, *loobemaya*. Go. Until later."

He walked off the dance floor. Nikos looked as if he meant to deliver some rejoinder, but Anna grabbed his hands, forced his attention back to her. "What are you doing here?"

Nikos's anger came back to focus on her. "The question, madam, is what are *you* doing here? Dancing with him? Dressed like that?"

"I can dress as I please—"

He interrupted her. "You will never see Victor Sinistyn again, do you understand?"

"No, I don't. You're not my husband. You're nothing—"

With a growl, he dragged her off the floor, through the crowds and out of the club. She struggled, unable to escape his iron grip.

Outside, the cooling desert air felt fresh against her overheated skin. She took several deep breaths, trying to calm her fears as he retrieved his motorcycle from the valet.

This was going to work. It *had* to work. She'd use the threat of Victor to force Nikos to give her joint custody of her son. And set her free.

Tossing a tip to the valet, Nikos threw a muscular leg over the motorcycle's seat. For a moment Anna's gaze lingered on his body, on the way his snug black T-shirt accentuated the muscles of his chest and his flat belly, on the tight curve of his backside in the dark designer jeans.

"Get on," he ordered, his eyes like ice.

Carefully, Anna climbed up behind him on the motorcycle. She gave a little squeak as he revved the engine and roared down the street without a word of warning.

She held him close, her body pressed against his back. Her tight suede halter top thrust her breasts upward, and they felt exquisitely sensitive, the nipples hardening as they brushed against the muscles of his back. She tightened her grip on his waist, her dark hair flying in the wind.

"You'll never go to that club again," he said in a low voice, barely audible over the roar of the engine.

"I'll do as I please."

"Promise me right now, or I swear to God I'll turn around and burn the place to the ground."

She felt his body tense beneath her grip as he waited. His deliciously hard body felt so good beneath her hands. It was enough to make her lose all rational thought.

Perhaps she could give in to this one request, she thought. She didn't want to go back to the stupid club again, anyway. She had no intention of letting Victor paw at her more on the dance floor.

Next time she'd meet him somewhere else. Like a library.

"All right," she said. "I promise."

She felt his body relax slightly. "Good."

A few moments later he pulled the motorcycle beneath the brilliant marquee of L'Hermitage Casino Resort.

Like the Parisian and Venetian hotels down the street, L'Hermitage's architecture was an imposing fantasy. Much of the design had been based upon the stately nineteenth-century palaces of St. Petersburg, but the centerpiece of the building was a reproduction of St. Basil's Cathedral in Red Square, with its distinctive onion-shaped domes.

Tossing his keys to the valet, he took her by the hand—more gently this time—and led her through the front door for her first inside look at the finished project that had consumed them both for nearly four years.

She gazed upward at the high ceiling as he led her through the main floor of the casino. The architecture had triangular shaped Russian arches over doors, watched over by painted angels. Soaring above the slot machines and roulette tables, a simulated horizon held the breathless hush of a starlit sky on a cold winter night.

"It's beautiful," she whispered.

He smiled at her then, an open, boyish smile, and it nearly took her breath away. "Wait until you see the rest."

On the other side of the main casino floor they entered the Moskva Shopping Complex, which was built like several outdoor streets within the casino. The storefronts and streetlights, the ambient light and even the sounds of birds far overhead, made Anna feel as if she was walking through a fairytale Russian city.

"It's just like I dreamed." She looked at the expensive shops, Gucci and Prada and Tiffany, and her fingers tightened around his. "You made our dream a reality."

He stared at her, then slowly shook his head. "We did it together, Anna. I couldn't have created L'Hermitage without you."

She blinked as tears filled her eyes. He appreciated

all the work she'd done, the heart she'd poured into her work.

He looked her full in the face. "I've missed you."

Anna felt her heart stop right in the middle of the ebb and flow of the busy street. The chic people hurrying into the stores seemed to blur around her. Could it be true? Just by seeing her with Victor, could Nikos have realized he missed her? Needed her?

Loved her?

Her heart gave a strange thump. Words trembled on her lips. Horrible words she couldn't possibly say, because they couldn't possibly be true. Could they?

"You…you've missed me?"

"Of course," he replied. "No other secretary has ever been your equal."

"Oh." The thump moved from her heart to her throat. She turned to face the large building behind her.

"Matryoshka," she murmured, over the miserable lump in her throat. She stared up at the restaurant's imposing domes of unpainted wood, like a miniature cathedral tucked inside the fairytale street. She had to change the subject before he realized what she'd been thinking. Before she despised herself more for being foolish enough to think he actually cared for her.

"Wait until you see the inside," he said, taking her hand. "You'll think you're inside the Terem Palace."

A slender, well-dressed *maître d'* stood at a podium just inside the restaurant.

"We'd like the table by the window," Nikos said.

The *maître d'* didn't bother looking up from his reservation page. "That particular table is booked for four months," he said, sounding bored. "And we have nothing available for tonight—not a thing—not even if you were the King of—"

Mid-sneer, the man glanced up. He saw Nikos, and his jaw went slack. He suddenly began to cough.

"One moment, sir," he said breathlessly. "We'll get your table ready, for you and for your lovely lady, straight away."

Two minutes later the *maître d'*, now fawning and polite, had left them at the best table in the restaurant. A little awed in spite of herself, Anna looked around.

The interior of Matryoshka had been designed in seventeenth-century Muscovite style, with intimate low ceilings made of stucco and covered with frescoes of interweaving flowers and the nesting dolls that inspired the restaurant's name. Elaborate tiled ovens and *kokosh-nik*-shaped arches were lit by flickering candles on the tables and torches on the walls.

As a waiter came to tell them about the specials, Nikos cut him off. "We'll both have the salmon with caviar and champagne sauce," he said, closing his menu. "And Scotch—neat."

"Wait." Anna stopped the waiter with a hand on his arm. "I would like Chicken Kiev, please. And *kulich* for dessert," she added, referring to the Easter fruitcake. "And sparkling water to drink." She closed her menu, matching Nikos glare for glare. "Not Scotch."

Caught in the crossfire, the waiter glanced nervously at Nikos, who nodded.

After the young man was gone, Nikos bit out, "I didn't mean the Scotch for you. I know you're nursing."

"Even if I weren't nursing I wouldn't want it. Or caviar, either. Ugh."

He gave her a humorless smile. "A Russian who dislikes caviar? Next you'll be telling me you have no taste for vodka."

"I don't appreciate you trying to order for me. I'm not a child."

"I was treating you like a lady," he said coolly, leaning back in his chair.

"Oh? And is that how you justify telling me who my friends can be?"

"Sinistyn's not your friend," Nikos bit out. "He'll use you and toss you aside."

She gave him an angry glare. "And you want to be the only one who does that to me?"

As the waiter placed their drinks on the table, Nikos looked affronted, furious. "You cannot even compare—"

"Save it. I've known Victor since I was eighteen. Our fathers were friends—although they chose to make their living in very different ways. I was Victor's secretary for five years. I know him better than you do."

Unfortunately she understood him well enough to know that everything Nikos said about him was true. But she wasn't going to say that.

Nikos's hands clenched on the table. "Just how *well* do you know him?"

Anna tilted her head and watched him narrowly. "He's asked me to marry him several times."

He glanced at the stained-glass window. The expression on his face was half hidden, but his jaw was hard. "What?"

"I've always said no, but that might change. I won't be your pawn, Nikos. I won't take your punishment forever.

I won't allow you to threaten me with losing my child. And if what it takes to match you is to marry Victor…"

She let her voice trail off.

Nikos blinked, very slowly. When he opened his eyes, for the first time since he'd dragged her back to Las Vegas, they were wary. He was looking at her not as a victim to punish but as a challenging adversary. "What do you want?"

"You know what I want. My freedom."

"I won't let you take Michael from me. Ever. Get that."

"Then you can expect a very prolonged custody battle. If Victor and I take you to court, it'll be splashed in the papers. A full media circus."

"Is that really what you want?" he said in disbelief. "The two of us pulling at our child like a rope in a tug-of-war?"

"Of course not!" She had no intention of starting a romance with Victor, let alone making him Misha's stepfather, but she was praying Nikos wouldn't call her bluff. "I don't want to ask Victor for help, but what choice have you given me?"

The torches around them flickered in silence for several seconds before Nikos tossed his napkin down on the table. "Fine. You win."

Nikos abruptly rose from the chair. Anna watched in amazement as he strode across the restaurant and out the door.

She'd won?

He was going to give her joint custody? He was going to let her leave Las Vegas? Let her have her own life back?

She could hardly believe it. In a few days she'd be back in New York, looking for a new job. She knew she wouldn't find anything as invigorating as working at Stavrakis, but at least she'd be able to take pride in supporting herself and her son. Nikos would insist on child support, of course, but she'd put that money into a trust fund for Misha later. That way it would be clear to everyone, including herself, that Nikos had no hold on her. She'd never give him power over her again.

And to make sure of that she wanted some space between them. The whole country would be a nice start.

Their dinners were served, and she took a bite of her Chicken Kiev. Delicious. She stared into the flickering flame of the torch on the wall. It had almost been too easy. She was actually disappointed Nikos had capitulated so quickly. After the way he'd treated her, her blood had been up for a fight.

"Enjoying your meal?" the waiter asked, refilling her water glass with a smile. "You look happy."

"I am."

"Because you're in love? I am too," the young man added, and before she could dispute his assumption he leaned forward to joyfully whisper, "I'm proposing to my girlfriend tonight."

"That's wonderful!"

"But what's this?" He peered at Nikos's untouched plate. "Mr. Stavrakis didn't like his salmon?"

"He, um, got called away." Anna handed the waiter her own empty plate, which she'd all but licked clean. If it weren't for the caviar spread over the salmon, she'd have eaten Nikos's dinner, too.

"In that case, I'll bring your dessert. An extra big

slice," he promised, then winked at her. "Everyone should celebrate tonight."

She definitely felt like celebrating. But as she dug into the fruitcake a few moments later she noticed her breasts were starting to hurt. Back at the estate, Misha would be getting hungry. She needed to return to the dance club, retrieve the Maserati and get back.

"Is there anything else I can do for you, miss?" the waiter asked.

"Um...the bill?"

"Mr. Stavrakis always takes care of his guests. I'd lose my job if I brought you a bill. Sorry. Standing orders."

She breathed a sigh of relief. Matryoshka was very expensive. As it had been Nikos's choice to bring her here, and he'd ditched her in the middle of the meal, her conscience would allow him to pay. Heck, his accountants would probably get a tax advantage out of it.

But just as she was about to leave Nikos sat down heavily in the chair across from her.

"What are you doing here?" she blurted out, chagrined. Could he have already gotten a lawyer to draw up the custody papers?

He frowned at the empty table. "Where is my dinner?"

"Long gone. My Chicken Kiev was delicious, though." She shook her head wryly. "Thanks for ditching me. I had a nice conversation with the waiter. He's in love. He's going to propose," she said airily.

"To you?" Nikos said sharply.

Anna snorted a derisive laugh. "Yes. To me. I have that kind of power over men."

He took a small sip of Scotch. Casually, almost dismissively, he tossed a small box on the table, pale blue as a robin's egg. "Here."

Frowning, she opened it.

Inside the box, nestled on black velvet, she saw a huge diamond ring set in platinum. The facets of the enormous stone, which had to be at least ten carats, sparkled up at her in the candlelight. It took her breath away.

She twisted her great-grandmother's stoneless ring around her finger nervously. Nikos's diamond was so big it wouldn't have even fit inside the Princess's empty setting. The diamond was bigger than a marble. Excessive to the point of tackiness. And yet...

She swallowed, looking up at him. "What is this? Some kind of trick?"

"No trick," he said. "We will be married tonight."

The rush that went through her then was like nothing she'd ever felt. *Nikos wanted to marry her.* Just as she'd dreamed for so long. Even when she'd known it was impossible—even when, as his secretary, she'd watched him go from one sexual conquest to another, she'd had secret dreams that she might someday be the woman to tame him.

"Put it on," Nikos said.

But it wasn't the earnest pleading of a lover—it was an order. Utterly cold and without emotion.

And just like that the pleasure in her heart evaporated.

Nikos didn't want to marry her.

He wanted to *own* her.

This was his way of dealing with the threat of Victor. Rather than calling for his lawyer, rather than negotiating for joint custody of Misha, he figured it was easier to just buy her off with a ring. He thought Anna could be purchased for the price of a two-hundred-thousand dollar trinket and some meaningless words.

"What do you take me for?" she said in a low voice.

"As my wife. To have—" his eyes raked over her "—and to hold."

She swallowed. His dark eyes were undressing her, right there in the restaurant. As if he were considering the very real possibility of pulling her to him, ripping off her clothes, and making love to her there on the table, with the entire restaurant watching.

He still intended to coldly seduce her. He still meant to take his pound of flesh for what she'd done. And if he were her husband, his power over her would increase tenfold.

*Just give in*, her thought whispered. Give in to her desire. Give in to his power. Then he couldn't send her away from Misha ever again. She would be his wife. She would be above Lindsey and the other women like her—she would be Mrs. Stavrakis. And though Nikos hated her now, perhaps someday...

*No.* She had to get a hold of herself. Even if someday Nikos forgave her, she would never, ever forgive him. He didn't love her. And it was worse than that. He didn't even trust her enough to work or to make any decisions about her own life.

He said he wanted to protect her, but he really wanted to lock her away, like a parakeet in a tiny gold cage.

Could she put aside every ounce of pride and self-preservation and marry a man who hated her? Allow herself to be bound to him forever?

"No," she whispered.

His dark eyebrows pushed together like a storm cloud. "What did you say?"

She trembled at his anger even as she braced herself for more. She wouldn't bend. She wouldn't submit. She wouldn't sell herself for the hopeless, destructive illusion that he might someday trust her, respect her, love her.

"I said no." Snapping the box shut, she held it out to him. "Sorry, Nikos. I'm not for sale."

## CHAPTER FIVE

NIKOS STARED AT HER, hardly able to believe his ears.

"Don't you understand?" he said. "I'm giving you what you wanted. I'm making you my wife."

"How very generous. But I only wanted that when I was in love with you. Not anymore." When he didn't take the box, she tossed it on the table between them. Such a small thing, but it separated them like a stone wall two feet thick. "Now I just want to be free."

She shifted in her chair, brushing her dark hair off her bare shoulders. He looked around the restaurant that they'd conceived together. To his fevered imagination it seemed that every man in the room was watching Anna. Her lovely pale skin, the dark hair cascading in riotous waves down her back, those almond-shaped turquoise eyes challenging him. The beige halter top barely covered her full breasts, and her dark low-rise jeans revealed her flat belly.

God, she was gorgeous. He'd never wanted her more.

"You will marry me, Anna," he said. "We both know it will happen."

"Death and taxes are inevitable. But marriage?" She gave him a humorless smile. "No."

"I don't particularly want to marry you, either. But my son's happiness means more to me than my own."

He saw her lips tighten at that. Good, so she understood how much he cared for Michael.

But there was more to it than that.

From the moment Nikos had seen Anna dancing with Victor Sinistyn in the club, something had changed in him that he couldn't explain. He only knew that Anna belonged to him and no other man. He had to stamp his possession on her for all the world to see.

The idea had haunted him. In the club, on his motorcycle, as he'd walked with Anna through the casino. He'd kept thinking it would be simple enough to marry her. Hell, they were already in Las Vegas. And once she wore his ring he knew she would be utterly loyal to those vows. There would be no more arguments or fear of betrayal. No custody battle splashed in the papers. It was the perfect solution.

He'd just never thought she would refuse him.

"You will marry me for the sake of our son."

"Never."

Nikos raked a hand through his dark hair in frustration. This wasn't how it was supposed to go. He was accustomed to his employees rushing to fulfill his orders, and his mistresses had always done the same.

"You will be rich—richer than your wildest dreams," he pointed out. "I will deny you nothing."

She snorted incredulously. "You think I care about that? If I'd wanted to marry for money, I could have done it long ago."

"Meaning you'd have married Victor Sinistyn?"

"Yes. I could have." She paused. "I could still."

Nikos tightened his hands into fists, cracking his

knuckles. A flood of unwelcome emotion swept through him.

He remembered watching Anna in the dance club, the way she'd swayed against Sinistyn, gyrating beneath the flashing lights. He remembered the way the skin on her taut belly had glistened, how her low-slung jeans had barely covered her hips as she swayed.

No other man but Nikos should touch her. Ever.

Especially not Victor Sinistyn. How could Nikos allow Anna to throw herself away on a man like that? How could he allow his son to have this man for a stepfather.

There was only one way to make sure that never happened. She would agree to his proposal.

He had to convince her.

"Why don't you give the ring to Lindsey?" Anna said sweetly as she rose from the table. "I'm sure she'd be more than willing to marry you. Now, if you'll excuse me, I need to go home and feed my son."

Home.

He had a sudden image of her in bed, and he relaxed. Bed was a place where they'd always understood one another very well. A slow smile spread across his lips. Once they were home he would take her in his arms and she would not be able to deny him anything...

"I will take you home," he said.

"But I left your car at the club—"

"That will be arranged. The fastest way to get to my estate is on the bike." He raised an eyebrow. "Unless you're afraid to be that close to me again?"

She tossed back her hair with a deliberate casualness that didn't fool him for a second. "Don't be ridiculous."

"Good." He rose from his chair, reaching out for her hand. "Let's go."

She stared at him for a moment, her eyes wide as the sea, then with obvious reluctance gave him her hand. It felt small and cool in his own. "Fine," she said with a sigh. "Take me."

Oh, he intended to.

But she hung back, glancing back at the table. "What about the ring? Are you just going to leave it?"

Nikos shrugged. Since the jewelry hadn't worked, it was of no further use to him. All he could think about now was that her skin felt warmer by the second. He yearned to touch her all over, to feel her hands on his body.

"Is everything all right, Mr. Stavrakis?" the waiter asked nervously behind him. "I hope there was no problem with your dinner?"

His eyes focused on the young waiter who'd served Anna earlier. He looked scared, holding a platter of dirty dishes on his shoulder.

"Your tip's on the table," Nikos replied abruptly. Then he turned back to push Anna out of the restaurant.

He heard a loud gasp, and the clatter of dishes falling to the floor as the waiter saw the ring, but he didn't wait for thanks. All he could think was that he had to get Anna home and in his bed. Within minutes they were roaring down the highway on his motorcycle.

THE MOON WAS FULL, casting shadows over the sagebrush and distant mountains. Anna clung to Nikos on the back of the motorcycle, her dark hair whipping wildly around her face as they sped across the wide moonlit desert.

She tightened her grip on his narrow waist, pressing her body against his. He was driving like a bullet, and the wind was cold against her bare arms and back. But that wasn't the reason she was shivering.

She was burning like a furnace, lit up from within.

She knew why Nikos was driving down the highway as if all the demons of hell were in hot pursuit. She'd seen it in his dark eyes. She'd felt it in the way he'd touched her. In the way he'd taken possession of her hand and pulled her from the casino.

He was going to make love to her. Until she couldn't see straight. Until she couldn't think.

Until she agreed to marry him.

She felt beads of sweat break out on her forehead, instantly wiped away by the cool desert wind.

It terrified her how badly she wanted him in return. She was barely keeping herself in check. She was afraid she'd give in.

To sleeping with him.

To everything.

Had anyone ever defied Nikos for long? Was it even possible?

She shivered again.

"Cold, my sweet?" Nikos asked in a husky voice as they pulled into the ten-car garage. Turning off the engine, he set the kickstand and gently took her hand, pulling her off the bike. He ran his fingers down the inside of her wrist as he pulled her close. "You won't be cold for long."

She backed away. "I—need to go feed Misha," she gasped out, and hurried down the hall. She was surprised and relieved beyond measure when he didn't follow her.

Afterward, as she closed the nursery door, leaving a well-fed slumbering baby behind her, she was just congratulating herself on escaping her fate when she heard his voice.

"I shouldn't have called you a bad mother. It's not true."

She whirled around to see Nikos step forward in the moonlit hallway, his face half hidden by shadows.

Gulping a breath, she looked down at the floor. "Nikos!"

He came closer and lightly brushed her wind-tangled hair off her shoulders. "I'm sorry I said it. You are good with him."

She knew that his brief kindness was part of his plan to wear her down, but unfortunately it was working. Those were words she'd been so desperate to hear, especially from him.

*Damn!* Biting her lip, she threw a look of longing at the guest bedroom the housekeeper had assigned her. It was only ten feet down the hall, but it might as well have been a million miles away as he took her in his arms.

He stared at the way her teeth rubbed against her lower lip. "You're so beautiful," he whispered, lightly tracing his finger against her cheek. "And so wild. So much passion behind that prim, dignified secretary. For all those years I never knew."

She started to tremble. She had to get out of here.

She had to escape. She was already perilously close to giving in.

Swallowing, she tried to pick a fight. "Where's Lindsey tonight?"

"I have no idea. I fired her."

"You did—what?"

"She was never my lover, Anna. She fed you lies out of some deluded hope that she might be someday. But she was never my type."

"What's your type?" she retorted feebly, trying to hide her shock about Lindsey.

He blinked, then shook his head, giving her a predatory smile. "Arrogant Russian-born women with black hair, cat-shaped eyes and a tart mouth." He leaned forward to breathe in her hair, whispering in her ear. "I remember the sweet taste of you. Tart and sweet all over, Anna…"

She struggled not to remember, not to feel anything as his voice washed over her senses. "Lindsey really wasn't your lover?"

"Since that first night we were together you've been the only one." He ran his finger gently along her lips. "You're the mother of my child. I need you, Anna. In my home. In my bed."

*Oh, my God.* She was dizzy with longing, unable to speak.

"You are meant to be my wife." He kissed her softly on the forehead, her cheeks. "It is fate."

"But I—I don't want you," she managed, her heart threatening to jump out of her ribcage.

"Prove it," he whispered. Encircling her body with his strong arms, he slowly traced his hand down her bare back. She could feel the warmth of his skin, the strength of his hand.

"I don't," she insisted, but her voice was so weak that even she didn't believe it.

He backed her up against the wall between a large plant and a Greek statue in the wide, dark hallway. "Are you sure?"

The only thing of which she was sure was that the strain of not reaching for him was causing her physical pain. She flattened her trembling palms against the wall as he gently ran his hand through her tangled dark hair. His fingers brushed against the sensitive flesh of her earlobe. He traced lightly down her neck.

"I always get what I want, and I've never wanted any woman like I want you…"

Lowering his mouth to hers, he kissed her. His lips was gentle and oh, so seductive. Pressing her hands against his chest, she willed herself to resist. To remember the cruel way he'd humiliated her before.

*I won't give in this time. I won't…*

But even as she made token resistance she felt her body surrender. Her head leaned back as his tongue teased her, as his lips seared her own. She felt her mind, soul, everything float away until only longing was left.

"No!" With her last bit of willpower she pushed him away. She tried to push past him toward her room, but he blocked her. She stumbled over her high-heeled sandals, kicking them off as she turned and ran down the hall. He pursued her, as single-minded as a wolf stalking a deer. She raced outside, banging the door behind her.

In the courtyard, dark clouds had spread across the sky, and she could smell coming rain. Silver threads of moonlight laced the sky, barely holding back the storm.

Barefoot, Anna tripped across the mosaic tiles of the courtyard, skirting the edge of the pool's shimmering water. Her pale skin glowed in the moonlight as she ran beneath the dark shadows of palm trees.

Nikos caught her in front of the enormous Moroccan fountain, his arms wrapping around her from behind.

"I need you, Anna," he said huskily in her ear, holding her body against his own. "And you need me. Don't deny it."

Kissing her neck from behind, he ran his hands over her, cupping her breasts in the suede.

Sucking in her breath, she whirled to face him. Angry words fell unspoken as she saw his face. His handsome, strong face, made somehow even more masculine with the dark bristles of a five o'clock shadow on his chin. In the snug black T-shirt and dark jeans he didn't look like a billionaire tycoon. He looked like a biker, dangerous and dark, and a devil in bed.

He was right. She wanted him.

Needed him.

Could so easily love him...

"I can't," she gasped aloud.

"Can't?" He held her even tighter.

In spite of her resolve, honesty poured out of her. "I can't fight you anymore..."

His sensual lips curved into a smile as he reached his hand behind her head and pulled her into a hot, hard kiss. She returned the kiss hungrily, tasting blood in the intensity of their mutual need. His blood? Hers? She didn't care. All she knew was that she'd been denied his touch for too long. If he stopped kissing her now she would die.

She wanted to possess him as thoroughly and savagely as he'd possessed her soul...

She pressed her hands against his back, desperate to pull him closer, but it wasn't enough. She brought her hands between them, beneath his shirt, running her hands up his taut belly. She heard him gasp as she explored the trail of hair up his chest, feeling the hard planes of his torso. He'd always been strong, but his muscles were bigger now, harder than they'd ever been. And more...

"What's this?" she murmured aloud, but didn't wait for an answer. She yanked on the black T-shirt, and he let her pull it off his body. She lightly traced a hard ridge across his naked collarbone, then found another one over his ribs.

"You have new scars," she whispered.

He shrugged, a deceptively careless gesture. "I worked some aggression out in the boxing ring while you were gone."

"I'm sorry—"

"I'm not. I'm stronger now. No one will ever have to do my fighting for me again."

Unlike most rich men, she thought in a daze. Unlike Victor.

Nikos ran his hands up and down her halter top, caressing the soft suede, pressing her breasts upward until they threatened to spill over. He reached beneath the top, cupping and weighing their fullness, then bent to nuzzle between them. The dark stubble of his chin was rough against her tender skin, sending prickles all over her body as he licked his way slowly to her neck. He sucked at the crook of her shoulder, causing pain and pleasure and a mark of possession.

She moaned softly, arching into him. He pushed her back roughly against the tiled wall of the courtyard. Her eyelids fluttered, and as if in a dream she saw the splash of colorful tile in the moonlight, heard the burble of the stone fountain.

She couldn't let this happen…

She couldn't stop herself from letting it happen…

Dazed and unsteady, she threw her arms back against the wall for support. He pressed his hands on the small of her back, pulling her closer, tighter. His naked chest pressed against her, the hard muscles of his arms wrapped around her bare arms. Their legs were tangled as she felt the naked skin of his taut belly against her own. He kissed her hard, running his hands through her hair.

He ran his hands along the sides of her jeans. Jeans! She cursed the choice. Why hadn't she worn a skirt? He grabbed her backside, lifting her up so she could wrap her legs around him. She could feel how hard he was, how ready for her. She wanted him to take her here, now, against the wall, before she had time to think.

"God, I want you," he whispered. "For the last year you're the only woman I've been able to think about. Just you. Only you."

She took a deep breath. "Then take me."

There. She'd said it. Right or wrong, she'd dared to admit what they both already knew: she wanted him. Her cheeks felt hot; she felt like a hoyden. She took a deep breath. "But please be gentle. My—my doctor said the first time I had sex after the baby might feel like... like I was a virgin. It might hurt."

He pulled back abruptly, giving her a searing look. "I would never hurt you, *agape mou*."

At that moment she believed him. "I know."

But he still hesitated, looking troubled. She realized that he was holding himself back because he didn't want to cause her pain. He still cared about her. For the first time she felt the magnitude of her own power over him, and it thrilled her.

She smiled up at him, tracing the beauty of his slightly crooked nose with her fingertip, touching his bare scars. He was a warrior, fierce and powerful, and frightening in his beauty.

But, powerful as he was, she realized she could match his fire.

Bracing her hands on his shoulders, she unwrapped her legs from his body. Backing away, she reached behind her and untied her halter top. It fell into her hands, leaving her upper body naked. Moonlight briefly drenched her skin in an opalescent glow the color of pearls, then disappeared behind the dark clouds that were rapidly covering the sky.

She stood in front of him in the semidarkness, straight and tall. She'd never been this brave before. Even during the months of their affair she'd always let him take the lead. Nervous at her own daring, she looked into his face.

His expression was strained. With a low growl he lifted her back into his arms, pressing her against the wall. The feeling of his skin against her own, without the halter top to separate them, was exquisite. But it wasn't enough—still not nearly enough.

Clasping her wrists tightly in one massive hand, he pulled her arms over her head, kissing down her body as he moved his other hand between her legs. Her earlier fear of pain was already forgotten as she moved against him, wanting to feel more. To feel *him*. Above her, she could hear the howl of rising wind, and she felt small drops of rain against her overheated skin. Her hair whipped wildly as she leaned her head back, hardly able to breathe, out of her mind with longing.

"I take it all back," she gasped. "Don't be gentle. Don't make me wait. Take me now."

He gave her a lazy smile as his fingers caressed her through her jeans. "You want me to take you here? Against the wall?"

"Yes. And I don't give a damn who might see." She only knew that if he kept stroking her through her jeans she was going to come any second.

But he didn't make a move to pull off her jeans. Instead he kept stroking her, moving his chest against hers, plundering her mouth with his own.

"Stop," she panted. Pushing his hand away, she strained toward him, her hands fumbling at his zipper. "I want to feel you inside me—"

"No." He grabbed her hands. "Wait."

A roll of thunder shattered the clouds and cold rain began to fall, splattering across the courtyard and pool. Wind howled across the desert, rattling the palm trees high above them as they stared at each other.

"I want you. But—" He blinked, as if trying to clear his mind of a fog, shaking his head like a wolf scattering water from his fur. "This is a mistake. When I make love to you again it will be in a bed…"

She saw a glimmer of hope. "My bedroom is—"

"As my wife," he finished.

They stared at each other in the moonlight, whipped by wind and hard rain. Anna was suddenly aware that she was standing half naked, with cold, hard rain sleeting down her bare breasts.

She'd just thrown herself at him.

*And he'd refused her.* Her cheeks flushed with shame.

"If you wait for me to marry you, you'll wait forever," she retorted, blinking back angry tears. He'd only been trying to prove his power over her, and she'd fallen for it yet again. She reached down to the tiled floor and snatched up her halter top, now ruined in the rain. Her hands shook as she tied the strings in back. Her teeth chattered as she said, "Just being your mistress nearly killed me. I will never be your wife, Nikos. Never."

Beneath the darkness of the desert storm she could barely see his face for shadows. But his voice was low and dangerous, resonant with the certainty that only came from power. "We'll see."

THE NEXT MORNING, Nikos growled at the housekeeper's cheery greeting as she brought his breakfast to the table. She set down a cup of strong Greek coffee and a plate of eggs, bacon and toast, then left. He stared blankly at the morning editions of the *Wall Street Journal* and the local *Review-Journal* and cursed himself for a fool.

He hadn't slept all night, and it was his own damned fault.

It was not in his nature to be patient, but he'd left Anna in the courtyard and gone to his bedroom alone. Where he'd tossed and turned until dawn.

He swore softly to himself. If he'd just made love to Anna last night, perhaps he'd already be free of this spell.

He took a gulp of the hot coffee. He'd need all the help he could get to make it through the day. He had to secure a new secretary to replace Lindsey, the negotiations for the land lease bid for his new casino resort project in Singapore were at a critical juncture, and all he could think about was getting Anna in bed. He was so wound up he couldn't see straight.

He was off his game. Just when his business urgently needed his attention. It was intolerable.

And the worst thing was he had no idea how to convince Anna to be his wife. It was the best thing for everyone. Damn it, why couldn't she see that?

He'd already reasoned with her. Fired Lindsey. Bought her a two-hundred-thousand-dollar ring. He'd offered Anna wealth and the protection of his name, and she'd thrown them back in his face.

Even seducing her hadn't made her agree to his proposal. For a man accustomed to negotiation, he was in a tough spot. What was left to offer?

"More toast, Mr. Stavrakis?"

He growled in reply. Accustomed to his moods, the housekeeper gave him a cheerful nod. "By the way, thank you for hiring Mrs. Burbridge. She's already popular among the staff. And such a sweet baby you have too, sir, if you don't mind me saying so."

"Thank you," he bit out, then picked up the nearest paper to signal the end of the conversation. After the housekeeper had left he took several bites of food, then threw his paper down and went to look for Anna.

He found her at the pool, and watched her for several seconds from the doorway before she saw him.

She was in the water, holding Michael. The baby was laughing and splashing as she skimmed him through the water in the warm morning sun. Anna held him close, pointing out things in the courtyard. "And those are palm trees, and a fountain. That's the blue sky, and the water is blue too. It's going to be hot today," she said to the baby, smiling. "So different from your great-grandmama's old palace, isn't it, Misha?"

Nikos envied her playful ease with the baby. He felt like an outsider looking at a loving family. It wasn't supposed to be this way. Having a child was his chance for a fresh start. To have a family of his own. To be the father he himself had never had. Damn it, how had everything gone so wrong?

It should have made him resent her, reminded him to hate her, but instead he felt only envy and a whisper of loneliness. Anna was simply in the pool doing nothing, splashing and wading, but he could tell she was having the time of her life because she loved just spending time with their child.

He'd been wrong to think about taking Michael away from her. Even if he'd been cruel enough to do it, Anna never would have accepted it. She would have fought him all the way. She had absolute loyalty and a single-minded devotion to those she loved.

His eyes went wide.

*That* was how he could get Anna to marry him.

Not jewelry. Not money. Not even sex.

Love. Love was the glue that would bind her.

He had to make Anna fall in love with him—fall so hard and fast that she'd not only marry him but would spend the rest of her life trying to get his love in return.

Which, of course, he wouldn't give her. He wasn't a fool. Loving her would make him weak when he most needed to be strong. How could he guard his family, protect them as they deserved, if his judgment was impaired? He'd never allowed himself to love anyone, and he never intended to.

But her loving him—that was something else. She had a character that was born for devotion. If she loved him it would ensure her loyalty for a lifetime. It would keep his son safe with a loving mother, and he'd be protected from stepfathers like Sinistyn.

It couldn't be that hard to make Anna love him, he reasoned. She'd said she loved him before, though he hadn't realized it at the time. All he needed to do was repeat those same conditions and she would do so again.

But she must never suspect what he was doing. She had to think she was falling for him of her own free will.

He narrowed his eyes, watching as Anna laughed with their baby, splashing in the pool, tilting her lovely pale face back to drink in the warm Nevada sun.

What carrot could he dangle in front of her to convince her to be with him and spend unguarded time together?

What if he allowed her to work as his secretary again? Just for a few days? Of course it would be temporary. And, hell, he'd actually be grateful for Anna's help in selecting a new secretary. Maybe she could even help polish the negotiations for the Singapore deal.

But it wouldn't take long. A week, maybe just a few days of working together. He'd put on the charm. He'd spout nonsense about his *feelings*, if that was what it took. He'd wine her and dine her until she surrendered her body and soul.

And what a body. Her skin was pale as a Russian winter, but she looked sexy as hell, barely decent beneath a tiny string bikini that matched the alluring turquoise of the water. She'd certainly never worn anything like *that* when she was his mistress. She'd never flaunted her curves, never tried once to tease him. She hadn't had to; she'd driven him wild even as a buttoned-up secretary who wore her hair in a bun and covered up her body with elegant loose-fitting suits.

But who was this siren in her place? String bikini today. Tight jeans and clinging halter top yesterday. Had Anna really changed so much?

He saw her give a worried glance at the sun and, cuddling the baby to her chest, she climbed up the wide pool steps. She pulled sunscreen out of the old, frayed diaper bag sitting on the stone table near the fountain. Sitting back on a nearby lounge chair, she sat the chubby baby down on her flat belly and playfully tickled him while slathering him with sunscreen.

She reached for a wide-brimmed hat on the edge of the stone table. Her nearly nude body stretched beneath the bikini, revealing the side swell of her breasts.

Mrs. Burbridge nearly ran into him as she hurried around the courtyard doorway.

"Oh! Excuse me, sir."

He'd been so intent on watching Anna that he hadn't heard the plump woman come up behind him. He straightened. "My fault, Mrs. Burbridge."

"I was just going to ask Mrs. Stav—er, Miss Rostoff—" she flushed with embarrassment as she tripped over the name "—if she wanted me to take the baby inside. She didn't sleep well last night, so I thought perhaps she'd like a bit of a rest."

"She didn't sleep well?"

"She has the room next to mine. I heard her pacing. Jet lag, I suppose, poor dear."

So Anna had slept as badly as he had. Nikos would be willing to bet money it hadn't been jet lag that had troubled her all night.

His lips curved up in a smile. *Perfect.* It was all coming together. By the end of the week—by the end of the day, if he was lucky—Mrs. Burbridge would never have to trip over Anna's name again. She would be Mrs. Stavrakis.

ANNA WAS BARELY back in the pool with Misha when she saw Mrs. Burbridge standing by the water's edge. But it wasn't the appearance of the Scotswoman that set her hackles on edge. It was the man behind her, who was staring at her like an ant under a microscope, as if he'd never seen a woman in a swimsuit before.

"Would you like me to take the bairn, Miss Rostoff?" Mrs. Burbridge asked. "I thought you might like a wee rest."

Since it was only ten o'clock in the morning, she was sure the "wee rest" was Nikos's idea. He wanted to get her alone, so he could finish his seduction and convince her to be his bride.

*Not in this lifetime.*

Anna turned to wade in the other direction, holding the baby close as if she feared the older woman might fling herself in the pool, orthopedic shoes and all, and wrestle Misha away. "No, thank you, Mrs. Burbridge. We're happy as we are."

She waited for Nikos to demand that she give up the baby, but to her surprise he didn't. "Obviously she's not tired," she heard him tell the nanny. "I think we'll just spend some time together as a family."

Anna heard Mrs. Burbridge leave and looked back, hoping that Nikos had left too. No such luck. He was standing by the pool, watching her with an inscrutable expression. His presence was like a dark cloud over the sun. It made her tense, remembering how easily she'd almost given herself to him last night, how much she still wanted to feel him inside her. The argument between longing and fury had kept her up all night. Twice she'd nearly weakened and gone to his room. It was only by the sheerest self-preservation that she hadn't woken up this morning in his bed, with a big engagement ring on her finger.

At least then she'd also have woken up with a big smile on her face. She shook the thought away.

"Well?" she said, giving him her haughtiest stare—

the one her mother had used to give to other people's servants when they sneered at their family as "charity cases" and purposefully ruined their meals or their laundry behind their employers' backs. Until Anna was eighteen, when her father had returned the family to New York and gone into business with Victor, their life had been full of insult and insecurity.

And after that Victor had had power over them. That was why she would never allow herself to be dependent upon someone else for her livelihood again. Better to starve in a garret and have her pride.

At least that was what she'd thought before she became a mother. Now she wasn't so sure. What was her own pride compared to the safety and well-being of her child?

"What do you want?" she demanded irritably.

Instead of answering, Nikos sat down on the tiled edge of the pool. He folded his legs Indian-style, looking strangely at ease, almost boyish. Her eyebrows rose at the sight of Nikos, in his elegant Italian wool trousers and crisp white shirt, sitting on the dusty tile floor of the courtyard. "I want you to teach me how to be a parent."

Her jaw dropped ever so slightly. "What do you mean?"

He glanced at Misha. "You know I never had a father. Not a real one, at any rate. I have no idea how to be one. I'm afraid to hold my own son."

Anna waited for him to point out that it was all her fault for stealing Misha for the first four months of his life, but again Nikos surprised her. He said instead, in a tone that was almost humble, "I need you to teach me how to be a father."

*It's a trick,* she warned herself, but for the life of her she couldn't see how. She licked her lips nervously. She glanced at the precious babe in her arms. He needed a good father, and, although she was far from a parenting expert, she was at least an expert on her own baby. How could she refuse?

"I suppose I could try," she said reluctantly.

"So you agree?"

"When do you want to start?"

"Now."

"Get a swimsuit, then."

"That would take too long." In a fluid motion, he pulled his shirt over his head and tossed it aside. Kicking off his shoes, he looked at her, and she suddenly realized what he was going to do.

"You can't be serious!"

"Anna, you know I'm *always* serious," he said, and jumped into the pool, trousers and all.

She turned away, protecting the baby from the enormous splash as he landed in the deep end of the pool. When he rose from the water his hair was plastered to his head. He spouted water like a fish, and his expensive Italian trousers were almost certainly ruined, but he was *laughing.*

Oh, my God. The sound of his laugh. She hadn't heard that for a long, long time. Nikos's laugh, so hearty and bold and rare, like a fine Greek wine, had first made her love him.

He swam over toward the shallow end, until his feet touched the bottom, and then he walked toward her, parting the water like a Greek god. He was six feet two inches, and the water only lapped his waistband when he reached her. His muscular torso glistened in the hot sun, and rivulets of water ran down his body. She nervously licked her lips as he put one hand on her bare shoulder and with the other gently caressed their baby's head.

"Will you show me how to hold him?"

She carefully set Misha in his arms, showing him how to hold the baby close to his chest.

"Hi," he said, looking down at the baby in his arms. "I know you've never had a father. This is my first time being one. We'll learn how to do this together."

Carefully, he moved deeper into the pool, until the baby laughed at the pleasurable feeling of the water against his skin. Nikos joined in his laughter as Misha joyfully splashed the water with his pudgy hands.

He kissed the baby's downy head and whispered, so low that Anna almost didn't hear, "I will always be here to help you swim, Michael."

Anna watched with her heart in her throat. She'd thought she was in danger before. But now, watching him with their son, holding him tenderly, she saw in Nikos everything she'd ever wanted. A strong man who wasn't afraid to be playful.

This was the father she wanted for her child.

The husband she'd always dreamed of for herself.

She tried to push those troublesome thoughts away. It wasn't the real Nikos, she told herself. He was trying to trick her, to lure her in for the sake of his revenge. He wouldn't stop until he'd crushed her, heart and soul.

For the rest of the morning she waited for Nikos to

revert to his usual arrogant, cold personality, but he never did.

They were like a happy family. It left her amazed. And shaken.

When she left the pool to go feed and change Misha for his nap, he climbed out behind her. The ruined Italian trousers dripped and sloshed water behind him. She glanced at them with a rueful smile. "Sorry about your pants."

"I'm not." He gave her a grin. He looked relaxed and something else…contented? Had she ever seen him look that way before? "Besides, I can get more. I haven't had that much fun in ages. I felt like a kid again."

She snorted. "If it was that great, maybe next time in the pool I'll wear a snowsuit."

"Please don't," he said lazily. "I like the bikini."

The look he cast over her made her suddenly feel warm all over, in a way that had nothing to do with the hot desert sun.

"You didn't like my outfit last night."

"That was different," he said. "That was for another man."

She waited for him to lash into her accusingly, demanding that she never see Sinistyn again, but he just turned away to head back into the house. "I'm going to slip into something a little less wet," he said with a wink. "After Michael's asleep come see me in the office, will you? I have a proposal."

A proposal? Thank heavens, she thought as she hurried back to the nursery with her cranky, yawning baby. Nikos's behavior had been starting to confuse her. But she knew that as soon as she met him in the office he would start tossing out demands. He'd try to kiss her senseless until she agreed to his marriage proposal.

That she could deal with. It was his new playfulness, his kindness and love for his son, that she didn't know how to handle.

She showed up at the office with a T-shirt and shorts over her bikini, ready for battle. She was so ready, in fact, that she could hardly wait for him to take her in his arms. All the kisses in the world wouldn't convince her to marry him, but since she'd managed to get through last night unscathed, she was willing—no, eager—to let him try…

But he didn't touch her. The enormous mahogany desk that filled his home office had a light lunch spread at one end, while he sat working at the other, surrounded by piles of disorganized papers that were also stacked on the floor. He somehow managed to ignore the mess, focusing on his laptop.

He was dressed now, in a T-shirt and casual button-down shirt. He greeted her with a smile and nodded toward the food. "I had the housekeeper bring lunch. I figured you'd be hungry."

"You figured right," she said, and went straight for the gourmet sandwiches and the fruit and cheese tray. Nursing left her hungrier than she'd ever been before, and thirstier too. She gulped down some sparkling water. She waited, but he still seemed intent on his laptop. She cleared her throat.

He looked up, as if he'd forgotten she was there.

"Um…why did you want me to join you here?" she asked, confused at his behavior. "You said you wanted to ask me something?"

"Oh. Right. I need your help. I'm closing my bid on the land lease for a new casino in Singapore, and since I fired Lindsey I have no executive assistant."

A thrill went through Anna. He wanted her back! She'd always taken such pride in her work, and she and Nikos had connected creating L'Hermitage. She tried to temper her growing hope. "But what about Margaret? Or Clementine in your New York office? They could quickly come up to speed."

"I need them where they are. The New York office are up to their necks getting zoning approval for the Battery co-op. And Margaret has her hands full with L'Hermitage. I need to hire someone new as my personal assistant, and I'll be leaving for Singapore in ten days. I need your help."

Her heart started to beat, thump, thump. Returning to work for Stavrakis Resorts would be a dream come true. She wondered if the baby would like traveling around the world.

"All right," she said, trying to hide her elation. "Since you need me."

"I was hoping you'd say that." He pushed a piece of paper down the desk.

To her confusion, Anna saw that it was a résumé. "What's this?"

"The first candidate." He looked at her with his velvety brown eyes, and a warm smile traced his lips. "To replace you."

## CHAPTER SIX

ANNA FELT AS IF she'd just been sucker-punched.

"Replace me?" She thrust the résumé back at him, as if it burned her fingers. "Why would I help you replace me? This job was my life. Why would I help you give it away? I'm not going to lift a finger for you."

"Good point," he said briskly, then pushed another official document toward her. "Would this convince you?"

She picked up the attached papers, frowning. "Another résumé will hardly—"

But, as she read the first words on the page, her jaw fell open and she collapsed back against the hard wooden chair.

"It's a custody agreement," she gasped when she could speak.

"Yes," he said pleasantly.

She fumbled through the pages, but her hands were shaking and the paperclip fell to the floor. Bending to pick it up, she looked up at him. "You're going to give me joint custody?"

"Call it incentive."

"What do you want in return?" she said guardedly.

"I'll sign the custody agreement if you help me find a good executive assistant within ten days."

She stared at him. "That's all? I just have to help you

find a new secretary and you'll give me joint custody of Misha? You'll let me leave?"

He gave a graceful shrug. "I'm a desperate man. I need this settled by the time I leave for Singapore."

She could hardly believe her ears. It was way too good to be true. "I thought you said you were going to make me suffer for betraying you?"

"As I said yesterday, I've come to appreciate your love and care for my son."

*Yeah, right.* "There's something you're not telling me."

"So suspicious," he said, then closed his laptop with a sigh. "You will, of course, agree never to see Victor Sinistyn again."

She nearly laughed aloud. At last it made sense. Perhaps he did want her help finding a new secretary, but it was Victor that really worried him. Her plan had worked better than she'd ever dared dream.

She opened her mouth to tell him she'd be perfectly happy to cross Victor's name permanently off her Christmas card list, but closed it as another thought occurred to her.

What if Nikos changed his mind before she found him a new assistant and he signed the custody agreement? If she agreed to stop seeing Victor she'd lose her only hold on Nikos. She couldn't play out her hand so easily.

"I'm not sure I can do that." She tilted her head, as if considering his offer. "Victor is a hard man to forget."

She saw a glint of something hard and flinty in Nikos's eyes, then it was veiled beneath a studiously careless expression. "It's your choice, of course."

"Whether I'm friends with Victor?"

"Whether you want joint custody of our son."

Hardly able to believe her own daring, she said, "Of course I do. But I'll need more than your signature on a custody agreement to give up a man who might be the love of my life."

His eyes were decidedly hard now, glittering like coal turning to diamonds under pressure. "What do you want?"

"You want a new secretary to replace me. Understandable. I want a new boss to replace *you*. Give me a glowing reference so I can find a good job in New York."

"I never agreed you could take our son to New York."

"What do you care? You'll be in Singapore—"

"And you'll never need to work again," he interrupted, not listening. "I will supply you with all the money you could possibly need to raise our child in comfort. Do not insult me."

"It's hardly an insult to wish to work."

"Your job now is to take care of our son."

"That's your job too, since you're his parent as well, but I haven't noticed you putting Stavrakis Resorts up for sale."

"The company is my son's legacy," he said. "I have no choice but to work."

"Neither do I."

"I will always support Michael. And you as well, for the rest of your life. I protect what is mine. You need never fear for money again."

"And my family, too? Will you support my mother and sister for all their lives as well?"

"A reasonable amount…" he started, then his gaze sharpened. "Why do you ask? Is your family in some kind of trouble?"

She really didn't want to discuss this. Backtracking furiously, she said, "I appreciate your offer of support, Nikos, I really do, but I don't want to be beholden to you for the rest of my life."

He drummed his fingers impatiently on the table. "So let me get this straight. You want our son to be raised by a nanny just so you can work as a secretary?"

"Are you implying my job is less important than yours?" she countered.

"No, I'm flat-out saying it. Stavrakis Resorts has thousands of employees around the world, all depending on the company for their salary. It's not even close to the same. In your case, I think the world can survive with one less typist."

"You know perfectly well there's more to what I do!" she said, outraged.

"Nothing in your job description could possibly be as important as—" He visibly restrained himself. He sat back in his leather chair and gave her a smile that didn't reach his eyes. "Anna, there's no reason we have to discuss this now. Until you help me find your replacement, it's all a moot point."

"I want to discuss it now," she said mutinously.

He sat in stillness, then gave a sigh. "Fine. Find me a new secretary—a good one—and I'll give you your job reference, if that's really what you want. God knows you deserve it."

"Even though I was *just a typist*?"

"You know I didn't mean that." He scowled. "Let me explain."

That surprised her. Nikos never explained, he just gave orders. "I'm listening."

Raking back his hair, he looked through the window. Outside, a gardener was riding a lawnmower across the expansive heavily watered lawn, a slash of green against barren brown mountains and harsh blue sky. "I barely saw my mother growing up. She was always working three jobs to keep a roof over our heads. By the time I was old enough to help support us she'd died. I never knew her except as a pale ghost with a broken heart."

He looked at Anna. "I never want my son, or you, to endure that kind of wretched life. I know I've given you no reason to accept anything from me, but please let me do this one thing. Let me give Michael the happy childhood I never had."

Anna swallowed. It was hard to ignore a plea like that. And harder still to ignore the pleas of her own heart. She didn't want to leave her baby all day long so she could go to work, but what choice did she have? It was either work or beg money from Nikos for the rest of her life.

*But maybe it wouldn't be like that.*

Stupid to even consider it. She'd trusted Nikos once before and she'd just been abandoned, fired, cheated on…

*He never cheated on me*, a voice whispered. *And, no matter how misguided and neanderthal his attempts were, he was only trying to keep us both comfortable and safe.*

She stomped on the thought. She wouldn't let herself weaken now and start going soft again. She wouldn't let Nikos get under her skin, no matter how vulnerable he looked asking for her help, or how warm his eyes had glowed when he'd laughed with their son. She wouldn't let herself fall back in love, no matter how wonderful he seemed to be at this moment.

She snatched the résumé back out of his hands, eager for distraction from her thoughts. "This is the job candidate you plan to interview first?"

"Yes, I thought—"

Skimming the page, she nearly jumped out of her chair. "Have you totally lost your mind? She has no secretarial experience. Her references are a strip club and—" she squinted her eyes "—a place called the Hot Mustang Ranch."

"I was trying to keep an open mind," he said defensively. "Your reference was Victor Sinistyn, but you were still the best damn secretary I've ever had."

"But there are three typos on her *résumé*. Even Lindsey wasn't this bad." She crumpled up the paper in her hands. "There's no point even doing an interview—not unless you need an erotic dancer with bordello experience."

"Fine," he said gruffly. "I'll have her sent away. Maybe your friend Victor will hire her at one of his clubs."

He held out his hand for the paper. As their fingers touched their eyes met, and an electric shock went through her. He looked at her so hungrily. She waited for him to take her in his arms, to kiss her senseless. To reach across the mahogany desk and take what she'd been aching for him to take.

She heard him take a long, slow breath. His fingers

slowly moved up her bare arm as they both leaned forward over the table.

There was a hard knock at the door, the sound of it swinging open. "Excuse me, sir, miss?"

Anna whirled around in her chair, blushing when she saw a maid standing in the doorway.

"I have standing orders not to be interrupted in my office," Nikos said in a controlled voice.

"Yes, sir. But, begging your pardon, it's Miss Rostoff who's wanted. Your sister's here, miss. She's quite agitated and said if we didn't get you she'd be calling the police and telling them you were being kept here against your will."

"Let me go!" Anna heard her sister's voice, shrill and frantic down the hall. "Get out of my way. Anna? Anna!"

Natalie pushed past the maid, nearly knocking the girl aside. Her linen shift dress was rumpled and dirty, as if it had been slept in.

She stopped abruptly when she saw Anna in her T-shirt and shorts, sitting casually on the desk near Nikos. Natalie's jaw dropped, then her eyes blazed through her thick glasses.

"You've got some nerve," she said to Anna. "Do you have any idea what's going on? I've been calling and calling, but you never called back. I thought you were in trouble. I thought he was keeping you prisoner again. And instead I find you lazing in luxury with the man you called your deadliest enemy!"

"Excuse us," Anna said hastily, and grabbed her sister's wrist, pulling her out of the office before she could repeat any of the insulting things Anna had once said about Nikos. She couldn't risk alienating him now—not when they'd finally made a fragile peace and he was actually considering joint custody.

She dragged Natalie into her bedroom and closed the door behind her.

"You've gone back to him, haven't you?" her sister said bitterly, rubbing her wrist. "Even after all the stuff he did. Ruining Father's company! Abandoning you! Cheating on you! Firing you because you were pregnant—with his baby! That's blatant sex discrimination. You should sue."

"Natalie, I'm not going to sue the father of my child."

"Why, when he's such a monster?"

Anna took a deep breath. "I blew things out of proportion. And I just found out that what I told you about Father's company…wasn't true."

"What?"

Anna looked at her young, idealistic sister and just couldn't bear to disillusion her by telling her about their father's embezzlement. "There were complications and problems that I didn't know about. Nikos didn't ruin the company. He was trying to save it when Father made some…bad choices."

Natalie looked at her keenly. "So if Nikos suddenly isn't so bad, why are you marrying Victor and moving to Russia?"

"What?"

"You don't know?" Staring at her in amazement, her younger sister, usually so trusting and sweet, gave a harsh laugh. "No, of course you don't. I've only left ten messages on your cellphone since yesterday. Victor

Sinistyn just bought great-grandmother's palace this morning from Mother. She sold it to him for a fraction of its value—two million off our debt, plus another twenty thousand to her in cash. Which she's already spent on clothes, of course. Victor is going to raze the old palace and build something new in its place. For you."

"For me? What are you talking about?"

"Vitya always seemed so strong, so handsome. Even after he quit his partnership with Father so suddenly I thought he was kind. I flew here last night to ask him to leave the palace alone. I thought he'd listen to me." She shook her head angrily. "But he just laughed. He said that the air in Las Vegas was getting unhealthy, and that he needed to raze the palace immediately because the two of you would be moving to St. Petersburg as soon as you were married."

"That's not true!" Anna gasped. "We're not getting married. He hasn't even proposed." *At least not lately,* she added silently.

"Well, he obviously thinks proposing is just a formality. Any reason why he'd think that?"

Anna paced across the thick blue carpet. "I've only seen him once since I got here! And even then it was only because…" Glancing right and left, as if she feared Nikos might be listening from the large walk-in closet or beneath the elegant canopied bed, Anna whispered, "Being Victor's friend is my only bargaining chip against Nikos to get joint custody. So I can leave here. So I can be free."

Natalie eyes widened, looking owlish beneath her glasses. "And you asked Vitya for help? When I went to his club I saw the kind of man he really is. He isn't our friend. If he were, he wouldn't have been loaning our parents money at that huge interest rate. I thought he was trying to help us. But now I think he only went into business with Father in the first place to be close to you. After you left to work for Nikos he dissolved the partnership and started loaning Father money instead." She took a deep breath. "I think since you wouldn't agree to marry him he's been drowning our family in debt to force your hand."

"It can't be true," Anna gasped. All right, so Victor had made advances the whole time she'd been his secretary. He'd chased off other suitors. He'd pressured her to marry him. He'd even gotten her father to try to use his influence over her. But Victor would never have deliberately hurt her family just to possess her.

Would he?

"It's the only thing that makes sense," Natalie pressed. "Why else does he keep loaning Mother money? He knows we have no way to repay it."

Anna rubbed her head wearily. "I don't know. But I'll figure it out. I'll handle this, Natalie, don't worry. As soon as I get custody of Misha I'll return to New York and find a job—"

"You still think he'll let you repay the money?" Natalie interrupted, looking at Anna as if seeing her for the first time. "If you think he's gone to all this trouble to let you set up some kind of payment plan, you're as delusional as Mother. Who's happy to take his money, by the way, because she's sure you'll marry him. Which you probably will. You always have to sacrifice yourself, don't you? Even when it does more harm than good.

You'll reward him after he's destroyed our family to get his hands on you."

"You don't know that's really true!"

"I don't?" Natalie shook her head. "You need to grow up and see the real world."

Her baby sister was telling *her* to grow up? "I do see the real world—"

"My whole life I've thought you were some kind of saint, you know? Sacrificing your own future to take care of us. When I wanted to study accounting so I could get a good job to help support our family you insisted I major in art instead—"

"I knew art was your passion!" Anna said, stung.

"Maybe." Natalie snorted derisively. "But it's no way to make a living. The truth is, you didn't *want* my help. You always have to be the one to do everything. God forbid you ever depend on someone else."

"I was trying to do the right thing for you!"

"Then why didn't you stand up to Victor ages ago and tell him to back off? Instead of running away to work for someone else? Why did you get pregnant by Nikos, then run away? Why are you still so desperate to run away from Nikos now? You're keen to stand up for others, but when it comes to yourself you just run away."

Anna stared at her, breathing heavily. "Natalie, please…" she whispered.

Natalie's eyes were hard. "You want to be strong? Fine. You got yourself in your mess. With Victor. With Nikos. Get yourself out of it. Just don't kid yourself that your choices are for us. All you've done is make things worse for *us*. Thanks. Thanks a lot."

Turning on her heel, she went for the door.

"Natalie!" She grabbed her sister's wrist. "Don't leave like this. Please."

"Let me go," Natalie said coldly. Her sister wrenched her arm away, and this time Anna released her.

After she left, Anna slowly sat down on the bed in the cool darkness of her room, still shocked by Natalie's attack. Her sister had always been the one person Anna could count on. She hadn't asked any questions when Anna had appeared on her doorstep in Russia, but had simply taken her in her arms and let her cry on her shoulder. She'd fought Nikos's armed henchmen to try to keep Misha safe.

Heartsick, Anna left her room and realized she'd blindly gone to Nikos's office to seek comfort. But his door was closed. She stared at the door, longing for him to take her in his strong arms and tell her everything would be okay. She would almost believe it if he was the one who said it. No doubt another example of her being *delusional*.

Was Natalie right?

Instead of being the one who'd saved and supported her family, had Anna been the cause of its ruin?

It was true that she'd never really stood up to Victor. He'd made passes at her, and Anna hadn't known how to deal with his flirtations, so she'd simply put up with them. She'd never told him flat-out to leave her alone. When they'd gotten to be too much, she'd run away to work for Nikos.

And as for Nikos… She'd known his faults, but she'd still fallen in love with him. She should have been more careful. Especially about jumping into his bed. What had she been thinking to allow herself to conceive a child with a man who not only wasn't her husband but didn't even love her?

The closed office door stared down at her reproachfully.

Turning away with a heavy heart, she went to the nursery, where Misha was still napping in his crib. She gently picked him up and cuddled him in the rocking chair. Tears filled her eyes as she stared out the window at the pool, where for a brief time that morning she'd felt like she was part of a happy family.

How could she fix everything she'd done wrong?

How could she make things right?

The one thing she couldn't do was ask Nikos—or anyone—for help. Natalie was right. Anna had caused this mess. She was the one who should take care of it. Alone.

Closing her eyes, she held her baby as she rocked back and forth. It was time to face reality.

Misha shouldn't suffer just because Anna had such a hard time being around his father. No matter how much she wanted to return to New York, she couldn't. She had to live close enough to Nikos that they could raise their son together. Misha deserved that much.

But she wouldn't marry Nikos either. She'd been careless enough to get pregnant, but she wouldn't make it worse by marrying him. She'd be miserable as his wife, committing herself to a man who didn't even love her.

Anna would share parenting with Nikos, but that was it. She needed her own place. Her own life. Her own job.

She sat up straight in her chair as her eyes flew open. She'd get Nikos to rehire her.

It was the perfect solution. She'd be able to travel with him around the world, so Misha would always see them both. Plus, working as his executive assistant was not only the best job she'd ever had, he'd also paid her a high salary that would be virtually impossible to find anywhere else. Enough so that she could set up a payment plan with Victor, which she'd force him to take.

It might be difficult to see Nikos every day, no doubt watching him date other women, but she'd deal with it. She would take responsibility for the choices she'd made.

Misha gave a little sigh. Opening his dark eyes, so much like his father's, he smiled up at her. Anna smiled back.

All she had to do was convince Nikos to hire her as his secretary—while keeping herself from falling into his arms—and everything else would fall into place.

It wouldn't be easy, but, hey—Nikos *had* asked for her help weeding out unsuitable résumés. She grinned. She'd pretend to go through them while taking over the secretarial job herself. She'd lull Nikos into complacency while she proved she could both work *and* be a good mother to his child. She'd prove to them both that she wasn't a screwup. She'd prove she could do it all.

"WHAT'S WRONG with this one?" Nikos demanded, exasperated. "Carmen Ortega has thirty years of experience working with CEOs of billion-dollar companies!"

"Those companies had shareholders," Anna said sweetly, tossing the résumé in the trash. "She's accustomed to toeing the line for many bosses instead of sticking to one. Too many cooks, you know."

No, he didn't. He had no idea what she was talking about. Nine days of looking through résumés, and Anna had found fault with every single one. But, since he'd asked specifically for her assistance, he had no choice but to continue this farce until he could get Anna to fall in love with him.

It was proving to be harder than he'd thought.

His plan had been to lure her with romantic dinners, gifts, and family outings. Instead, work had somehow taken over. She'd turned the romantic dinners into working meals, taking notes in shorthand between dainty bites of Cavaleri's pasta *primavera* and *pad thai*. When he'd given her flowers and chocolates, she'd thanked him gravely for remembering Secretaries' Day. Secretaries' Day! As if there was any damn way he'd remember some made-up holiday like that!

The family outings with baby Michael, including splashing in the pool, taking walks along the edge of the desert, and strolling through L'Hermitage, had certainly been enjoyable. Nikos had relished holding his son as they walked across the casino floor, through the Moskva Shopping Complex and into the elegant, soaring lobby of the turn-of-the-century-styled hotel. "This will all be yours someday," he'd whispered into his son's ear, and he'd been filled with pride.

But, though Anna seemed glad that he was learning to be a father, she didn't seem at all inclined to fall at his feet for that alone.

At least the time had made a difference at his home office. The piled-up papers were gone, sorted and filed.

His appointments had already been reorganized to better suit his schedule, with no more double-bookings. In nine short days Anna had mended Lindsey's ineptitude with efficiency and poise.

He looked around his office. A man could get used to this, he thought with satisfaction. Then he stopped himself cold. No, he *couldn't* get used to this. He couldn't let himself. After the ten days was over Anna would return to full-time motherhood. Her place was at home, in luxury and comfort, raising their son.

It had been nice working from home for the last week, though, instead of going to his office at the casino as usual. He'd seen a lot of Michael, too, since Anna was still feeding him every three hours. She usually had him in the office with them for much of the afternoon. Right now the baby was in the nursery, taking his afternoon nap, but just a few moments ago he'd been lying on a mat on the floor, batting at the dangling toys of his playgym while he gurgled and laughed. Remembering, a smile formed on Nikos's lips.

He shook himself. What kind of work environment was this? In spite of Anna's organization, his work habits were slipping. His usual sixteen or eighteen-hour days just weren't possible when he was constantly being distracted by the laughter of his son and the gorgeous vision of Anna in a slim-fitting white shirt and black pencil skirt, crossing her killer legs while she took dictation.

No, he had to stick to his plan. Anna would be free of the burden of work, and he'd find some other secretary. He'd make do for the sake of his son having a happy childhood, and return to his eighteen-hour work days.

He'd shown his son the empire that would soon be his; he couldn't slack off on the job now.

But he was leaving tomorrow. He only had tonight to make Anna fall for him before he left for Singapore, and, while he still believed he'd achieve his goal, it might be time to get creative. He'd soon have no choice but to…ugh…talk more about *feelings*. He had no idea how to do that, but he'd improvise. How hard could it be? He'd talk about his childhood. Didn't women swoon over stories of poverty and misery?

"What are you doing?" he asked, suddenly distracted by the vision of Anna's sweet backside in the form-fitting black skirt as she knelt near the trash can and leaned forward on her hands. Wild images went through him.

"This must have bounced off the rim." She picked up the crumpled résumé from the floor, then spotted something behind the can. Nikos groaned inwardly as she saw the pale blue envelope that he'd tossed there early this morning.

Leaning back on her haunches, she picked it up and read the envelope. "It's postmarked from Greece."

Nikos grabbed a new résumé. "Have you looked at this one?"

She refused to be distracted, and held the blue envelope a little higher. "When did you get this letter?"

"Yesterday," he said, grinding his teeth.

She pushed back a long tendril that had escaped from her sleek chignon. "It hasn't been opened, but it was in the trash."

"And your point is?"

"Aren't you going to read it?"

"I think my actions are self-explanatory."

"But if your father's widow wrote all the way from Greece to try to mend the breach in your family…"

"There is no breach, because there is no family," he said shortly. "My father meant nothing to me, and now he's dead, so why should I care about his widow? She can write me or not. That is her choice. I'm perfectly capable of throwing her letters in the trash without your advice."

He still remembered all too well the first letter he'd received from the Greek woman. She'd broken the news of his father's death, and informed him that he'd left Nikos a share in his shipping business—the same shipping business that Nikos had tried to crush as an adult. Worse, she'd told him that his father had been the secret investor who had helped Nikos create Stavrakis Resorts. His father had been the one to help Nikos build his very first hotel.

Shaken, Nikos had still refused to go to the funeral, or meet his half-siblings. He'd also refused the shares in the company. He hadn't wanted any part of the family who'd been more important to his father than he and his mother had been.

But it was the kindness in her letter that had shocked him the most. She'd been so gentle, when he'd expected only hate. The confusion and pain had driven him to Anna's house. He'd instinctively sought her comfort, her arms, her bed, and they'd conceived Michael…

Anna gave him a piercing turquoise glance, as if she guessed his thoughts. "But how can you still hate your father now that you know that he helped you?"

"If I'd known he was the investor behind the venture capital firm that financed my first hotel, I would have tossed the money back in his face."

"But—"

"He was a married man when he seduced my mother. He got her pregnant, then sent her packing to New York. The man is nothing to me."

"But your stepmother—"

"Don't ever call her that again."

"Your—your father's widow said he tried to send you money every month of your childhood. Your mother was the one who always sent it back."

Yes, he remembered what the Greek woman had said—that his father had always loved Nikos, that he'd tried to visit and send child support but his proud mother had refused. She'd even said that his father hadn't wanted his mother to go to New York, that he'd been heartbroken when she'd left. She'd said his mother was the one who had refused to let him see his son.

Nikos didn't know who to believe.

His mother, of course, he told himself furiously. She had died taking care of him. She deserved his loyalty.

The last thing Nikos wanted to do was read another of the Greek woman's letters. The past was dead and gone. Better to let it remain buried.

Unfortunately, Anna didn't see it that way. Her lips pressed in a determined line. "I'm going to read the letter."

He grabbed her hand as she reached for the letter opener on his desk. "You're quick to arrange my family affairs. Is it to avoid dealing with your own?"

She hesitated. "What do you mean?"

"Why did your sister come here? You've evaded the question for over a week. I'd like an answer."

She tugged on her hand, but he held her fast. "It's nothing," she mumbled. "A family quarrel."

"Does it have anything to do with Victor Sinistyn?"

She pulled away with a savage force that he hadn't expected. "Just stay out of it! I don't need your pity and I don't need your help. I can handle it on my own—"

She grabbed at the letter opener with a trembling hand, plunging the sharp edge of the blade into the side of the blue envelope with far too much vigor. It sliced her palm, and she squelched a scream, holding out her bleeding hand.

"Let me see your hand," Nikos demanded.

She turned her face away in a fruitless attempt to hide her tears. He was relieved that she didn't resist as he gently took her hand. Blood from the cut smudged against the cuff of his shirt as he narrowly examined the wound.

"I don't think you'll need stitches." He'd been hurt enough times while sparring in his boxing club to be a pretty good judge. "Let's just clean it in case of infection."

He led her into the adjoining bathroom, and she followed him, seemingly in a daze. She winced as he placed her hand under the running water. He dried it off softly with a thick white cotton handtowel.

"This might sting a little," he said, before he applied the antiseptic he kept in the cabinet for any injuries he got working out at the club.

She closed her eyes. His hand tightened over her fingers and he felt a strangely agonizing beat of his heart that he was hurting her, even though it was for her own good.

He placed the small bandage over the cut. "All done."

She opened her eyes. "Thank you." She started to pull away, but he stopped her.

"Anna, tell me what hold Sinistyn has got over you."

"He doesn't."

"You're a terrible liar."

"I don't need your charity, and I don't want your help," she said. "It's my family's private business." But even as she spoke the words he could see the tremor of her swanlike throat, the nervous flutter of her dark lashes.

"Not if it affects my son."

Her eyes went wide. "You think I would endanger Misha?"

He glowered at her silently until he saw her blush. Good. Let her remember her worldwide travels to unheated ramshackle apartments on her own.

"Go to hell," she said, and left him. But she'd barely gone three steps back into his office before he caught her unhurt hand.

"Tell me, or I'll beat it out of Sinistyn. Or maybe I'll just ask Cooper to track down Natalie. I doubt she's gone far."

"Please don't." She lowered her gaze to her clasped hands, then sank slowly into the hard wooden chair by his desk. "All right. I'll tell you. We're in debt."

"How much?"

She took a deep breath, still unable to meet his eyes. "It was six million, but now it's four." She suddenly gave a hysterical laugh and leaned forward, rubbing her temples. "It's at a thirty-five percent interest rate and compounding daily. That's why we were at my great-grandmother's palace, trying to get it into decent shape to find a buyer. But the palace needs a fortune in renovations to make it livable."

"You should have asked me for the money."

"You think I'd sell myself for a palace?"

"Anna!"

"Thank you for your kind offer, but we found a buyer already."

"For the palace, or for you?" he asked, trying to spur her into energy. Anything to make her eyes look less dead and defeated than they did at this moment. But she didn't even rise to his bait.

"Both, I think," she said dully. "Victor bought the palace from my mother for two million dollars. That's why we only owe him four million instead of six. He's planning to raze the palace and build a new house as a wedding present to me."

"What?" he exploded.

"Victor has wanted me for a long time." Rubbing the back of her neck wearily, she rose from the chair and started to pace. "He's been lending my parents money over the years because he knew that eventually we'd default. I think it was his way to…to back me into a corner."

Rage went through Nikos. Looking at the circles under her eyes, he wanted to rip the other man apart. "I'll kill him."

She shook her head. "No. I can handle him. I'll talk to Victor, make him understand that I don't love him and I'll never be his wife. If you want to help me, there's just one thing you can do. One thing that would really, really help me."

"What's that?" Nikos asked, relieved at her admission that she had no intention of marrying Victor Sinistyn.

She looked at him with a painful expression of hope in her lovely almond-shaped eyes. "Hire me back as your secretary so I can pay back our family's debt."

"I told you. You don't have to worry about the debt. I'll handle it," Nikos said. *And I'll start by destroying Sinistyn,* he vowed privately.

"Please, just hire me back," she begged—Anna the proud, who never begged for anything.

He took her hand. He wanted to cover her with kisses, let her know that she was safe, let her know that he'd never let anyone hurt her again. "I'll keep you safe, and your family, too. I swear to you on my life."

"I just need a job." She licked her lips nervously—full pink lips that were made to be kissed. For a moment he couldn't stop looking at her mouth. Why hadn't he bedded her yet? Why hadn't he kissed her every hour, every moment? He tried to remember as she continued desperately, "I'll work from home so I can still take good care of the baby. And you'll be glad to have me back in your office, I promise. I'll make you so glad—"

"No," he said harshly, furious at how tempted he was to give in to her. Hell, he'd love to have her as his secretary again. His life was so much easier with Anna by his side. And it was hard for him to deny her anything when he wanted to kiss her so badly. But he couldn't be selfish. Not now. "I don't want you as my secretary. I want you as my wife."

"Nikos, please," she whispered, with those full pink lips. She crossed her arms over her chest, pushing her breasts upward beneath her slim white shirt. "I need this so badly—"

So did he.

Taking her in his arms, he kissed her.

# CHAPTER SEVEN

ANNA COULD NOT even try to stop him. His kiss was hot, demanding. She felt his fingers run down her neck and along her back, and her whole body seemed to relax like a sigh. For a brief moment she thought she could put all her cares and worries aside. She was safe in his arms. Maybe Nikos could protect her, care for her. Love her…

His tongue brushed against hers as he deepened the kiss, caressing her in an erotic dance that left her breathless. She leaned against him with a sigh.

"Anna," he whispered, so softly that the words were a mere breath against her skin. "You belong with me. Always."

He pressed her against the desk, kissing the vulnerable spot between her neck and shoulder until prickles of longing spread across her body. He ran his hands through her hair, causing bobby pins to scatter to the floor and her hair to tumble out of its chignon around her shoulders. She braced herself with an unsteady hand against his muscled shoulder. His fingers played with the waistband of her black pencil skirt, then moved beneath her fitted white shirt. A gasp escaped her as she felt his wide fingers splay lightly against the skin of her belly.

Without warning he lifted her up on the desk, crushing papers beneath her weight, cradling her to his body. He spread her legs to wrap them around him. Through his finely cut trousers, she could feel how badly he wanted her.

She wanted him too. But she was afraid. Afraid to trust too much, to give too much. What if she let herself depend on him and he crushed her?

She couldn't let herself give in to her desire. If she agreed to be his wife it would mean disaster. She couldn't give herself away to a man who didn't love her!

He drew away. "You're trembling."

Grasping at straws, she indicated the résumés, their laptops, the appointment calendars spread across his large mahogany desk. "We can't do this," she panted. "There's too much at stake—"

With an angry growl, he swept everything on the desk to the floor. Not even seeming to notice the crash of the laptops as they hit the carpet, he pushed her backward against the glossy wood of the desk. "Here. Now."

"Nikos—"

He leaned forward, pressing his body against hers. His face inches from hers, his dark eyes pierced hers as he looked into her own searchingly. "Tell me that you don't want this. Tell me you don't want *me*."

Licking her lips, she tried to speak the words. But the lies could not form themselves on her mouth when all she wanted to do was kiss him all over and feel his naked skin against her body.

She closed her eyes as she felt him slowly unbuttoning her shirt. He kissed her bare skin with each newly revealed inch until he finally pulled the shirt off her body. Without even knowing what she was doing, she whispered, "Please."

He stopped. "Please what?"

*Please hurry.*

*Please make love to me now.*

*Please love me...*

"Wait," she gasped. To her surprise, he released her, and, bereft of his touch, she opened her eyes.

He pushed himself up on one arm, looking down at her, and the expression on his face was one she'd never seen before. No, that wasn't true. She'd seen it once. The night they'd conceived Misha. Nikos Stavrakis, the ruthless billionaire, was watching her with a vulnerable light in his dark eyes. As if she alone had the power to hurt him. Or save him.

"What is it, *zoe mou*?" he asked softly.

"I'm afraid," she blurted out, then stopped, aghast.

"Of what?"

"I'm afraid you'll hurt me," she whispered.

A smile suddenly curved his lips, softening the hard angles of his handsome face as he gently brushed her cheek with his hand. "I would never hurt you, *agape mou*. Never."

And at that moment she believed him.

"I will be gentle. I swear to you on my life." With two easy movements he pulled off her skirt, murmuring with awe, "You are so beautiful."

She reached up for him, unbuttoning his crisp linen shirt. Unlike his easy removal of her clothes, her fingers felt clumsy. They trembled in excitement, until finally she gave up on the last button and ripped off the shirt in her impatience.

"That was my favorite shirt," he said, amused.

"Stupid of you to wear it today," she murmured.

Growling under his breath, he braced himself with his knees on the desk over her and slowly stroked down her full breasts, beneath the lacy fabric of her bra, until the only sound she could make was a moan.

He unhooked the front clasp of her bra and pulled the fabric off her body, tossing it to the floor. "Beautiful," he breathed again, cupping them in his hands, and she arched her back against the desk, straining to bring him closer to her. He lowered his head to taste her breasts. Then abruptly stopped.

Wondering why, she looked down and saw that a small trickle of milk had escaped her left breast. She felt a squirm of embarrassment, then defiance. She was a nursing mother. She wouldn't, couldn't, be ashamed of it. But still…

He raised a dark eyebrow at her, then lowered his head and slowly licked the other breast with his rough tongue. She sighed with pleasure. She gasped as he lowered his head between her legs.

He worked his tongue with agonizing slowness, spreading her wide to taste the very heart of her. The full thickness of his tongue seemed to touch every nerve ending of her body, leaving her quivering and taut with longing.

Gripping his hair with her hands, she stared up at the ceiling, knowing she should make him stop, that she should pull away, but she couldn't. She was naked in his office, her thighs spread wide on his mahogany desk, and her boss—the playboy desired by women far more beautiful than she—was lapping her with his tongue until she thought she would explode.

And then she did. She heard a loud cry and realized it had come from her own mouth. For a few seconds afterward all she could do was breathe, and Nikos took her in his arms, holding her close as he whispered endearments. Anna realized that he wasn't even all the way naked. But he was all the way hard. She could feel that through his tailored pants, pressing against her. And yet he wasn't trying to make love to her.

Why not?

She started to stroke him through the fabric, but he caught her hands. His eyes, looking down at her, were vulnerable. "Marry me, Anna. Be my wife."

*Yes.*

*Yes.*

*God, yes.*

"I can't." It felt horrible to say. Ungenerous and so, so wrong. And it wasn't what she wanted. Especially when it made him abruptly pull away. "We can raise our son together, but I can't marry you, Nikos. It would never work."

"So you say." He pulled away from her and without even looking in her direction started to put on his shirt.

She sat up, still naked, feeling dizzy. "Don't you understand? We'd never be happy together."

"No, I don't understand. I see only a spoiled woman who is determined to toss away happiness with both hands."

"You don't love me—" she started, praying he would argue.

Instead, he cut her off with, "And you don't love me." His face, so warm and loving just moments before, now expressed icy contempt. "But we both love our son. I am trying to do what's best for him. I wish you would do the same."

"I am!" she said, stung.

"Right." He rapidly buttoned up his shirt. "What have I done to make you hate me, Anna? What did I do that was so horrible? What have I ever done except try to take care of all of us? One of us has to take responsibility for the family we've created. Especially since you obviously don't give a damn."

"Wait—that's not true—you know it's not true!"

His lip curled as he turned to go. "I'm going to go find Sinistyn and handle him once and for all. Before he talks his way into becoming Michael's stepfather. Because apparently you have a problem telling him no. Unlike me."

"I'm not trying to hurt you. I just don't want you to get involved."

"Too late."

"It's not your problem, it's mine. I should be the one to—"

"My God, you really don't trust me at all, do you? No matter what I do or say, you won't accept my help. You'd rather fight me. You'd rather put both yourself and our son in danger." He stopped in the doorway. "I always admired you, Anna. A pity the good sense you have as a secretary is lacking in you as a woman."

His words struck her to the bone. His face was in shadow as he added quietly, "Look through the résumés, Anna. Find me a new secretary. When I come back, give me a name. I'm done fighting with you."

NIKOS WAS GRIM as he rode in the back of his limo, poring through documents about the last-minute details of the Singapore land lease bid as his chauffeur drove him back to the casino.

He'd lost his temper.

He never lost his temper.

Damn it, Anna was really starting to get to him. He'd accused her of letting her emotions run her reason, but he had just done the same.

The way he'd shouted at her. It made him wince now. It had not gone according to plan. Yelling at her was no way to make her fall in love. Even he knew that.

He sighed, leaning his head against the darkened glass and staring out at the empty, barren landscape as the Nevada desert flew by. He'd felt so close. His soul had soared when he'd felt her tremble beneath his tongue. He'd felt sure that she would say yes to his proposal. Why else had he restrained himself, when he could think of nothing but having her in his bed? He'd said that he wanted to make love to her only as his wife, and that was still true.

He ground his teeth. Forget those stupid scruples. He only had twenty-four hours to close the deal. Next time he wouldn't hesitate. He wouldn't relent. He'd seduce her, and he'd get both his satisfaction and her agreement to his proposal. And before she had a chance to change her mind he'd take her straight to one of the all-night wedding chapels and get it all nailed down.

He glanced at the document still in his briefcase. His lawyers had already drawn up the standard prenuptial agreement: if the marriage should end, both parties would end up with what they'd started with. Leaving Anna virtually penniless.

He didn't intend for her to suffer. On the contrary,

he meant for her to live in luxury. He'd even keep her snooty mother in Hermès handbags. Anything to make Anna happy. The prenup was for one reason only—to make sure that Anna would never have any incentive to walk away from their marriage.

He twisted his neck, cracking the joints to relieve the stress, and revised his tattered gameplan. Tonight was his last night to close the deal. After he'd finished with Sinistyn he'd go straight home, make love to Anna until she couldn't see straight, and then she'd sign the prenup. Then they'd go to the courthouse for a license and, from there, a drive-thru chapel.

He flexed his hands, trying to make himself relax. Anna was getting under his skin—probably because they were spending so much time together, blending home and work. It had been wonderful, in a way, having her back in the office. Best damn secretary he'd ever had. Together they were the perfect team. Unbeatable.

*No.* He pushed the thought away. He'd already made up his mind, and tonight it would be done. He'd get a new secretary, take Anna as his wife, and keep his home and work life separate—the way they were supposed to be. He'd enjoy Anna at night, see his son every day, and go back to putting in eighteen-hour days at the office. That was the life that made sense to him. That was a life he could control.

But Anna *had* to marry him. Without that everything else fell apart.

Rubbing his hand against his forehead, he sighed. It was time for him to play his last card. He had no choice. He was leaving for Singapore tomorrow, to meet with government officials and make sure Stavrakis Resorts' land lease bid was successful. The new casino resort would be an important asset in his son's fortune.

But first he had to close the deal with Anna.

He would tell her he loved her.

He'd never said the words before—to anyone. And even tonight it would be a lie. He would lie to make her capitulate, to make her love him in return. He'd told himself that he'd never say those three words to anyone, but he'd give up that tiny slice of honor now. He'd do far more than that to protect his family.

He'd tell her he loved her, and make her believe it. He had to convince her he meant it. Convince her he'd make a good husband. Convince her he was worthy of her love, even if it all was a lie…

He had a sudden memory of Anna in his bed, naked, with tousled hair and a sweetly seductive smile, looking up at him with honest, trusting eyes.

He shook the disturbing image away. As his chauffeur pulled up to the private garage on the third level parking deck of L'Hermitage, he focused instead on his meeting with Victor Sinistyn, whom he'd called on the drive into town.

He couldn't blame the man for wanting Anna for himself. Nikos ground his teeth as he strode into his private elevator. Any man would want Anna. But Sinistyn had gone too far, trying to force her into a marriage against her will. Trying to *buy* her through trickery and putting pressure on her family.

Images of Anna went through his mind: laughing in the pool last week, splashing with their child, smiling up at Nikos in the bright sunlight. She was so beautiful, so vibrant, so warm and alive. How *dare* Sinistyn try to imprison her? How dare he try to seize by manipulation and force something he had no right to call his own?

"It's time you picked on someone your own size," Nikos muttered under his breath as he entered his private office.

"What was that, sir?" Margaret, the senior administrative assistant for the casino, was filling in on some rudimentary duties as his executive secretary. She temporarily sat in Anna's old desk outside his office.

"Please let me know when Victor Sinistyn arrives." Closing the door behind him, he went to the outside windows and stared down at Las Vegas Boulevard, watching the hectic traffic below. He went to the crystal decanter and started to pour himself a small bourbon, then stopped.

Was it possible that he was doing the same thing as Sinistyn? Trying to possess Anna when he had no right?

No, he told himself fiercely. It wasn't the same at all. Sinistyn was trying to force Anna to marry him to satisfy his own selfish lust. Nikos just wanted to protect his family. To protect his son.

*But still,* the voice of conscience, rusty from disuse, whispered in his mind, *you're going to make her fall in love with you on false pretenses, to bind her to you forever. Isn't that just as bad?*

He tried to shake the thought out of his mind, but it wouldn't go away. He paced back and forth through his office, trying to concentrate on Sinistyn, the Singapore deal—anything but his plans for Anna. In the end he gave up, and pummeled the boxing bag in the corner of his office with his bare hands to clear his mind. The pain helped him forget. Helped him focus.

There was blood on two knuckles when he went over to the wall of one-sided windows that overlooked the main casino floor. He glanced down, impatiently looking at his watch. Sinistyn was two minutes late.

Then his eyes sharpened.

Sinistyn wasn't late. He was already in the casino downstairs, beneath the high crystal chandeliers, in between the gilded nineteenth-century columns and wealthy, attractive gamblers at the roulette tables and slot machines.

He wasn't alone, either. He'd brought two hulking bodyguards from his club. But he wasn't talking to them.

He was talking to Anna.

*Anna*. Still wearing the slim white shirt and black skirt, but sexier than ever, with her long, long legs and glossy black pumps. Her dark hair, which he'd mussed so thoroughly nearly making love to her on his desk, cascaded down her shoulders. Her lips were full, pink and bruised, as if she'd just come from bed.

She was too enticing—innocence and sin wrapped up into one luscious package.

Nikos cursed under his breath. She'd defied his direct orders and come down here to intercept Sinistyn. He clenched his jaw. From this distance he couldn't read the expressions on their faces. What was she saying to him? What was he saying to her? His hands clenched into fists as he strode out of his office to the elevator.

When he reached the casino floor he signaled

Cooper, his head of security, to follow with two body-guards. Trailing bodyguards in his wake, he stalked through the noise of slot machines and gamblers toward Anna and Sinistyn, barely able to keep his fury in check.

Why couldn't she trust him to handle things? Not even once? Why did she always have to make everything *so damned hard*?

"Sinistyn," he said coldly, grabbing the man's shoulder. "Let's go upstairs to talk." He gave Anna a look. "Leave."

"I'm staying," she said, raising her chin.

He heard Sinistyn snicker under his breath. Nikos ground his teeth. "Let me handle this."

"This isn't your fight. It's mine." To Nikos's shock, she turned to Victor Sinistyn and put her hand on his hairy arm, looking deep and soulfully into his eyes. "Victor, I'm sorry this has gone so far. It's my fault."

"About time you came to your senses, *loobemaya*. I've waited long enough for you to be my wife." Looking up from her cleavage with a triumphant half-smile, he locked eyes with Nikos. "About time you chose the better man."

Nikos felt a strange lurch in his chest. A sick feeling spread through his body. She'd chosen Sinistyn over him? She trusted that man over him?

"No." Anna was shaking her head at Sinistyn. "That's what I'm trying to tell you. I'm sorry, but I don't love you, Victor. I never have. I should have made it clear from the first time you flirted with me, ten years ago. I will never be with you. No matter how much money you loan my parents. Never."

The smug expression disappeared from Sinistyn's face. He looked dangerous and hard. "You don't know what you're saying."

"You bought the palace for nothing. I'll pay you back the money we owe. But I don't want you."

His eyes became hooded, his face flushed with anger. "At the club last week you made me think differently."

She took a deep breath and looked him straight in the eye. "I was going to ask for your help to get custody of my son. It was wrong of me. But then you were wrong to loan my parents millions of dollars at a thirty-five percent interest rate while claiming to be our friend."

"Your father promised that you would be mine. When we were in business together he said he'd convince you—"

"He tried, but I refused. We've known each other for a long time, Victor. It is time for us to be honest. I will never be your wife, but I will pay back every dime we owe you. Can we at least part as friends?"

She held out her hand.

But Victor's expression was hard as he looked from her outstretched hand to her face. He grabbed her arm roughly, causing her to cry out.

"I waited for you," he said softly. "I've tried to be nice. But it seems there's only one language you'll understand. You're mine, Anna. Mine."

He drew back a fist. Sucking in her breath, she winced in anticipation.

Quick as a flash, Nikos stepped between them, grabbing the other man's hand. He knocked him off balance with a hard right hook and shoved him to the ground.

"Don't touch her," Nikos shouted. "Not now. Not ever."

His body was crying out for the man's blood. He wanted to bash Victor Sinistyn into a pulp for threatening her. He wanted to kill the man for trying to hurt her.

Then he heard Anna's soft moan.

Nikos realized that his own bodyguards were barely keeping Sinistyn's men in check, and that at any moment a full brawl would break out in his own casino. They were already being watched by gamblers, gawkers and slack-jawed tourists, a couple of whom were holding cameras in anticipation of the coming action.

Breathing hard, Nikos jerked away from Sinistyn. "Get him out of here," he ordered Cooper. Cooper nodded, and with a single gesture a phalanx of security guards appeared.

"Follow me, gentlemen," Cooper said, holding out his arm in an ironic gesture.

One of Sinistyn's bodyguards tried to help his boss to his feet, but the Russian jerked his arm away and rose slowly on his own.

"You'll regret this, Stavrakis," Sinistyn said, and then his eyes shifted to Anna. "You'll both regret this."

He stormed out, followed closely by his shamefaced bodyguards.

"I'll make sure he doesn't get back in," Cooper said quietly. "And post extra guards on the night watch." He said loudly to the crowd, "Show's over, folks. The waitresses will be out to make sure everyone's getting their drinks."

Nikos felt Anna in his arms as she threw herself against his chest. "Oh, Nikos, I'm so sorry. It's all my fault."

At her touch, he slowly came back to himself. He looked down at her, stroking her hair.

"Everything you said was right," she said tearfully. "Everything. I should have trusted you. I've been a fool. A selfish, cowardly fool." She pressed her face against his shirt with a sob, then looked up at him, tears streaming down her pale cheeks. "I ran away when you were only trying to protect us. Can you ever forgive me?"

NIKOS HAD BEEN RIGHT about Victor.

Anna's stomach hurt. She'd known Victor was bad, but she'd never thought he'd actually want to hurt her. Natalie had also tried to tell her, but she wouldn't listen.

Nikos had been right about everything. Maybe he'd been bossy and controlling, but at least his motives had been good. Strong and loyal and true, he'd put their new little family first in his life. Why hadn't she done the same? Why hadn't she been brave enough to stay and fight, rather than believe the worst of him?

"Forgive me," she said again.

His dark eyes were unreadable as he softly touched her lips with his finger. "There is nothing to forgive."

She was suddenly aware of the curious stares of onlookers and the noise of the slot machines. "Before you leave for Asia, I need to talk to you."

"Let's go upstairs." He hugged her close to his body, guiding her gently toward the private elevator. His body felt warm against hers. She wrapped her hand around his muscular waist, enveloped in the scent of him—clean, but with a hint of something dangerous, as searing as the desert sun.

She knew the risk of reaching for the sun. Its heat and fire could consume her.

But she was suddenly so tired of feeling frozen inside.

Nikos had made it clear that he was done fighting with her. She'd been praying that she would have changed his mind by now, that she'd have proved she could both be a good mother and a good employee. But it was too late. He didn't want her as his secretary. He wanted her to fulfill their deal.

She'd blown it.

Once they were upstairs he'd demand the name of his new secretary. She'd give it to him, and tomorrow he would fly off for Singapore. There would be nothing left for her to do but pack for a new life in New York.

A new life that, for all its freedoms, would be missing one thing she wanted desperately. The man she loved.

She loved him. There. She'd admitted it—if only to herself. But he didn't want to hire her, and without his love she didn't want to marry him. There was nothing left to say.

Except that if their relationship had to end she wanted one last night to remember. One night to laugh with him again. To be daring. To be bold. One night where she allowed herself to love him with her whole heart.

One night to prove how much she trusted him.

But, as much as she knew he wanted her, he'd already refused her too many times, holding out for marriage. She licked her lips, glancing at him from beneath her lashes. Before he left, could she make him change his mind—just for one night?

She'd never seduced a man in her life, but maybe it was time to try.

Marveling at her own boldness as she crossed the casino floor with his arm around her, she ran her fingers surreptitiously along his waistband, stroking his flat belly through his shirt. "You changed your shirt."

She heard his intake of breath, but his voice was even as he replied, "You ripped up the last one."

"Sorry." She rubbed her breast against his side as they walked. She heard a slight growl from his throat.

"What are you doing?"

"What do you mean?" she asked innocently.

He picked up his pace toward the elevator, and the moment the doors were closed behind them he was on her. Pressing her against the cool metal wall, he kissed her savagely, running his hands up and down her body.

"God, you drive me crazy," he whispered against her skin. "I want you, Anna. It's killing me."

"Good." She reached for his shirt and saw his expression as she untucked the fabric and ran her hands underneath, exploring his flat belly and the muscular chest covered with dark hair. "This time you're not going to refuse me," she said, using a tone she'd heard him use many times—the tone no one could refuse. She unbuttoned his shirt, her fingers somehow moving deftly, as if she'd been seducing men all her life. "You're not going to make me wait. You're not going to demand that I marry you."

"Anna." His breathing was coming harder. "We both know—"

"Later." She already knew what he was going to say, and she didn't want to hear a word of it. She didn't want to think about the résumés in her purse, or the fact that Nikos had finally decided to let her go. Tomorrow she'd face those cold, hard facts. But tonight she'd stop time. She'd have one perfect night with him that could be crystallized in her memory forever—something to remember during all the cold and lonely nights.

Tonight she would give herself to him completely.

*I love you, Nikos. I love you.*

"Did you say something?" he murmured.

Oh, my God, had she whispered those words aloud? She had to distract him.

"I said *no talking*." She reached for his waist. Unbuckling his belt, she pulled it out of the loops and tossed it to the floor of the elevator. She slowly stroked his bare belly beneath his shirt, swaying her body against his.

With a taunting smile, she undid the top button of his pants.

He gave an audible gasp and grabbed her wrists, yanking them tight above her head. "Is this what you want?" he choked out. "Hard and fast? Here in the elevator?"

She struggled against the shackles of his hands, wanting to touch him, to feel his naked skin against her own. Her whole body ached for him.

The elevator dinged as it reached their floor, and the doors slid open. She felt drunk, drugged with desire, as with a throaty growl Nikos picked her up, carrying her roughly into the penthouse.

Against a backdrop of two-story-high windows, the only color was a minimalist red sofa against white walls and white carpet. He took her swiftly into his enormous bedroom. He pressed a button on the wall and the room suddenly glowed with firelight. She'd wondered what this room would be like. It was spartan, empty, and ghostly white. The floor was white tile, covered by a white fur rug in front of a white adobe fireplace. Surrounded by oceans of unused space, the king-size bed sat, pristine and untouched, in the center of the room.

Nikos started to kiss her again, and she closed her eyes. She forgot where she was, forgot everything. He lowered her gently to the enormous mattress, caressing her long hair. He stroked her cheek, down her neck, then placed his hand softly between her breasts, over her heart.

"Last chance to leave," he growled.

Deliberately, she leaned back against his bed.

Unblinking as a wolf, he stared at her. Her eyes devoured his bare chest. Dark hair covered his torso, tightening to a vertical line that disappeared beneath the waistband of his exquisitely tailored pants.

His clothes were elegant and fine. The uniform of a wealthy, civilized man. But his body was something else, something more. As he discarded his clothes, tossing them on the white tile floor, he revealed the savage warrior beneath.

He stood in front of her, naked and unselfconscious. His muscles were hard, wide. She saw the old scars, almost faded, brought into stark relief by new white lines across his ribs and collarbone. She saw how much he wanted her. Most of all she saw his dark eyes, hungry with need. She sat up, reaching for him, holding out her arms.

He was on her in an instant, pressing her back roughly against the luxuriant softness of the bed.

*"Agape mou,"* he whispered. "I have waited so long. Wanted you for so long…"

Reaching his broad hands beneath her back, he unzipped her skirt. He pulled her shirt over her head and tossed them both to the floor. The stroke of the fabric, the sheen of his breath, sent prickles of longing up and down her skin. As he kissed slowly down her body, between her breasts and down her belly, it was all she could do not to blurt out the three forbidden words.

Kissing her, he pushed her back against the soft goosedown comforter, spreading his hands wide as he caressed her body, making her shiver as he ran his fingers over her white panties and bra.

He covered her with his naked body, pressing her into the soft folds of the thick comforter. She felt as if she was drowning. She clutched at him like a life preserver, gasping as he unhooked her bra and freed her breasts. He slowly moved his body up against hers, rubbing his chest against her, pressing his naked hardness between her legs as he sucked on her neck, her shoulder, her earlobes. Holding her tightly, he ran his tongue around the tender edge of her ear, slowly moving inward until he made her gasp as he penetrated the center with his tongue. She turned her face to him, grabbing the back of his head as she kissed him hungrily.

Then she pulled away, looking into his eyes.

She had to say the words. She couldn't keep them inside anymore.

"Nikos, I love you."

## CHAPTER EIGHT

Nikos froze. "What?"

"I love you." Anna's face looked bare, vulnerable, as she repeated the words.

Nikos had tried for the last hour to speak those same three words—the simple lie that would close the deal and give him the upper hand. But he'd been unable to force the words out of his mouth. He hadn't wanted to say them, hadn't wanted to lie to her. He'd let himself hope that making love to her would be enough.

*Tsou.* No. It was now or never. He had to act now, or it was all over.

He pictured his son with a man like Sinistyn as his stepfather. He imagined Anna in another man's arms, and his lips pressed into a line. To protect his family he'd do anything, say anything, sacrifice anything.

Even his honor.

Watching his face with a troubled expression, Anna rushed to say, "I know you don't love me back, and it's okay—"

"I love you, too." He spoke the words quickly, spitting them out as if they were a live grenade in his mouth.

"You love me?" Anna stared at him in amazement, as if she couldn't believe what she'd heard.

"Yes." His voice was low, strained.

Her whole face started to light up from within, like

a thousand Christmas candles glowing at once. "You love me?" she repeated in a whisper, her eyes filling with tears. If he'd truly loved her, the joy on her face would have been enough to keep him warm through a thousand cold, dark winters. "I never expected—I never dreamed—Oh, Nikos…"

She kissed him then with a passion so pure and sweet it was unlike anything he'd ever known. He returned her kiss with fervor, desperate to forget the lie he'd told, to wipe his sin clean through the fire of his longing for her. He wanted her. He wanted every part of her. Her beauty and innocence and goodness. He kissed her back with all the hard, brutal honesty in his soul.

He ran his hands down the length of her soft skin, kissing her lips, her breasts, sucking the tips of her fingers as she reached for him, trying to pull him closer. The way she moved, the sway and tremble of her body beneath him, brought him perilously close to exploding. Only the thin barrier of fabric kept him from seizing her hips and plunging himself into her. The image had barely crossed his mind before he kissed down her belly, running his hands beneath the fabric, gently nudging her panties down as his kisses went lower. He pulled the cotton down with his teeth even as he ran his fingers between her splayed legs, lightly tracing upward from the sensitive area behind her knees to her inner thighs. He reached his hands beneath her panties and pulled them down. His tongue descended on her, spreading and licking her wide. As he ran his tongue over her hot nub, swirling in a circular motion, she writhed and moaned beneath him.

"No—" she gasped, trying to push him away. "I want you inside me—"

But he was merciless. Instead of stopping, he reached a thick finger inside her, then another finger. He pushed into her as his tongue licked and lapped her. She arched violently, her body snapping back against the bed, and he felt her shake and tremble as she came.

Feeling like he was going to explode, he lifted up on his arms and positioned himself between her legs. He found her wet core, pressing right into her, then hesitated, panting from the effort of restraint. He didn't want to hurt her. He would have to go slowly...

But Anna, more merciful than he, took things into her own hands. As he gritted his teeth, aching as he pushed himself slowly inside her, she reached behind him and yanked his naked buttocks toward her, forcing him through the tight sheath, impaling her. He heard her gasp, and he tried to pull back, but the pleasure of being buried deep inside her after all the months of longing was too much. He moaned her name softly, moving inside her, and took her in his arms, kissing her.

He'd never known it could be like this.

IT HURT WHEN HE PUSHED into her. Had he always been this big?

Then he kissed her. His tongue twined around hers, caressing her deeply, and as her body relaxed the pleasure returned, built, intensified.

*He loves me*, she thought in amazement. Her eyes fluttered open and she saw the expression on his face as he was kissing her. It was worshipful. Devout. Intent. *He loves me.*

Her body relaxed. She didn't have to leave him, ever. Her heart was flooded with joy such as she'd never known before. He'd never said *I love you* before.

With those three words her whole world had changed.

Somehow everything would work out. Why not? What problem was insurmountable, what miracles were impossible, when Nikos loved her?

Running his hands along her breasts, he slowly pushed into her again. Her nerves grew taut. She wanted him, wanted more. She lifted her hips to meet his thrust, holding on to his shoulders. But the bed was far too soft, swallowing her into the comforter under his weight.

With a growl of frustration he lifted her up from the bed, careful not to pull out as he wrapped her naked body around him. In five long steps he crossed the firelit room to the nearest wall—the thick windows that over-looked the Las Vegas Strip, twenty floors below. Thick, unbreakable windows that she herself had discussed with the architects—but she'd never dreamed she would put them to use like this.

Anna moaned as he pressed her naked body against the windows. She glanced down at his tanned skin, at the ripple of his hard muscles in the flickering firelight. She tightened her legs around his rock-hard buttocks as he pushed into her. A groan came from his lips as he thrust into her again and again, causing her full breasts to move with each force of his thrust. Leaning forward, he bit her neck as the pleasure began to spiral within her, even deeper and harder than she'd felt before. Her whole body began to shake, so tense that she could hardly breathe for want of him. She felt him explode inside her with a shout, and she screamed, rocked hard against the windows behind her, as she was devoured by the most intense pleasure she'd ever known.

She fell forward onto him, weak and spent. He lifted her in his arms and lowered her to the white bearskin rug in front of the fire. Murmuring her name tenderly, kissing her face, he held her close.

It took Anna several minutes to open her eyes, but when she did Nikos was looking down at her. His dark eyes were fierce, guarded.

"Anna—" he said, then stopped.

She licked her lips uncertainly. Was he already thinking that he'd made a mistake telling her he loved her? Or maybe she'd imagined the whole thing? Suddenly she felt afraid. For a long moment she heard only the low roar of the fire.

He reached down to caress her cheek. "I don't want to be like Sinistyn. Answer me this one last time, and I promise you I will never ask again." He took a deep breath. "Will you marry me?"

A rush of relief and joy went through her.

"Yes," she said.

He visibly exhaled. "Tonight? Right now?"

She snickered, playfully tugging on his ear. "We'll have to get a license, won't we? The courthouse closed hours ago."

"I'll call the judge at home—"

"No. Let's do this right. Please."

"Tomorrow, then?" he growled. "First thing in the morning?"

"All right," she said, kissing his cheek and smiling.

"You're really going to marry me?"

"Yes!"

"Say it again," he ordered, holding her close.

She laughed out of pure happiness. "Nikos, I'll marry you."

As Nikos held Anna in his arms through the long, interminable night, he stared up at the moonlight creeping slowly across the ceiling above the wide bed. He held her close, listening to her sighs of sleep against his bare shoulder. She was so sweet. So trusting.

And he'd deceived her.

*I did what I had to do,* he told himself fiercely. Anna would be his forever. Michael would have a permanent family. He'd saved his family. He'd matched his wits against hers, laying siege against her heart until it fell, like a golden city overrun by a savage army.

But he'd never thought winning would feel like this.

He'd lied to her. Now, even holding her in his arms, so warm and soft against him, he felt cold. He stared down at her lovely face in the shadows and moonlight. She was smiling in her sleep, pressing her body against his. She was radiating warmth and contentment. She believed that he finally loved her. She believed in happy endings—even for a man like him.

His whole body was racked with tension. But even as he tried to justify what he'd done the thought that she would learn soon enough about his lie pounded through him. She wouldn't be satisfied with an unlimited bank account in lieu of his love. She would demand things of him—emotion, energy, vulnerability—that he simply couldn't give. Not even if he tried. He just wasn't made that way.

And as soon as she found out how she'd been deceived, her joy would be snuffed out like a candle. It would cause the bright new light in her to go out, perhaps forever.

Shortly before dawn he heard snuffling moans from the next room, where Mrs. Burbridge had brought their baby to spend the night. At their son's cries, Anna stirred in his arms.

She gently pushed out of his embrace and crept into the baby's room to nurse, before returning back into his bed.

"Nikos?" Anna whispered.

He kept his breathing even, feigning sleep.

"Thank you," she said, so quietly it was barely audible. "I have the home I dreamed of, the family I dreamed of. I don't know what I did to deserve this. Thank you for loving me."

God, this was intolerable. He turned on his side, pulling away from her, every nerve taut. As soon as he was sure she was really asleep, he sat up in bed. Feeling bone-weary, he raked his hands through his hair and rose slowly from the bed.

Glancing at Anna, slumbering peacefully beneath the white goosedown comforter, he came to a decision. He looked at the clock. It was almost six. He'd intended to have her sign the prenuptial agreement as soon as she woke, then drive straight to the courthouse for a license. He'd planned for them to be married at a drive-thru chapel before breakfast.

But, no matter how pure his motives, now that he held

her fate in the palm of his hand he just couldn't do it. He couldn't take her honesty and trust and love and use them as weapons against her. He couldn't break her heart and destroy her life, no matter how good his motives might be.

Anna Rostoff deserved a man who could love her with his whole heart.

If he wasn't that man, he had to let her go.

A fine time to grow a conscience, Nikos thought bleakly. Apparently he did have one last bit of honor left.

He gave Anna one final, lingering glance. Her dark hair was sprawled across his pillow, her creamy skin like ivory against the white thousand-count sheets. Her cheeks still glowed pink, a remnant of their lovemaking, and her lips curved into a soft smile as she sighed in her sleep.

It was an image he knew he'd never see again.

ANNA WOKE IN A FLOOD of early-morning light with one bright thought: today was her wedding day!

She stretched her limbs against the luxurious sheets with a contented yawn. Her body felt sore. A good kind of sore. She smiled to herself, almost blushing as she remembered everything Nikos had done to her last night. She'd woken up twice for the baby, but, as worn out as she'd been from their lovemaking, with Nikos's hard body curled protectively around hers she'd still had an amazing night's sleep.

She glanced over to the wall of windows, revealing the wide blue Nevada sky from the twentieth-floor penthouse. She'd never felt happy like this before. Safe. Optimistic. Secure. For the first time in her whole life she not only had a home, she had someone who would actually watch over and protect her, instead of just looking out for their own interests. And she had someone she could protect and love in return not because she had to, but because she wanted to.

She and Nikos would be partners, in work as in life. Together they'd be as unbreakable as tempered steel.

It was an exquisitely heady feeling. She wanted to do cartwheels across the penthouse.

She wanted to kiss Nikos *right now.*

Where was he? In the kitchen, making her breakfast? Humming to herself, she rose from the bed and threw on a satin robe, barely stopping long enough to loosely tie the belt to cover her naked body. She paused briefly outside the door of the second bedroom, where Misha was sleeping. She heard only blessed silence.

She smiled to herself. With any luck she and Nikos would have time for more than a kiss before their child woke up demanding breakfast.

She went down the hall and found the kitchen, but it was empty. The immaculate white counters looked as if they'd never even been touched. Nikos was probably already working in his office. Wouldn't he be surprised and happy if she made him coffee, eggs and toast?

Looking in the bare cupboards and refrigerator, she made a face. Even she couldn't manage to manufacture breakfast out of sugar cubes, Greek olives and ice. She turned away when she heard voices down the hall. She followed the sound, stopping outside the door at the other end of the hall.

Muffled through the door, she heard a man's voice

say, "Sir, in my opinion you're making an enormous mistake. As your attorney, I must advise—"

"Since I'm paying you five hundred dollars an hour, I won't waste more time discussing it. I've heard your complaints. Thank you for your assistance. There's the door."

Anna's ear was pressed against the wood; she jumped as the door was flung open and an older man in a dark gray suit came through it.

He gave her a sharp glance, then a scowl. "Congratulations, miss." He put on his hat and stomped out of the apartment with his briefcase.

"Anna. You're awake," Nikos said. "Come in."

His face was dark, half hidden in the shadows of morning where he sat behind a black lacquer desk. The furniture here was as sleek and soulless as everything else in this penthouse. Anna suddenly felt uneasy.

"I thought you were going to wake me up," she said. "Early-morning wedding and all that." She glanced behind her. "Why was your lawyer here? Oh. He brought the prenup?"

His eyes flicked at her in surprise. "You knew I wanted you to sign a prenuptial agreement?"

"I assumed you would. I mean, of course you'd want me to sign one. You're a wealthy man," she said lamely, even as disappointment surged through her. He didn't trust her. He honestly thought she cared about his money, that she'd try to take it. He thought they were at risk of getting a divorce. It cast a pall over her happiness.

Then she realized what he'd said. "Wait a minute. You *wanted* for me to sign a prenup? But not any more?"

"No," he said quietly. "Not any more."

She blinked as the joy came back through her. He'd realized he could trust her!

"Nikos," she breathed. She crossed the room in five steps and, pulling back his chair, climbed in his lap and threw her arms around him. "You won't regret it," she murmured against the warm skin of his neck. "I'll never let you down. I'll be true to you until the day I die. We're going to be so happy..."

She kissed him then, a long, lingering kiss that held her whole heart in every breath.

"Stop, Anna. Just stop." Pushing her off his lap, he stood up, rubbing his temples. His whole body was tense. He didn't seem like a man who was about to get married. He seemed miserable. And furious. Like a wounded lion with a thorn in his paw. He seemed both hurt and dangerous.

"What is it?" she asked warily. "What's wrong?"

He picked up a file from his desk and held it out to her without a word, careful not to let their hands touch. Pulling the papers out of the file, she looked down at the first page and her knees felt weak.

She looked up at him slowly, her mouth dry. "I don't...I don't understand."

"There's nothing to understand. I'm giving you joint custody. You can live wherever you like, and I'll provide you with a generous allowance. Enough to clear your family's debt. Enough to support your mother and sister. My brownstone in the Upper East Side will be transferred to your name. My son will have every support, the best schools, vacations abroad—whatever you think best. All I ask is that I have visitation at will, as well as some arrangement to be made for holidays."

Her head was spinning. "But I don't need custody papers. Once we're married we—"

He was shaking his head grimly. "That was a fairy-tale, Anna, nothing more. I wanted you in my bed, that's all."

"No." She frowned at him, feeling like she'd fallen into some strange nightmare. "You could have had me in your bed long ago. You were the one who insisted we wait. You've done everything under the sun to convince me to marry you. Why would you change your mind now? It doesn't make sense."

He gave her a careless smile. "I guess I'm just not marriage material."

"But you are!" she gasped. "I know you are. You've changed over the last weeks. You've become the husband I've always wanted, the father I dreamed of for Misha. Kind, brave, strong." She closed her eyes, a thousand images going through her of all the time they'd spent together over the last weeks. Working together. Laughing. Nikos playing with their child. "All the time we've spent together—"

"It was a trick, Anna. God, don't you get it? It was all an act. I wanted you. I would have pretended anything to win you. It was pride, I suppose. I couldn't stand the thought of you leaving me. But now—" he shrugged. "The charade's already growing old. I don't want the burden of a wife or the full-time care of a child. I want my freedom."

"It's not true! You're lying!"

He grabbed her wrist, searing her with his hot dark

gaze. "You know me," he said cruelly. "You know how I am. So many beautiful women, so little time. Did you really think I could ever settle down with one woman? With you?"

She felt like she'd just gotten punched. She looked up into his face as tears filled her eyes. "Why are you saying this?"

For an instant something like regret and pain washed over his handsome face. "It's better for you to be free," he said finally. "Forget about me, Anna. You deserve a man who will truly love you."

"But *you* love me. You said so," she whispered.

He shook his head, and now his eyes were only cold. "I lied. I don't love anyone. I don't know how."

At those words, all the hope she'd been holding in her chest disappeared.

Nikos didn't love her. He'd chased her out of pride, out of his determination to possess her, to beat his rival. But now that she'd given him her heart he was already bored with her.

For the first time she believed him, and she felt sick. She turned away.

"Fine." She was relieved that her voice didn't tremble. She tried to remember the plan she'd once had—the plan that had sounded so wonderful before she'd fallen back in love with Nikos. "I guess I'll…I'll go back to New York and get a job."

"No." His voice was dark, inexorable. "I told you. You'll never need to work again."

She looked up at him, pressing her fingernails into her palms to fight back tears. She had her pride too—too much pride to ever cry in front of him again.

"I won't take a penny from a man who doesn't love me. I'm going to find a job. Whether you give me a recommendation or not."

He blinked at her, then turned away, clenching his jaw. "I didn't want it to end like this."

"How did you expect it to end?"

He didn't answer the question. His dark eyes looked haunted as he gazed down at her. "You're right. If you truly want to work, I can't stop you. I have no right to stop you," he said in a low voice. "All I can do is ask that you make the decision carefully. And I know you will. I see now that you'll always look out for Misha. I just have one favor to ask. When you marry, choose well. Choose carefully for our son."

"I thought I had," she said softly. Her feelings were rushing through her, almost uncontrollable. He'd finally agreed that she could work, but even that didn't matter anymore. She wanted to wrap her arms around him, to weep, to beg him not to leave her.

But she was the great-granddaughter of a princess. She was Misha's mother and she had to be strong. Anna clung to her dignity and pride. They were all she had left.

Reaching into her purse, she quietly handed him two pieces of paper. "Here."

"What are these?" he said, sounding shaken.

"The two best résumés for an executive secretary. I lied when I said they weren't any good because I hoped you'd hire me instead. But now that I'm leaving I don't want the company to suffer. I care too much about the company. I care too much about you. I love you."

"Anna—"

She stepped away from him, looking into his eyes. "Goodbye, Nikos. Good luck."

She turned to go, still praying he'd stop her.

He didn't.

Going into the next room, she found the overnight bag Mrs. Burbridge had packed for her the previous night and put on a T-shirt and jeans. She carefully placed the custody agreement into her old diaper bag. She fed and changed Misha and cuddled him close.

Taking a deep breath, she glanced down the hall, hoping against hope that Nikos would appear, put his strong arms around her, and tell her this had all been a horrible mistake.

But Nikos's office door remained closed.

He didn't even care enough to say goodbye. He was probably already phoning the employment agency about the résumés. Or maybe he was calling some sexy show-girl to ask for a date.

Apparently she was easy to replace. In every way.

Straightening, she held on to the frayed edges of her dignity and walked out of the penthouse where, just an hour ago, she'd thought she found love and security at last. She wouldn't let herself cry. Not in his casino, where his men and his security cameras were everywhere.

She managed to hold back her sobs until she reached the sidewalk on Las Vegas Boulevard. Where to now? There was a taxi stand at the hotel across the street. She could barely see through her tears as she stepped off the curb. Just in time she saw the van barreling toward her in the sparse early-morning traffic. She jumped back on the sidewalk in a cold sweat, frightened at how close she'd come to walking into traffic with her son.

"Just who I was looking for," a cold voice said. She looked up with a gasp to see Victor sitting inside the van's open door with several of his men. "What? No snappy comeback? Not so brave when you're alone, are you? Grab the kid," he ordered.

Anna started to fight and scream, trying to run away, but it was hopeless. When Misha was ripped from her arms she immediately surrendered. Ten seconds later she was tied up in the back of the van, on her way to hell. Victor faced her with cold eyes and an oily smile.

"You have a choice to make, *loobemaya*. What happens next is up to you."

NIKOS HAD A SICK feeling in his gut.

Pacing around his L'Hermitage penthouse, he poured himself a bourbon, then put it down untasted. He went to his home office, started to check his email, then closed the laptop without reading a single message. He finally went to the window overlooking Las Vegas. Twenty floors above the city, he had a clear view. He could see the wide desert beyond the city to the far mountains. It seemed to stretch forever. The emptiness was everywhere.

Especially here.

*I did the right thing letting her go,* he told himself. But the sick feeling only got worse. His knees felt weak, as if he'd just run twenty miles without stopping, or gone twenty rounds with a heavyweight champ; he sank into the sleek red-upholstered chair by the edge of the window. He put his head in his hands.

It was the silence that was killing him.

The absolute silence of his beautifully decorated apartment. No baby laughter. No lullabies from Anna. No voices at all. Just dead silence.

He could call one of his trusted employees, like Cooper. He could call acquaintances from the club. He could call any of a dozen women he'd dated. They would be here in less than ten minutes to fill his home with noise.

But he didn't want them.

He wanted his family.

He wanted *her*. His secretary. His lover. His friend.

"*I had to give her up*," he repeated to himself, raking his hand through his hair. I didn't love her.

"Are you sure about that, sir?" a Scottish voice said from behind him.

Nikos jumped when he realized he'd spoken his last words aloud. Mrs. Burbridge was standing in the doorway, her hands folded in front of her. A sharp reply rose to his lips, but her plump face looked so gentle and understanding he bit back the words. Instead, he muttered, "Of course I'm sure."

"You told me to pick up the baby early this morning, as you'd be going to a wedding, but I've arrived to find an open door, no wee babe, and no bride. Am I to understand the wedding's off?"

"They're both gone," he said wearily. He went to his desk, sat down and opened his checkbook. "Your job here is done, Mrs. Burbridge. I'm sorry to bring you so far for just a few weeks. I'll compensate you—"

She reached over and shut the checkbook with a bang. "Where are they, sir? Anna and your child?"

"I let them go," he said, resting his head in his hands. "My son deserved a mother."

"But the bairn was happy enough. So was his mother, I thought. Why send them away?"

"Because Anna deserves better," he exploded. "She deserves a man who can love her. She's been through enough. From her family. From me. I just want her to be happy."

"And you? You don't look terribly happy."

He gave a bitter laugh. "I'll get by. But Anna..." He rubbed the back of his head wearily. "I couldn't let her down. She loved me. Marrying me would have ruined her life."

"Her happiness means more to you than your own?"

"She's the mother of my son. The best damn partner I ever had at work. My friend. My lover. Of course I want her to be happy. It's all I want."

The Scotswoman raised her head and looked at him. Her eyes were kind, but sad. "Sir, what do you think love *is*?"

For a second he just stared at her. Then his heart started to pound in his chest.

"Oh, my God," he whispered.

Was it possible that she was right? That he *loved* Anna?

He didn't just want her in his bed, that was true. He didn't just enjoy her company, appreciate her skills as a mother or respect her perfect secretarial work.

He wanted her face to be the first he woke up to and the last he saw before he slept.

He wanted to see her face light up when she had a business idea, or when she was splashing around in the pool with their son.

He wanted her to be happy. To work as his secretary if that was what it took to make her glow from the inside out. Her happiness was everything.

That was love?

Oh, my God. *He loved her.* He didn't deserve her, but what if he could spend the rest of his life striving to make her happy?

Because without Anna he now realized that his life was empty. His fortune, his business empire—meant nothing. Without her this penthouse was no better than his childhood tenement, and his life was just as lonely and hungry.

Money didn't matter.

Love mattered.

Family mattered.

*Oh, my God. Anna.*

"Bless you," he said to Mrs. Burbridge. He raced down the hall to the door. He had to find Anna—now, at once.

He stopped short when he saw Cooper standing outside his door. The burly bodyguard's face was white and drawn.

"Boss—"

But at that moment Nikos saw the bundle in Cooper's arms. His baby son, wrapped in a blanket. Michael's little face was red and miserable as he cried.

"We found him at the front entrance to the casino," Cooper said. "Alone."

Nikos's heart stopped in his throat as he took his son in his arms. "Alone?"

The burly man nodded grimly. "A valet said a van stopped beneath the marquee, left the baby on the ground, and drove away."

Nikos held his son close, crooning to him softly, rocking him back and forth against his chest, just like Anna had taught him. The baby's tears subsided. Michael was comforted, but Nikos was not. "Anna wouldn't let herself be separated from Misha."

Looking miserable, Cooper handed him a letter. Nikos scanned it quickly.

*Nikos*

*I've realized that sharing custody will never work. I'm in love with Victor Sinistyn and leaving with him for South America. You once said I was no kind of mother, and I guess you were right. Trying to keep our baby safe and warm would be too much effort where we're going. Please don't bother trying to find me. Raise our son well.*
*Anna*

"Boss?" Cooper repeated unhappily. His voice echoed in the private outside hallway against the steel of the elevator doors. "What do you want me to do?"

Nikos's heart was pounding. She'd left him. The moment he'd realized he loved her with all his heart, she'd left him. His worst fear had come true.

But something nagged at him, overriding the pain,

and he read the letter again. A mere hour after she'd left Nikos she'd decided to leave both him and Misha behind for a life with Victor Sinistyn?

Maybe it *was* her handwriting, but he didn't believe a word of it.

"She's in trouble," Nikos said slowly. "Someone forced her to write this letter."

"You think she's been kidnapped?"

"Sinistyn," he breathed. The man had made it clear he wanted Anna, and when Nikos had shoved her out of L'Hermitage without bodyguards he'd handed her to him on a silver plate. He cursed himself under his breath. "Get the plane ready."

"It's ready now—for your trip to Asia."

"Screw Singapore. Let Haverstock take the bid," he said, throwing away the billion-dollar deal to his chief rival without a thought.

"Where are we going to look for her? South America?"

Nikos shook his head. "Sinistyn put that in to throw us off the track. No. He's going someplace else. Somewhere private. Somewhere my power does not easily reach." He glanced down at the letter, forcing himself to read it again slowly.

> *You once said I was no kind of mother...*
> *Trying to keep our baby safe and warm would*
> *be too much effort where we're going...*

He sucked in his breath. She was trying to tell him where they were going. Folding the letter, he shoved it at Cooper. "They're going to Russia."

"Let me guess, boss," Cooper said sourly. "You want to handle this alone."

Nikos gently handed the baby to Mrs. Burbridge. Kissing his son goodbye, he turned to face Cooper with rage surging through his veins. "Hell, no. I want every man we've got on the plane within the hour. And get Yuri Andropov on the phone. It's time to call in a favor."

## CHAPTER NINE

ANNA SHIFTED SLIGHTLY in her chair, trying to shift the cords that bound her wrists without attracting the attention of Victor or his goons. Her hands felt hot and sweaty with the effort, but the rest of her felt like ice as she worked the broken tines of her great-grandmother's ring against the rope.

On the car ride from St. Petersburg she'd briefly felt the spring sun on her face, but the backroom of the Rostov Palace felt cold as ever. Especially as she'd listened to Victor's men ransack the Princess's china in the kitchen. Biting her lip, she watched as Victor and one of his men set up an old black-and-white television near the fire.

"It's not working. We'll miss the game," the bodyguard complained in Russian, trying to position the antenna.

"It'll be fine," Victor snapped in the same language. He took the antenna then, realizing that there was no electricity, dropped it in disgust. "Go help with dinner."

"Why can't *she* make us dinner?" the man grumbled, nodding at Anna. "Make the woman useful for once."

Victor glanced back at her, and she froze.

"Oh, she will be useful. But only to me. Get out, I said. I want some time with my future bride."

As Victor approached she pressed her wrists against

her T-shirt, hoping he wouldn't notice that one of the cords binding her to the chair was finally starting to fray.

She'd been praying that customs officials would discover her when they arrived in St. Petersburg, but Victor's connections, along with a well-placed bribe, had allowed his private plane to arrive unmolested.

At least her baby was safe, thousands of miles away with Nikos. She'd bought her child's safety with that horrible letter Victor had forced her to write. Would Nikos see her clues?

*Maybe he won't even care,* she thought hollowly. He'd made it clear that he wanted her permanently out of his life, and this was about as permanent as it could get.

Victor pulled off her gag. "Here," he said, sounding amused. "Scream all you want. No one will hear you."

But she didn't scream. She just pulled away from his touch, glaring at him.

He laughed, folding his arms as he looked around them. "I can see I need to renovate my so-called palace. No heat. No electricity. And all they've found in the kitchen so far are potatoes and teabags."

"I hope you starve," she replied pleasantly.

"That's not a very kind thing to say to your future husband, is it? You and I both need to keep up our strength. I'll send one of the boys to the grocery store. And as for heat…we can supply that on our own, later." He gave her a sly smile. "Any requests? You've been refusing food and drink for hours." He ran his hand down her arm, making her shudder with revulsion. "You must eat something."

"So you can drug me? No thanks."

"Ah, *loobemaya*," Victor said softly, brushing back a tendril of her hair. "I wouldn't go to so much trouble if I didn't love you so much."

"You call this love?"

"Until Stavrakis's spell wears off, and you understand it's really me you want, I need to keep you close. You will realize how much you want me." His voice sounded threatening as, massaging her shoulder hard enough to leave a bruise, he added softly, "Very soon."

Ignoring the loud sounds of crashing china and slamming cabinet doors in the kitchen, Anna pulled her shoulder away from his hand. "I love Nikos, and I always will."

He yanked back her hair, causing her head to jerk back. Anna dimly heard men shouting from the kitchen, but all she could see was Victor's sadistic face, inches away from her own. "Forget him. Forget his baby. I will give you others. I will fill you with my child tonight. You belong to me now. You will learn to obey my will. You will learn to crave my touch—"

He forced his lips on hers in a painful ravishment that was meant to teach fear. And it worked. For the first time Anna began to feel truly scared of what he would do to her.

When he pulled away, Victor smiled at the expression on her face. He ran a hand up the inner thigh of her jeans.

"You have no right," she whispered, shaking.

"This is my country. I have half the police in my

pocket. Here, you are my slave." He reached to fondle a breast, and without thinking she brought up her bound wrists to block him. His smile stretched to a grin. "Yes," he breathed. "Fight me. That's what I want. Stavrakis isn't here to save you. You'll never see him or your precious son again. You're mine. You're totally in my power—"

"Let her go."

Victor looked up with a gasp. Anna saw Nikos standing in the kitchen doorway and almost sobbed aloud.

Nikos's face had an expression she'd never seen before—as cold and deadly as the gun he was pointing at Sinistyn.

Victor looked up with an intake of breath which he quickly masked with a sneer. "You're as good as dead, Stavrakis. My men will—"

"Your men will do nothing. They barely tried. When they saw they were outnumbered, most of them gave up without a fight." He cocked the gun, assessing his aim at Victor's head. "Some loyalty you inspire, Sinistyn."

With a single smooth movement Victor twisted behind Anna, using her body to block his own. "Come closer and I'll kill her."

He put his beefy hands around her neck. Anna flinched, then struggled, unable to breathe. As he slowly tightened his grip, the room around her seemed to shimmer and fade.

Nikos uncocked the gun, pointing it at the ceiling. "You really are a coward."

"It's easy to throw insults when you have a gun."

"Let her go, damn you!" Nikos threw the gun on

the floor, then straightened with a scornful expression. "Even now I'm unarmed, I know you won't fight me. I'm stronger, faster, smarter than you—"

"Shut up!" Victor screamed, releasing Anna's throat. She took a long, shuddering gasp of air and felt the world right itself around her.

Victor stormed toward Nikos, lunging for the gun.

Nikos kicked it into the roaring fireplace and threw himself at the other man's midsection. The two men fought while Anna watched in terror, desperately struggling with the cords that bound her to the chair. Victor lashed out wildly, hitting Nikos's jaw with his knee. Nikos's head snapped back, but he fought grimly, as if he were in the battle he'd trained for all his life. With a crunching uppercut to the chin, Nikos knocked Victor to the floor.

Gasping for air, Victor slid back, scuttling like a crab. Reaching into the fireplace, he picked up the gun with his sleeve and pushed himself up against the wall, panting.

"Now you're going to die." Victor shot a crazed look from Nikos to Anna. "And you're going to watch. After this, only his ghost will haunt us." He cocked the gun, pointing it at Nikos with triumph.

"No!" Anna screamed, desperately struggling with the cord. By some miracle it snapped open against her wrist. She threw herself from the chair, flinging her body in front of Nikos as Victor squeezed the trigger.

She closed her eyes, waiting to feel the bullet tear through her body.

Instead, she just heard a soft *click*.

The gun was empty!

Victor shook the gun with impotent fury.

Nikos turned to one side, tucking her protectively behind him as he faced Victor. "Guess I forgot the bullets. Sorry."

With a scream of frustration Victor threw the gun at him, but Nikos dodged it easily. It clattered to the floor.

Nikos glanced at it with a derisive snort. He raised an eyebrow, giving Victor the darkly arrogant look that Anna had once despised. But she appreciated it now. She knew he used all his arrogance, all his strength and power, to protect the people he loved.

"Fight me, Sinistyn," Nikos demanded coldly. "Just you and me."

Victor swore in Russian, shaking his head. He looked straight at Anna, muttering all the sadistic things he'd do to her if Nikos wasn't there to protect her.

Anna felt her cheeks grow hot with horror. Nikos didn't speak Russian, but when he saw the effect the man's words were having on her he strode forward grimly.

With a yelp, Victor turned and ran in the other direction. But Nikos caught up with him, grabbing his shoulder and whirling him around.

"Like scaring women, do you?" He punched Victor in the face—once, twice. "Too much of a coward to fight someone your own size? Fight me, damn you! Or are you going to just let me kill you?" Nikos's eyes narrowed and he looked dangerous indeed. "Don't think I won't."

Victor started fighting dirty. He tried to knee Nikos in the groin, to trip him. When Nikos blocked him, he stumbled back to the fireplace and grabbed a sharp iron poker.

"I'll stab you like a pig, you Greek bastard," he panted, swinging the poker at Nikos's face.

He blocked it with his right arm, but Anna heard the crunch of bone and saw the way Nikos's right hand hung at a strange angle.

Victor had broken his wrist. She trembled with fury. She started to run at Victor, to fight him two to one, but Nikos stopped her with a hard glance.

With his left hand he wrenched the poker away and threw Victor to the floor. He held him to the ground with one hand against his neck. Anna watched in horror as he tightened his grip.

"How does it feel to be vulnerable?" Nikos demanded.

"Nikos, let him go," Anna sobbed.

"Why? Do you think he would have let *you* go?" he demanded, not looking at her. "Did he ever show mercy to anyone weaker? Why should I let him live after what he's done to you?"

Slowly she put her hands against his shoulders, feeling the hard tension of his muscles. "Do it for us. Please, my love, let him go so we can go back to our son."

Abruptly, he released his choke-hold on the other man and rose to his feet. She had one brief vision of his face, and she thought she saw tears in his eyes as, without a word, he took her in his arms and held her tightly.

Nikos looked down at her as he held her tenderly to his chest. His dark eyes were shining.

"Thank you, *agape mou*," he whispered, brushing her cheek softly with his hand. "Thank you for trying to take that bullet. There weren't any bullets, but you didn't know that. You…you saved me. In so many ways."

"And you started early," a man said from the doorway in heavily accented English. Anna looked up to see a man in a Russian police uniform, with half a dozen policemen behind him. "We missed it."

"I couldn't wait, Yuri." Nikos jerked his head toward Victor, still stretched out on the floor. "There he is."

The man called Yuri smiled. "You said you were calling in a favor. I wish I had to pay more favors like this. We've wanted Sinistyn a long time, but he was untouchable. Now, with your testimony and influence, he won't see the sun again for a long time." The policeman looked with concern at Nikos's wrist. "My friend, you are hurt."

"It's nothing—"

"It's his wrist. I think it's broken. We need a doctor right away," Anna said, then looked up anxiously at the face of the man she loved. "Please, Nikos. I need you to be well."

"All right," he muttered. "Get the doctor."

Turning away from the policeman, he sank into a nearby chair and pulled her into his lap. "Anna, before the doctor starts filling me with drugs, I have to tell you something. I should have told you this a long time ago, but I was too stupid to see it and too stubborn to admit it—even to myself. I really do love you."

"Nikos, I love—"

"Please let me finish, while I can still get this out." He took a deep breath. "You saved me. From a life that was empty. I was stupid to prevent you from working, or doing anything else that brings you joy. If it makes you happy, I want you to work. As my secretary, as vice-president, as any damn thing you want."

Tears filled her eyes even as she gave him a mischievous smile. "I think I'd make a good CEO."

"Cocky." He returned her grin. "You always were the only one who could stand up to me. I need that in my life. Someone to keep me in my place."

As she looked into his handsome face she barely heard the noises of the swarming police, or Victor's whining complaints as they took him away.

"Your place is with me." She cupped his jaw, rough with dark stubble, in her hands. "As long as we're together, anyplace in the world is my home. But there's something that I have to ask you. Something I've never said before to anyone." He'd called her cocky, but what she wanted to ask him now terrified her. She took a deep breath. "Nikos, will you marry me?"

For answer, his smile lit his face from within, his dark eyes shining at her with hope and love. "I thought you'd never ask."

"I TOLD YOU WE SHOULD have gotten married at the drive-thru chapel in Vegas," Anna whispered when she reached the end of the aisle.

"And miss all this? Never," he whispered back with a wink.

As the priest began to speak the words that would bind them together for all time Nikos knew he should pay attention, but all he could do was look at his bride. Beneath the hot Greek sun, on the edge of a rocky cliff overlooking the Aegean Sea, they were surrounded by flowers and a small audience of people who loved them. It was a simple wedding, plain by some standards, but he knew in his heart it was what Anna wanted.

And, looking at her now, he knew he'd never be able to deny her anything. Her turquoise eyes, a mixture of sea and sky, smiled at him as he lifted her veil. She wore a white shift that made her look like a medieval maiden.

Her engagement ring, a four-carat diamond in an antique gold setting, sparkled from her finger. He'd given it to her two nights ago. She'd tried to refuse it until she'd realized that he'd found the original stone from her great-grandmother's wedding ring. Now it was one of her greatest treasures.

The way she'd thanked him had made him forget all about the cast on his wrist. Remembering that night, and every night since they'd returned from Russia, still made his body feel hot from the inside out. He could hardly wait to give Anna her honeymoon present—Rostov Palace, which he'd bought from Sinistyn's confiscated estates. Sinistyn didn't need it anymore, as he'd be living out his days in a Russian prison.

Nikos glanced around him at family and friends and the sea and the bright blue sky. *Justice.* Another thing he'd thought existed only in fairytales, along with love and happy endings.

He'd not only held his wedding in his parents' hometown, but, at Anna's urging, he'd invited his father's family—Eudocia Dounas and her three daughters—to the wedding. To his surprise they'd all come, bringing their husbands and children. He now had a family. Siblings, nieces, nephews. He didn't know them yet, but he would.

Near his family sat Anna's mother who, in another wedding-day miracle, was not only on her best behavior, but had pinched his cheek and declared it was "about time" the two were married. Anna had spent last night talking to her sister, barring Nikos from her bedroom because it was "bad luck" for him to see her. Now, Natalie was bouncing Misha on her knee while she watched the wedding, smiling through her tears. And he could see his son's two new top teeth in his smile as he watched his parents wed.

It was a day for families to join together.

All right, he'd admit it. It wasn't just Anna who'd wanted this kind of wedding. He had wanted it as well. In some way he'd wanted this all his life.

Family.

Home.

Love.

As Anna said the words that made her his wife her voice was sweet and true. He barely remembered repeating the words himself, but he must have done so since before he knew it the priest was speaking in accented English, declaring them husband and wife, and he was kissing the bride. Over the sound of the crashing surf he heard their family and friends behind them burst into applause, and a noisy cheer from Cooper. But as he kissed her, holding her tightly in his arms, all he could feel was the pounding of his heart against hers.

She pulled back, caressing his face as she grinned up at him through tears. "See?" she whispered. "Wasn't that better than having Elvis marry us?"

Hiding a grin, he looked down at her solemnly. "I'm yours to command now, Mrs. Stavrakis."

"Mine to command?" She paused, pretending to consider her options, and then leaned forward to whisper in his ear. "In that case, my first order is that you take me to bed."

"Leaving our guests to start the reception?"

She gave him a wicked smile. "They won't miss us."

"They won't even notice," he agreed with a grin. He picked her up in his arms and, to the delighted gasps of the crowd, he turned to carry her back to his villa.

"Ah, Anna. I can tell I'm going to have a hard life with you," he observed with a sigh, and he kissed her with all his heart.

\* \* \* \* \*

# REQUEST YOUR FREE BOOKS!

*If you enjoyed this story from*
USA TODAY *bestselling author Lucy Monroe,*
*here is an exclusive sneak peak from her brand-new*
*Harlequin Presents® title FOR DUTY'S SAKE,*
*part of the* ROYAL BRIDES *duet, available June 2011.*

*Heroine Angele decides to release Sheikh Zahir from their
decade-old betrothal pact—she'd rather set the man she love
free than wed him knowing he doesn't return her feelings!*

*But will Zahir give her the wedding night she's always
dreamed of…without taking her hand in marriage?*

SHE MADE IT TO ZAHIR'S ROOM WITHOUT FURTHER INCIDEN
Then she stood in front of the lever that would swing a
ancient wardrobe within the room open like a door, an
gathered her courage. This was it. The moment she'd crave
far longer than anyone else would ever know.

She reached out to pull the lever, but the "door" was al
ready opening. It swung inward to a room lit by numerou
candles.

Clad in the traditional wedding garments of the Zohra roy
al family, Zahir looked at her with an expression so seriou
it made her breath catch. "I began to think you had change
your mind."

Unable to speak, she shook her head.

"Your wedding night awaits." He stepped back. "Come."

Her heart hammering, she followed him into the candlel
room, but jerked when he reached behind her, and the
blushed at her jumpiness.

"Be at peace. I am only closing the access to the corridor.

"How did you know I was in the corridor?"

Zahir merely shrugged, but there was an odd expressio

his eyes, the soft light of the candles giving his angular cheeks a burnished glow that almost looked like a blush.

He reached out and cupped her cheek. "You look beautiful."

"Do I?"

"Oh, yes." His hand slipped around her head and settled against her nape. He used the hold to gently tug her forward until their bodies were a mere breath apart. "You are a minx. How did I not realize this before?"

"Minx is such an old-fashioned word."

"I am an old-fashioned guy."

"You think?"

"In some ways, I am very traditional."

Then, before she could answer, he lowered his head, and he finally got the kiss she'd always wanted.

And it was every bit as tender and romantic as she could ever have hoped. Letting out a little sigh of pleasure, she let her lips part slightly.

Zahir's tongue swept inside, claiming her mouth with unhesitating, if gentle, demand. Her arms moved of their own volition, her hands clasping behind his neck as she melted into him....

*Will Zahir let Angele walk away from their marriage after sharing such passion? Or can he tempt her to reconsider?*

*Find out in FOR DUTY'S SAKE*
*by* USA TODAY *bestselling author Lucy Monroe.*

*Available June 2011,*
*exclusively from Harlequin Presents®.*

**Harlequin** *Presents*

## EXTRA

IF YOU ENJOYED THIS STORY
BY *USA TODAY* BESTSELLING AUTHOR

# JENNIE LUCAS

YOU'LL LOVE

# RECKLESS NIGHT IN RIO

PART OF THE NEW MINISERIES

## ONE NIGHT IN...

*A night with these men is never enough!*

From the heat of the desert to the cosmopolitan
flair of Madrid, from sultry Brazil to opulent London,
seduction is a language that knows no bounds!
Real heroes know that sometimes actions speak
louder than words....

ALSO AVAILABLE:
## A SPANISH AWAKENING
by **KIM LAWRENCE**

*COMING JULY 2011 FROM HARLEQUIN PRESENTS® EXTRA*